BLOOD CHILD

Also Published By Dawn Publishing

Slave Boy – Book One in the Democ'Chu Series

by Nath Brye (2020)

Break Down to Wake Up – Journey Beyond the Now

curated by Jocelyn Bellows (2020)

Unlocked – Discover Your Hidden Keys

by Carmelle Crinnion (2020)

Becoming the Champion – V1 Awareness

by Korey Carpenter(2020)

Becoming Annie – The Biography of a Curious Woman

by Dawn Bates (2020)

Standing in Strength – Inspirational Stories of Power Unleashed

curated by Laarni Mulvey (2021)

The Sacral Series by Dawn Bates:

Moana – One Woman's Journey Back to Self (2020)

Leila – A life Renewed One Blank Canvas at a Time (2020)

Pandora – Melting the Ice One Dive at a Time (2021)

The Trilogy of Life Itself by Dawn Bates:

Friday Bridge – Becoming a Muslim, Becoming Everyone's Business (2nd Edition, 2017)

Walaahi – A firsthand account of living through the Egyptian Uprising and why I walked away from Islaam (2017)

Crossing The Line – A Journey of Purpose and Self-Belief (2017)

BLOOD CHILD

Book Two of The Democ'Chu Series

NATH BRYE

Dawn Publishing

Published by Dawn Publishing
www.dawnbates.com
The moral right of the author has been asserted.

For quantity sales or media enquiries, please contact the publisher at the website address above.

Cataloguing-in-Publication entry is available from the British Library.

ISBN:
978-1-913973-26-1 (paperback)
978-1-913973-27-8 (ebook)

Book cover Illustration – Ben Sampey (aka Sampey)
Book cover design – Jerry Lampson

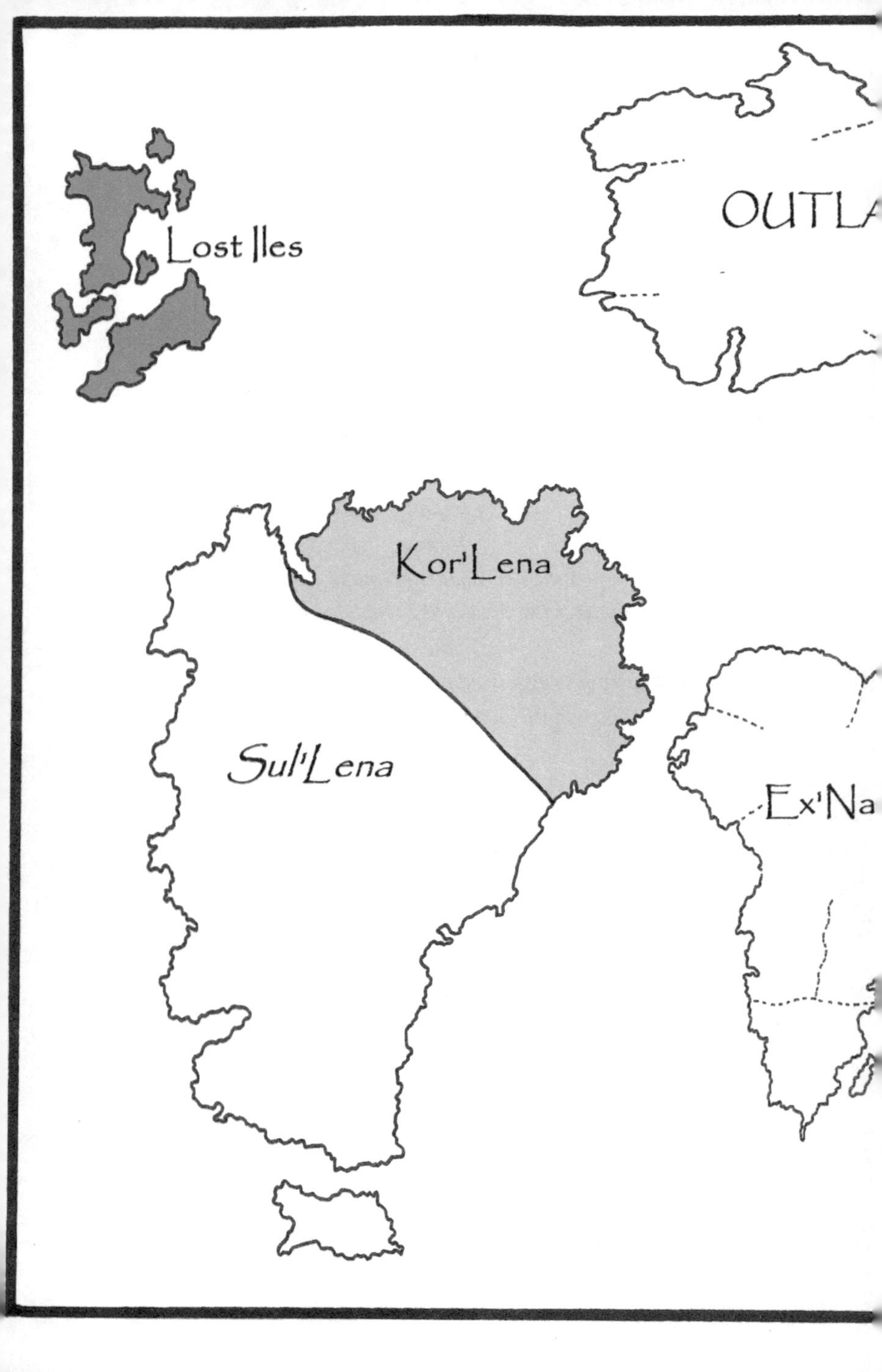
Lost Iles
OUTLA
Kor'Lena
Sul'Lena
Ex'Na

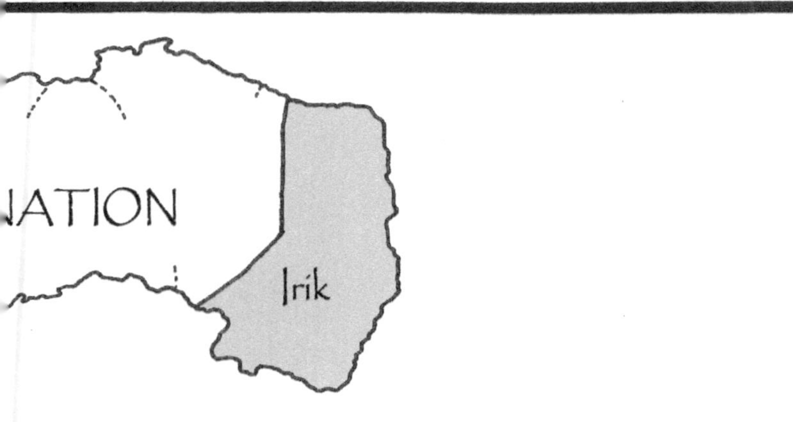

'North-West World Map'

Gratitude

Christine, you have once again done an amazing job proofing my work. I promise the next one will be easier as I continue to grow my skills and improve my typing. Thank you.

Sampey, once again your art is beyond compare and it would never be a Democ'Chu novel without your art. I look forward to continuing to work with you and I am really looking forward to stage two of my tattoo work.

Dawn. How good have you been to get me here? Amazing is what you have been! But here we are, the second novel finished and complete. Two down, not many to go. We got this!

The former slaves arrived in the middle of winter; the news of their journey from the other side of the Outlander nation spreading quickly throughout the city of Valik. Their story was told on every street corner as the people of Irik marvelled at where the former slaves had come from.

The former slaves had adjusted to their new lives better than expected, although there were a few struggles. The pit-rats first shock was the change in culture. Everywhere they looked, they saw a race of people that looked exactly like their previous masters. This made them uneasy, but they gradually started to accept that the people looked like their former masters, they were not the same at all. The fact that they were surrounded by mainly blonde giants that shared the same build, hair colour, facial expressions and language was quite an adjustment. The people of Irik dressed differently and, of course, were generally a friendlier and kinder race of people. They did not walk around armed to the teeth or owned slaves. They treated the former pit-rats with respect, laughed more and appreciated human life. It was a definite difference from the Outlanders that the former slaves were used to. The cities and towns which they had visited were cleaner, the buildings were well-planned and constructed. The many centuries of separation from the Outlanders clearly showing in the way the people of Irik had progressed.

Joren, the Captain of the Bloodchildren, was delighted in hearing all of the stories of his newest members, some true and others not so true. He was amazed how quickly their story had travelled around his country. Joren and the other members of the Bloodchildren were surprised just how well they had adapted to their new situation.

It was explained by Silent-Boy that as slaves, change was a constant companion in their lives and they had learnt to adapt quickly. Ten of the former slaves had, of course, not joined the mercenary company and had made their way to the seaside fishing village. It was a village that was short of young men and a plentiful supply of young women. Joren knew they would do well and noticed those who had chosen to leave, were the youngest of the former slaves. Demon-boy had explained that they had not been in the slave camp as long as the others, and would adapt quicker to a peaceful way of life. The other sixteen that had joined his company were fitting in well with the training and the other mercenaries. There was some suspicion from the older mercenaries and his First Sergeant Dolac clearly did not like them. His distaste for the former slaves evident in everything he said.

That is not to say everything was going perfect. There had been three incidents of drunken fighting in the town with the pit-rats drinking too much, then causing fights. Fights they won easily. Fortunately, no one had been killed. Joren understood that the former slaves had never known freedom and it was a new thing for them. He understood the adjustment needed for such a shift in their lives. However, he was really not happy having to bail the pit-rats from the city guard cells. Demon-boy and Silent-boy had both explained that drinking was a rare pleasure when they were slaves, and often when they got hold of something to drink, they would over indulge to numb out the pain of their lives. The last incident saw Bulldog-boy beat two men of the city guard badly over an argument. He had been fined, which Joren had paid, and sentenced to two weeks in the cells that saw Bulldog-boy taken away from the training. After getting a dressing down from Joren, Bulldog-boy was keeping his head low and avoiding notice. Demon-boy and Silent-boy had also received some of that dressing down, and both had kept a better watch on their troubled brother. He was a brother that was struggling more than most in their new situation.

Joren, of course, also kept his eye on both Demon-boy and Silent-boy. Both had leadership potential and had a good basic understanding of tactics and strategy. Where they learnt this from as slaves, he had no idea; he would have to ask them. Both were fantastic fighters, and it was this reason that his First Sergeant Dolac said nothing in front of the former slaves. He too recognised the former slaves' skill with weapons. He was the one that had to duel with Demon-boy before they were accepted into the company.

As he watched his new recruits train, he could not help but remember a situation two weeks ago that brought a smile to his face. He closed his eyes and looked back, the memory still fresh in his mind.

On arrival to the company camp, they had to give their names to the company clerk in order for him to register them. All they had was their slave nicknames and these were not suitable. When told they had to choose names, they all looked blank. There was silence in the clerk's office as the pit-rats looked at each other in confusion, until Funny-boy started laughing at the problem. All of the others joined in the laughter, realising they were in a situation they never thought they would be in. It was Demon-boy who spoke first. The memory was not only a fine one for Joren, but it was beautiful and almost brought a tear to his eyes. Demon-boy stood, and the other pit-rats stopped their laughter.

"I have a name!" said Demon-boy.

"And, what is it?" asked the clerk, quickly running out of patience.

"I name myself Corvin. Corvin Demonchild," said Demon-boy with a fire in his eyes and silent pride showing on his face.

All of the former slaves stood and banged their right fist on their chests in respect before seating themselves once more. Joren did not know where that name came from or the importance of it, until it was later explained by Silent-boy. The one called Bulldog-boy stood next as the clerk waited.

"I name myself Irikson Bulldog."

The others once again banged their fists on their chest but remained sitting. Joren was touched that he had taken the name of his own country. It was a respectful way to honour the country that had given them their freedom. Silent-boy stood next.

"I name myself Jorga Silent."

There was more banging of fists as the clerk looked on, getting fed up. He was old and quite bitter, and did not see the emotion of the scene before him, let alone appreciate it. Joren did!

"Hurry up, we have not got all day!" snapped the clerk as Funny-boy stood.

"What is your name, old man?" he asked the clerk.

"What does that matter?"

Funny-boy looked at him hard without blinking; a pure evil stare, all the while flexing his huge arm and shoulder muscles. When Funny-boy stood, his size would intimidate anyone and he had been the most noticeable of all the pit-rats as he walked around the town of Valik, where the Bloodchildren Company was based. The dark colour of his skin making him stand out in the country of Irik; most of the Valik inhabitants' conversations were regarding him. He was quiet and kept to himself, which added to the mystery. He often walked around with a calm face or a small smile. He had a friendly face that seemed almost out of place on his huge body.

He stood there, staring at the clerk, his dark brown eyes serious, the huge muscles of his chest and arms contracting. The move was not lost on the clerk.

"I am called Lorka, son of Mirac," he said nervously.

Funny-boy smiled, his infectious grin spreading to the others who waited. Funny-boy then spoke his new name.

"I name myself Lorka. Lorka Soon-dead," he said.

The others laughed and banged their fists to their chests again as the clerk muttered angrily to himself while writing down the name. Joren had to hold himself from laughing and could not believe that someone would name themselves such, but he knew the former slaves had a dark sense of humour. This is how they survived.

Four more names came, all of the others banging their fists on their chests in respect as each name was called out by the former slaves. There was Bordix Era, taking his first name from the town where the former slaves first reached their freedom, and his last name from the province where he had fought his first death bout. Then came Norda Trainer, his first name was all he could remember of his family and his last name another reference to their slavery that Joren did not understand. Next was Mirac Now-dead. The others all laughed louder than before at another former slave naming himself after the clerk's father who was now no longer alive, a not-so-subtle insult that had all the others laughing loudly. The former slaves bent over in howls of laughter and tears streaming down their faces. This time Joren could not hide his humour and bent over laughing as well, earning a scowl from the old clerk.

Lastly, the youngest of them stood. Slightly shorter than the rest, wired muscle and a very youthful face. He looked no older than fifteen summers of age.

"I name myself Youst Silent," said the youngling.

It was later explained that the youngling had escaped before he had any death bouts. The first man he had killed was in the Outlander province of Youst during a battle. His last name he chooses in respect to Jorga Silent, who came over and banged his hand on the youth's shoulder. The pair were inseparable, and it was clear Jorga was the young one's mentor.

For the rest of his life, he will remember the naming ceremony with fondness. If it were not such an intimate situation, he would get his favourite poet to turn it into a saga, to bring warmth to their hearts in the depth of winter.

At the end of the second week of training, it was clear the former slaves were much fitter than any of his other mercenaries. He thought this would cause jealousy, especially from his more senior men. Apart from the basic suspicion they had, the former slaves being in better shape did not cause jealousy. Most of his mercenaries viewed the former slaves in awe.

Joren adjusted himself on the stone seat, easing his body to ease the muscles of his right leg. He was still fit, but less training had started to show, and he was gaining weight. His body was still in good shape and he looked younger than his forty-five summers. His chestnut brown hair now showing many grey patches. He looked on as the new recruits continued to train, he thought back to another problem the former slaves had run into. The largest one was explaining currency and their monthly pay to them. They knew they were getting paid, but as they had no concept of money or the value of the coins, he had to explain it. He had sat them down and explained it, slowly. They picked it up much faster when Jorga Silent had asked questions of what basic items costed in Irik. Once Joren had seen where Jorga was going with this chain of thought, explanation became much easier. He smiled at the memory and once again, he drifted back to the barracks hall with all the former slaves, two weeks ago when they had arrived.

"Okay, now we come to payment!" said Joren.

All of the former pit-rats had hushed themselves and listened.

"The going rate for mercenaries in Irik is one Sulvic and five Boric coins a month! I pay slightly better, and you will get two Sulvic coins a month," he said.

The first to raise the amount was Irik Bulldog.

"That does not sound like much!"

The others listened on. As Jorga Silent spoke next.

"We have never earned money before so don't quite understand how much you are paying us. That is probably why it does not sound like much."

The others nodded.

"Keep in mind that included in your contracts is many things you do not have to pay for. You get free uniform, weapons, free lodging in the barracks, two meals a day and I pay for medical treatment if you are injured. The pay is purely for personal things you want. Also, during summer when we are working, you get a small monthly bonus of one Sulvic coin and at the end of the season, if the company earns a bonus, half this goes straight to all the fighting men."

He could see the former slaves think their way through this and most of them were nodding. They understood now, their pay was for personal stuff, as he supplied almost everything else. Then, Jorga Silent spoke again.

"In Valik, how much here is the price of a meal? Or the price of a mug of ale?"

At first, Joren did not know where he was going with these questions but answered them quickly.

"A good meal at one of the taverns will cost you three Boric coins, a mug of ale costs three Iric coins," he said.

Straight away, they all look confused and he realised they had no idea of the worth of each coin. So, he explained.

"The Iric is our basic coin made from basic iron," he said, pulling a couple from his money pouch at his side and throwing a few to the mercenaries, before continuing.

"Three of these will buy you a mug of ale. Ten of these Iric are worth the same as one Boric." He then pulled a bronze boric from his pouch and threw that to the mercenaries so they could inspect it.

"Three of these Boric coins will get you a decent meal and a drink in most taverns."

He then pulled a couple of Sulvic coins next and threw them to the former slaves.

"Ten Boric coins are worth the same as one Sulvic coin. Five Sulvic coins will buy you a good dagger in most of the blacksmiths here in the city, although if you want a really good one, it may cost more. A cheaper dagger around two Sulvic coins."

He could see now they were understanding the way his people's currency worked. Corvin Demon-child spoke next, holding up the Sulvic coin.

"We get two of these Sulvic coins a month?"

"Yes," said Joren.

"We get three of these when working?" asked Corvin.

"Yes," Joren said again.

"So, we are getting paid one basic dagger a month," said Jorga Silent.

All of the former slaves started smiling, now fully understanding how the currency system in Irik worked.

Joren had no Golic coins on himself, so did not bother explaining this to them.

"How much for the company of a lovely woman for the evening?" asked Irikson Bulldog.

All of the others laughed. It was no secret that Irikson was looking forward to sleeping with a woman. He often went on about it and some of the pit-rats had joked that was what kept him going in their trek for freedom. Joren himself smiled knowing that of all of the former slaves, it would be Irikson to ask that question. He smiled as he replied.

"The going rate I have been told, is five Boric for a tumble with one of the 'Coin-Wives'."

The former slaves cheered. Joren could see Irikson trying to work it out in his head, how many working girls he could afford to pay for each month. The former slaves, of course, had no education and did not have their numbers. He told Irik before the question could be asked.

"This means Irik, you will be able to afford to hire four Coin-Wives a month if you wanted!"

The room exploded with cheers and Irik sat there with a huge grin on his face.

Joren pulled out his charcoal pencil and continued to jot down notes of his new recruits. He was noting their strengths and weakness, not that there were many weaknesses so far. In a few weeks, he would assign the new recruits to squads. He had an idea or two and would discuss them with his First Sergeant when he got the chance. He looked forward to watching their progress!

Chapter One

The forty-five new recruits ran around the track at an easy lope. They had done five of the twenty circuits they had to complete. The track was similar to the one they had in their slave training camp except for a few differences, both were of roughly equal distance. The track they now trained on was a distance of 400 Lai. Where the slave training camp track was dirt that would turn to mud in the first rains, this track was compressed clay on top of a bottom layer of small stones to aid drainage. Also, instead of being grassy area or vegetable garden infield, like it had been in the slave camp, it held a large, roofed area held up by massive wooden posts. Also, hanging from the roof around the entire perimeter was rolled up canvas. When this was untied and lowered, it enclosed the massive space like a tent that kept out the worst snow and rain. This meant it could be used in the foulest of weather. The former slaves where not even sweating as the made their way around the track. The new recruits, however, had a light moisture on the skin of their foreheads. It was easy to see the pit-rats were a little bored as they were talking as they jogged.

"Two weeks of this and I am already bored!" said Lorka.

Irikson nodded with a sour look on his face.

"I thought they were being easy on us in the first two weeks and the training would intensify, but still we jog around this track at this slow pace," said Irikson.

Jorga said nothing, just smiling.

"Perhaps, we pick up the pace then?" suggest Corvin.

All four of them nodded with smiles when Corvin called out.

"Pit-rats! Training speed!" yelled Corvin.

The former slaves all stuck to Corvin as he increased his pace, a pace they were more familiar with. At first, the other recruits had kept up with the quickened pace but after two laps started to lag behind. Within ten laps, the other recruits had been overtaken by the pit-rats. The former slaves all stayed silent and stuck as a tight group as they continued at a pace they were satisfied with. First Sergeant Dolac and Captain Joren had been watching.

"What is this?" asked Dolac as he started to step forward.

"No. Leave them. I want to see if they can keep the pace they started!"

Dolac sat back down and they watched as the former slaves continued to race around the track. After twenty laps had been completed by the former slaves instead of stopping, they eased their pace to a jog; the same speed as they had started the morning run and continued for another five laps to stretch their muscles.

By the time the other recruits had finished their own twenty laps, the former slaves could be seen sitting down on the edge of the track stretching their legs in different exercises.

First Sergeant Dolac walked over to the group, and regardless of what the Captain thought, he wanted answers.

"Why did you increase the pace? I gave no such order?" he said loudly.

The former slaves looked up and said nothing, just looked at the First Sergeant.

"WELL?" he shouted.

Corvin stood with a look on his face that all of the other pit-rats knew all too well. His eyes wide and the veins starting to show on his forehead. Jorga also stood and spoke first before Corvin could say something stupid or insulting.

"We are used to a faster pace than this. This slower pace is no good for us," said Jorga.

"FASTER?" yelled the First Sergeant.

Captain Joren joined the First Sergeant but said nothing.

"Yes, faster. We trained to exhaustion most days in our slavery, which is why we are so much fitter and stronger than anyone in this camp," said Corvin, his temper still simmering below the service.

It was a slight insult, both Jorga and Lorka looked at the ground.

Captain Joren knew his First Sergeant's temper, but wanted to see how Corvin and the others reacted. To see if they could be diplomatic when they needed to be, especially as the First Sergeant out-ranked them.

"Well then, I will have to show you how the Bloodchildren train harder and faster."

Dolac did not see the half smiles of the former slaves, nor did he see the look of resignation from the other new recruits.

"Twenty more circuits, at the same speed you just ran. GO!" shouted the First Sergeant.

They all stood and took off. The former slaves running as a tight group and once again leaving the other recruits behind.

The Captain and First Sergeant both looked on.

"You really think, Dolac, that they will not be able to handle another run?"

"I'll make them run until they collapse," said the First Sergeant.

"I doubt they will collapse. The new recruits may, however!"

They continued to watch as the two groups made their way around the track, at different speeds, of course.

"They are fitter than any of our men, are they not?" asked the Captain.

"Yes," said First Sergeant in a barely audible answer.

"Well, perhaps they have an idea or two on training that we do not have."

First Sergeant said nothing, then turned to look at his Captain.

"What are you thinking, Captain?"

"I am thinking of making Jorga and Corvin - corporals of their own squads!"

It was said slowly, without pause.

"Corporals? I have already chosen the three new corporals for the new season!"

"Yes, you have, but I want to see what the two of them can do with a squad each."

"They are not corporal material!"

"Yes, they are, and you know it, Dolac! Both of them have a good basic knowledge of strategy and tactics, and how they got this knowledge as slaves, I have no idea. Jorga has a better grasp of these things than Corvin, but what Corvin lacks in tactics and strategy, he more than makes up for in leadership skills. You can see the former slaves follow his word without question. He is a natural leader, but he does not even know it.

"I can't believe this, Captain! We need experienced corporals to lead the squads. Not two slaves!"

The Captain stopped watching the runners and turned on his First Sergeant.

"Experience? The two of them lead an escape! They got themselves and the slaves across the length of the Outlander nation and they spent the bulk of their lives fighting for their lives in the pits. You say they have no experience?"

The First Sergeant knew the Captain had already made up his mind and nothing he could say or do would change that. He resigned himself to the Captain's decision, but he still was not happy with it. He also knew the Captain was correct in his assessment, but his own arrogance and dislike for the former slaves was clouding his judgement.

"What squads?"

"I'll give Jorga Eighth Squad and I'll give Corvin Seventh Squad. I will let Third Sergeant Waynix decide who runs Ninth. They are his section, after all."

"How will you place the former slaves?"

"I will leave that up to the new corporals and Sergeant Waynix."

"Do I get to choose the replacements for my squads?"

"Yes. You can have first pick," replied the Captain.

He knew the First Sergeant would pick the best recruits to replace his lost men.

"When will you tell them?"

"This afternoon after their history lesson."

First Sergeant grunted and said nothing further.

"I don't understand," queried Corvin.

"You and your fellows were not taught this as you were slaves, no offence," said Captain Joren.

"None taken," replied Corvin.

Corvin was sitting in the Captain's office. He thought it was a meeting to do with training and surprised to find it was the Captain passing on a few things and teaching him more of the culture of the people of Irik.

"You kept track of what day it was - first day, second day," said Joren.

"Yes," said Corvin, still not understanding.

"We have words that mean multiple days."

"Okay. So, what is the word 'month' mean?"

"One month is twenty-eight days long. There is sixteen months in a full season. So, spring lasts for four months, as does summer, autumn and winter," said Joren.

"So, there is four months for each of the different seasons?" asked Corvin.

"Yes, Corvin. I see your number lessons are coming along. Also, we call a full season, a year."

Corvin smiled.

"Yes sir, but very slowly. Jorga is picking up his numbers very quickly but the rest of us are taking a lot longer."

"It is to be expected, Corvin. You were alive for one task only; the Outlander Bastards had no need to teach you numbers or letters. In fact, apart from the chiefs and some of their retainers, I doubt many of the bastards have their numbers or letters either."

Corvin smiled again. Hearing his Captain refer to the Outlanders in the same fashion as the former slaves always brought a smile to his face. It reminded him how different the Outlanders and the people of Irik were to each other.

"So, why twenty-eight days per month?" asked Corvin.

"I am not sure, Corvin. The people of Ex'Na, who pride themselves on their knowledge, came up with the system over 700 years ago. The country is the birthplace of knowledge in the known world."

Corvin's heart jumped as the Captain mentioned Ex'Na. According to the Smith, there was a good chance Corvin and Irikson came from that land as they both has a basic understanding of the language. Corvin had not yet opened up to the Captain regarding this information. He would have to find out more about this country.

"We keep track of the seasons. The years, I mean?" asked Corvin.

"Yes, we do. We are currently in the year of 1341."

"Confusing, I am sorry."

"Don't be sorry, Corvin. It's all new to you and you did not grow learning this along the way like most children do."

"So, if I have this right, seven days in a week, twenty-eight days or four weeks make up a month, and there is sixteen months for a year, and a year is a full season?" asked Corvin.

"Correct," said Joren.

Corvin was starting to understand.

"So, children are taught this by their parents? They are taught numbers, letters and the different names for the seasons?" asked Corvin.

"Yes. Here in Irik, it is the parents that teach their children. Although, not all children here are taught these things; it all depends on their station. The richer families will teach these children or pay others to teach their children. They see it as a way to give their children every advantage they can and they are right, of course. The poorer families may teach their children basic numbers, but not letters."

"What about the other countries?"

"It depends on the country. Ex'Na, for example, is considered to be the centre of the world and they send their children to various places to be taught. In fact, as I understand, a child will spend five-to-eight-years learning at these places. I forget what they call these places. When a child there turns five-years-old, they get sent to a building with many children of a similar age to be taught their letters and numbers," explained Joren.

"Everyday?" asked Corvin.

"Yes. They get seventh day off, but apart from that, they are there every day. They even have places where adults can go to continue their learning."

Corvin took it all in. He would struggle to explain the things he was learning to the others, and he was struggling.

"All nations do this?" asked Corvin.

"No. Ex'Na is considered the most advanced nation so they teach their people from a young age. A country called Kor'Lena also has some places of learning for their young ones but not on the same scale as Ex'Na. Here in Irik, we leave it up to the parents to teach their children, although there have been some talks by our leading council, that we have a place of learning like Ex'Na."

"You think Irik should have these places of learning?" asked Corvin.

"Yes, I do. Not to the same level of Ex'Na, but a place where our children can learn basic skills like letters, numbers and other useful things would be a bloody good idea."

"Clearly, the Outlanders do not," said Corvin.

"No. They don't. Also, Sul'Lena which is the neighbouring country to Kor'Lena does not either."

Corvin mulled over everything the Captain was saying.

"So much to learn."

The Captain laughed.

"Yes, but not all in one sitting. You had best get back to your training. We will talk again soon. I may even add some lessons to your day for you and your fellows to catch up on some knowledge that you do not have."

"One last question, Captain," said Corvin.

"Yes?"

"What is a Lai?" asked Corvin.

"It's a unit of measurement. They have measuring sticks but it is about one long stride. Why do you ask?"

"I heard it said the other day."

The Captain stood up. He took one step.

"That is roughly one Lai," explained the Captain.

"Then, what is a Melai?" asked Corvin.

"A thousand Lai."

"A thousand?" asked Corvin.

"Yes. A Lai is a smaller measurement. We use it in many situations. A Melai is a thousand steps roughly. We use 'Melai' when we are measuring large distances. For example, they distance from here to Bordix, where you first arrived, is roughly 450 Melai," explained the Captain.

Corvin struggled through the number, converting it in his head.

"So, it is 450,000 steps from here to Bordix?" asked Corvin.

"Very good, Corvin. Yes, that is correct," said the Captain, sitting down again.

"So much to learn," Corvin said again.

"Get back to your training. You will learn but as I said before, not all in one sitting."

Corvin smiled, then left. The Captain poured himself some wine and leaned back. Normally, he would not spend any time with the new recruits, but Corvin and the former slaves where different. He enjoyed the expression on Corvin's face as he was learning. Corvin soaked it all up like sponge and Joren wondered what Corvin could have been if not taken by the Outlander bastards all those years ago.

The new recruits were seated in the meeting hall. The meeting hall had enough seating for the entire company but was only half full, as the new recruits all sat in the front. In the back, was a couple members of the company slowly sipping from their ale mugs. The meeting hall was tall with a high ceiling and had enough seating for the entire company of the Bloodchildren. The outside was of solid stonework, neat and straight with a height of three men standing on each other's shoulders. The inside was a light wood that had been oiled. These wooden walls ran from floor to ceiling; when the fireplace and the candles were lit, it reflected the light off the walls and brightened up the hall.

The former slaves and other recruits had slowly begun to meet the other members of the company, but the established mercenaries were a little stand-offish. Jorga had discussed this with Corvin and they both agreed, it would be this way until the new recruits had proved themselves in battle.

The day had been harder on the new recruits as first Sergeant had done his best to run them off their feet. Of course, the former slaves took it in their stride, the other new recruits were not taking it so well; some falling over and not being able to move from exhaustion.

"A history lesson apparently," said Irikson as he sipped his mug of ale.

"Whose history?" asked Lorka.

"The Bloodchildren's history!" said Jorga.

They all hushed as the Captain stood in front of them.

"Tonight, you will hear of our history. The history of the Bloodchildren!" said the Captain.

He stood straight and looked over the new recruits. Most of them looked exhausted from the day's training, and just looked at the drink and food in front of them. However, the former slaves were eating and drinking their fill. The Captain continued.

"We, the Bloodchildren, have been around for a while and we have a rich history. I will pass you over to Sergeant Emric, who will take the lesson tonight."

Second Sergeant Emric strode forward. He was a solid muscular man that stood just on six feet tall. His shoulder length black hair matching the blackness in his eyes and he looked younger than his thirty-one years. The new recruits had seen him around the base but of course, never had any interaction with him. He had been with the company for the last decade, once starting out as a new recruit like all the others before him. He stood in front of them and looked over the assembled recruits. He waited for a few minutes before launching into his lesson.

"A hundred and nine years! That is how long the Bloodchildren have existed. That is how long the tradition of this company goes back."

He waited for that to sink in. He looked around the hall looking at all the new recruits, the future of the company. All were listening, all were focused on him and he felt a small amount of pride as continued to talk.

"A hundred and nine years ago, First Captain Joren formed this company. There was a war in the lands to the south, a land called Ex'Na. This land had asked for fighting men to help in a small civil war they were fighting. First Captain Joren, a sailor by trade, saw a chance to make money. He gathered two hundred rough men who he knew could handle themselves well and set sail for this land in the south. His men and himself fought well in that war and built a reputation as fearless fighters! Ferocious fighters! At the end of that little war, his men had been reduced to a hundred and five fighting men from the original two hundred. He was paid a large bonus for all he and his men accomplished in the war and the King of Ex'Na had been heard calling our men the children of blood, in reference to the way they fought. On returning to Irik, First Captain Joren took the next step and made it official and the company was formed. He chose the name Bloodchildren and after paying off the men who had fought with him, but wanted to return to what they were doing previously, sent out a call for recruits to build the company."

Second Sergeant took a sip from his own ale cup, looked around the hall and saw the new recruits hanging on his words.

"The decisions that First Captain Joren made a century ago, laid the foundations for what we are today. He decided that when his men were not fighting, they would be training. He decided his company would always have a maximum of a hundred and five men! The exact number of men that survived the first war. The company would be made up of a captain, three sergeants, a clerk and one hundred fighting men. With the money he had made from the first war, they had fought in; he purchased this land. A hundred and nine years ago, this land was nothing but empty hills and sold cheaply. He had the large stone wall which we now have circling our camp built. The settlement outside slowly sprang up over the years until it was a town of some size and named Valik."

He took another sip of his ale.

"Since those early days, the Bloodchildren have stuck to the traditions First Captain Joren started. ALL of the company Captains are called Joren in honour of the First Captain. Our current Captain Joren is the fifth to take on the role. So, he is known as Fifth Captain Joren. The next to replace him will be called Sixth Captain Joren. Over the years, our base here at Valik has evolved. Once a basic training camp, is now the walled-in base you live in and train in today. Each Captain adding and improving to our base here. Fifth Captain Joren was the one that had the large indoor training area built inside the running track. This was completed three years ago."

Second Sergeant stopped to catch his breath before launching into the final part of his speech.

"As new recruits, you are responsible for upholding the honour and traditions of the original Bloodchildren. Over the next month, you will learn more of our history and traditions that we have here. Over the next month, you will hear stories of our most famous battles and of the heroes of the company. Listen to these stories, take heart and courage from these stories. Most all remember our motto here at the Bloodchildren! Train hard. Fight harder. Die hardest!"

He looked over the assembled crowd one last time as his speech came to an end. He saw some fire in the eyes of the new recruits. He smiled, stepped over to his seat and sat back down. Captain Joren now stood back in front of the recruits.

"You have just heard a brief history of the Bloodchildren. You will hear more in the coming weeks as Second Sergeant Emric has said. Our history is just as important as our future! Now off with you all and enjoy your day off!" he said with a smile.

The new recruits cheered as tomorrow was seventh day. For the Mercenaries, it was a day free from training or other duties.

The former slaves were in high spirits as they drank ale in at the tavern in Valik. It was a tavern called the 'Bald Goat' that welcomed the mercenaries, the owner Keloc knowing full well the mercenaries would spend many coins on drink and food but because of their training and discipline, not act out or cause too many problems.

"Proud history!" said Jorga as he put his ale cup down.

"Yes," replied Corvin.

They both turned as they heard the laughter from the other end of the table. They watched as Irikson picked himself up off the ground with a curse. As usual, Irikson was drunk. He muttered curses as he righted his stool. They both smiled at the fiery man.

"Did you find out what Captain wanted to speak to us about in the morning?" asked Corvin.

"No, he just said he wanted to speak to both of us after first light," replied Jorga.

"I can't imagine what we have done wrong!" said Corvin looking into space.

"Agreed. We have performed all of the training and duties asked of us. Since Irikson beat the two city-watch, we have all kept ourselves in line," said Jorga.

"Do you think it has anything to do with Irikson picking a fight with First Sergeant last week when he was drunk?"

Irikson had been in the tavern on the eve of seventh day, out-drinking everyone as usual. First Sergeant had come in and made a comment about Irikson's drunkenness. Which, of course, Irikson being highly emotionally charged, took the comment as a challenge. He had offered to fight the First Sergeant outside. The First Sergeant was about to accept when Second Sergeant that had been sitting at another table diffused the situation by asking Irikson to join him in a drinking contest.

"I'm not sure. First Sergeant is petty, but I doubt he would go running to the Captain," said Corvin.

"Who knows? He certainly does not hide his bad feeling towards us!" said Jorga.

"No, he does not!"

Another cheer went up as Irikson and Lorka started an arm wrestle. Corvin stared into space, thinking of the past.

"Thinking of Smith?" asked Lorka.

Corvin smiled and looked at his friend.

"I was."

"Not an easy man to forget. I miss him," said Jorga as he put his hand on Corvin's shoulder.

"Aye. We all miss him."

"He would be proud of you, Snow Weasel!" said Jorga.

A smile spread across Corvin's face and he looked at his friend.

"He would be proud of all of us for getting out," corrected Corvin.

Jorga also smiled.

"Was not bloody easy and we lost a few."

"We lost more than a few!" said Corvin.

Just then, the old Third Sergeant Waynix arrived at their table.

"Corvin, Jorga" Waynix nodded as he greeted them.

"Sergeant," they both replied.

"Captain wants to see you both if you do not mind coming back to the camp?"

They looked at each other before Jorga spoke.

"Not at all, Sergeant," said Jorga.

They finished their ales in one and stood, following the Third Sergeant out of the tavern.

"Please be seated, both of you," said Captain Joren as they entered his work room.

They both sat down in the chairs in front of his desk. They were both a little nervous as they had no clue what they or anyone of the former slaves had done wrong.

Joren saw their nervous faces and smiled. "Relax, both of you. Neither of you have done anything wrong."

Once the two had got comfortable, Joren continued. "Firstly, I want to say I am impressed by the level of fitness of all the former slaves. Never in my life have I seen anyone in better physical condition. I know this comes from your former life, but it's still impressive."

It was Jorga that spoke first. "Thank you, Captain."

"You have both seen how we train here at the Bloodchildren and I wanted to know your thoughts!"

"Thoughts?" said Corvin.

"Yes, your thoughts or ideas. All of you are superbly fit, strong and well disciplined. If I had one hundred of you, I would be the most well paid company in this nation!" said the Captain.

The two looked at each other. Jorga nodded to Corvin to continue.

"We have some ideas where you could improve, yes," said Corvin after thinking about it.

"Great," replied the Captain.

Jorga went to speak but was cut off by the Captain.

"I do not need to hear these ideas!"

They both looked very confused and Corvin could feel his anger rising. Before he could say something insulting, the Captain continued.

"Instead, I want you both to SHOW me!"

If they were confused before, they were even more

confused now. The Captain looked at their confused faces and laughed, loud and long.

"I am promoting you both!" he finally said.

"Promoting?" they both said in unison.

"Yes. Both of you are now promoted to Corporals. Jorga, I am giving you command of Eighth Squad. Corvin, I am giving you Seventh squad. You have full authority over training for the rest of the winter. Third Sergeant Waynix will oversee you both as he is in charge of Seventh, Eighth and Ninth squad. He has agreed to let you have full authority over the training of the recruits."

Jorga was smiling, as was Corvin. Then they both started laughing.

"What's so funny?" asked the Captain.

"We apologise, Captain. We both thought we were in trouble when you asked to speak to us," said Jorga.

Corvin still smiling, nodded. Captain Joren also smiled.

"Far from it!" he said.

"How did Third Sergeant take the news he was not in charge of the training?" asked Corvin.

The Captain nodded, well satisfied that Corvin was starting to learn and be more aware of the politics within the company.

"He is fine with it, but then again, it was partly his idea. He said he was quite excited to see what the both of you could do!"

"Excited?" asked Jorga.

"Yes, very excited," said the Captain, before continuing.

"Keep in mind, Sergeant Waynix is a well-seasoned soldier and has more life behind him than anyone else in the company. He is fifty-three years old and recognises good soldiering when he sees it."

Both looked very surprised. Jorga looked over at Corvin, seeing a little pride in his eyes. He then turned to the Captain.

"I think we are both surprised that he has let us have full authority over training two squads," said Jorga.

"Not two squads, but all of the recruits in his section. All three squads!"

"ALL three?" said Corvin.

"Yes. All three!"

Both of the former slaves said nothing. They sat in silence taking in the promotion. The Captain had to nudge them along.

"Do you accept?" asked the Captain.

"I accept and I am honoured to be a corporal," said Jorga.

The Captain looked to Corvin.

"Yes. I also accept and feel honoured, Captain. Thank you." The last words almost a whisper.

"That's what I wanted to hear. The unlucky ones have already been sent to their homes and told to try again next year", said the Captain as he rose.

The other two stood as well as the Captain reached out to shake their hands.

"Tomorrow is a rest day. Enjoy it and then take charge of your squads."

"Yes, sir," they both said.

Both of the former slaves were deep in discussion as they made their way back to the tavern.

On arrival at the tavern, they found where Waynix was sitting and joined him.

"Congratulations, boys," he said as the two sat down.

"Thank you," they both said.

"Although, I think we are a little more than just boys!" said Corvin.

"Aye, but at my age, you are all boys," replied Waynix with a chuckle.

"Why all three squads?" asked Jorga.

"No point in having one squad not being able to keep up with the other two is there?" he replied.

Jorga nodded as Corvin continued.

"Thank you for having faith in us, Sergeant."

"You and your boys are the fittest men I have ever seen, and I have been amongst soldiers and mercenaries my whole life. You all fight like wounded cats, can run all day and have more discipline than the Infantry of Mealus. Well, disciplined when sober!" said the Sergeant, with a wicked smile.

"Infantry from where?" asked Corvin.

"It does not matter, but I am looking forward to what you can do with the new recruits!"

"That's what the Captain just said," said Jorga.

"I will still be there to oversee, of course. I enjoy learning different techniques for training," said Waynix.

"Have the squads been sorted then?" asked Jorga.

"That is another reason I wanted to chat to you both. First Sergeant Dolac has gone through the recruits and chosen the fourteen he needs for replacements in the other squads under himself and Second Sergeant Emric," said Sergeant Waynix.

"Any of them former slaves?" asked Corvin.

"No. He has chosen none of your former pit-rats. If he had, I would have said no and taken the matter to the Captain. I want to keep you all together as much as possible," said Sergeant Waynix.

"Good, and thank you," said Jorga.

Sergeant Waynix smiled.

"Who has he taken?" asked Corvin.

"I have a list of names here," he said, pulling out a piece of parchment.

He began reading the names as he knew neither of the corporals had their letters and could not read. Once he had finished reading the fifteen names, Jorga smiled.

"He has taken the best of Irik recruits!" said Jorga.

"Yes," Corvin said, with a little annoyance.

"For now. Once you have finished training the rest of the recruits, I am sure they will be more than a match," said the Sergeant.

"Thank you for your confidence in us," said Corvin.

The two corporals said nothing for a time.

"Out with-it, boys! If you have something to say, just say it," said Waynix.

Corvin smiled, then spoke.

"Captain said we start on first day. We would like to start tomorrow! Can you have all of the recruits meet on the training field at sunrise?"

"Looking to piss some people off, are you? No better way of doing that than taking away their day off!"

"We won't be taking their day off away from them. We want to set in motion certain ideas and let them know that next month will be hard," said Corvin.

"Okay. What else?"

"We will send them on a short run to stretch their legs and it is time someone taught them to stretch. We have a couple of recruits with pulled muscles already," said Jorga.

"I can do that, I'll spread the word soon. Anything else?"

"No, Sergeant, not at the moment."

"Well, enjoy your night then, boys and I'll make sure word is passed around to meet tomorrow. I am giving you both plenty of freedom to train as you see fit and I will not interfere. All I ask of you is to include me in your planning and discussions. Although I am looking forward to seeing what you can do, I do myself have a good amount of experience, as you can both tell from my grey hairs in my beard."

They both chuckled and stood.

"We will, Sergeant. Thanks again for giving us the three squads. We can both say they will be very much fitter within the next month."

"You're welcome, lads. I'll see you at sunrise," said Waynix as he raised his mug of ale.

As they both walked towards the bar to get more drinks, they continued to talk.

"So, what will we be doing first?" said Jorga.

"I think we will introduce them to hell runs. That and strength training to start with," said Corvin.

"Good idea. I suggest we stop all fight training and focus on fitness for the next couple of weeks. Once they have got used to the new training, then we introduce unarmed combat, then weapons training," suggested Jorga.

"Agreed. Any training from the bastard Outlanders that we should leave out?" asked Corvin.

"Object lessons," whispered Jorga.

They had stopped at the bar top and Corvin turned to Jorga. He placed his hand on Jorga's shoulder and squeezed lightly. At that moment, they both thought of Trainer. They were sad but had hearts filled with hope.

"He would be proud of us!" said Corvin in reply.

"Not if we don't get these recruits fit, he won't," said Jorga with a smile.

Corvin laughed aloud.

They ordered drinks, then returned to their friends. They agreed to say nothing and surprise the former slaves in the morning.

"Alright lads, gather in close," said Third Sergeant Waynix.

He looked over the thirty recruits under his command and could see a lot of angry faces. Soldiers and Mercenaries did not like having their day off taken away from them. He hid a smile and watched them all gather round. One of the recruits raised his hand and he nodded to him.

"What do you have us doing today, Sergeant?" spoke the recruit.

"I will not have you doing anything, recruit. I did not ask for you all to be here this morning. Your two new corporals asked me to assemble you all here," said Waynix

The recruits all looked at each other, whispering started to take hold when Waynix shouted out.

"These are your two new Corporals - Corporal Corvin and Corporal Jorga!"

The whispering stopped as the two new corporals strode forward and stood beside the Third Sergeant. Corvin and Jorga looked at the former slaves, along with the smiles and nods coming from them. The other recruits looked a little fearful. They all knew these two had led the slaves out of the Outlander nations. Some were in awe, but most where a little standoffish and even fearful.

"With me overseeing, these two are now completely in charge of your training for the rest of the winter. They speak with my voice and my permission. You will obey them as if I am giving the order. Is that clear?"

A chorus of "Yes, Sergeant" went around the group. Corvin took a step forward and began to speak.

"For the next month, all training will be fitness. Weapons training will be put on hold. Jorga and I will be introducing you to some new ways of training. Many of you have been annoyed that you cannot keep up with those of us that escaped the Outlander bastards. Many of you have not believed the stories we have told of how we got as fit as we are. Well, now you will get to experience that training," said Corvin.

The former slaves all nodding their heads and smiling. They knew that copying their training from the slave camp was a good idea. Whereas the other recruits really had no idea of what was about to hit them. Jorga stepped forward.

"We have called you here this morning to let you know and advise a few things. The first thing we will suggest, is seeking your beds earlier. Training will be hard and you will need a good night's sleep. Trust me, you will not want to do this training with a sore head from drinking too much ale the night before!" said Jorga.

The former slaves all laughed, and the new recruits just nodded.

Corvin nodded and spoke again.

"Secondly. We suggest you learn from each other. The men that escaped from slavery are no different from the recruits raised here in Irik. They are not special! They do not have something you do not! They have just had different lives. If those of you are struggling, ask for help. Those of us that did the long trek can pass on our knowledge of training. In return, you can pass on your knowledge on how to live. Think about that for a second, all of you. You men that were born and raised here in Irik can teach us something that all of us that did the long trek are struggling with."

The recruits from Irik looked puzzled, as did the former slaves. All was silent when Corvin continued.

"You can teach us, the former slaves, how to be free!"

The faces across all the recruits now had large smiles across them. There was laughter coming from a few of the recruits. Lorka that had been standing next to the largest of the recruits from Irik, a mere few inches shorter than himself, laid his hand on the man's shoulder.

"You can teach us how to drink and the best way to haggle prices with Coin-Wives!"

All of the recruits roared with laughter. Jorga and Corvin shared a look and a smile. Lorka, as was his way, had crossed the gap in a few words and a joke. Third Sergeant Waynix was also smiling. He was looking forward to seeing how the two new corporals would bridge the gap between the former slaves and those recruits that were from Irik. He was not disappointed. Corvin continued.

"I would suggest you enjoy your day off but before that, since Lorka can't bloody well learn to take anything serious, he can lead us all in a few simple exercises to stretch our muscles."

The recruits laughed again.

"Aye, Corporal," said Lorka.

"All hit the field and do a slow five laps. Lorka, you set the pace," said Jorga.

All of the recruits followed Lorka and began to slowly run around the track. As they jogged, Lorka explained the importance of stretching.

"That went better than I thought," said Corvin.

"You two handled that well," said Waynix.

"The work is just beginning," said Jorga.

"Yes. We need the Irik recruits feeling a part of it and not sitting on the outside looking in," replied Corvin.

"Well, enjoy the morning. In a week or two, we will discuss squad placements."

"Yes, sir," they both replied, before running off to join the others.

Third Sergeant watched as they caught up and ran at the back of the pack as it made its way slowly around the training track. He watched as the three squads did a slow five laps, then stop and make their way into the covered area in the field. He walked over to watch and listen. Jorga was instructing the recruits and taking them through a set of exercises that he had never seen before. He listened to the explanation but most of it went over his head. Something about stretching the muscles from the day before. This Jorga explained would cool off the muscles and help them feel more refreshed for the next day. He would ask some questions of the two new corporals another time. He could see the other former slaves, hauntingly at first begin to help the Irik recruits. Suggesting or showing how to complete the stretching. The Irik recruits listened and soaked up all they could. Third Sergeant Waynix smiled again. He thought back to the speech Corvin had given, in particular the part where he said the former slaves *"We're nothing special!"* He believed differently. They were all special. As he walked away, he started to look forward to the coming season. He would have thirty superbly fit soldiers under him. It would be a good season.

Chapter Two

The morning started with a light workout. The recruits, led by Jorga and Corvin, completed ten laps of the track at a light jog. The group ran closely together, shoulder to shoulder, as instructed by the two new corporals. At the end of the ten laps, they all stopped and Lorka took the recruits through the first stretches of the day.

"We do these stretches after our first run, to warm them up. If we push the body straight into the hard work without first warming them up, you will injure yourself," said Lorka.

Corvin who was bent over stretching his legs smiled to himself. At the slave training camp, the slaves were drawn to Lorka, then known as Funny-boy. Drawn to his smiling face, his gentle good humour and his natural way with people. He possessed a natural warmth that radiated out and drew people to him. Here he was again, helping bridging the gap between the former slaves and the other recruits. Corvin looked up and saw the recruits from Irik hanging on his words. Looking over at Jorga, they caught each other's eyes and smiled.

They had finished stretching and all stood. Lorka looked over at Corvin, who smiled and nodded his head.

"Now we have all stretched. I want to see us all run four more laps of the track. Irikson will set the pace! I want to see you all stick together in a group. Once you have run the four laps, all meet in the indoor training area. You are all going to be introduced to something we call 'hell runs'."

"You bastard!" some of the former slaves muttered.

The recruits from Irik looked confused, but Corvin knew they would not be confused for long.

The group set off around the track as Irikson lead from the front. He was talking to the recruits as he ran, encouraging them, including them and making feel a part of the group. Listening at the rear of the group, Corvin, Lorka and Jorga ran behind them. Trying not to laugh when Irikson shared an off-colour story regarding him, the old cook from the training camp and an incident in the vegetable garden. He heard giggles from many of the group. Corvin realised something he had not thought of before. He was surrounded by some supportive men, some good men and some amazing men.

They finished the run and walked over to the indoor training area. The night before Corvin and Jorga had placed white painted rocks at regular intervals throughout the space, to replicate the set up from the hell runs they used to do in the training camp.

"Gather round everyone," said Corvin.

The recruits all gathered around and waited.

"We said we would introduce you to hell runs. Those of us that were slaves used to do these every day. They bring a world of pain and to be honest, we hated them. However, they are the best exercise we did for fitness," said Corvin.

"PIT-RATS on the line!" yelled Jorga.

The former slaves stepped up to the line.

"Watch what we do," said Corvin.

"AWAY!" shouted Jorga.

The former slaves took off at full run, stopping at every line of rocks, touching the ground and sprinting back to the starting position. The two new corporals had joined in and ran with the group. As the former slaves ran, they all battled with their own thoughts. These runs brought back many memories they had tried to forget about. As they sprinted back from the last line of rocks they were breathing heavily. They stopped and caught their breath.

"What you just saw, was what we call a hell run. We call them this because after a few of them, you feel like you are in hell. We will split into two evenly-matched groups. Whilst one group runs, the other catches its breath," said Corvin.

One of the Irik recruits that Corvin knew by face alone, raised his hand.

"Yes," said Jorga.

"One of these looks hard but I would hardly call them hell runs!" said the recruit.

Lorka laughed loudly and the other former slaves smiled.

"What you saw, is one run. We do twenty of these!" said Corvin.

The look on the faces of the recruits from Irik was one of surprise - an unwanted surprise.

"That is why we run in two groups. One is running and the other is resting," said Jorga.

"Eventually by the end of the first month, we will cease to run as two groups and run as one group, with only a small rest in the middle," replied Corvin.

Third Sergeant Waynix had walked in and was watching. He had witnessed the example of the hell run and was glad he did not have to do it. He watched Corvin and Jorga sort all the recruits into two groups. He noticed they had spread the former slaves evenly amongst the two groups. Jorga lead one group, and Corvin the other. Corvin's group lined up first.

"Away," said Jorga.

The first group took off. The recruits from Irik were a few steps behind the former slaves.

"We stay in a line as a group. We start the run together and we end the run together!" Corvin yelled out.

Sergeant Waynix smiled again to himself. He watched both groups go through the hell runs and was surprised once again at the stamina of the former slaves. The Irik recruits struggled, all of them had never done anything so tiring in their lives. Almost all had dropped out and did not complete the full twenty, barely being able to breathe. Yet, once the hell-runs had been completed, they were not criticised or ridiculed. In fact, the opposite happened which surprised him. Once all the recruits had caught their breath, they sat down in a group, Corvin and Jorga facing them.

"Those of you that did not finish the hell runs, do not be ashamed. You will not be teased for not finishing. All we ask is you try your hardest," said Corvin.

Jorga jumped in and added his thoughts.

"If you can remember at which point you dropped out, remember that number. Tomorrow, push that little bit further, try and beat what you did today," said Jorga.

The recruits from Irik nodded and felt better about the situation. The former slaves however had not done these runs in a while and most of them had only just finished them. If they had been asked to do another five, they would not have been able too. Corvin saw this and spoke on it.

"Irik men, look around at the former slaves! They too are out of breath and barely finished the runs. We have not trained this hard in a few months and believe me when I say we struggled as well," said Corvin.

"Youst. How you feeling?" asked Jorga.

"Like shit, Corporal. That hurt and I hated it!" said Youst.

All of the recruits laughed. Corvin smiled at the youth's honesty.

"Trust me, after a month of every morning, you will all be fitter and stronger," said Jorga.

The day continued with new exercises. Corvin and Jorga had sourced wheelbarrows yesterday and spent their day off filling them with rocks. They were lined up next to the track. The recruits from Irik had paid no attention to them, the former slaves had and knew what was coming. The next two hours before lunch was spent running a circuit with a wheelbarrow filled with rocks. The pace was not as fast as the pace during the hell-runs, but it still hurt. The former slaves once again had not done these rock-runs for a while and muscles they had not used in a while were hurting. Of course, the recruits from Irik had never done these rock-runs before and had discovered pain in muscles they never knew existed. Sergeant Waynix watched as the two group took turns in running around the track pushing the wheelbarrows. He watched as all of the former slaves kept up the encouragement and talked constantly with the Irik recruits.

Once they had finished, the wheelbarrows were parked up beside the track and the recruits were stretching once again. Once done, they all made their way to the cookhouse for their midday meal. Third Sergeant had already had a conversation with the cook. The two new corporals had asked for different food for the recruits. The cook had checked with the Third Sergeant to make sure it was okay; he had said yes. The midday meal, which usually would have been meat and starchy vegetables, was now a vegetable broth with a little bread and a selection of dried fruit. Third Sergeant did not know why the two new corporals had done this. He would have to ask them. He sat down by himself in the cook house and shared the same meal as the recruits. He watched the interaction of the recruits and noticed the former slaves had spread themselves around all the recruits, not sat by themselves. He knew they were trying to encourage a sense of community and was pleased with the thought.

For the next week, the training stayed the same. Hell runs, rock runs, strength exercises in the afternoon and then finishing the day with more laps of the training track. The new recruits whether former slaves or recruits from Irik, all fell on their evening meals with gusto before collapsing in their beds. There had been some resentment when the fight training had been stopped to focus on fitness training, but even by the end of the first week, ALL the recruits had improved. Sergeant Waynix had not watched everyday but rather let the two corporals get on with it. By the end of the third week since midwinter, he invited the two corporals to a meal at the tavern called the Wandering Warrior. This tavern was on the other side of the settlement and not visited by the mercenaries as it was a bit more expensive. The officers from the Bloodchildren often visited it if they wanted someplace quiet to discuss anything that was a little more private. The two corporals walked in and saw Sergeant Waynix. They walked over and the Third Sergeant smiled.

"Thank you both for coming, have a seat," he said.

Both sat down. Both of the former slaves had come to terms with the relationship of their Sergeant and were a lot more comfortable around him. The last three weeks since being made corporals, they had spoken to him daily, giving reports and to the delight of the Third Sergeant, asking for advice.

"Thank you, Sergeant," said Jorga.

"How goes the new fitness training?" the Sergeant asked.

"You have not been watching?" asked Corvin as he dug into the roast meat that was sitting in the middle of the table on a huge platter.

"I have been watching but want to know your thoughts," said Sergeant Waynix.

"Good. Very good in fact," said Jorga.

"Yes. It's going well," agreed Corvin.

Sergeant Waynix said nothing, inviting the corporals to continue.

"The fitness has improved for all the recruits, including the former slaves. The recruits are training well together and there are some friendships being formed," said Jorga.

Corvin just nodded.

"Good to hear. Now we have twenty-eight recruits to put into three squads. Also, we need to choose a new corporal to lead the Ninth Squad."

Both the corporals nodded their agreement. They had not yet had the chance to discuss the make-up of the squads between themselves. They had just concentrated on getting the fitness to a better standard.

"I have an idea or two!" said the Sergeant.

They both nodded.

"I was thinking of your ex-slave Irikson to lead the Ninth squad."

Jorga and Corvin looked at each other in surprise and both shook their heads.

"Not a good idea," said Corvin.

"It's not? Why?" asked the Sergeant.

"He is too emotionally charged. Yes, he is good at helping out with training and may be once he has grown up a bit. He could be a corporal, but even though I call the man my brother, I could not trust him to lead a squad. He is the type of person that would forget his orders and charge in to combat recklessly and waste his men's lives," said Jorga.

"Agreed. I am surprised you would think of him after the problems he and his drinking have caused," said Corvin.

"Yes, he caused a few problems, but he has kept his head down lately. So, who do you see leading the Ninth Squad?" asked the Sergeant.

He was quietly happy. He knew Irikson was not suitable to be a corporal but in a way, it was a small test for the two new corporals.

"It needs to be an Irik recruit," said Corvin.

"Yes, it does. If the squads are all lead by former slaves, it would affect morale and reinforce that we are special and better than them. We can't have that!" said Jorga.

Corvin racked his brain, running his mind through the faces of the Irik men. Jorga did the same. There were a few silent moments when Corvin finally lifted his head and returned to the conversation.

"Torin," said Corvin.

Jorga nodded his head.

"Agreed. Torin has a calm way about him but knows how to fight. He is one tough man but knows how to follow orders. He also has the respect of not only the Irik recruits, but is well liked by the former slaves," said Jorga.

"Interesting. He is a good man, but I admit I did not see him as a corporal. He sits back and follows, but never have I seen him want to lead," said the Sergeant.

"That's why he is a good choice," said Corvin.

"Explain?" said the Sergeant.

Corvin tried to put his thoughts into words, but once again, it was Jorga that spoke.

"He sits back and follows, yes. When he is sitting back, he

is listening and listening well. It may seem he is unassuming, but he thinks well. Also, he cares for those around him which will be a benefit when we start fighting. I have had a practice bout against him! Trust me, he is the closest of the Irik recruits to a fighting equal to the former slaves. No offence intended, Sergeant," said Jorga.

"None taken," replied the Sergeant.

"Yes. He has the qualities and if he were under me, I would have full confidence in him. I would however make a suggestion," Corvin left the words hanging.

"Go on," said the Sergeant.

"I would spread the former slaves out amongst all the squads. I know it seemed it would be a good idea to have all of us in the same squads, but that may seem to those Irik men, we are above them. Instead spread us out. If you decide to make Torin the corporal, I suggest adding Norda and Lorka to his squad," said Corvin.

Jorga nodded his head in agreement.

"Yes. Both of those are good men and would support him well. Especially Lorka! He has a way about him that would do well in the Ninth Squad. He would be perfect for supporting Torin. Also, having a couple of former slaves under an Irik man would be good for morale," said Jorga.

"I see where you are coming from. Yes, it's a good idea," said the Sergeant.

"Who would you place in the other squads, Jorga?" asked Corvin.

"In your squad, I would put Irikson. He works best at your side anyhow and it is possibly the best way to keep him in line. Also, Mirac, Pula, Celix and Maddik. They would be a good fit. In my squad, I would take Youst, Bordix, Benik and Samik. Also put Thomik, Liok and Kamik in Ninth Squad. As for the Irik recruits, I think they will fit into any of the squads with no problem," said Jorga.

Corvin nodded and looked to the Sergeant.

"Well, you two have pretty much solved the problem of how to fit in the former slaves into which squad. I can see that spreading all of your fellows throughout the squads will spread experience. Much longer and I can retire!" said the Sergeant, with huge grin.

For the rest of the evening, the three of them discussed which Irik recruit would go where over a few mugs of ale. The three of them discussed problems of uniting the squads and came up with ways to get around them. Late into the night they talked, the two former slaves now fully at ease with the Third Sergeant. The Third Sergeant happy to pass on his knowledge to two young men that appreciated his experience and soaked up all he could share.

Seventh day had arrived again and the recruits left over from the ones that First Sergeant had taken, were stretching and talking quietly amongst themselves after their morning stretching run. It was an overcast day after another night of snowfall. The air was as chilly as the former slaves had encountered in the Outlander nation. The difference was they had warmer clothing than they had in the training camp or indeed when they were slaves. Third Sergeant Waynix had arrived.

"Listen up boys, I have an announcement to make," said Sergeant Waynix.

All of the recruits had stopped their stretching and sat on the ground under the roofed in training area.

"I have been watching you all train and I am happy with how the training is going,"

A small cheer went around the group.

"We are getting closer to the fighting season and it is time we appoint you all to your squads," said the Sergeant.

The news got all of their attention. They straightened and sat up. He read through all of the members of the Seventh and Eighth Squads. Corvin and Jorga had explained to Lorka and Norda of the situation of Ninth Squad last night and had also told them who the corporal would be. They had agreed and felt no hard feelings towards the decision.

"To the rest of you that I have not read out, will be Ninth Squad. Ninth Squad needs a corporal and after talking with the other two corporals, it has been decided Torin will be Ninth Squad's corporal. Torin, stand and be recognised."

A cheer went up of those gathered. Not only were the Irik recruits cheering but also the former slaves. They had all got to know Torin and formed friendships with him. Torin, with a surprised look on his face, stood up and walked forward. He shook the hands of the other corporals and also the Third Sergeant. He had no words and was not expecting this.

"I am sure you will lead your squad well, Torin. From now, on you will be included in our end of week meetings," said the Sergeant.

"Yes, Sergeant."

"Good. Enjoy your day off today and I will see you all back here on first day," said the Sergeant before leaving.

What followed was many of the men jumping up to congratulate the new corporal. He was smiling from ear to ear and accepted all the congratulations with genuine thanks.

"It's only a few weeks until the season and already, we have a few offers come in for our services," said the Captain.

The three sergeants of the Bloodchildren sat around the

Captains desk like they did every winter, ready to discuss the many offers they received. Ready to offer advice to the Captain, although the final choice was always his.

"What's the offers?" asked Third Sergeant Waynix.

"We have three so far," said the Captain.

He looked around at his Sergeants before continuing.

"The first is from the Duke of DuNoor in Ex'Na. He wants our company to join his soldiers for a job in Renis in the far south!"

"That arrogant bastard still owes us from five years ago, does he not?" said Second Sergeant Emric.

"He does!" said the Captain.

"Has he mentioned this payment he still owes us?" asked Sergeant Dolac.

"Promised to pay what he owes at the end of the upcoming season!" said the Captain.

"Will he?" asked Waynix.

"No. I doubt he will!" said the Captain.

"Then, I advise no," said Emric.

"Agreed," said Waynix.

"Yep, screw him," said Dolac.

"Okay, that offer is gone," said the Captain, as he screwed up the letter.

"The next offer is once again from Nedia in Ex'Na. They want us to help protect their sea border from raiders," said the Captain.

"From our Outlander cousins, you mean! Is it good money?" asked Dolac.

"Two hundred Golic coins for the summer, then a further fifty Golic coins if we prevent the raiders along the coastline which we would be appointed to. It's an easy task and not too risky. It will be easy money!" said the Captain.

"What's the last offer?" asked Emric.

"The king of Sul'Lena is calling all mercenaries companies he can. He has made a very rich offer for a job. Although, he has not said what the job is," replied the Captain.

"It will be a murderous job, it always is," said Waynix.

"True," agreed Emric.

"Money good?" ask Dolac.

"Three times the amount of the Nedia offer. Six hundred Golic coins for the summer. However, we all know of the King from Sul'Lena. He is a murdering savage and will be up to no good. We have all fought against his savages before, I did not think we would want to fight with him," said the Captain.

"I would not want to," said Waynix.

"The money, however, is not trivial. The work may be murderous but that is what we do. Is there a bonus?" asked Dolac.

"No. A straight six hundred Golic for the summer, although he mentions there could be plunder," replied the Captain.

"We work for coin, not plunder," said Emric, with feeling.

"Agreed," said Waynix.

"To be honest, I have heard of companies who get sent in against hard targets towards the end of the season. They get wiped out and of course, he does not have anyone left to pay," said Emric.

"I have heard that rumour as well," added the Captain.

"It is a good amount of money! said Dolac.

"Okay, I have made my mind up," stated Waynix.

"You have, old friend?" asked the Captain.

"Yes. We have many new recruits this year to rebuild from last year's bloody disaster at Maraken. Since almost half our number will be fresh recruits, I offer my advice to take up the offer from Nedia. It will give a chance to let our new recruits experience a season and let them settle in. If there is some fighting, then well and fine, that is what we get paid to do. I would not suggest going anywhere near Sul'Lena," said Waynix.

"I agree. I advise the same view. It should be Nedia," offered Emric.

"I'm against it. I suggest we throw them into the thick of it and go for the better offer from Sul'Lena!" said Dolac.

The three Sergeants all looked at each other as the Captain made up his mind. He looked at each of his sergeants in turn before speaking.

"No. I agree with Emric and Waynix on this. We take the company to Nedia."

Dolac looked at his Captain, a little pissed off. The Captain looked back.

"Remember last season, Dolac? We lost almost half our number! We cannot afford to do that again or the Bloodchildren will not survive," said the Captain.

"What of the other companies?" asked Waynix.

"Jooma's Hounds from Nedia are taking up the offer of Sul'Lena. Of course, the Greenhawks are going with the Duke of DuNoor on his 'job' in Renis," replied the Captain.

The three Sergeants did not miss the emphasis on the word job and laughed.

"As to the others, I am not sure. I have not heard anything yet."

"So, it's decided then, Captain?" asked Dolac.

"Yes, First Sergeant, it is. We finish the training and go to Nedia and potentially have a few scraps with the Outlanders if they decide to raid," said the Captain.

"Okay. I best start training my men for beach operations then," said Emric, as he got himself up.

The meeting broke up as the Sergeants left. As Third Sergeant Waynix went to leave, the Captain called out to him.

"How are the former slaves working out?"

"Good sir. Very good. They have some very effective training routines that they are putting all the squads through. I have no doubt, the three squads under me will be the most disciplined and fittest of all the squads," said Waynix.

"Good to hear. Are they working with the Irik recruits or remain how shall we say, aloof?" asked the Captain.

"No, sir. They are working as one," said Waynix.

He then quickly told him of the arrangement of squads. Captain was pleasantly surprised.

"It is working well. It sounds like they have a good grasp of things?" said the Captain.

"Yes, sir. As I said, they are working out well."

"Good, keep me up to date."

"Yes, sir."

All of the new recruits were at the Bald Goat Tavern enjoying a few ales. It was seventh day. They all knew they had training in the morning, but no-one seemed to care. They had toasted and celebrated the promotion of Torin, who accepted it in good humour. Most of the new recruits were drunk. As was his way, Irikson was off trying to secure himself the services of a Coin-Wife before he was too drunk. Corvin knew he would be haggling, trying to get her price down. The waitress plonked down another tray of drinks for the group at the table that consisted of Lorka, Corvin, Jorga and Torin. The new corporal asking many questions of the two other corporals and being proud to be a part of their circle. Lorka drank in silence.

"There you go, lads," said Nani, as she walked away.

A few of the recruits from other tables called for her to

come over and chat. She never did, of course. Nani never did give the mercenaries the time of day.

"Perhaps we should say something to the squads, perhaps tell them to leave Nani alone," said Jorga.

"Nah. She is alright. Very worldly is our Nani," replied Torin.

"Worldly?" asked Corvin.

"Aye. Worldly. I chatted to her a few times. She has more life experience than her eighteen years suggests," said Torin.

The other cocked their eyebrows as they waited for an explanation.

"She was a barmaid at a tavern in Iriksec, the capital. She has been exposed to sailors all her life. She knows how to handle herself. In fact, if you ever need anything out of the ordinary, I am sure Nani could point you in the right direction," said Torin.

"What do you mean out of the ordinary?" asked Lorka.

"If you need a special Coin-Wife that will do stuff the others won't, or if you need some cheap spirits with no questions asked, I suggest you talk to Nani," replied Torin.

"Really?" said Lorka surprised.

"Yep," said Torin.

"Excuse me," said Jorga and got up. He walked towards Nani.

"Where do we think he is going?" asked Corvin.

"I would say he is going to ask Nani for something unusual!" grinned Torin.

They all laughed and Corvin watched his friend. He was indeed talking to Nani at the bar. Jorga had never sort out company of the Coin-wives. Corvin himself had not either, after the betrayal of the cook in Hura, he was not interested in women. He was not sure why; he just focused all his energy on the men under his command and he had no time for anything else. He was brought back to the conversation by an off-colour joke of Lorka.

"Well, he is a big lad, perhaps he needs special type of woman!" he said suggestively.

Torin and Lorka laughed whereas Corvin saw Jorga walking away and heading for the door. He went to jump up and intercept him but when he got up, Jorga was already gone. He had left the tavern. He sat back down and the three of them continued to discuss the upcoming training. The evening ended with the three of them heading back to the barracks a little drunk. On his way to his cell, he stopped past Jorga's cell. He was not there. Corvin stared into the empty cell for a little time, then continued to his own bed. A massive day of training tomorrow so he had better get some rest.

That night, Jorga had found the small building by the north wall that Nani had sent him to. He knocked on the large door. After a moment, a small shutter on the door slid open, and he saw a small round face staring at him.

"What do you want?" asked the woman's voice.

Jorga wanted to turn around and walk away. He was scared!

"Well? Do not just stand there. What do you want?" said the voice.

Finally, Jorga spoke in a quiet voice.

"Nani from the Bald Goat sent me," he said.

"Why would she do that?" said the voice.

"She said you could help me! She said I could find here what I am looking for, what other taverns cannot give me."

The shutter closed and all of a sudden, the door was opened. Standing there was a woman in a plain brown dress and a grey woollen shawl. Her hair was grey, but she was not old. She looked late twenties and had a welcoming smile.

"Then come in stranger!" said the woman.

Her voice softer and more welcoming. Her smile was warm and radiated welcome. Jorga took a breath and stepped through the door, which was closed and bolted quickly behind him. As he entered the tavern, he was surprised. Looking around the small room was many two-seater couches, with men, young and old seated in them. Some men were sitting and holding hands, others with their arms around each other. They looked at the newcomer. All knew of him and heard the stories, Jorga, the huge new mercenary that had grown up in Irik but had been stolen from them and thrown into a life of slavery. Taking his arm, the woman led him to the bar and asked the barmaid to pore a drink for their new guest.

"What is it you are after, Jorga?" said the woman that had opened the door.

Jorga looked around.

"What they have," he finally said, pointing at two men sitting on a couch, holding hands and talking quietly.

He was seated in an empty two-seater and quickly a man around his age with blonde hair and large blue eyes joined him. He sipped the wine he had been given and relaxed.

The night had been one of wonder for the huge former slave. Although he did not take up the offer to go to the back rooms, he was still happy. Happy to sit, talk and learn. He must have fallen asleep on the two-seater as he was gently shaken at dawn by the woman that had greeted him. As he walked away from the small hidden tavern at the north wall, he felt content at first, then worried as he started to think up excuses for his whereabouts when his fellow mercenaries asked him, which he knew they would.

"Where did you get to last night?" asked Corvin.

Jorga looked at him, then looked at the ground. They had finished their morning of hell-runs and everyone was off to the cook house for their midday meal.

"Went for a walk," said Jorga, still looking at the ground.

Corvin knew his friend better than anyone. He was silent and did not appear to say much to those around him. He was always listening and thinking, but over the last two days, he had that faraway look. As the others left them, Corvin rounded on Jorga.

"My friend. What's the matter? I saw you talking to Nani and then you vanished when I stood up," enquired Corvin.

"I asked her about something, is all. She pointed me in the right direction."

"What direction was that? The boys all joked you needed a special lady to handle the size of your rod. Is that what it was about?"

Jorga was still looking at the ground.

"Well, my friend? If you can't tell me, who else can you tell?" asked Corvin.

"I asked her if she knew anywhere I could go to see my needs filled. She looked surprised but pointed me to a small tavern by the north wall that is hidden," he said after some time.

"That's what I thought!" said Corvin.

Jorga said nothing.

"You do not need to be ashamed of it, brother! We all have needs!"

"Mine are different," whispered Jorga.

"Not that different my friend."

Jorga finally looked up and Corvin saw a small tear running down his face from his right eye. He was shocked. He knew Jorga was actually quite a gentle person despite his size and fighting ability. He had never seen him so quiet, so quietly upset.

"Brother, what is it?"

"Men," said Jorga.

"Men what?"

"Men. I wanted to sleep with men!" said Jorga.

"Like in the slave camps? You miss sharing a room with them?"

"No. I want to sleep with men, the way the others sleep with Coin-Wives."

Corvin was not shocked, just did not understand. He had never heard of men sleeping with other men. "I do not understand."

"The way the others are attracted to women, crave attention from women, want to hold and kiss a woman, I want to do the same with other men."

"You want to have sex with other men?" Corvin asked quietly.

More tears came down Jorga's face.

"Yes."

Corvin did not understand at all. The surprise and confusion running through his head in equal measure as he tried to understand what he had just been told. However, he did know his brother-slave and did not care who he wanted to be friendly with.

"And?" asked Corvin.

"And what?" said Jorga.

"And... so what!" said Corvin.

"What do you mean?"

"Do you really feel that I would think less of you? Do you really think I would judge you or no longer call you brother? Do you really think I would love you less?" asked Corvin.

It was Jorga's turn to look surprised as he stared at his friend. Corvin was also surprised, he had never used the word 'love' before. It was the only word he could use in that moment. Corvin continued.

"Yes, I am surprised, I did not see it before. I have never heard of men being with other men and I will not pretend to understand it. To be honest, I could not care less. You are my brother!"

Jorga grabbed Corvin and wrapped him in a big bear hug and held him. He cried quietly, the acceptance from Corvin washing away most of the sadness he felt. The sadness of what he had been hiding for so long, the sadness of being different from all the other men in the Bloodchildren and amongst the former slaves. They let go of each other and Jorga spoke.

"I did not understand it either. I had never heard of men being with other men. All I knew was how I felt. We were kept isolated in our slave camps and there is much we do not know or understand."

"Yes. I am sure there is a lot we do not know, but we will learn. Why is the tavern you went to such a secret?" asked Corvin.

"From what I learnt at this tavern, men who want to be with other men are not well liked and even though it is common knowledge to most, it is never spoken about. It has to be with being different, they said. Other countries have the same problems as explained to me last night. Look at how we are treated by some of the older mercenaries here. We are different, therefore they do not like us," explained Jorga.

"There is truth in that," replied Corvin.

"So, to stay safe and not draw attention to themselves, they meet in private. Hence, the need for a secret tavern," said Jorga.

Explaining it all to Corvin was like lifting a weight of his shoulders. He felt at peace with himself and who he was.

Corvin looked at his brother-slave. The smile on his face the largest Corvin had ever seen. Tears ran freely down his cheeks. Corvin was not sure what to say, so decided to be honest and turn it into humour.

"Were your needs seen to then?" asked Corvin.

Jorga laughed his big, rich laugh.

"Yes. The small bar I was sent to is private and has a small clientele. It is where men go to be social with other men," said Corvin, as they walked toward the cook house.

"By social, you mean kiss?"

"Yes, amongst other things."

"They accepted you into the bar, I assume?"

"Yes. When I arrived, I said Nani had sent me. Then they asked what I wanted."

"And, you said?"

"I said I wanted to be with other men!" said Jorga, who was already finding it easier to say.

"Will you go back?"

"Every chance I get. I have never understood why I have never wanted a woman. It was not until Sick-boy pointed out to me one day in the training camp."

That was a name Corvin had not thought of in a while.

"Pointed out what? Sick-boy was not usually one I would trust to give any advice."

"He said that like him, I was attracted to men," said Jorga.

"He was attracted to men?"

"So, he said yes."

"So, you have been holding on to this for the last five to seven years?"

"Yes."

"Well, brother," said Corvin as he laid his hand on the bigger man's shoulder as they walked. "I am glad you have found a way to have your needs met and no longer have to hide it from me."

"Thank you," Jorga said slowly.

"Now that we have that sorted and you trust me enough to tell me anything, perhaps we grab some food?"

Jorga laughed.

"Agreed Brother!"

They walked into the cook house. Jorga now relieved he had shared a large part of himself which he had been hiding. Corvin relieved his friend was now more relaxed. They approached the table when Irikson called out.

"You two been kissing behind the training shed again?" joked Irikson.

Corvin was about to say something when Jorga laughed out loudly. He looked at his friend as they sat down. He could see how comfortable his friend was again. He smiled as the two started sharing insults.

"I would not kiss the nice corporal here; I am saving myself for you, Irikson!" said Jorga.

"Not without buying me a few drinks and asking nicely, you're not!" said Irikson.

The room erupted with laughter as the insults flew back and forth.

Chapter Three

The last week of winter had arrived. The last storms of the season lashing the land with a light snow and much rain. Of course, this froze everything and made training difficult. It had been six weeks since Jorga and Corvin had been made corporals and taken over the training of Seventh, Eighth and Ninth Squad. The three squads were in good shape, mentally and physically. The Tenth Squad had also joined the three squads under Waynix. The Tenth Squad was made up of exclusively archers. They trained and practiced their skills with the bows outside of the camp on the edge of town. The new recruits had seen them around but had not been given the chance to know them. Since they had joined the training, they had learned of their role within the Bloodchildren. Jorga and Corvin had often discussed why the company did not have more archers. Although they themselves had no experience of the bow, they had seen it used to good effect in their escape from the Outlanders. Archers killed more than a few slaves on their escape across the land of the Outlanders. They soon came to respect the skills of a good archer.

After the winter of training, the Irik squad members were now able to keep up with the former slaves on the training field. The gap that had existed between the two groups was now gone. As Third Sergeant Waynix watched the four squads complete more hell-runs, he was pleased to see all of the recruits move as one. He continued to watch as they finished up; all of the recruits broke into their different squads for stretching and strength exercises. He waved the three corporals over to him. They gave out orders and trotted over to where he was standing.

"Cold morning, Sergeant!" said Torin.

"It's cold enough to want to go back to your beds, that is for sure," said the Sergeant.

All three now stood before him,

"What training is planned for this afternoon?" the Sergeant asked the three of them,

"Weapons training, Sergeant," replied Jorga.

The three corporals had re-introduced weapons training in the afternoons two weeks ago. All of the recruits felt better practicing with their weapons. Of course, the former slaves tutoring the Irik recruits in all the skills and tricks they had learnt in the fighting pits. Most of the training had centred on the short sword and shield the Bloodchildren preferred. However, the former slaves had also given some basic knife and axe training as you never know what weapons you may find in your hand when the fighting started.

"Good. How is the weapons training going?" asked the Sergeant.

"Coming along nicely, Sergeant," said Corvin, before continuing. "All of the squad members are efficient with short sword and shield, and have picked those skills up very quickly. We are falling behind a little when it comes to fighting as a squad and I have asked a corporal from the

Fifth Squad to come over and train with us this afternoon. He mentioned a few nights ago, he was happy to give a hand."

Sergeant Waynix nodded.

"The squads are rounding out nicely and the three of you have done well considering the challenges. Remember, training will only take you so far. The squads will learn so much more on the field of battle."

"Agreed, Sergeant, but we would prefer not to lose any men in our first action," said Jorga.

"I know, but you will plus it is always a surprise who falls first and who survives. I have learnt over the years that even though I have good experience of fighting men, I still get it wrong," the Sergeant added.

The three corporals just nodded silently.

"The reason for my visit is tomorrow morning, it is time to fit out the squads with their armour and weapons."

All three smiled.

"The armour has arrived then?" asked Corvin.

"Yes, it arrived yesterday morning," confirmed the Sergeant.

"That will put a few smiles on a few faces," smiled Torin.

"Not for long!" Corvin responded.

Torin and the Sergeant looked at Corvin as they did not understand his comment. Corvin saw the confusion.

"It means for the rest of the week, we will be training in full armour. That means hell-runs in armour, fight training in armour and if the weather clears, rock-runs in armour!" said Corvin.

"Yes, it would have been better to have the armour sooner to get the men used to the weight of it. Even the former slaves are going to struggle. Remember, we have never worn armour before. It will be a hard couple of weeks for all of us."

The Sergeant and Corporal Torin realised what they were saying.

"To be honest, I never thought of that, but hearing you say it makes a lot of sense," said the Sergeant.

Torin looked at the other two corporals.

"I did not think of that either. Yes, the next few weeks are going to be hard. Shall we tell the men?"

"No. We fit out with our new equipment in the morning, I am sure it will take all morning. Then after lunch, we get them straight into it," said Corvin.

The other nodded.

"Good. Tell the men to meet at the barracks after first light. Please remind the men not to hassle old Lorka too much. He is old and angry, but very good at what he does!" said the Sergeant.

Jorga and Corvin laughed remembering the back to the beginning of winter when they had signed up to the company.

"We will pass that on," said Jorga.

"See you at first light then, Corporals."

"Yes, Sergeant," they all said.

The morning had started with a simple stretching run. The three squads running back and forth in the roofed training area. They had carried out their stretches and once completed, followed the corporals over to the main armoury. On arriving at the large building, they were greeted by the Captain and Third Sergeant Waynix.

"Gather round my lads," said the Captain.

The three squads gathered around the Captain, standing in a semi-circle around him.

"When you first signed up, it was explained that I would

provide weapons and armour. You have trained hard throughout the winter; you have a basic understanding of what it means to be a part of the Bloodchildren. With the new season only weeks away, it is time for you to look like Bloodchildren!"

Cheers went around the large room in the armoury. The armoury building was two stories tall with a large basement beneath their feet. The Basement was used to store amour and weapons, the top story of the building used to store uniforms and smaller items. The ground level was split into two by a wall running through the middle of the building. Half of the ground floor was used as a workshop, repairing armour and clothing. The other half of the ground floor, the room they stood in, had large tables running around every wall. On those tables were large wooden crates and bundles. Every one of the new recruits eyed the packages and boxes with smiles on their faces.

"Lorka, step forward!" shouted Sergeant Waynix.

The huge former slave stepped forward.

"Off with that shirt!" said the Sergeant.

He took off his shirt revealing a huge, well-muscled frame. Although the former slaves and the Irik men knew of his strength and size, it never failed to amaze them when they saw his naked torso. Well-corded muscle covered him, his shoulders were great slabs of muscle. Of course, his back was covered in old scars from the whip. Most of the former slaves carried these whip scars on their bodies. Eight weeks ago, there would have many questions being asked by the Irik men. However, all of the Irik men had been told of the escape in great details. Corvin had encouraged the former slaves to share their stories with the Irik men. Firstly, to help the former slaves off load some of the burden, and secondly to draw the Irik men in closer. To share with them the details and struggles, to include them in the pain they received on a daily basis. The bond these Irik men now shared with the former slaves was strong.

"First off, on goes your padded shirt," said the Sergeant.

The Sergeant threw a grey/white shirt to Lorka. It was a standard shirt but had no sleeves. Lorka put it on and it fitted well, which surprised the big man.

"Yes, Lorka. We had to have a few made a little larger than normal to fit you and a few others," smiled the Sergeant.

"I hope you had bigger underclothes made for him as well! The ones he has barely contain him," said Torin.

All of the assembled recruits laughed as did the Captain.

Lorka was feeling the shirt fabric with his hands as the Sergeant explained.

"On the shoulders, there is extra padding sewn in as well as on the chest and back," he said, pointing out the padding. "This is to make your amour a little more comfortable and stop it rubbing your skin raw," he continued.

"Now the top shirt," said the Captain, throwing another shirt to Lorka.

He put it on. It was a thick weave of a fabric he did not know. The shirt was a dark red, the same colour of human blood.

"The shirts are made of two different types of wool. Goat's wool for strength and lightness, and sheep's wool for warmth and to keep cost down," informed the Sergeant.

The shirt seemed a little snug on Lorka, but he moved his arms around and smiled, as there was still plenty of movement.

"Now for the armour!" said the Captain.

Sergeant Waynix had walked over to the table behind them and grabbed the leather armour. He walked back to Lorka and helped him fit it. Once it was put on, the recruits saw how it was tightened together from straps and buckles down the left side. Lorka stood tall letting the other recruits get a good look. Even though they had all joined up, this was the first time any of them had seen the armour they would be wearing. The mercenaries did not wear it in during the winter. The recruits all cheered as Lorka's smile beamed back at them. The armour was thick brown leather and covered his entire torso, stopping just below his belt. It was also sleeveless giving the arms room to manoeuvre.

"As you can see, the chest has had thicker leather added to offer better protection along the back and belly. This armour will stop a knife and sword in close quarters. However, it will not stop a large axe or an arrow from a good bow," said the Sergeant, as he handed Lorka another bundle.

"Forearm protectors," said the Captain.

Lorka needed a hand with these. Sergeant helped him strap them on.

"These protect your forearms and hands. Once again, it will protect from cuts from the likes of a dagger, knife or sword. Anything large will smash the bones in your wrists. For added strength, there is small strips of steel running the length of the forearm protectors. These steel strips are inserted between the two layers of leather that make up the protectors," demonstrated the Captain.

The leather was the same thickness as the armour. When Lorka closed his fingers into a fist, he saw the leather started just above his knuckles. It ran all the way up his forearm and stopped just short of his elbow. He gave the protectors a few solid whacks with his fist and smiled. Next, he was handed a leather helmet that the recruits had seen before. It was also of brown leather with reinforced steel straps between two layers of hardened leather. Lorka put it on. In the middle of the helmet, at the height of his forehead, was the number 9. This was shining steel that had been buffed until it was bright and shiny.

The Sergeant also passed him leg guards that fitted over his woollen trousers. These protectors fitted from the top of his boots to just below his knee. Like the other armour, it was two layers of hardened leather with steel strap reinforcing between them.

"Weapons time," said the Sergeant.

The Captain threw a short sword to Lorka, who caught it easily. He stepped back out of the way and gave it a few swings to check the balance; it was good. The grip was of leather straps over wood hilt. The blade itself was short and very sharp. The steel shining in the light of the lamps. The Sergeant strapped the leather baldric around Lorka's waist. Once done, Lorka sheathed the sword into the holder on the left side. On his right side was a good-sized dagger that Lorka drew. He tested the edge with his thumb before replacing the knife.

"I have added a refinement to the back if you would turn around, please Lorka," said the Captain.

Lorka spun around.

"As you can see between the shoulder blades at the top of the back, I have six extra small iron loops riveted in. This is so all Bloodchildren can carry a backup weapon. You would have all heard of last year's slaughter that we were a part of. After discussion, we decided having backup weapons is a bloody good idea. Secondly, I know the former pit rats have weapons they favour in a fight, so now they can carry their personal weapons as well."

Another small cheer went up from all the former slaves. Lorka turned around smiling. He now had somewhere to carry his huge two-handed axe which Corvin had found for him in the battle of Youst.

"Everyone, go around the tables and grab your uniform; two shirts and two padded shirts per mercenary!" encouraged the Captain, with a smile.

The comment was not lost on any of the recruits. This was the first time they had been referred to as mercenaries and not recruits. They all smiled with plenty of smacks on the back going on. Then, like children, they fell on the items with laughs and banter. Corvin approached the Captain.

"Thank you Captain, for the addition of those rings. It would be strange going into a fight without the weapons I trust. I am sure all of the former slaves feel the same," said Corvin.

"A pleasure, Corvin. As I said, the other seasoned mercenaries had asked for it as well. After last year's debacle, they all insisted being supplied with back up weapons. Better get yourself fitted up, my lad," he said, slapping his hand on Corvin's shoulder.

"Thank you, sir," said Corvin and he walked over to join the others.

That afternoon, much to the groaning of ALL of the newly fitted out recruits, they had completed hell-runs and strength exercises wearing all their new armour. None of the new recruits had realised quite how heavy the new armour would be. All recruits struggled during the hell-runs. During the weapon and fight training, they were all breathing hard.

"It's going to take a bit to get used to this new armour, brother!" said Irikson.

"Yes, harder than I thought it would be," said Corvin.

"We do not have that long to get used to it either, apparently we sail in three weeks," said Torin.

They were all on the ground doing their stretches, a task made a lot harder when wearing armour.

"We have no choice. If we are going to get used to all this, we need to practice," said Jorga.

The others gathered round nodded.

"Well, that armour certainly slowed down the squads," said the Captain.

"Yes. I doubt it will slow them down for long. Another couple of weeks and they will have it sorted," replied Sergeant Waynix, with confidence.

"No doubt!"

The Captain and the Third Sergeant had been watching the training for the afternoon, watching and listening for the frustration shown by the three squads. Clearly, they felt hampered by their armour. They talked for a further hour, when they were interrupted.

"Sir. Captain, sir," said the company clerk Lorka.

"Yes."

The clerk handed the Captain a sealed package. He then stood as the Captain opened it. The Captain read it and as he got further through the letter, his face took on a surprised and angry look. Once he finished, he screwed it up.

"Fuck them all the way to hell!" said the Captain.

"What is it?" asked Sergeant.

"Lorka. Please go and get the other sergeants and corporals to assemble in my ready room immediately," requested the Captain.

"Straight away, Captain," responded the clerk, as he walked away.

"Captain?"

"We now know what the general of Sul'Lena wanted us for! It looks like they have kicked off with Kor'Lena again!"

"You're joking!"

"Wish I was," said the Captain.

"Well, it is probably due to happen again. Why are you so pissed off? It will not affect us.

"Just turn down the general of Sul'Lena," said the Sergeant.

"It was not the general of Sul'Lena that sent the letter, my old friend."

The Sergeant looked at the Captain, puzzled.

"It was a letter from the council of Kor'Lena, asking for our help."

"Fuck it!" said the Sergeant.

"Yes."

"We cannot say no, can we?"

"No. We cannot! Grab your three new corporals and I will see you in the ready room."

Torin, Corvin and Jorga arrived at the Captain's ready room. They had never been here before but walked in confidently. The room was attached to the Captain's residence. It was a large rectangle room with no windows and only one door leading in. As they walked in, they felt the warmth of the room hit them. On the long wall to the right was a large fireplace, with a fire burning fiercely and the light from the fireplace reflecting off the polished wood panel walls. The only item in the room was a long rectangular, wooden, polished table with fifteen chairs around it. At the head of the table, there was just one chair, where the Captain was seated. Six chairs went down each side of the table with the foot of the table having two chairs. At the foot of the table sat Third Sergeant Waynix and beside him, the company clerk. Sergeant Waynix pointed to the three empty seats on his left.

"Seat yourselves, Corporals and do not be shy. Help yourselves to the food and drink." said the Captain.

The new corporals sat themselves down. There was assorted finger food and jugs full of ale on the table.

"Corvin, Jorga and Torin. Welcome to the ready room," said the Second Sergeant Emric.

The three new corporals smiled as the corporals of the other squads banged their fists on their armoured chests repeatedly.

"No mucking around, my lads. I have just had an emergency letter placed in my hands," said the Captain.

All of the mercenaries sitting around the tables went silent.

"Looks like Sul'Lena has decided it's time to have ago at invading its neighbour again."

Swearwords ran round the table and looks of disgust was shared by all of the more experienced mercenaries. The three new corporals and a few others looked confused. It was Second Sergeant Emric that explained.

"Sul'Lena and its neighbour Kor'Lena have been at war for the last seventy-five years. It has been an ongoing war. It never ends, it just calms down for a while and fighting stops. Then, without warning, it erupts again."

Corvin raised his hand.

"Yes, Corvin?" said the Captain.

"How long have they not been fighting for?" asked Corvin.

"This time, they have been in quiet for thirty-seven years," said Third Sergeant Waynix.

"Then why start up again?" asked Corporal Yelix of Fourth Squad.

"Sul'Lena is always the aggressor. They stop for a couple of decades, then decide to have another go at invading. This will be the third time fighting has kicked off since they started fighting seventy-five years ago!" said the Captain.

"How does this affect us? I thought you had already picked out the job for the summer season?" asked Yelix.

"I had. Unfortunately, this takes precedence!" said the Captain.

Second Sergeant Emric delved into the explanation.

"The last time hostilities erupted, the Bloodchildren were on another job. Our then Captain was close friends with a senior member of the council of Kor'Lena. This friend had requested help, but there was no way we could make it. Sul'Lena almost won the war and made it over the wall into Kor'Lena. Our Captain apologised and promised that no matter what we were doing or where we were, we would come running the next time fighting erupted. The Bloodchildren keep their promises."

The Captain looked to the end of the table to where Corvin and Jorga were sitting. He saw the confusion on their faces.

"Corvin. Jorga. You looked confused?"

"Yes, Captain," said Jorga before continuing. "We are paid to fight. So, I do not see the problem!" said Jorga.

First Sergeant Dolac answered.

"We fight skirmishes, we take on guard duties, track down and take down criminal gangs. All of these things are how we earn a living. Fighting brutal wars is not what we want. It is too easy for the company to get wiped out," he said.

"It will not be bad as most wars, as Kor'Lena has a large wall snaking its way across the width of their country. From the sea, all the way to the mountains in the west. We will be given a small section of wall to hold and defend," said Sergeant Waynix.

"Will that make the newest three squads a liability?" asked Corvin.

"A liability?" asked Sergeant Dolac.

"We have not trained to defend walls. Also, the former slaves are used to fighting on the offensive. We have no idea how to hold a wall!" said Jorga.

"It's easy. You stand on the wall to stab and slash anyone climbing the ladder trying to get up. Trust me, your stamina and fitness training will hold you in good stead," said the Captain.

Corvin nodded but was not convinced.

"When do we leave?" asked Sergeant Waynix.

"Five days!" said the Captain.

"Five days?" said a lot of the corporals in unison.

Jorga and Corvin swore under their breaths and earned a dirty look from Sergeant Waynix. The Captain held up his hands for calm.

"Yes, five days. We need to gather our equipment and be in the capital in ten days. Which means, we leave here in five days," said the Captain.

Sergeant Emric looked at the newest corporals.

"You will be caught up on all the history of where we are going, once aboard the ship. It's a good four-week journey to Kor'Lena. That's plenty of time for me to teach you and your men the customs and history. Also, your men will start learning some of the more basic language they speak in Lena!" said Sergeant Emric.

"Anything special that we need to take with us?" asked Corvin.

"No," said the Captain.

"As we are defending the wall, most of our equipment will be left behind. The men only need to take the tools of the trade and a pack with spare clothing. I would suggest taking some warm clothing and you will be issued with cloaks as well. The sea voyage this early in the season will be cold," said Sergeant Emric.

Corvin, Torin, Jorga nodded.

"Meeting over! Inform your men all that has been said here and inform them of the timeline. If there is any gear needed that you do not have, get a full list to me by the end of the day," said the Captain.

He then looked over at the new corporals.

"Get your men to the armoury again after the evening meal, please. We will issue you and your men with travel packs, cloaks and some warmer clothing," said the Captain.

"Yes, sir," the three said.

All of the men left the room except Third Sergeant Waynix. He approached the Captain who was talking with the clerk. He sat down in an empty chair next to the Captain and waited. The clerk quickly left the room and soon, it was just the Captain and Third Sergeant left.

"I know what you are going to say Waynix."

"I do not need to repeat it then, Captain, do I?" Waynix said with a smile.

The Captain took a deep breath, then spoke.

"I know I promised you that you would not take part again if the Bloodchildren went to war."

"I am too old. I cannot keep up."

"Defending a wall is a lot easier and it will not be as bad as last season."

"Well, I lost all three of my squads in Maraken. I left thirty bodies buried in the ground when we came back. I cannot do it again, Captain."

"What can I do? I need your experience, Waynix."

"Promote a corporal! I'm getting too old to go on campaign and it is only a few years until I retire anyway and look for a soft job."

"You cannot squeeze one more in for me?" asked the Captain.

"I cannot, Joren."

"Who the hell are we going to promote? There are experienced corporals in Squads One and Two, but which one?"

"No. The Seventh. Eighth and Ninth Squad will not accept them. It has to be a corporal from within my own ranks!"

"They are all fresh, Waynix," said the Captain, with a slight look of annoyance.

"Yes, they are. For the first time in our history, you already have two new corporals with more fighting experience than any other corporal in the company."

"True," said the Captain.

"You have two to choose from."

"I assume you are talking of Corvin and Jorga?"

"Yes."

"You know First Sergeant will throw a fit if I promote either of the former slaves!"

"Let him. I no longer care what First Sergeant thinks."

The Captain stared into space. He could not think of going into action without his experienced Sergeant beside him.

"I am not happy about this, friend!" said the Captain finally.

"You have no choice. I'm not looking forward to a cold sea voyage, let alone sleeping on hard ground again. My days in the field are done, Joren."

The Captain looked at his most experienced Sergeant. He knew it could not be easy admitting he was no longer able to handle life in the field.

"So, which one?" asked the Captain.

"It all depends on what you need!" said the Sergeant.

"What do you mean?"

"If you need a sergeant that has a good grasp of tactics and strategy, then you promote Jorga. If you need a sergeant that the men will follow into any situation without question, then promote Corvin."

The Captain looked at the face of his Sergeant.

"Your recommendation?"

"I have none. As I said, it all depends on what you need."

"I need a sergeant that has the respect of his men! A sergeant that will charge into a fight and have his men jump after him without being asked to! I need a sergeant that leads from the front and can keep his men under control!"

"Then you need Corvin!" smiled the Sergeant.

The Captain smiled.

"I'm still not happy with you not coming with me!"

"You will get over it," said the Sergeant with a smile.

"Go tell Corvin to report to me immediately. Then get back here once he has left, we need to share a few drinks, you and I," said the Captain.

"Yes, sir," said Sergeant Waynix, standing up with a smile.

"Sit down, Corvin!" said the Captain.

"Sir."

Corvin sat down removing his helmet and placing it on the floor.

"I won't keep you long, as I know that you have lot to do before we leave here."

"Thank you, sir. Actually, my squad is under control, once we have our travel packs, we will be good to go," said Corvin.

"Trust me, Corvin, you are about to have many more tasks thrown onto the broad shoulders of yours," the Captain said with a smile.

"I do not understand!" said Corvin.

"Sergeant Waynix has asked to retire and will not be coming to Kor'Lena with us."

"And?" said Corvin, feeling a little panic well up inside himself.

"I am promoting you to Third Sergeant, Corvin."

Corvin was shocked. He had not expected this and never wanted it.

"Me, sir?"

"Yes, Corvin. You may be young, but you lead well, and everyone knows you fight well."

"I am not ready, sir. Jorga would be a better choice."

"No, Corvin. He would not!"

"He is smarter than I, he has a better grasp of strategy and tactics, and as you well know, more in control of his emotions!"

"That's not what I need. I need someone who will jump and his men follow. I need someone that leads from the front."

Corvin went quiet. To say this was unexpected, was an understatement.

"I do not know what to say, sir!" said Corvin.

"Then say nothing, Third Sergeant Corvin. Take your new helmet and go get your squads under control," he said, passing along the new helmet that had the logo for Third Sergeant on it.

"Who will you promote to corporal of the Seventh Squad, Captain?" he said as he stood.

"I'll promote no one. That is your job, Sergeant," said the Captain, still smiling.

"I will do my best, sir. What happens to Sergeant Waynix?"

"He retires! He finds a soft job somewhere and live a comfortable life."

"That is such a waste, sir!"

"A waste, Sergeant?"

"His experience and knowledge. Leaving now is a waste, Captain."

"Yes, it is, but there is nothing I can do."

"May the new Sergeant make a suggestion?"

"You may."

Standing up in front of the Captain, his confidence finally started to find a hold in his person. He took a breather and started.

"Promote him as well to a new position!"

"A new position?"

"Yes. Sergeant of Recruits. While we are away fighting, task him with taking on more recruits and training them through the summer. It will make the most of his abilities and that way, you can continue to use his experience and knowledge."

The Captain was impressed, very impressed. He wished he had thought of that.

Corvin continued.

"If you let him take on additional fifty recruits, he should have the weak ones weeded out and the strong ones ready to replace the losses we have in the coming conflict."

The Captain nodded his head.

"You think you are not smart, Corvin? That is brilliant!"

"Thank you, sir," said Corvin, smiling for the first time in the meeting.

"Send him to me now and go get your squads ready and tell them the news."

"Yes, sir."

Corvin put the new helmet on his head and left.

Corvin walked into the barracks of the Seventh, Eighth and Ninth Squad. He pushed open the door to the casual room and walked in. Jorga was the first to see him in his new helmet. Jorga's eyes lit up and he smiled.

"New Sergeant in the room!" called out Jorga.

All of the members of the squads stood and turned. When they saw who was now standing before them wearing the helmet of the Third Sergeant, a huge cheer went up around the room with the mercenaries banging their fists on their armoured chests.

Corvin looked around the assembled men and felt powerful emotions well up inside of himself. He once thought he had everything when he had escaped with his brother-slaves! He once thought he had everything when he was made corporal! However, staring around the room at the smiling faces, the eager faces and the proud faces, he knew he could not ask for much more in this life. He went to speak but was unable to. He continued to look around and his eyes rested on every one of the former slaves. He saw how proud they were, that one of their own, once a slave was now a sergeant. Finally, once the clapping and cheering had finished, he spoke.

"Third Sergeant Waynix, has been promoted to Sergeant of Recruits. He will be staying behind to train more men. As you can see, I have been promoted to replace him," said Third Sergeant Corvin.

The cheers went up around the room again. He motioned for them to settle.

"I will be appointing a new Corporal of the Seventh Squad soon. For now, focus on the things you need to take with you. As you have been instructed, we will be issued more warm clothing, a cloak and a travel backpack later today. All you will need with you is your spare clothing and our tools of the trade. The only other items I would suggest you take is perhaps an extra water skin or two."

He looked around at the eager young fighters.

"We have been training hard all winter, it is now time to show the other squads that we may be new recruits, but we can do more than just keep up!"

There was a cheer around the room.

"It is time to show the Captain our skills in battle!"

The cheer around the room got louder.

"It's time to show the bastards we face, that the Bloodchildren do not mess around!"

The cheer went louder and could be heard around the base.

"It is time, we went to battle!"

The loud cheer that went up could be heard in the settlement beyond the walls. Captain sitting in his study with Waynix smiled.

"Pretty motivated, these lads of yours," said the Captain.

Recruit Sergeant Waynix smiled.

"Brother, can I have a word?" said Irikson.

Corvin turned from his packing his pack.

"Of course, brother," he replied.

"I have a bad feeling!"

"Bad feeling? About what?"

"This war we are going to, something feels bad about it."

"Anything in particular?"

"No. Just does not feel right."

Corvin looked at Irikson's face. Irikson was an emotionally-charged person; his emotions changing by the hour. He was not the most mentally stable person, but in a fight or facing a new situation, he is one of the people in this world that Corvin wanted by his side.

"Going to war does not feel right?" said Corvin finally.

"No, it has more to do with where we are going. I cannot put it into words. It is just the feeling I get."

Corvin looked up and saw Lorka walking across the training yard. Corvin called out to him and waved him over. He ran over.

"Sergeant," Lorka said, with a huge grin on his face.

Corvin and Irikson both smiled. Lorka never failed in his teasing of Corvin.

"Irikson is having a bad feeling," said Corvin.

Lorka raised his eyebrows in surprise.

"Anything in particular?" said Lorka.

"This coming war!" said Irikson.

"You seem to get these feelings when a time of change is on us," said Lorka.

"Yes, he does," said Corvin.

"What does it mean now?" asked Lorka.

"I am not sure. It just does not feel right. The only words that come to mind is we are saying goodbye to this place, this company, these new friends," said Irison.

Jorga joined them and asked what was going on. They quickly filled him in.

"It does not mean we are going to die, perhaps it just means a time of change," said Jorga.

Irikson nodded before Corvin spoke.

"What do we do?" asked Lorka.

"There's not much we can do. Sorry if I feel sceptical brother, but I have never been one to think too much about the future," said Jorga.

"There is not much we can do, but if the main feeling you are having is we are saying goodbye to this place, then perhaps it is as Jorga suggested. It is a time of change," said Corvin.

"As Lorka said, what do we do?" said Irikson.

Corvin thought about it before speaking.

"Pass on the word to all the former slaves but keep it from others. Tell all former slaves to pack ALL their belongings for the trip. We all do not own much so should all fit into our new packs. If they have to leave some items behind, then so be it. If you feel we are saying goodbye to this place, then let's prepare for that," said Corvin.

Lorka and Irikson nodded but Jorga was not convinced.

"You want us to take all we own? I know we do not own much but it would still add extra weight to our packs," said Jorga.

"Yes, it will. Remember what Smith taught us 'expect the best but prepare for the worst'. At best, it means we are carrying a little extra weight with us. At worst, life turns badly once again but we have everything we own on us and are not attached to this place," said Corvin.

Once again Lorka and Irikson nodded. Even Jorga could see the wisdom.

"I see what you mean even though I am unconvinced," said Jorga.

Corvin put his hand on Jorga's shoulder. "Thank you, brother. I know you were born in this country and it is your home. The rest of us, although happy with the new lives we have been granted, are not so attached. I just want us to be prepared."

Jorga smiled. "You are wrong, brother. This is not my home. My home is wherever in this world the three of you are!"

They all smiled and clapped Jorga on the shoulder.

"Okay, pass the word to our brother slaves. Leave nothing behind that you would miss if we did not return."

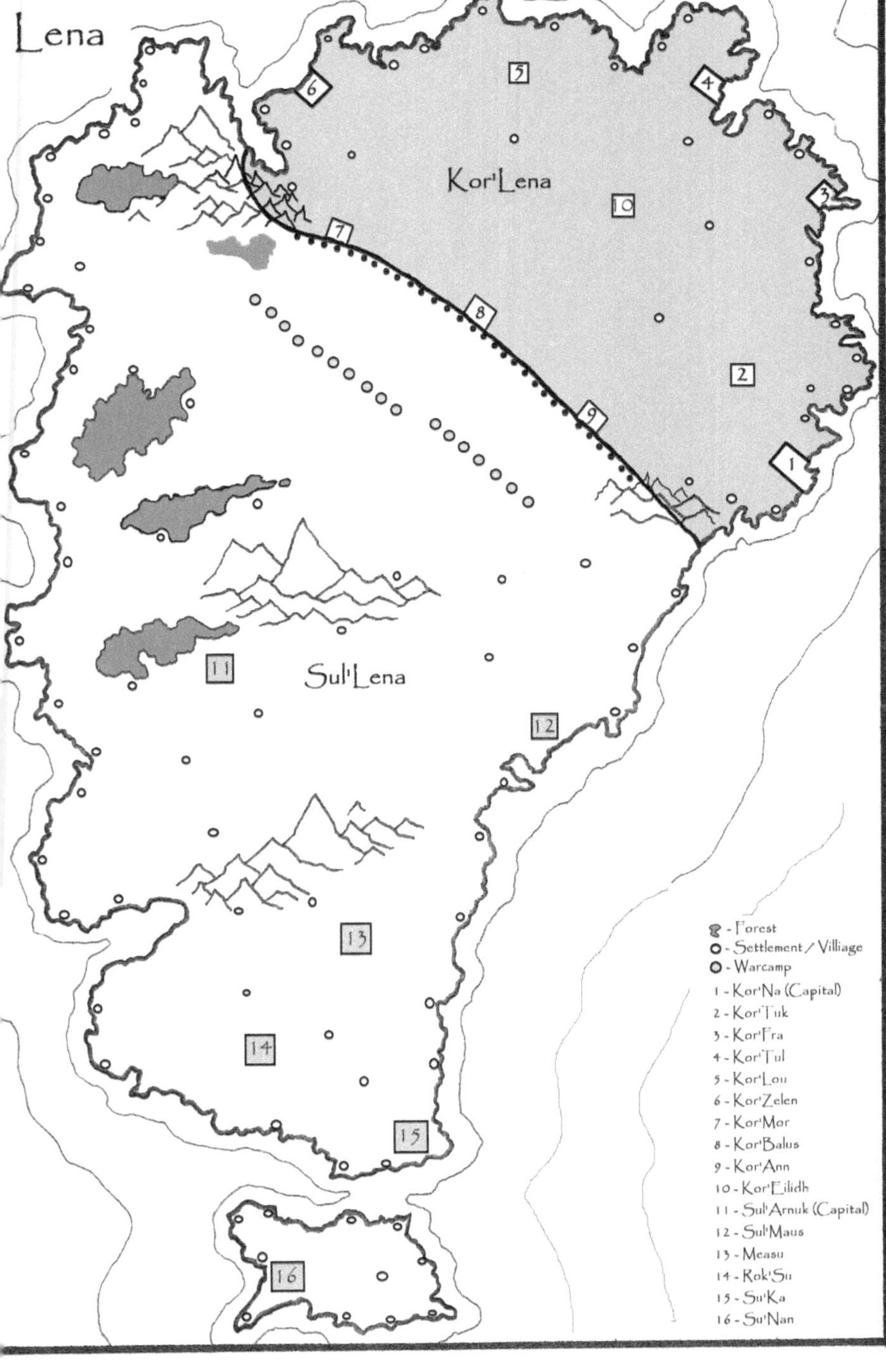

Lena
Kor'Lena
Sul'Lena
6
5
4
3
7
10
8
2
9
1
11
12
13
14
15
16
- Forest
- Settlement / Villiage
- Warcamp
1 - Kor'Na (Capital)
2 - Kor'Tuk
3 - Kor'Fra
4 - Kor'Tul
5 - Kor'Lou
6 - Kor'Zelen
7 - Kor'Mor
8 - Kor'Balus
9 - Kor'Ann
10 - Kor'Eilidh
11 - Sul'Arnuk (Capital)
12 - Sul'Maus
13 - Measu
14 - Rok'Su
15 - Su'Ka
16 - Su'Nan

Chapter Four

The days passed very quickly. Corvin and his corporals had worked frantically to organise their squads in time. There was time only for light runs and only a few hours of training. With his promotion, Corvin had come out of his shell a little. He delegated many tasks to his corporals and was rewarded with support and no complaining. The three squads under him had already been fitted with their uniforms and weapons. On the day after the announcement, they were off to Kor'Lena. They had been fitted and given their travel gear; backpacks made with an oiled leather. The straps made from wide leather and padded, to be as comfortable as possible. In these packs, there was spare clothing, small clothes, a mercenary's aid kit that consisted of bandages, pain paste, needle and thread plus other small items to help with minor injuries. There was a small eating kit consisting of a wooden bowl, a wooden mug, fork, spoon, and of course, a sharp knife. Three water skins were strapped to the left side, with the right side holding their warm travelling cloak tied by further leather straps sewn into the backpack. Their sleeping bag was rolled and tied to the top of their pack. An experienced corporal from the third squad had spent a few hours showing the three squads how to pack their gear into the backpack and get the weight even. He also showed them all a trick of making sure their backpack straps stayed in place and did not slide down or move to their arms.

"Trust me, the weight of the backpack may not seem like much but if the straps slip to your arms, the straps will rub your skin raw," he said.

Using corded rope, he had shown them all how to tie the straps together once the packs were on. He had also shown them how to cut the cord quickly if they needed to drop the packs in a hurry when they needed to fight.

Corvin, Lorka, Jorga and Irikson had spent a few evenings discussing how they were feeling and the strangeness of it all. They had seemed to just get settled into their new life and now they were off on their first season of fighting. The word of Irikson's uneasy feeling was quietly spread around the former pit rats. Once it was explained to them, they took heed and packed all they owned into their new packs, which as Lorka had said, was not much.

Within no time, they were in wagons heading for the capital of Iriksec to board their ship. The excitement could be seen on the faces of the new recruits. The news had been told to them by Corvin and from that moment, they hardly seemed to stop. Everything happened so quickly! Five days of gathering their equipment and trying to learn as much of the destination as they could without getting in the way of the other squads. Learning from the other more experienced mercenaries was not easy. They were busy with their own preparations and to be honest, were being tight-lipped. All the new recruits knew, was what Corvin had learned and passed on. They would have to wait until they were on ship and received further instruction. Of course, Corvin had extra duties and things to think of. He needed a new corporal and also one more recruit, both for Seventh Squad as with his promotion, they were down to nine. One day before they were due to leave to greet their ship, had still not made up his mind. He managed to catch up with Waynix, the freshly promoted Sergeant of Recruits on the day before they were due to leave.

"Yes, Sergeant Corvin, how can I help?" said Waynix with a smile.

Corvin smiled back and shook the hand he was offered.

"Do you have a moment, Sergeant?" said Corvin.

"I do and call me Waynix. We are of equal rank now!"

"I need advice."

"Advice on what, Corvin?"

"Picking a replacement corporal for Seventh Squad."

"Oh. No idea on who to choose?"

"No, I do not. I have been running the faces and names through my head for the last three days trying to come up with the right person to lead the squad, but no one stands out."

"Sometimes, it's a very hard choice indeed."

"Yes."

"Put in the front of your mind what you are heading to! You will be defending a wall which is slightly easier than attacking the wall. You need someone who the Seventh Squad will respond to. I do not mean hear an order and then follow it. Anyone can give out orders. You are looking for a corporal that will jump into battle and the squad will follow him in without being told to. Someone the squad will jump with before asking why. Does that make sense?" said Waynix.

"No. Not really."

"Okay, put it this way. When you arrived at our border, the Outlanders were close behind you. You thought for a few minutes you had to fight them. Thankfully, you did not. However, imagine if you charged them with weapons drawn but had not said anything to your former slaves, would you be fighting alone?"

"No, the others would have followed, without question or being told to do so. They would have been right beside me."

"Exactly Corvin. They would have followed you without been told to. That is what you are looking for in a corporal in this situation. That was the original reason I wanted you and Jorga to be corporals."

"What about jumping before thinking? You have told us many times to size up a situation and think before you leap."

"Yes, I have but that comes from experience and can be learned. Having a corporal that the squad instinctively follows cannot be taught. Does that make things clearer?"

"Yes."

"Who are you thinking of now? Who comes to mind?"

"Irikson!"

Waynix laughed.

"Yes. Irikson! He has kept his head down over the winter months since his time in the cell and I think he has grown up a little since then."

"I am still a little unconvinced," said Corvin.

"I mentioned him to you originally to be a corporal."

"Yes, you did."

"That was actually a test for yourself and Jorga. At the time, Irikson was not suitable to be given a squad. He still may not be, but he has come along nicely in the last couple of months."

Corvin thought about it before continuing.

"Is that your advice then, Waynix?"

"No. I have given my advice and told you what you need.

The decision is yours to make and then live with," said Waynix with a smile.

Corvin said nothing.

"Talk to him. Sound him out and find out if he thinks he is up to it!"

"Talk to him?" questioned Corvin.

"Yes. See what he thinks."

Corvin was not convinced but nodded his head.

"You do not have to name someone straight away. You can take the time off the ship to see who would best fit the role."

"No. Sorry Waynix, I do need someone now. It will give them the time before the ship berths to get their squad in hand so when the fighting starts, the squad knows who they are following."

Waynix, once again impressed with the insight, put his hand on Corvin's shoulder.

"Then make your choice!"

"I will. Thank you, Waynix."

Corvin had gone looking for Irikson straight away and found him lying on his bed in his room in the barracks. He sat down on the end of the bed as Irikson greeted him.

"Sergeant," he said, with a teasing smile.

Corvin still got teased by the former slaves regarding his elevation, but knew it came from genuine pride and not jealousy.

"Irikson, I have a question for you!"

"Sure. What did you want to know?"

Corvin had been planning the conversation in his head since he left Waynix.

"Who do you think would make a good corporal for Seventh Squad?"

Irikson thought about before answering.

"Don't know. No one comes to mind as taking over from you."

"What about you?"

"Me?"

"Yes, you."

"You know I have had my problems, especially when I first got here."

"Yes, you have. Since then, you have sorted yourself out. Also, all of the members of the three squads like you and in some way look up to you. I need someone to support me. Someone to lead that squad and make quick decisions when I am not there."

"You want me to do this?"

"You do not think you can support me?" asked Corvin.

"Of course, I would. I have always supported you, brother!"

"Yes, you have. All I ask is you keep supporting me, but this time by helping eight others support me as well!"

Irikson thought about it before speaking further.

"You know, I am not a very clever man. I do not understand all the things Smith used to teach you and Jorga about armies and such. I know nothing about leading men," said Irikson.

"You will learn but I think you know more than you think. You want the promotion?"

"I'll have to behave myself more, won't I?"

"Yes, you will!"

"You will help me and teach me?"

Corvin smiled, knowing he had approached the situation just right.

"Of course, I'll teach you."

"I'll have to stop spending most of my time with the Coin-Wives and spend less time drinking, won't I?"

"Not a bad idea," said Corvin still smiling.

"Well, it is about time I grew up a bit then!"

"Yes, it is. You want the job?"

"If it supports you, brother, and you can help me, I will take it."

"Then get off that bed, Corporal Irikson, and go get your squad in hand!"

Irik jumped up. Corvin also stood and offered his brother his arm, but Irikson ignored it and hugged him. Once they stepped back from each other, Corvin ducked into the corridor and returned with his old helmet. The helmet that had the Seventh Squad corporal insignia on it. He threw it at Irikson who caught it and put it on his head. He smiled.

"Thank you for trusting me, brother!" said Irikson.

"Go inform your squad and make sure they are ready. We leave tomorrow."

The travel by wagons would take five days. The entire company was there, all ten squads. Each squad had its own wagon. One squad had their gear piled up in the back. The wagon hitched to two large draught horses, the largest horses Corvin had ever seen. Ten wagons filled with mercenaries and their gear. At the very back was one further wagon with the company smith and cook, the wagon filled with the tools and food they needed. Corvin sat in the front next to the driver of the wagon set aside for Seventh Squad. He was keeping an eye on Irikson and so far was pleased. In the day, he had taken control of the squad, he had shown maturity and leadership. Corvin thought back to the conversation with Lorka.

"Could be the making of him!" is all Lorka had said.

Corvin sat in the wagon on the third day listening to Irikson teach his squad. He was telling them about different moves he had himself learnt in the ring and the squad members were listening with intent. There had been no arguments when Irikson was named Corporal of the Seventh Squad. He saw a few of the faces in the men under them and saw a little jealousy there. He expected it. He and Jorga were very lucky they had faced no opposition when being named corporals. They had full support from all the men around them. He knew Irikson would be a different matter. Although he was likeable and a great fighter, he could be moody and sometimes emotional. Although he had made no enemies with the Bloodchildren, Corvin new many of the mercenaries in the company were a little stand offish and tended to avoid Irikson's company. The promotion would hopefully give Irikson the chance to change this. Rivalries and clashes of egos were always present when any number of men worked and fought together, and the Bloodchildren were no different. However, the Captain kept a tight rein on the men under him. Corvin would do the same and tell Jorga to also keep an eye on Irikson. Corvin looked over the landscape and thought back to the day they had been loading the wagons, making ready for their departure.

"Sergeant Corvin, you are wanted at the gate," said Lorka, the old aide of the Captain's.

"By who?" asked Corvin.

"Some young man. He is being escorted by one of the border guards from Bordix," replied old Lorka.

"On my way!" said Corvin.

He was moving towards the main gate when Jorga fell in step beside him.

"Where are we off to?" Jorga asked.

"The gate. Apparently, there is someone that wants to talk to me."

"Who?"

"Not sure."

"This should be interesting," said Jorga with a smile.

As they reached the open gates, they saw two men standing there. One clearly a guard from the border town of Bordix and the other instantly recognisable. Medium height, slim muscular build and standing there with a surly half smile on his face. Both Corvin and Jorga were shocked, they did not think they would see him again. However, here he was, standing at the gate. As they reached the pair, the guard saw the symbols on Corvin's helmet and spoke.

"Greetings, Sergeant. This man made it to our town. He has been asking to see you for the last three days. The mayor asked I bring him here," said the guard.

"Sergeant? You are moving up in the world, Demon-boy," said Sick-boy.

Corvin and Jorga stopped and stared at Sick-boy. They were not unhappy to see him but Sick-boy had never been a part of their circle in the slave training camp and had stuck to himself. They looked him up and down. Corvin was unsure how he was feeling but finally spoke.

"I am surprised you made it, but I am happy you have," said Corvin.

Sick-boy laughed his sick little laugh before the guard spoke again.

"I am to release him into your care and return, Sergeant."

"That is acceptable," said Jorga.

With that, the guard turned and walked away. Jorga stepped forward and placed his hand on top off Sick-boy's shoulder.

"We were never close you and I, but I am glad you made it out of that shit hole," said Jorga.

"I was never close to anyone, and me making it here was a close

*thing, Silent-boy. I followed the carnage you boys left in your wake,"
Sick-boy replied.*

"He is known as Jorga now. I am known as Corvin."

*"You took the Smith's name? Good for you," replied Sick-boy, with
genuine pleasure.*

The three stood in silence looking at each other.

"Are you going to invite me in?" asked Sick-boy.

"I'll take him to my room, fetch Lorka and Irikson," said Corvin.

Jorga nodded and left.

"Follow me," said Corvin.

*They walked to Corvin's room in silence. Sick-boy looking around at
the home of the Bloodchildren, taking in all he saw. They arrived at
Corvin's room and sat down in the group lounge that his squads shared.
Corvin had poured five mugs of ale before passing one to Sick-boy, then
seating himself. Sick-boy sipped it and said nothing. They waited in
silence. Nothing was said and Corvin did not know how he felt. He was
happy Sick-boy had made it out, but to be honest, he did not trust him
and if he were here looking to join the Bloodchildren, he would be turned
away if Corvin had anything to do with it. The others arrived. Irikson
sat down and grabbed a mug. Lorka smiled and walked up and patted
Sick-boy on the head.*

"You made it, you sick little man!" said Lorka.

"Just," said Sick-boy.

*"What happened? We last saw you when we were leaving the
drinking hall," said Jorga.*

*"Yes. We thought you would have been with us when we left
Hurarock," said Irikson.*

"I told you I would go my own way, and I did," said Sick-boy.

"So where did you go?" asked Corvin again.

*"Once we left the drinking hall, I headed to the slave huts. I found
cook and her helpers, I beat them, cut them a few times, then cut their
throats," said Sick-boy.*

He was smiling and it showed the others he had not changed in any way, not that they expected him to improve. He had always been a little deranged, which is why he had the name Sick-boy.

"You tortured a woman?" asked Lorka.

The cook had been the one to betray them all, and the reason the Smith had been tortured to death. Still, cutting a woman's throat after beating her, did not sit well with the others.

"Of course. I may not have been as close to the Smith as you four, but he was still a good man and did not deserve what they did to him. He was always patient with me, and never judged me the way you lot did. Yes, he knew some of my life story, whereas you lot didn't. He was one of the few people in that camp I did not dislike. The cook needed to die, painfully."

"Well, maybe you are correct," said Corvin.

"We don't disagree, she needed to die," said Irikson.

"You are just a little squeamish when it comes to killing women," said Sick-boy.

"Yes, we are, and that is how it should be," said Corvin.

"Well, I do not feel the same way," said Sick-boy.

"What happened after you had your fun with the cook and her helpers?" asked Corvin.

"I went on a little bit of a rampage, to be honest," said Sick-boy.

"A little bit of a rampage?" asked Lorka.

"I met up with some of the other pit-rats. We hid in alleys and ambushed the bastards, killing many. We were moving around the settlement looking for chief bastard but could not seem to find him. We ran into a large troop of the bastards. The small group was almost wiped out, only me and another survived. It was at that point, we decided that we needed to get out. We made our way to the gates and dodging guards the whole way. We waited for you lot but thought we must have missed you. We found the tree where the Smith was still hanging from. We cut him down and dragged his body away. We were some distance from the road when we saw you lot running through the shadows, heading west. We could not shout out and draw attention to

ourselves, so I told the young pit-rat to try and catch up with you. He ran off."

"No one caught up to us, he must have been caught. Who was he?" asked Jorga.

"Not good with names, you know that," said Sick-boy.

"What did you do with the Smith?" asked Corvin, a blank look on his face.

"I carried the body into the hills and hid in the forest there. Once I saw chief bastard leave with all his men, I made a fire and burned his body," said Sick-boy.

"That was dangerous," said Jorga.

"Yes, but it needed to be done. I was not letting those bastards get their hands on his body. It took many hours, but I reduced him to ash."

"How did you get here? It is not an easy journey and we only just made it," said Corvin.

"Does it matter?" said Sick-boy.

"You are here now, so you no doubt want a place with us?" said Lorka.

"No. You can play soldiers, but I will go my own way, as I always do," said Sick-boy.

"You came all this way just to say hi and then leave? We have never got on with you, although we do owe you for helping us out of there, for taking care of the Smith's body and killing the cook," said Irikson.

"You owe me nothing. I came here for this," said Sick-boy.

He reached into a small bag he had at his feet and pulled out a large wooden jug. It had a wooden lid, and the lid was sealed to the jug with wax. He handed it to Corvin.

"What is this?" asked Corvin.

"Smith's ashes, Demon-boy. Thought you may want them," said Sick-boy.

All were silent. Corvin did not expect this. He held the jug in his hands and like the others, fought back tears. His friends looked at the jug and it was a while before someone spoke.

"Thank you," said Lorka.

"Yes, thank you, Sick-boy. This means much," said Corvin.

"You're welcome," replied Sick-boy.

"So how did you get here?" asked Irikson.

"No. That story is for me and me alone," said Sick-boy standing.

"We could make a place for you here, if you wanted it," said Jorga.

"No. I will go. This life is not for me, you lot are not for me," said Sick-boy.

Corvin held the jug in one hand and with his right hand, held it out for Sick-boy. Sick-boy looked at it, then shook it.

"I don't hate you, but none of you are my friends, none of you are my family. I will go and find those," said Sick-boy.

One by one they all shook his hand. They escorted him down to the gate and he did not even say goodbye. He walked away but stopped a few paces from them. He turned and looked at them.

"If any of you had called me brother in that place, if any of you had taken the time to learn of me and my story, things may have been different," he spoke.

With that, he walked away.

Corvin and the others had felt guilty and had talked long into the night. Sick-boy had been right, they had never made the effort to learn of Sick-boy or his journey. It was not an easy guilt to swallow, but it was theirs and they would have to deal with it.

The wagons pulled over to a field and parked up. The men all jumped off their wagons and started the routine of making camp. After the first night camping under the stars, the new recruits had learned what needed to be done from the more senior members of the company and the instruction handed down from the Captain. Some squads were sent to gather wood for the cook fires, another squad was in charge of digging firepits for the cook fires. One squad was charged with watering the horses and then picketing them not far away amongst the fresh grass, coming up for the spring. There were still patches of snow on the ground and the air was still cold at night. The former slaves had taught the other recruits under Corvin, to sleep right up against each other at night. This helped the squads keep warm.

Once the cook fires were going, the squads had a bit of free time. Irikson, Torin and Jorga used this time to take their squads on a light run to stretch any kinks they had from sitting in the wagons for a full day. Other squads of the company sat around talking and generally doing nothing. Tenth Squad, being full of archers, went hunting to get some small game which added to the food supply they had brought with them. Corvin knew this was more to keep their eye in with a bow as it was to add food.

Once everyone was settled Corvin walked off to meet with the other Sergeants and the Captain. He found them standing some distance off the road talking together. As he approached, the Captain looked up.

"How is your section, Sergeant Corvin?" asked the Captain.

"Good, Captain. They are travelling well and are behaving themselves," Corvin replied.

Second Sergeant Emric smiled, whereas First Sergeant Dolac just stared. Corvin could not work out what Dolac's problem was. He was never hostile; in fact, he was never anything. He pretty much ignored Corvin and his former slaves. He was the only one not to congratulate Corvin on his promotion. He had never been rude either, to Corvin's face at least. Corvin was happy to be ignored and hoped the situation never arose where the two clashed. There would be only one outcome and the Captain would not be happy. He cleared his mind back to the present when the Captain asked another question.

"The lads in your squads not asking too many questions?"

Corvin understood what the Captain was meaning. The rush to get the company ready and on the road had not left much time for explanation of what the season held for them.

"No, Captain. The former slaves are not affected. The other members seem a little confused but generally are also just getting on with the job at hand," said Corvin.

"I'm not surprised your former slaves are unaffected, they do not have the understanding of the bigger picture!" said Dolac.

The barb was not lost on Corvin, Emric or the Captain.

The Captain said nothing and just watched the exchange, he wanted to see how Corvin would handle it. Emric went to say something but saw the Captain shake his head.

Corvin looked into the face of the First Sergeant and took a step closer.

"It is not knowing the bigger picture as you put it, First Sergeant, that saves lives. As slaves, our lives are constantly changing and slaves that cannot keep up, get killed. We are used to rapid change," responded Corvin.

Dolac scoffed.

"You would do well to remember that, First Sergeant," said Corvin.

"Yes, he would," said the Captain.

"Corvin, your squads are on guard duty tonight. You can roster them how you like, as long as one full squad is awake guarding the company," said Emric.

"No problem. Any advice how to roster for this guard duty?" asked Corvin.

"One squad guard from dinner time until after midnight,

the second squad guards from midnight until dawn," replied Emric.

"Okay. I do have a question if I may?" said Corvin.

"Certainly, Corvin," said the Captain.

"Why are we guarding? Is your own country dangerous for a company of this size?" asked Corvin.

It was asked genuinely. Dolac scoffed again and turned away to hide his smile.

"The guard is not needed in our own land, but once we reach the ship and indeed our destination, night guards will be needed. This gets the men used to it and also prepares the most inexperienced of our company to the guard duty," said the Captain.

"The men who take the second shift can sleep in the wagon the next day?" asked Corvin.

"Yes, but do not let them sleep too long, just a few hours. They can catch up on sleep the next night," said Emric.

"The reason I have called for you is this," the Captain continued.

"I have had a letter arrive by fast horse from our ship. It is stocked and ready to go but the Sea-Captain wanted to let me know that he is a few sailors short for the journey. This means all of our men will be helping out with all chores on the ship. Any problems?"

All of the three sergeants nodded there was no problem.

"Secondly, it is roughly four-weeks sailing to get to Kor'Lena if we have no storms. During that time, the lessons will start and be held every morning for a few hours. I have hired three retired sailors that came from Kor'Lena to give a brief history and also teach basic language skills. They live in Iriksec now and only cost me a few coins and their keep. Corvin, get your men up to speed as quickly as possible especially with the language. I do not expect your men to be fluent in two weeks…"

Emric laughed and Corvin smiled.

"At least, have a rough understanding of the basics of the language. The more senior men in our company already have a good grasp of the language. Both Dolac and Emric are fluent."

"Yes, Captain," said Corvin.

"Also, Corvin, pay close attention to the history between Kor'Lena and Sul'Lena. Kor'Lena can be a little strange in their customs and if you do not have a grasp of where the two nations have come from, there could be problems."

Corvin nodded.

"Any idea of where they will station us?" asked Emric.

"No. I have had no more news from Kor'Lena. I sent a courier bird straight away with a reply to say we would be there in roughly five weeks," said the Captain.

"If we get the weather," said Dolac.

"Yes. If we get good weather," said the Captain.

"Anything else, Captain? I want to check on my squads," said Corvin.

"No, that is all Corvin. We will talk again tonight once we have reached our next camp site," replied the Captain.

Corvin nodded to them all and left.

"You really want to piss him off?" asked Emric.

"I do not care either way, to be honest!" said Dolac.

"He calls you out, there will be trouble!" said Emric.

"Yes. He has already beaten you once in a practice bout. You want to face him again?" asked the Captain.

"We all know there is a difference between practice bouts and real fights," said Dolac.

"I do not see where this anger comes from Dolac," said Emric.

"It's not anger. I just do not like him. For a former slave, he walks too tall. He needs to be taught humility," scoffed Dolac.

"Not by you, though. Remember, I let my men sort out their own quarrels and do not interfere, unless it endangers the company as a whole. You would not do anything to do that, would you?" asked the Captain.

"No, Captain. It would not come to that," replied Dolac.

Emric laughed and said, "I'll see to my squads."

The three broke off and went on their way. Dolac thought back to the Third Sergeant. He had tried to keep an open mind and deal with Corvin like he would any other fighting man, but he hated his arrogance, his walking around with his head held high as if he had never been a slave. A slave! That is what life had chosen for Corvin, he should learn his place. Maybe it needed to be taught to him.

After five days of journey by wagon, the convoy arrived at the gates of Iriksec, the capital of Irik. The former slaves thought they were amazed at the size of Bordix, the border town they had reached during their escape. Nothing prepared them for the size of Iriksec. The city could be seen from when the sun rose in the morning of the fifth day, and all day as they travelled towards it, the men spoke little. Now as the convoy started to make its way through the immense gates, the former slaves, the pit-rats, looked astonished. The said nothing but took it all in like a child seeing something wonderful for the first time; many stared with mouths open.

The wall around Iriksec was even taller than the border wall between the Outlander Nation and Irik. Corvin estimated it was as tall as five grown men standing on each other's shoulders. The stone used in the construction was a dark grey with small flecks of lighter grey or white through it. There was two gates side by side. The individual gates were of a stout, thick wood. The gates wide enough to let two wagons side by side through at a time. The gate on their right, the one they were entering was the one Emric had said was the entry gate. The other gate solely for those leaving. As they rode through the gate, Corvin and the other pit-rats were amazed at how deep the wall was. It took them longer to get through the tunnel that they imagined. Emric had warned Corvin and said the wall was fifty lai wide. Even though the former pit-rats had been learning their numbers and letters, the numbers meant nothing to Corvin until he travelled through it. Corvin worked out in his head that it was as wide as 25 tall men lying in a line on the ground. Once they reached the sunshine, they came into the city itself; stone buildings everywhere. Either side of the main road, they looked like it led straight to the docks, tall buildings ran either side of the road, tall as some of the tallest trees Corvin had seen. Emric said the night before that the buildings where all five to six storeys high. Corvin had not believed him, but now he did!

People were everywhere! In fact, Corvin had never seen this many people in his life. Once again, all the former slaves thought they had seen what they thought to be all the people in the world when they entered Bordix. Nothing prepared them for the sight of the thousands and thousands that walked the streets and plied their trade. Emric had explained to Corvin's three squads that over 60,000 people lived here. A number that meant nothing to the former pit-rats. It was Torin, Corporal of the Ninth Squad that explained it.

"Think of triple the number of Bordix, and you will be close," said Torin.

The smell that assaulted them was horrible. Even though

Bordix had been a large town, it did not have the amount of people living this closely to each other or the same smells. The smells of street stalls cooking their food was new to the pit-rats. There also seemed to be a heavy smell of burnt oil hanging in the air. Corvin would have to ask Emric.

It took the convoy an hour to reach the docks. The size of the ships here once again shocked the former slaves. Corvin, of course, had only ever been on one ship and he was locked into the hold for the journey. Seeing the ships brought back sad memories and he tried to block the thoughts. He would have to speak to the pit-rats latter in the evening.

Corvin jumped down from his wagon and ran forward as they reached the docks. He reached the wagon Emric was driving and joined him in the front seat.

"Big?" said Emric.

"That's one way of putting it. There are many open mouths in my squads, including mine."

Emric laughed.

Corvin watched the ships as they headed along the stone causeway. The ships where all different sizes but shared the same colour. A rich brown with an oily sheen, except one. Further along the row of ships that were docked, Corvin could make out a ship with two masts when the others had three. It was a rich dark red. Corvin pointed. Emric looked to where Corvin pointed.

"Ah. Our destination. That lad is the 'Blood Storm', our transport ship," said Emric.

"The company owns a ship?"

"Yes. The Captain thought it a good idea to have our own ship. We have owned the ship for six years now."

"Why do we need our own ship? Can we not pay someone else to transport us? It must be expensive."

"Cheaper than you think. The main reason is when we go

off on jobs, the ship comes with us. It then waits out the season to bring us home. It comes from over a decade ago when the Bloodchildren got stuck."

"I have heard that story. You got stuck at the bottom of Ex'Na with no ships around!"

"Yes. We had to march for twenty-five days to arrive at a port that had a ship willing to take us. We got back late in autumn and the sea voyage was very rough. After that, the Captain decided we needed our own vessel. We hire sailors at the beginning of every season and then they leave us at the end. It works out cheaper."

"You painted it?"

"Yes. Captain paid for a red dye to be painted over the outside of the ship before the protective oils where added. It has faded a bit over the last six years to an acceptable colour."

"It looks like blood!"

"It does now! When we first got it painted, the crews painting it used the wrong dye. It was closer to a pink-red."

Corvin laughed.

"Pink red?"

"Yes. Not very menacing!" Emric said, with a twinkle of a smile in his eyes.

Corvin laughed again.

"We had to paint a darker red over the top of it. For many years, the lighter red still had the ship looking bright. Once it faded, we got the desired colour. If she ever sinks, I do not think the Captain will paint a replacement."

As they reached the ship and came to a halt, Corvin along with many others new to the company, took in the full size of the ship. According to Emric, it had two levels under the main deck. The bottom hold was for storage of equipment and stores. The middle deck was living quarters. The second level or living quarters was broken up into four sections. The front of the ship, or Bow, was the sleeping quarters for the Third Section as well as the Tenth Squad. The next section along that was Bow/Mid was the sleeping quarters for the Second Section under Sergeant Emric. Next along called Amidships, was the kitchen area called a galley; used by the cooks for cooking and used by the men for eating. It only had enough room for one section at a time to eat, so as Emric had said, all the sections have different eating times throughout the day. The stern was taken up by the quarters for the section First Sergeant Dolac commanded. Corvin took all this in and would have to explain this all to his squads, most of them had never seen a ship, let alone sailed on one.

All of the squads had unloaded themselves and their travel backpacks from the wagons and been loaded straight away onto the Bloodchild. The three squads under Corvin along with the Tenth Squad were led down into the second level and their sleeping quarters. On entering, Corvin noticed candles burning around the large room. All around the walls and indeed in the middle, was what Emric had described as sleeping hammocks. A thick piece of canvas that supported a man whilst he slept. These were stacked three high with hooks close by for all the men to hang their back packs and weapons. Much laughter was had when Irikson, the clown of the group these days, tried getting into one. He quickly fell out and landed on his arse. Every member of the four squads laughed, long and hard.

"You try it, you bastards!" said Irikson, as he got himself up of the deck and rubbed his backside.

Luckily, their guider, one of the senior sailors, gave a quick demonstration on how to get into these hammocks. He climbed the small ladder and got straight into the highest hammock that Irikson had difficulty with. He grabbed the hammock and seemed to shuffle his way onto it, moving his body in time with the swinging hammock.

"See? Easy."

"Bastard!" muttered Irikson.

The squads all laughed again.

Corvin was glad they were all laughing. It lightens the mood and for some of the former slaves, being down in a hold of a ship again brought back a flood of memories, none of them good.

"Everyone, get your gear sorted and hung up, choose your playmate for the night."

Corvin said making a comment about the hammocks that set the squads all of laughing again.

"Then once that is done, assemble on the top deck for a briefing."

Corvin found a hammock near the door and close to a candle lamp and hung his gear up. He left with the sailor and headed back up to the top deck.

"Where do the sailors sleep?" asked Corvin.

"We have smaller quarters in the bottom hold. There is usually only thirty of us, so we are all rammed into together in a smaller space with our hammocks four high. Easier this trip as we are sailing short of crew with only eighteen of us."

"Yes, I have been told we will be learning to sail. Is that not a little tight down in the hold?"

"Yes, but the bottom of the ship rolls less. So, a better sleep. Also, we are usually up on deck more, so do not need a lot of room."

Corvin just nodded and continued to follow.

Chapter Five

"Bloodchildren, listen up!" shouted Captain Joren.

All of the company had assembled on deck to hear a briefing from the Captain. As always, Sergeant Dolac was on his right, looking over the assembled men.

Emric and Corvin were both standing with their men. The crew of eighteen climbing all over the ship, getting it ready to sail.

"Now that you have all your gear stowed, there is a few things that need to be passed on."

The men of the company all listened up and stood to attention.

"As some of you have heard, we do not have enough sailors for this trip, so all of you will be taking your turn to help out the sailors. A roster has been set up for duty, switching between guard duty and watch duty on the ship. The Sergeants will all be told of the roster soon and will pass on the information to you all. If we have good weather, we should be at sea for roughly twenty-eight days. If we have rough weather, a little bit longer."

"Do you think we will have good weather, Captain?" said a voice from amongst the men.

"Predict the weather? Are you mad?"

This got the assembled men laughing.

"Not even the gods can predict the weather," said the Captain.

This got more laughs from the men. Corvin was pretty sure who the voice belonged to and would have a word with Irikson later about it.

"Also, for the newer men in the company, I have hired some men from Kor'Lena to teach you about their history and also to learn the basics of the language. Even some of the more experienced men could use more tutoring on the language."

This got the more experienced men laughing.

"All we need to learn Captain is 'No'. Where are the drinks? Where are the Coin-Wives?" shouted the voice.

This got all of the men including the sailors laughing once more. Corvin could see the Captain was now slightly irritated and that reflected badly on his section, if the Captain knew who the voice belonged to. He caught the eye of Emric who was holding back his laugh and winked at Corvin. Corvin shook his head in disappointment that made Emric smile. He then looked over at Jorga who was also suppressing a smile. Corvin shook his head; Jorga nodded once and slowly drifted back into the mass of men, looking for Irikson to no doubt tell him to shut his mouth.

"We set sail on the turning tide which I have been told is only a few hours away, so get yourself back to your quarters where you will be informed of the roster. Obey the sailors if they ask you to do something, obey the master of the ship Captain Loreen as he speaks with my voice, and keep your minds on the job at hand. Dismissed!"

"The roster is a three-day roster. Three days of guard duty, then three days of working with the sailors, then three days off. The three days off, I am told, will be split into history lessons and information we need to know about the people of Kor'Lena. Language lessons will be every day, no matter what you are doing. These will be fitted around our duties. Those of you not doing anything during the day are reminded to make as little noise as possible when in these quarters as others will be sleeping. We are allowed up on deck and the Captain has said to be mindful of not getting in the sailor's way. Is this understood?" said Corvin.

"Aye," spread around the room. Corvin eyed Irikson and was going to say something in private but thought a little mention in front of the men would not hurt.

"Irikson, do you have any idea who was shouting out comments to the Captain?"

"No, Sergeant. I have asked my squad and we have no idea," said Irikson, with a serious look on his face.

Corvin smiled.

"Well, we all need to make sure we do not annoy Captain Joren. We have enough work to do on the voyage and would hate to be given extra dirty jobs now, would we, men?"

The men all smiled and looked at their feet including Irikson, who was trying not to laugh. Lorka stood at the back and caught Corvin's eye. Lorka had that huge smile of his and Corvin tried his hardest not to laugh.

"Our section has the first three days off. Then after that, Seventh Squad has watch duties, Eighth and Ninth Squad have guard duties. I will tell the corporals more in the next hour or so. For now, you are free to return to the main deck. The Captain has let us all witness our first departure from the top deck. Dismissed."

The men all departed for the top deck accept Irikson,

Lorka and Jorga, who gathered around Corvin. As the last men departed, Corvin turned to them.

"Some of us do not have good memories of being inside a ship!"

The other three only nodded

"I want the three of you to keep an eye out over all of the pit-rats. If they look like they are struggling, then support them. I have already spoken to the Captain and he has agreed that even though he does not like giving special treatment, all of the pit-rats are allowed up on deck when they feel the confines of the ship are getting too much."

"That's good of him," said Irikson.

"Yes. I am surprised he had not punished you for your little comments!" said Corvin.

"He knew it was me?"

"Of course, he knew!" lied Corvin.

"We'll watch over you too, Sergeant," said Lorka.

"Yes, we will," said Jorga.

"Thank you both. It feels a little different this time around and I am surrounded by you lot. However, getting to sleep may be a whole different feeling."

"We'd better get up on deck and get a good spot," said Jorga.

With that, the four of them made their way to the top deck.

Corvin did not sleep the first night, or the second night, either. It was the third night into their voyage on the Bloodchild and he was lying in his hammock trying to get to sleep. As the last two nights, he was once again struggling. It was not the rocking of the ship or the snoring of the thirty other men around him that kept him awake. He had suffered flashbacks of his time as a child when he was thrown into the hold of a ship, when he was first captured. His mind would not stop and the thoughts of Trainer and the children crying would constantly run through his mind. After two hours, he gave up and quietly got himself up. He wrapped his warm overcoat around himself and made his way to the top deck. He arrived and made his way to the Aft section. Some of the sailors who were on night duty were watching the sails and rigging, talking amongst themselves. The Fourth Squad was on guard and watch duty this night. They had scattered themselves around the top deck, keeping an eye out over the dark ocean, looking for any trouble. They would walk over to each other for quiet conversations before walking off back to their stations. Corvin knew there was little trouble expected. The Outlander raiders would not raid a ship this size. The former pit-rats had discussed it last night and all agreed, they would love the opportunity to hit the Outlanders and all hoped they would be attacked. As he reached the bow, he came up on Yelix, the Corporal of Fourth Squad. A corporal that he did not know well.

"Evening, Yelix," said Corvin.

"Evening, Sergeant Corvin. Can't sleep again?" Yelix replied.

"No."

"You will get used to the ship, Sergeant. It just takes a while for the body to adjust to the rolling of the ship."

Yelix was twenty-five years of age. He was the same height as Corvin but a little thinner in the shoulders and arms. His speed in the training bouts was legendary. He was sword champ of the Second Section and Corvin was looking forward to testing his skill against him. Unlike the other men of Irik, he had dark brown hair and instead of growing a beard, kept his face clean shaven. He had a hard face that was softened by two dark brown eyes. He was in his fifth season with the company and according to Second Sergeant Emric, a solid man.

"It is not the rocking of the ship that keeps me awake," said Corvin.

"What then?"

Most of the company had heard stories of the former slaves. Corvin's own squads knew better than most but none of them knew the intimate details of their slavery apart from the former slaves themselves. For a reason he did not know, Corvin launched into his tale. He told Emric of the nights stuck in the hold as a child, the story of the boy across the way that turned out to be Trainer using gestures to keep him calm. He told of the nights sitting in his own urine, whilst the other children around him cried themselves to sleep. Corvin told it and managed to stay calm for a change. The memories still hurt, even when discussing with Jorga, Lorka and Irikson. He finished his tale and kept quiet.

"That is one hell of a story, Sergeant. Thanks for sharing it. We had all heard stories of course, of you and your fellows, but until now I have never known any of the details," said Yelix.

"Thanks for listening, Corporal. I think it helps to speak of it."

"Not much else to do on the night watch. We have as much chance of being attacked by Outlanders as we do being raided by fish."

Corvin smiled.

"I do not envy your life, Sergeant, or the others that arrived with you, but I will say something if I may?"

"Go ahead."

"I do envy you and your fellows for your strength and

fighting skills. I am not bad with a sword and known to be handy. I have been in many skirmishes over the last five seasons but never seen men with the same level of ability as you and the former pit-rats, as you call them."

Corvin nodded. "Thank you, Corporal."

"I'm looking forward to a few training bouts. Will be good to face someone else and perhaps learn some new tricks," said Yelix.

"We can arrange that. Perhaps once we have reached our destination?"

"That would be good, Sergeant. I look forward to facing that speed of yours," said Yelix with a grin.

"I best get my head down. Enjoy the rest of the watch.

Corvin smiled and walked away. He was feeling a little more relaxed and headed back to his bed.

"No, it is pronounced 'Ku-Larka', not 'Koo-Lara'. You need to make the sound at the start a little stronger," said Lenor, the translator from Kor'Lena.

It was Seventh and Eighth Squad sitting in the galley receiving another lesson in the language of Kor'Lena. Corvin was present with the squads and had finally got some sleep the previous night. His talking with Yelix adding a little bit of balm to the wound that Corvin carried. As Corvin had no fixed duties other than keeping an eye on his squad, he was free to take as many lessons as he wanted. He had made himself attend them every day no matter what squad was being taught. Emric had said that as Sergeants, they needed to lead the way and have a good understanding of the language and customs. Because of this, Corvin sat in every morning and learnt. Some of the mercenaries in his squads were taking to it well but a few others needed extra help; one of these was Lorka. He was not stupid by any means, but he struggled with the language, but he kept at it and concentrated.

The lessons had started with the basic words like no, yes, hello, I do not understand and words like that. Lenor had said to Corvin that hopefully by the second week, they would be able to understand most of the more common words and be able to communicate on a very basic level. As Corvin found speaking the language was not the problem, but rather listening and understanding when someone spoke it to you was the hardest. When Loren demonstrated by talking in conversation to Emric, Corvin could not believe how fast they were speaking. The words all flowed into one another and he had found it hard to single out the words he knew. Lorka made the comment that got them all laughing.

"When do you stop for breath? I guess you lot cannot eat whilst you are talking, your food would go cold!"

It was not like Lorka to run down another culture and Corvin knew the large warrior was getting frustrated at not being able to accomplish a task. Ninth Squad was on work duty this morning, so would have their lesson on the afternoon. Corvin would be there to see how his squad was going and join in the lessons.

"Corvin, if I said to you 'Kuma mor veneer', you would reply?"

"No thanks, not happy to do that!" said Corvin.

All the men present laughed as none of them knew what Lenor was saying.

"In the language of Lena, please Corvin," said Lenor.

"Urelana Nu," said Corvin.

Which, of course, meant 'I don't understand'. It was the phrase the mercenaries had learnt first.

"Good, Corvin. Your pronunciation is coming along nicely," said Lenor.

Lenor was supposedly a retired sailor from Kor'Lena but a lot of them suspected he was something else. Corvin did not know the word for it, but a title given to someone that helps others learn for a living.

For the next two hours before lunch, the Seventh and Eighth Squad worked their way through with Lenor. Corvin looked over at Irikson and smiled. He was listening intently and for once, was taking something seriously. Jorga was also concentrating and was one of the better students. Jorga was the brightest of all the former slaves and was indeed the only one who had his letters and numbers as well as could read and write well. He had learnt in the evenings over the winter, learning them from Emric. Corvin wished he had joined Jorga, but of course, he never knew Jorga was learning these skills. For now, Corvin would have to make do with knowing his numbers, which all of the former slaves had learnt quickly in order to know how much items cost. None of the former slaves wanted to be disadvantaged when dealing with the local merchants.

"You can use your elbow, its solid bone and thrown in the right direction can cause some damage," said Lorka.

Lorka and Irikson where taking the Seventh Squad through some unarmed combat training on the top deck of the amidships. Corvin had been chatting with Emric and watching the training as well.

"Let me demonstrate!" said Irikson

Irikson squared off against Lorka and they started fighting. Irikson ducking and weaving as Lorka threw punches.

Lorka although was quick, was not as quick as Irikson. Irikson ducked a flying right cross that came in quick, then stepped in and slammed an elbow into the stomach of Lorka.

"Hold," called Jorga, who was also watching and helping out.

Lorka was bent over catching his breath that had whooshed out when Irikson had connected. Irikson turned to his squad.

"See? The elbow is your best short-range weapon when fighting unarmed. Imagine that hit if I had aimed for his throat! He would not be able to breathe and would not be able to fight for some time," said Irikson.

Corvin turned back to Emric.

"Is your training always full contact?" asked Emric.

"Yes," said Corvin.

"We are seven days into our voyage and many of your squad members are carrying small injuries and most have bruises."

"Yes. Fight training needs to be full contact. If it does not hurt, then you won't learn."

"True. I'm more concerned that a serious injury will happen before the fighting actually starts."

Corvin smiled. His relationship with Emric had grown over the last few weeks since his promotion and he found himself seeking him out whenever he had a question to ask.

"I'll have a word with the corporals then."

"How are your squads?"

"Good. Irikson is taking his squad in hand and they seem to be open to his ideas."

"That is one way of putting it. The rumour I hear is they almost worship him."

Corvin smiled again. The Seventh Squad had adapted much quicker to Irikson's influence than expected. He was known amongst the former slaves as being a little crazy and jumping before thinking into any situation life threw at him. He was, of course, a fearsome fighter and could be very quick to anger. However, his jokes and his foolhardiness seemed to bring out something into the squad that Corvin as a corporal, could not. They followed in his footsteps and the confidence coming from the squad could be seen.

"He is getting more out of them than I could, that is for sure," said Corvin.

Emric laughed.

"You did very well by them, lad. In fact, there are no squad's fitter or stronger than yours in the entire company. I look forward to seeing what you can do on the battlefield," said Emric.

"I thought we would be guarding a wall?"

"Figure of speech, lad."

"In fact, I am a little worried about that."

"Worried? About what?" said Emric, surprised at what he was hearing.

"The former slaves may be good in a pit, one on one, but in a group battle with hundreds around us, things will be very different!"

"Yes, they will. You know that, your fellows who escaped with you know that and you have trained in groups since you arrived. Trust me! You will learn more in battle and I am sure you and your squads will handle it well!"

"Thank you. Still, I worry. I don't want to lose any more of the former slaves. We have lost enough!"

Emric nodded.

"I understand that. As a sergeant, all you can do is train your men to be stronger, and faster. Teach them and prepare them for as many situations as you can. Once battle starts, it can sometimes be pure chance, as I have told you before, it will amaze you as to who survives and who does not. As I also said, defending a wall is a lot easier than taking one."

Corvin nodded. They both continued to watch as Irikson was working one on one with a member of his squad.

"Sergeants," said Captain Joren as he sat beside them.

"Captain."

"Captain."

"I see your squads are still training, it's good to see."

"Thank you, Captain. Thought it would be a good way to for Irikson to get to know his squad better. When it comes to teaching a man to use his fists, Irikson is one of the better trainers," said Corvin.

"Judging how many punches he is landing on those poor lads; I would say he knows them intimately by now!" said Emric.

Corvin smiled and the Captain laughed.

"It's working, however. The Seventh Squad are reacting well to him," said Corvin.

"Good. The lessons are they going okay?" asked the Captain.

"A few are struggling with the language," replied Corvin.

"You are not expected to speak it fluently Corvin," said Emric.

"Just enough basic words to prevent any major misunderstanding. They are a proud bunch, and it is easy to offend them," said the Captain.

"So I have heard," replied Corvin.

"Your lads understand the history?" asked the Captain.

Corvin thought back to the large history lesson they had received the day before. All three of his squads had been there as well as Tenth Squad. The lesson started with Lenor going back to the time when the country of Lena had been one. Corvin could remember the lesson almost word for word.

"*To understand the two different countries you have to go back to the beginning when they were one country. In the year 1080, King Meruk died. His two sons spent time arguing over who the best king for the future would be. As was custom, it was up to them to discuss and choose who would inherit the throne. They argued for a full year until a furious public argument in the king's court took place.*

The eldest son Sul-Meruk was a mean, vicious person who wanted to lead the armies on conquest and invade the neighbouring country of Ex'Na. The youngest son, Kor-Meruk was more peaceful, reasonable and intelligent. He did not want to go to war. He knew the way to a rich nation was through peaceful trade with their neighbours. During the argument Sul-Meruk stormed out of the throne room. He went south to his home to raise his armies. Kor-Meruk stayed in the North and prepared to defend. This is the start of the great Civil War.

A year later after raising all the southern forces, Prince Sul-Meruk marched north. Prince Kor-Meruk, however, had not spent the time idle. He had gathered the forces loyal to himself in the north and dug in. He had not raced south with all speed but had stopped one hundred Mila South of the Aula mountain ranges. His forces being of twenty-five thousand fighters, had dug long trench lines and placed his forces in defensive position across the whole country width.

When his brother arrived with his forty-nine thousand men, he ran head long into those defensive positions. For twenty-two years, the war raged across this defensive line, with the princes both middle aged by the end of it. No ground was won or lost as both sides were stuck in a violent stale mate. The southern forces could not push through the defences that had been dug, and the northern forces not having the numbers to push back, so it was a meat grinder with both sides battling every day.

Prince Kor-Meruk was not a stupid man and knew the war would be a stalemate so had prepared for this. As the war was being fought, the northern engineers and workers were busy completing more permanent fortifications 100 Mila back from the fighting lines. A massive wall of stone that ran from the Aula Mountains all the way to the sea had been erected. They called it 'The Dark Wall', which was eight Lai tall or as tall as three grown men, and twelve Lai wide. The fact that this had been built with such speed was a testament to the quality of engineers the North had.

The war had ended thousands and thousands of lives. The South that had more numbers was able to reinforce quickly, the North not so much."

The information coming thick and fast as Lenor took time to get a sip of water before continuing.

"In the year 1105, once the great Aula wall was completed, Prince Kor-Meruk had slowly started moving his troops back to the wall position and instead of sending any reinforcements to the fighting lines, garrisoned them in at the wall. This had to be done carefully because if he left his lines too light, his brother's forces would push through.

Then on the last night of fall in 1105, they retreated north as fast they could.

The next morning a large attack was staged, but of course when the southern forces attacked, they found all fortifications empty. Prince Sul-Meruk gathered all his forces then sent word all down the fighting line to speed North with all haste. His forces did this and the next day ran into the new Aula Wall. For four days the southern forces threw themselves at the wall. The death rate was enormous for the southerners, whereas the northerners hardly lost troops. Finally, a truce was called and the two brothers met at the large gate of the Wall.

A treaty was made that afternoon and witnessed by both sides' advisors and generals. The country of Lena was separated into two kingdoms, with one brother ruling over the south, now called Sul'Lena and the other to rule over the north, Kor'Lena.

The south lost around one hundred and seventy-five thousand men over the twenty-two years, which depleted the south of all able-bodied men for many decades and twenty-five thousand of those lost in the last week when they tried to overrun the new wall. The North lost one hundred and *ten thousand soldiers and although not as many as the south, it hurt more as the north was not as heavily populated.*

After the Civil War, both brothers retreated back to their new capitals. Much work needed to be done to save their kingdoms. The south, although with more resources and manpower, suffered more as the prince had pressed all able-bodied men into his armies. There would be a shortage of food for many years to come and a shortage of workers, materials and coin.

The north fared slightly better as the Prince had held back some men and also had all the woman in the country trained in the work men normally did. Whilst the men had been fighting, the rest of the north were working to support their troops supplying food, weapons etc. Also, Prince Kor-Meruk had the foresight to have new granaries built and had brought in at great expense food stuffs from the neighbouring Ex'Na. He had also hired engineers and advisors from Ex'Na to help with his wall. This is when the ties between the two kingdoms begun. They had been close ever since."

"Well, Corvin?" asked the Captain.

"Yes, Captain. The men now have a good understanding of the history."

"Good. Lena is sometimes called the 'Mercenary's Paradise' for all the work they give out to fighting men," said Emric.

"Yes. They have been going to war on and off ever since. Well, I should say the southerners, a ruthless uncivilised bunch, keep deciding every few decades to have another go," said the Captain.

"They do not learn?" asked Corvin.

"No," said Emric.

"They do seem a little more serious this time. According to the message we received asking for help, the Sul'Lenans have gathered quite a few brotherhoods or mercenary companies as well as their own army. We will find out more once we make landfall," added the Captain.

"Have the southerners hired any more companies from Irik?" asked Corvin.

"No. Our fellow companies would not work for the southerners. Also, the mercenary's companies from Ex'Na would not work for them either. Well, maybe the current Duke of DuNoor would, he is an arsehole. No, most of the hired men will come from the lands of Maraken," said the Captain.

"Bloody savages," spat Emric.

"Yes. Furious fighters and lots of them. Do you know of the people of Maraken?" asked the Captain, looking at Corvin.

"No, Captain. I only know the name of the country as have heard it mentioned a few times by your veterans," replied Corvin.

"Yes, it is where we lost almost half the company last season. We got stuck in a trap and couldn't get out. We lost a few good men on that trip," said Emric.

"Yes, we did. Well, the Maraken's are a tribal people that roam. Their tribes can be as big as five or six thousand people or as small as fifty. They all have alliances with different tribes and to be honest, I could never work out their politics or keep up with them. The problem is they have professional companies like ours that they send out into the world. If you have the gold, you can buy all the warriors of the whole tribe for a season. If you have enough gold, you can buy many tribes."

"So, we could be facing a few thousand of these warriors?" asked Corvin.

"Yes," said the Captain.

"What are they like?" asked Corvin.

Emric looked away as he spoke.

"They are dark-skinned like Lorka, but not nearly as big. They are heavy set but are quite a bit shorter. However, they are also bloody insane, the lot of them. I once saw a warrior's weapon snap and he beat the guy he was fighting to death with the blunt end. All the while screaming and frothing at the mouth," said the Captain.

"Yes. One of them alone is a handful because they are so unpredictable. Gather a few hundred of them together and it becomes a bloody nightmare," said Emric.

"Do they fight well together, or do they just rush the line?" asked Corvin.

"Rush the line and try and overwhelm their enemy with savagery. Although they are not stupid and can be a little tricky. They don't know tactics as such, its more..." the Captain paused trying to think of the correct word.

"They like to play tricks," finished Emric.

"Yes, that is the best way to put it. They enjoy fighting and they enjoy playing tricks," said the Captain.

"Tricks?" asked Corvin.

"They get great amusement out of tricking an enemy. They find that about as much fun as they do cutting people to pieces," said Emric.

"Yes. I remember once we faced them last season. On patrol, we came across a recent battle with dead bodies everywhere. I asked the two squads with me to spread out and look for survivors. As they were doing this, the dead bodies came to life and sixty or so Maraken warriors started attacking us," said the Captain.

"Lost six men before we could retreat. We did not even fight, just ran and still we lost men. Tricky bastards," said Emric.

"I'll have to remember that, nice trick," said Corvin with a smile.

Both the Captain and Emric laughed aloud.

"I best move off and check in with the First Section," said Captain Joren.

Corvin and Emric sat in conversation for some time, discussing tactics. Emric telling of different situations he had been in over the years and Corvin soaking all of the information up like a sponge.

Corvin was moving across the deck looking for his corporals. He walked past First Sergeant Dolac who was talking to two of his own men. They saw Corvin and laughed.

"Is there a problem, First Sergeant?" asked Corvin as he walked past.

His anger was rising as it often did when he was around the First Sergeant.

"Nothing for a former slave to worry about!" said the First Sergeant.

Corvin's hands slowly rested on his weapons at his belts. The two corporals noticed this and stepped back, also resting their hands on their weapons. Dolac just smiled

"Not thinking of drawing your weapons on me, are you Corvin?" said First Sergeant.

"I'm just adjusting my belt, do not want it to rub me the wrong way. I get pissed off when things rub me the wrong way," said Corvin.

The violence in his voice was not missed by the two corporals of the First Sergeant. Corvin, however, managed to get a hold of himself and walk away.

"If you do not mind me saying First Sergeant, he needs to be taught a lesson. Strutting around here like he owns the ship," said Corporal Geren of the Second Squad.

"Yes, he does," agreed Dolac.

"Perhaps call him out, sir? He may be good with weapons, but I have seen you in a fist fight, you are unstoppable," said Corporal Urik of the Third Squad.

"Yes. I can handle myself in a fist fight. Different skills as you both know. We will see if I can keep pressing him into doing something stupid. You never know, he may do something stupid like drawing his weapons on me," said Dolac.

"That's a whipping offence!" said Geren.

"Yes, it is. Have to play it well, however, and do it carefully," said Dolac.

The two corporals nodded and continued their conversation about all the former slaves.

"What is that angry face for?" asked Jorga.

"First Sergeant," is all Corvin said.

"Ah, I understand. Perhaps we should cut his throat?" said Jorga.

"Wish we could, but life here at the Bloodchildren is too good to do something stupid like that."

"I know brother, just trying to help you walk through your own emotions."

"How is the fight training going?" he asked as he watched Irikson who was still drilling his squad.

"Good, Sergeant. They are coming together. They seem to respond to Irikson. I'm surprised," replied Jorga.

"You did say it would be good for him to take on more responsibility."

"Yes. I was right, but when am I ever wrong?" asked Jorga with a smile.

Corvin's bad mood evaporated and he too smiled.

"Saw you last night talking to the Corporal of Fourth Squad, Yelix, I think his name is," said Corvin.

Jorga looked at his feet again and said nothing. It was the same reaction Jorga had when Corvin had questioned him on his whereabouts on the night he had visited the secret tavern. Corvin put one and one together but said nothing. He just looked at his brother and waited. Finally, Jorga looked up.

"I got to visit that tavern again before we left. I saw him there in the corner with a man. I had not had a chance to speak to him of it. So last night finally had the courage to talk to him," said Jorga

"You and he?" asked Corvin.

"No, brother. He has a partner, a man he spends all his time with. I just needed to talk to him about who I am. Having someone within the company who understands what it is I feel, is very comforting."

"I am glad you have someone who understands, I am just jealous it is not me. I am sorry," said Corvin.

"You have nothing to be sorry for, brother," said Jorga.

Jorga put his hand on Corvin's shoulder and squeezed it.

"Just be careful on this ship, brother. I wish it were not so, but most of the men in the Bloodchildren would not understand at all."

"That is what Yelix said, but we will speak many times over the season, I am sure," said Jorga.

"Are you going to tell Lorka and Irikson?" asked Corvin.

"I have," said Jorga.

"What was their reaction?" said Corvin with a smile.

"Lorka wrapped me in a hug and understood. He said there were men in his village where he grew up that lived together as man and wife. He then told me that he better not catch me looking at him when he is undressing," said Jorga.

Corvin laughed loudly and Jorga joined in. Once they have got themselves back under control, Corvin replied.

"Of course, he turned it into a joke. Irikson?"

"He said he didn't care. He just patted me on the shoulder and told me it changes nothing. It was not the reaction I was expecting," said Jorga.

"Yes. Not much bothers Irikson, does it?" said Corvin.

"No, it seems not."

They both continued to watch the fight training. Jorga looked over at Corvin, then watched Irikson. He could not have asked for a better family than he had found in that slave camp so many years before. He doubted his real family would have been as accepting of who he was, if he had never been taken. It had been a journey for him, accepting who he was, and his brothers would never know how he had turned that uncurtaining, that lack of knowledge and understanding into anger. An anger he had used in the pits. It was not a peace he had found; more he was now comfortable in his own skin. He did not care if others did not accept him. His three brothers accepted him, and he now accepted himself. No one else mattered.

Chapter Six

The weather was chilly and many of the Bloodchildren wore their sea cloaks when out and about on deck to keep warm. Spring was here but the wind was still quite cold. The former slaves who grew up with very little clothing found the weather comfortable. They walked around in a tunic only. The only time they wore their cloak was when it rained. The former slaves were not used to rain. Yes, they had seen it in their life time but living so far north, it snowed more than rained. Corvin had explained this to the First Sergeant during a meeting of the senior members.

"Do your fellow slaves not feel the cold?" said the First Sergeant, with a smile on his face.

"Former slaves," said Corvin.

His relationship with the First Sergeant had not improved after he was promoted. Corvin thought it would be easier once he had gained rank but he thought wrong. The relationship was still strained and although he hid it well, Corvin knew the First Sergeant looked at the former pit-rats with contempt.

"Whatever," replied the First Sergeant.

"Your lads used to the cold then?" asked Second Sergeant Emric.

"Yes. We remember we grew up with very little clothing, working in the fields and other such work before we got thrown into the pits. We got used to the cold," Corvin replied.

"It will be interesting to see how your lads handle Kor-Lena. The weather is a lot warmer," said the Captain.

"So, I have been told. To be honest, I am not sure how we are going to handle it. Any suggestions?" asked Corvin.

"Keep up your water intake," said First Sergeant with a sneer.

The Captain ignored the way it was said. He could not take sides openly as it would lessen Corvin. He knew Corvin would have to work it out for himself. He may, however, say something in private to his First Sergeant.

"Another thing to remember, Corvin, is to rest in the shade whenever you can. The sun can sap the strength of your men very quickly," advised the Captain.

"Agreed. Also, before we dock, I will gather your men together and give a quick lesson on how to fight the heat. A few little tricks that myself and my corporals learnt last season fighting in Maraken," said Emric.

"That would be good," said Corvin.

"I am sure your men will do fine, Corvin," said the Captain.

First Sergeant continued to sneer before walking off with the Captain. Emric shook his head.

"What the fuck is his problem? What have myself or the former pit-rats done?" said Corvin.

"I am not sure, lad," replied Emric, frowning in confusion.

"All winter, we have received the brunt of his dislike for us.

If any other man, I would call out and happily slice his throat open for him," said Corvin, his anger rising.

He had been patient all winter during the training. He had tried to remain calm and prove to the Captain he was in control, especially when he had been promoted. His patience was wearing thin and he really wanted to challenge the First Sergeant.

"It would improve his looks," said Emric.

Corvin smiled a dark little smile.

"We are a Brotherhood, Corvin. Mercenaries, not barmaids. I am sure the Captain will not have a problem if you two fight, just make sure it is without weapons," said Emric.

"I won't get in trouble?"

"Of course not, lad. Tensions always flare and problems arise when you have strong fighting men working and living so close together. It is only natural."

"The Captain won't mind?"

"Hell lad, he probably expects it! As I said, it is only natural, and a few fights now and then are expected. That is the difference between being a soldier and a mercenary. Soldiers will get whipped for fighting. Mercenaries will not! It is allowed and a good way sometimes to let two men work out their differences. The Captain lets the men under him sort out their own differences," explained Emric.

Corvin looked at Emric. He stood up and looked to where the Captain and the First Sergeant were standing at the front of the ship.

"Good to know," said Corvin, as he walked towards the front of the ship.

Emric enjoyed the look on Corvin's face, he stood up and followed.

"This should be interesting," he said to himself.

"As I said, First Sergeant, it should be a lot easier than last season and the coin is good," reminded the Captain.

First Sergeant nodded but said nothing. He turned quickly when he heard his name shouted.

"First Sergeant," shouted Corvin as he approached.

The First Sergeant smiled as he saw the anger in Corvin's face. The Captain looked to Second Sergeant Emric for an explanation but all he got from him was a wink. The Captain hid a smile.

"What, Corvin?" asked the First Sergeant.

"As I understand it, you should address me as Third Sergeant Corvin," said Corvin, stopping a few paces away from him.

The raised voice of Corvin had been noticed by the sailors and mercenaries alike. They had all stopped and some had approached the three senior men of the Bloodchildren.

"Is that right, 'FORMER' slave?"

"If you have a problem with myself or my fellows, perhaps we should sort that out now."

First Sergeant unbuckled his belt and dropped it, along with his weapons to the deck. The Captain and Second Sergeant stepped back. Corvin dropped his belt to the deck as well and stepped forward.

First Sergeant stepped forward and was about to throw another insult at Corvin again but never got the chance. A straight left came at him and connected with his nose. He went to raise his hands, but a right cross followed, connecting with the side of his head and knocking him to the deck. He shook his head, and then went to stand. Corvin, however, did not allow that and came in quick, his knee connecting with

First Sergeant's head. Corvin stepped back to give the First Sergeant room to get up.

"GET UP, OUTLANDER SCUM! We are just getting started," yelled Corvin, in a voice they probably heard back in Irik.

Being called an Outlander was the biggest insult for any man who lived in Irik. Dolac raised himself up and then charged. He slowed before he reached Corvin, he was an experienced fighter and knew not to rush in like an idiot. As he slowed, he threw a quick left followed by a right uppercut that both missed. This is when Corvin exploded into action. He grabbed Dolac and pulled him into a head-butt, shattering Dolac's nose, then followed with a four-punch combination he had learnt from Irikson. A fast left, step to the right and throw a quick right cross, step to the right and throw another right cross before throwing a powerful left uppercut. An uppercut that smashed into the already broken nose of Dolac and dropped him to the ground. Dolac was knocked over but not knocked out. He lay there holding his nose. He looked at Corvin with hate in his eyes.

"Hold," said the Captain.

Corvin stepped back. His anger was still coursing through him and he wanted nothing more but to continue. Before he turned and walked away, he wanted to give Dolac something to think about.

"Next time you disrespect me or any of my former slave brothers, I will call you out with weapons and I promise you will not survive. Scum!" said Corvin.

Corvin stormed off, heading towards the decks below.

"I better go and speak to him," said Emric.

"No. I will. You see to Dolac, explain a few things," said the Captain.

Corvin sat in the dark bunk room, his back against the side of the ship drinking the water from his waterskin. He was breathing hard, not because he was tired from the fight, but because he was trying to calm himself. He was so enraged, he did not notice the look of hate on the faces of the members of First Sergeants section. Nor did he see the smiles and pride on the faces of the men of his own section.

"About time you stuck up for yourself," said the Captain as he approached.

Corvin looked up and saw a blank look on his Captain's face. He said nothing. The Captain sat beside him and handed Corvin his own waterskin.

"Try this."

Corvin took the waterskin and took a small sip. He smiled as the waterskin contained Firemer.

"I thought drink was not allowed on board?"

"Captain's privilege."

Corvin took another sip and handed the waterskin back to his Captain, who also took a sip.

"I am in trouble for the fight?"

"No, lad. I'm just surprised it took you so long. He has been baiting you all winter."

"Yes, he has. I have stayed patient, but I can only take so much and I am getting tired of it."

"Unity in a company like the Bloodchildren often takes time."

"Unity? I do not know the word."

"Working together, relationship."

"Oh. Do the Bloodchildren often have fighting?"

"Sometimes, yes. It is mainly when we take on new

recruits. Usually, it ends once the company has fought together. Once the men fight side by side, a bond is formed."

"So Dolac with be less of a bastard once he has seen us in battle?"

The Captain laughed, then took another sip before continuing.

"Maybe, maybe not. It takes a while for a fighting unit to get along. Take yourself and your fellow former slaves. Why do you all trust each other so much?"

"We grew up together, we trained together, we fought together and we escaped together."

"Exactly. You all have a close bond and nothing will shake that. A bond that has grown over many years, a bond formed in many battles. It is not so different in this situation. It will take time for all of the former pit-rats to be accepted completely by members of the Bloodchildren. Most of you have done better than other new recruits, being accepted quicker and forming friendships because of your abilities. Men like Dolac and a few other of the senior members of this company will take longer."

Corvin said nothing, just listened.

"You know our rules. What happens if a member of this company kills another?"

"Death by hanging," said Corvin quickly.

"Which is why I would not, if I were you, call out Dolac with weapons. I cannot make any exceptions Corvin, even for talented men like you. Fighting with fists to sort through problems is fine. It sometimes relieves tension and goes a long way towards getting problems out in the open. Fighting with weapons and killing another member, well, let's just say it goes against all of our traditions and I won't have it."

Corvin was not quite yet in control of himself.

"If he baits me further, Captain, the thought of hanging will not stop me. I will destroy him," said Corvin.

The Captain said nothing. He knew Corvin's blood was still fired up. After a few minutes of silence, Corvin was just starting to calm down.

"I just wish I knew where his dislike comes from. You know what will happen if he treats some of the other former pit-rats like he treats me?"

"Yes. I will be hanging one of your fellows for killing him."

"Yes. Especially someone like Irikson. I have problems with my anger, I know. I have been working hard to fit in and keep it under control. Someone like Irikson, however, will cut his throat without a doubt. He has calmed down somewhat, and he is starting to grow up, we all are. After a life like we have had, insults from someone like Dolac do not go unpunished."

"I know, lad."

"What will happen now? Will I face any more insults from Dolac?"

"I doubt it. He will have learnt to keep his mouth shut. It is his section I am worried about."

"His section? You think they will come at me?"

"No, but they follow Dolac in everything. I think your section may face some attitude for the fight is all."

"Attitude, we can handle. Will it come to more fights?"

"No. Two men fighting through some problems is common place. Sections fighting? How would that turn out, lad?"

"Good point!"

The Captain stood up and tied his waterskin to his belt.

"Search out, Dolac. Talk. He is one of the best Sergeants in Irik. I have him as my first for a reason."

"I may do, but not yet. I'll let his face heal a bit first," said Corvin, with his little half smile.

The Captain also smiled, then turned and left.

"You think our squads will face problems?" asked Jorga.

"No, nothing serious, but we may face some dirty looks and dirty talk from them. It is important to keep our squads from doing anything stupid. The Captain will not mind the occasional fight, but it has to be one on one, and it cannot be a brawl involving entire squads," said Corvin.

Corvin had called a meeting of all his Corporals. Jorga, Irikson and Torin had joined him. The only none Corporal to be there was, of course, Lorka.

"I wish I had been there to see you drop the bastard on his arse," said Irikson.

"As do I," said Lorka.

"It needed to happen but the Captain, I am sure, will not want the dislike between me and Dolac to be taken up by the squads," said Corvin.

"I'll keep a close eye on my squad and make sure they are too busy," said Torin.

"We all will. The fight needed to happen, plus I wish I was there also to see that bastard get his face broken," said Jorga with a smile.

The others laughed and Lorka patted Corvin on the shoulder.

"Your squad, I think will get the worst of it, Irikson. They know you are a little headstrong, so they will try and bait you," said Corvin.

Irikson looked at the ground and nodded.

"I will make sure none of the squad members does anything stupid. I can't promise I won't!"

Corvin smiled.

"No. You enjoy doing stupid things," said Torin.

They all laughed.

"I am not saying accept all the shit you are given. Do not start anything, do not pull weapons or let entire squads get into fights," stated Corvin.

He looked around and all four nodded.

"Now that's out of the way, we have an additional training session tomorrow with Second Sergeant Emric," said Corvin.

"Us or all the squads?" said Torin.

"Only myself and the Corporals of Third Section," said Corvin.

"Training for what?" asked Jorga.

"How to deal with the warmer climate once we get to Kor'Lena. The weather there is a lot warmer than we are used to, so I have asked Emric to help us and give advice on how to deal with it," said Corvin.

"That makes sense. We are used to colder weather. Even now on the ship, it's warmer than I used to," said Lorka.

"Yes, fighting in the warmer season will take some getting used to," said Torin.

"I have said we will meet Emric just after sunrise. I'll see you all then," said Corvin.

"Aye," they all agreed.

The week had gone fast with all of the Bloodchildren busy preparing. Corvin's squads were kept slightly busier as Corvin and his Corporals where mindful of their men performing well. Corvin had organised other lessons and more training for all of the men in his section. He did not want the new recruits to be at a disadvantage by lack of knowledge. Also, if he kept them busy, they would be less likely to react badly to the insults from the First Section. He was happy with the way his section was shaping up. Irikson had truly taken ownership of the Seventh Squad and Corvin was proud of him. Jorga and Torin had their squads well in hand as well. The language lessons were going well with Corvin and his Corporals, at least having a good basic understanding in how to speak Kor'Lenan. They were not fluent, but Corvin was confident they could deal with most situations.

As the weather was warmer, Corvin decided to include some hard training to get used to the warmer climate. With the Captains permission, he had marked out lines along the port side of the ship. With many of the other mercenaries watching in silence, Seventh, Eighth and Ninth Squad took turns at completing hell runs. The sweat that poured off the men was a testament to how warm it was. The squads gritted their teeth and pushed their way through the runs. The Captain watched and saw the determination on the faces of the men, not willing to give up in front of the rest of the company. Some of the other men of the company had seen the hell runs before, others had heard of them. All were amazed at the spectacle in front of them. No doubt in the rest of the companies mind now that the Third Section was the fittest.

The Captain was talking to Second Sergeant Emric and watching the Third Section.

"Is that Corporal of the Fourth Squad, Yelix, I see running with Corvin and the Seventh Squad?" asked the Captain.

"Yes, Captain. Yelix has his squad spread out amongst Corvin's squad for training purposes. He asked my permission this morning. Yelix is impressed with how fit the Third Section is and had formed a good friendship with Corvin," replied Emric.

Both watched as the Seventh Squad finished its run and collapsed on the deck, gasping for air. The Eighth Squad stood on the line, and from a shouted command, took off on their run.

"How many times do they do this?" asked the Captain.

"Twenty times I think, Captain?" Emric replied.

"Twenty?"

"Yes. It was training they learnt in Hura."

They both continued to watch as Eighth Squad finished their run. Emric looked over to the starboard side of the ship, and saw First Sergeant Dolac and his Corporals watching and chatting.

He smiled but said nothing to the Captain. Dolac had been quiet after his beating at the hands of Corvin. Nothing further had been said between them. Although Emric was now aware of the small insults the First Section threw at the men of the Third Section. So far, the Third Section had given them dirty looks, said nothing, and continued with whatever task they were doing. Emric knew it would not be much longer before there was another fight or two. He said as much to the Captain.

"Yes. I have heard some grumblings, although Corvin has said nothing yet," replied the Captain.

"He won't. He will stand on his own two feet and I am sure so will the men of the Third Section."

"That is what concerns me. The last thing I want is a pitched battle on the decks between the First Section and the Third Section," said the Captain.

"A battle the Third Section would win," said Emric with a smile.

"I would expect your section to jump in between them, Emric, to calm things down."

"I am confident they would," said Emric.

Emric, however, was not that confident. In fact, he would not be surprised if his section jumps in to help out the Third Section. His section and Corvin's section were working together well and many friendships were being formed. He had noticed that the men of his section had withdrawn from any friendship of the First Section and that worried him. It didn't surprise him; his section were good men, sound men and fair men. They did not like bullies and that is what Dolac and his men were becoming. He would not speak of it to the Captain.

They both watched as the hell runs were completed. All of the men sat down where they could and gasped for air. It was clear the heat made this run so much harder than they were used to. They all drank water and caught their breath. Both the Captain and Second Sergeant Emric noticed a corporal from the First Section making his way towards the seated Third Section.

"Here is trouble, sir," said Emric.

"If that idiot starts anything, Dolac will find himself in some hot water," replied the Captain.

Corporal Geren of the Second Squad walked over, with a small smile on his face. He of all the First Section had hated Corvin the most for his promotion. He had been told by Sergeant Dolac that he was next in line for promotion to a Sergeant. He stopped short of all the seated men and sneered.

"Good runs. It must be good to train and get yourself used to the idea of running from the enemy," said Corporal Geren.

It was spoken loud enough to be heard across the deck. Corvin's look was murderous as he was about to step forward and speak to the corporal; he did out rank him, but Irikson stood up and walked towards him. The look on his face was worse than Corvin's. Corvin wanted to rein him in but couldn't. If he did, Irikson would lose face in front of his men. The situation was heading for disaster and unfortunately, there was nothing he could do to stop it. He thought of shouting out to Dolac to take his man in hand, but this also would make Irikson and the rest of the Third Section lose face. No, Irikson had reached the Corporal and was standing less than a Lai from him. Corvin just hoped Irikson didn't kill him.

Irikson was about to say something when Torin came up to him and interrupted Irikson

"Brother, I have got this. You owe me for taking your guard duty last night. I'll take this as payment," said Torin.

Corvin smiled. Irikson stood still and said nothing. He nodded once and walked backwards and sat down.

"Did you say something, scum?" said Torin.

"Scum?" asked Geren.

"What, are you deaf as well as ugly?" said Torin.

Geren was a good fighter and very experienced. He swung a quick right hook at Torin. Torin, however, had been trained by Corvin, Irikson, Jorga and Lorka. His hand-to-hand combat was almost as good as theirs. He did not even move; he just lowered his head and Geren's fist struck the crown of his head, a move taught to him by Lorka. Everyone heard the loud crack as the wrist of Corporal Geren's broke; he howled. Torin threw a quick left jab that connected to Geren's throat, a punch taught to him by Corvin. He followed that by a straight right that connected to Geren's left eye, which spun Geren to the deck. He lay there, out cold.

Corvin was smiling, as was the rest of the Third Section.

Two more corporals of the First Section walked forward

and stood in front of Torin. Corporal Kalin of First Squad and Corporal Urik from Third Squad.

"You broke his wrist; we can't have that," said Urik.

The entire Third Section was about to move when Corvin's voice rang out.

"Third Section, stand down," shouted Corvin.

Corvin then caught Lorka's eye and nodded. Lorka moved forward. He dropped his armour to the ground and stripped his undershirt. When he arrived by Torin's side, he was shirtless. His large frame, dark brown and huge, on show for everyone to see. The two corporals from the First Section, all of sudden not so sure of themselves.

Yelix also joined Torin. In fact, it was Yelix that spoke.

"Are we finished here?" questioned Yelix.

"You take their side?" asked Kalin.

"Over you two and the bully you call a Sergeant? Count on it," said Yelix.

"You insulting our Sergeant now?" said Urik.

"He leads you to this, so yes, we are. These former slaves have more honour than any of First Section. If you speak another word of insult to any of the Third Section, the Second Section will get involved. Do you understand?" asked Yelix.

The two corporals were now on thin ice. They had not expected Torin to get involved and truly did not expect Yelix to get involved either. Irikson was their target, and everyone on the deck knew it.

"You make yourself clear," said Urik.

"Good. We would hate to have seen the First Section get their arses handed to them by combined men of the Second and Third Section. Captain would be disappointed," said Torin.

The two corporals walked away, losing face. The look on

First Sergeant Dolac's face was plain to see. Anger, hate and disgust. It had not worked out at all as he had planned.

"Well, that was a surprise. I dare say there should be no more problems. Yelix is a good man," said the Captain, with a stern look on his face.

He was glad there had been no escalation and was impressed with Yelix, but it was still clear he was less than happy that there was a problem to begin with.

"Yes, Captain, he is. I was not surprised, Yelix thinks much of the Third Section and is close to them. Although, sir, I was not amused at him volunteering the entire Second Section like he did. I will have to have a few words to him," said Emric.

"Yes, a good idea. We now have a split in the company and it's all Dolac's fault. I'll talk to Corvin and the other Corporals later and remind them of a few things, although the Third Section has done nothing wrong," said the Captain.

"Dolac, sir?"

"Tell him I want to see him in my quarters, now."

"Yes, sir."

"You are an idiot!" bellowed the Captain.

Sergeant Dolac stood and took the yelling. He was pissed off his plan to drop the Third Section into trouble had not worked, and even more pissed off he was now taking the brunt of the Captain's anger.

"How is this my fault, sir?" asked Dolac.

"Do not even play innocent in this, Dolac. You have been looking down on the Third Section since they were formed. I can see it, your men can see and dammit man, all of the company can see it. You do not even see it, do you?"

"See what, sir?" asked Dolac.

He had no idea what the Captain as on about.

"The spilt in the company?" screamed the Captain.

"The split?" asked Dolac confused.

"Right now, the First Section stands on one side, and the Second and Third Section stand on the other side. Your section stands alone, Dolac, and is despised by the two other sections. You almost let your section start a mass brawl on the deck."

"It would not have gone that far, sir. Just a couple of Corporals fighting."

"That is why you are an idiot. You still do not see it. Your section could not handle the Third Section in a fight, let alone the Second Section at the same time."

Dolac said nothing. He actually had not seen the split, now he could. He was even angrier now, but still blamed the Third Section.

"You realise how close you are to being demoted?" asked the Captain.

"Demoted?"

"Yes. If that fight had kicked off between the sections, I would have stripped you of Sergeant and returned you to the ranks."

"I am your longest serving Sergeant," said Dolac, looking straight at the Captain for the first time.

"Which means you should know bloody better, but no. You think up some scheme to get at the former slaves, who for some bloody reason you hate, when they have done nothing wrong to you or your men. It goes badly and you expect not to get in trouble? Once we reach shore, there will be punishment for this. You will not get away with this stupidity. For now, you will spread the word amongst your men. One more incident like this, I will completely re-arrange the sections. You will be busted to the ranks as well as your three corporals. And trust me, you would not like where I place you," said the Captain.

Dolac was shocked. Clearly, he had not expected this.

"Dismissed!"

"Yes, sir," said Dolac. He walked back out on the main deck, stood for a few seconds and breathed. He did not notice Emric standing beside him.

"That went well!" said Emric.

"Shut it," said Dolac.

"No. I don't think so," said Emric.

"Going to give me lecture as well, Second Sergeant?"

"No, just passing on that I had a word with all of the Second Section. They have been told that they now have my permission to destroy any man from the First Section if they start any trouble. They have been told that if they see any bad behaviour from the First Section, towards the Third Section, they have my permission to end it with force," said Emric.

Emric walked off to see the Captain, leaving Dolac with his own thoughts.

"I should have killed him," said Irikson

Corvin looked at Torin. "Probably, but then you would be hanging from the rigging, a rope around your neck. I'm not ready to lose you yet. Well done. You saved a lot of bruises and punishment coming our way."

"Do not mention it, Sergeant," said Torin.

"Good punches by the way, beautiful timing," said Corvin.

The gathered corporals of the Third Section smiled, including Torin.

"Good teachers," said Torin.

At that moment Yelix approached as the other stood in the bow of the ship.

Before Yelix could speak, Corvin moved towards him and held out his arm. Yelix took it in the warrior's grip.

"Thank you, Yelix. Your support will never be forgotten by me or any member of the Third Section," said Corvin.

"My pleasure," Yelix responded with a smile.

One by one all of the Corporals took turns gripping Yelix's arm in thank you. Once done, Yelix spoke.

"Here's a head up. Second Sergeant Emric has told all members of the Second Section, they have his permission to deal harshly with any members of the First Section if they see this happen again. In other words, your men have the full support of the Second Section," said Yelix.

"Good to hear," said Torin.

"Yes, but that now causes a split in the company," said Corvin.

"Yes, it does, not that I know how that will affect us," said Irikson.

"No. We will have to trust in the Captain," said Jorga.

They all nodded their agreement.

The Third Section, along with elements of the Second Section, continued to train. The relationship between the two sections now cemented in a strong bond. Members of the First Section were now alienated and alone. Although they deserved this, Corvin spread the word to his men to stop this. Of course, it was Lorka, huge Lorka with his jokes and smile that started to bridge the gap.

Men from the Second Squad were struggling with the

spare mainsail. They had aired it out to stop mould growing, then trying to fold it up again and put it away. Lorka arrived and used his strength to help them. As they were folding, he told them the story of Irikson's run in with the cook back at the slave camp. By the end of the tale, a few were chuckling and all were smiling. Corvin had watched it. It was a start!

Training, however, came to a halt when land was sighted. They had been at sea for five weeks. Longer than a normal journey but the weather was still rough. The ship had to slow down to dodge large ice floes that still floated in the sea. As the Bloodchild approached the harbour of Kor'Na, all mercenaries were on deck. The newest squads had a good position at the bow of the ship. As the ship approached the harbour, they were all silent, staring at the massive city before them. They had all been impressed with the size of Iriksec, the capital of Irik, but nothing prepared them for the size of settlement they sailed into. Captain had called it a city, another new word they had all learnt. Before they knew of a village, a town or a settlement. Irik and the Outlander Nation had plenty of those, but they did not have a city.

As the ship got closer, they began to see the size of the buildings in the Capital. Buildings so tall, they would never have imagined they could be built by men. The men around Corvin where pointing at the tallest structure, which rose above everything else. It was not as Corvin would describe as beautiful or graceful. It was just, there, like a mountain. A huge, tall grey rock building that reminded Corvin of a mountain. He stared at it and did not notice Second Sergeant Emric had moved alongside him.

"It is called Concik. It is the building that houses the council," said Second Sergeant.

"It's huge," said Corvin.

"Yes. It took them twelve years to build it apparently."

"Hard to imagine men building anything that big," said Corvin.

"For you and your men, yes, it would be hard to imagine. If you ever get to Ex'Na, you will see a few buildings that are even larger," Emric replied.

It took most of the morning for the Bloodchild to be towed slowly into its berth in the harbour. If the former slaves thought the harbour at Iriksec was large, nothing prepared them for the harbour of Kor'Na, the capital of Kor'Lena. There were so many ships berthed and offloading their cargo. Smaller vessels, larger vessels and everything in between. There was even a four-master tied to the wharf across from them. It was almost double the size of the Bloodchild. Corvin lent across to Emric.

"How many men does that hold?" he asked.

"None, Corvin. That is a cargo ship, no doubt full of grain or other food stuffs."

As the Bloodchild was being tied to the wharf, the Captain's voice could be heard.

"All men gather your equipment. We will be getting off shortly," shouted the Captain.

He was first down the gangplank and was greeted by an official in a long, red tunic that went past his knees. Corvin did not get a decent look as he shouted at his section to follow the Captain's orders. He himself went down and grabbed his stuff, eager to be off the ship and standing on solid ground once more. He was filled with nervous energy, as was the rest of his section. After grabbing his bag and weapons, he shouted at his men to hurry up and made his way back to the top deck.

The company were off the ship smartly. The Captain had already received instructions and the members of the Bloodchildren had marched out of the harbour, through the streets off Kor'Na and straight out the main gate. They got a quick look at the city as they walked past and Corvin knew many of his fellow pit-rats were amazed at what they saw. They were amazed at how many people walked the streets as well as the buildings which towered above them. Even though this was the biggest settlement they had seen, it did not take them long before they had walked past the main gates. Gates and a wall that made the fortifications of Iriksec seem small.

The Captain had explained that they had been redirected to their section of wall and had to walk there as fast as they could. Their destination was some place called Kor'Mor which was some kind of armed town to the north-west of them. Captain had said there was supposed to be wagons to take them, but all the wagons had been pressed into taking supplies to the wall. He explained it was roughly a ten day walk to their destination. There was one wagon that held the company cook and blacksmith. This carried all the food they needed and had to last until they arrived.

Corvin's section brought up the rear, which he was happy about. It kept distance between his section and the First Section. Nothing more had been said of the events on the ship. Anytime he saw Sergeant Dolac, Dolac looked away or just stared at Corvin, saying nothing. Also, the First Section men had caused no further problems. Of course, the Second Section and the Third Section had grown even closer. This pleased Corvin and it was good to be accepted by at least some of the Bloodchildren. He spoke to Emric a few times and had a long conversation with the Captain. His section had not got in trouble at all and all he was told, was to keep his head down and concentrate on his duties. The Captain assured him there would be no further problems. As Corvin marched at the head of his section, he did his best not to think of the recent events. He would take it as it comes. He heard the men behind him laughing. Lorka was once again entertaining the men; Corvin smiled. He was with his brothers and that is all that mattered.

Chapter Seven

The first day of walking was hard. The Third Section under Corvin were without a doubt the fittest in the company. Unfortunately, they were not used to the armour and carrying their packs over long periods and long distances, especially in the warmer climate. The pace that had been set was not a hard one, the Captain taking it easy on the first day. The company had the left the city of Kor'Na behind around midday and the sun started to set as they were stopping to make camp. Apparently, they had covered ten Melai today, which was impressive, but the Captain had said he expected around twenty Melai tomorrow. They would be picking up the pace and walking a full day.

As the Third Section sorted themselves out and dumped their gear, Corvin ordered the corporals to put the men through stretching before the meal was ready. Once the men had sorted themselves out, Corvin headed towards the front to speak to the Captain. As he walked, he got nods from the men of the Second Section, a warm smile and many nods. The corporals of the Second Section said hello and smiled warmly.

Corvin smiled back and continued to walk. As he reached the First Section, he kept his eyes to the front. He was not at ease around the First Section after what had happened. He knew they were all scowling at him. He did not care, but right at this moment, could not be bothered dealing with it. Someone called out to him and he stopped.

"Sergeant Corvin," said Corporal Geren with a nod.

"Corporal Geren," Corvin returned the greeting.

Corvin focused, expecting more trouble and waited for the trouble to start again.

"I doubt you and your fellows are used this heat, Sergeant. How are they handling it?" asked Corporal Geren.

The question was asked with genuine interest and respect, which threw Corvin.

"It's harder than we thought, yes," he replied.

"If you do not mind me suggesting, if you wet some cloth, which the men should all have, then tie it in place around your heads during the heat, it will a lot more comfortable," said Geren.

Corvin did not know what to make of the man. He was the one that started the last trouble on the ship. He looked around and saw some of the First Section had indeed got large pieces of cloth tied around their heads under their helmets.

"It helps?" asked Corvin.

"It does, Sergeant. Every time we take a water break, you just add a little more water to it. I just thought I would make the suggestion," said Geren.

"Thank you, Corporal. I will pass that along," said Corvin.

"Righto Sergeant, I better let you carry on. I would not want to piss off the Captain," he said with a smile.

"Thank you, Corporal. You better get some food and water in you," said Corvin.

Corvin walked away not knowing what to think of the exchange. He was trying to think what game Geren was playing at but could think of anything apart from genuine help; surprisingly. He would have to talk to Emric about it.

Corvin reached the Captain who was talking to Sergeant Emric. Sergeant Dolac reached the Captain at the same time.

"How are the men?" asked the Captain.

"Mine are fine, all fit and healthy Captain," said Dolac.

"Mine as well, although I have one man with a twisted ankle. We have strapped it and he will sit on the back of the food wagon, if that is okay?" said Emric.

"That's fine, Sergeant. How about your men, Corvin?" said the Captain.

"Made it, sir. I'll be honest, it was a struggle, especially for the former slaves. We are just not used to this heat," said Corvin.

"So, there is something that the Third Section does not excel at?" said Dolac.

Corvin squinted his eyes, then took a relaxing breath.

"Yes, First Sergeant Dolac. We know how to fight, outshine the First Section in everything we do but you are right, this heat is bloody hard," said Corvin.

Out of the corner of his eyes, he saw Sergeant Emric trying to hide a smile, and even the Captain had humour in his eyes.

"Well, get the men rested and fed. Keep in mind, this is just spring. Once summer is upon us, it will be a lot hotter. Although by then, I think your men will be used to it. First Section has guard duty tonight. The next night, it is the Second Section, then the Third Section the night after that.

That is the roster until we reach our destination," said the Captain.

All three of the Sergeants nodded.

"How many days, Captain?" asked Corvin.

"Roughly ten days, Sergeant," said the Captain.

Corvin nodded.

"Although there is a small chance that the original wagons that were supposed to cart us, may come available and catch up to us. However, we are not counting on it happening," said Emric.

Corvin nodded again.

"Thank you, I will pass it on to the men and I will not mention the wagons. No point in giving the men false hope," said Corvin with a smile.

"Good idea. In fact, we should all do the same," suggested Emric.

"Agreed," said the Captain.

Even Dolac nodded his agreement.

"Anything else, sir?" asked Corvin.

"No, Corvin. As you were," said the Captain.

Corvin nodded to Emric as well as Dolac, then he turned and walked away.

As Corvin walked off, Emric caught up.

"Everything under control?" asked the Second Sergeant.

"Yes. The heat was hard as I said," replied Corvin.

Emric nodded.

"The Corporal Geren, what sort of man is he?" asked Corvin.

Emric looked at Corvin.

"Why do you ask?"

"He greeted me before, politely, and has offered some advice to combat the heat," said Corvin.

"What did he suggest?" asked Emric.

"He suggested cloth tied around our heads that had been soaked in water."

"Yep, a valuable suggestion. We do that in the full heat of summer. Some do it now in spring. It's a good suggestion," said Emric.

"Why would he give it to me? He is from the First Section, the one that started the recent problems," said Corvin.

"Not sure. Before the incident, he was a solid man. He was never seen to be a bully or a hard arse like Dolac, but he was with the Second Section until his promotion to corporal. He trained under me and I found him to be a very dependable man. Whether fighting or training," said Emric.

"Okay, feeling guilty, you think? Or trying to be tricky and it's leading to something else?" asked Corvin.

"No, it will be genuine. I think the fight he picked on the ship, he was put up to by Dolac and the other two corporals. He has only been in the position since the end of last summer. Perhaps he was trying to prove himself. I certainly did not want him to leave the Second Section," said Emric.

"Okay. I'll take it at face value. If I get a chance alone with him, I will thank him again and see why he would help," said Corvin.

"Do not let Dolac see you," Emric said with a smile.

Corvin placed his hand on Emric's shoulder and smiled.

"Maybe I'll do it in front of him," laughed Corvin.

Emric laughed, waved him off and returned to his men.

Corvin was still smiling when he reached his section. He called in the corporals and gave them the information he got from the Captain. He also mentioned the suggestion from Corporal Geren. They were all surprised. Corvin suggested keeping an open mind when dealing with the corporal from now on. They nodded and went back to their men.

The next day was much the same. The same road that was a mixture of dirt and small stones. There was no wind to speak of and the day was as warm as yesterday. They were on travel rations and last night's meal was similar to the food Corvin had grown up with as a slave. Porridge, although last night's dinner had dried beef through it. The former slaves ate the food without complaint. They were used to this type of food. Some of the Irik men could be heard grumbling. Corvin smiled.

During the morning Corvin had a decent chance to look around and see the landscape. Flat, very flat. There looked to be a forest to their right, many Melai away. To their left, the men could just see a large settlement. It was only the towers of this town that gave it away. Emric had explained that was the first wall town and called Kor'Ann. He explained that there were three main towns along the wall. These were oversized military camps and were there for one purpose. To feed and house the soldiers watching and guarding the wall. Corvin could not see the wall yet, but was assured by Emric that as they got closer to Kor'Balus, he would indeed see the wall. The road they were walking snaked and turned closer to the wall over the next day or two. Apparently, the road travelled in parallel beside the wall for the last days of travel. Corvin had passed on the info to his corporals, who in turn passed it on to the men.

Lunch was travel rations and a type of cake, flat and the same size of a hand with the fingers stretched out. It was made of oats, wheat and some other ingredients Corvin could not pick out. It was hard and the joke went around the men that if they made the flat cakes bigger, they could use them as shields. Corporal Geren had once again passed on some advice to Corvin. He suggested wetting the flat cake with some water. It worked, it was easier to eat and Corvin discovered it was filling and actually had some flavour. He still could not see where Geren was coming from, so continued to accept the advice and take it as sincere. Along with the flat cake, the men were given some dried fruit. The men were a little quiet, until Lorka started entertaining them, at the expense of Irikson.

"This food is nothing to rave about," stated Irikson with feeling.

"Perhaps you should have a word to the cook. You have a way with cooks," said Lorka, his grin broad across his face.

All the former slaves laughed, whereas the men from Irik, just looked on confused.

"Shut your mouth," said Irikson.

This got Lorka smiling bigger and got more chuckles from the former slaves that knew the story. The Irik men just looked more confused.

"He has a way with cooks?" said Torin.

He knew the story, of course, but had never shared it.

"Yep, a special way with cooks. He was very close to the cook in our old slave camp. Weren't you, Irikson?" said Lorka.

"I did say for you to shut it!" said Irikson.

The laughter spread through the Third Section. Corvin smiled.

"Tell them about it, Irikson," said Corvin.

"I do believe, Sergeant, that you can shove it up your arse," said Irikson, his face like thunder.

The Third Section roared with laughter. The Second Section, who were quite close, slowly shuffled over to see what was going on. Half of the Second Section was now close enough to hear.

"I think the first encounter was in the garden, was it not, Lorka?" teased Corvin further.

"Yes, Sergeant, it was. What were you doing in the garden at the time of night, Irikson?" asked Lorka.

"He must be passionate about his gardening," said Jorga with a smile.

"You bastards!" Irikson said.

"Yes, so the story goes. Irikson was doing some late-night gardening when he was caught by the cook. She was an amazingly, good-looking woman, was she not, Sergeant?" said Lorka.

"Stunning," said Corvin.

"Apparently, she made a pass at you, Irikson!" said Jorga.

"She did not make a pass at me, she just commented how strong my young body was, that's all," said Irikson.

The assembled men all laughed.

"And?" encouraged Corvin.

"She said she had never seen anyone of my age with hands quite so big," said Irikson.

"How old where you?" asked Jorga.

"I was fifteen summers old," said Irik.

"So, you were in the garden, topless, doing some gardening in the dead of night and the cook was complimenting your strong looking body and the size of your hands?" said Torin.

This set the men to giggling, waiting to see where the story was going.

"Yes," said Irikson.

"What the hell were you doing with no shirt?" said Lorka.

"None of your business," said Irikson.

"Then what happened?" asked Corvin.

He was trying to hide his laugh, not doing a very good job.

"She made a comment that if my hands were so large, what else of mine was larger than life," said Irikson.

The assembled men roared with laughter, some with tears falling down their faces.

"Then what did you do?" asked Lorka.

"You bloody well know what I did. She blocked the path, so I had run through the cabbages to get away from her," said Irikson.

The men roared with laughter again, Corvin joining in, feeling the stress of the warm day leaving him. He stood up and as he walked past Irikson, he placed his hand on his shoulder.

"You are very lucky that we called you Bulldog-boy, rather than Cabbage-boy," said Corvin.

"Should have called him 'Cooks-Plaything'," said Jorga.

The entire Third Section and half of the Second Section that were listening roared again, so loud the rest of the company looked in their direction to see what was going on. Corvin smiling to himself walked to a tree to relieve his bladder. On returning and sitting down next to Jorga, the men were still giggling. Until Corporal Yelix who was smiling spoke.

"So, what happened to this cook? You should have brought her with you," said Yelix.

The former slaves all went quiet and looked at the ground. He had killed the mood, although he did not know what he had said wrong. He saw the effect of his question and apologised quickly.

"My apologies. I did not mean to bring back bad memories," said Yelix.

Corvin looked around at his brother-slaves, all of who were staring at the ground, no doubt remembering the Smith.

Jorga nudged Corvin and whispered, "Tell them, Snow-Weasel."

Corvin nodded.

"No need to apologise, Yelix. It does bring back bad memories for those that escaped."

"As I said, I am sorry. I'm sure if you could have got her out, you would have," said Yelix.

"No," said Jorga.

Yelix and the other men from Irik looked puzzled.

"She was a spy for the masters. She passed on any information she could and in the end, betrayed us. Because of her, two of our mentors were brutally murdered," said Corvin.

"One was a blacksmith, our father figure. Without him, a lot of us would have been killed by the masters. So many times, he stopped us from doing something stupid. He was strung up, tortured and then killed. He was such a special man, that our Sergeant took his first name as a way for us to remember him by," said Jorga, placing his hand on Corvin's shoulder and squeezing it.

"The other was our fight trainer. Without him, we would not have lasted in the fight pits. He was hacked to pieces in front of our eyes. No, the cook was not someone we cared about," said Corvin.

"What happened to this cook?" asked a voice.

Corvin turned and saw it was Sergeant Emric. If anyone else had asked, he would have not answered.

"She was killed, by one of us," said Jorga.

"Some of you know of the last former slave that made it out and arrived at the camp of the Bloodchildren, a few months after we did. He killed her, in fact knowing him, he would have tortured her and then killed her. His nickname was Sick-boy, because well, he was sick, in the head. He enjoyed giving pain, and in the fight-pits, would draw out the fights to inflict as much pain as he could," said Corvin.

The assembled men were all quiet. Torturing a woman and killing her did not sit well with them, but then any reasonable man would feel uncomfortable with harming a woman. Before there was laughter, now all silent.

"Probably a good thing. If Sick-boy did not do what he did, she would still be chasing our brother here with the large hands," said Lorka.

All the assembled men roared with laughter again. As was Lorka's way, he cut through the tension with a simple comment. Corvin looked over at him and smiled. Lorka winked and went back to his food.

"She bloody would, too. She'd probably swim behind the ship, all the way here," said Youst.

"Bugger off, the lot of you," said Irikson.

The men laughed again. Jorga leaned in and whispered to Corvin.

"Speaking of it helps. The men of Irik are now our brothers. We need to share with them."

Corvin only nodded. Once again, reminded of the special men he was surrounded by.

The march continued, as Emric had said the walk took them closer to the wall. Once they got closer to it, all of the Third Section were amazed at the size of it. It was the tallest wall they had ever seen. It was dark grey, almost black in colour. The stones were cut and shaped from the volcanic rock that was said to be in ample supply in the mountains to the northeast of them. Corvin did not know how any men could get over it. There was no gate that could be seen. The Captain had explained there was only three gates, heavy fortified in each of the towns that were placed along the walls. Kor'Ann, Kor'Balus and Kor'Mor. The last city being their destination. Corvin had no idea how tall it was until Emric had explained.

"Just over twenty Lai tall, Corvin. Ten men standing on top of each other's shoulders would not quite reach the top," said Emric.

Such size was hard to imagine for all of the former slaves. On the fifth day, they reached Kor'Balus that was apparently the halfway mark in their journey. They made camp across from the town in the open fields. The Captain and Sergeant Dolac had gone in with the cook and the wagon to purchase some fresh food. The Captain deciding it was time for a decent meal. That evening, all the men shared roast mutton and some mugs of ale. This picked up the men and Corvin could feel the Third Section were more at ease. They had got used to walking with their packs by now and Corvin was proud of all of his section. On this night, the Captain did not bother setting a guard duty. He wanted everyone to get a good night sleep, and unless the city fell, they would all be safe.

To everyone's surprise, including the Captain, twelve wagons arrived during the night with supplies for Kor'Balus. When the men woke in the morning, the wagons were all parked up and ready to take them the rest of the way. The leader of the wagons had been given clear instructions to offload the food, then get the Bloodchildren to Kor'Mor as quickly as possible. The wagons were large, weathered wood wagons with a huge flatbed on the back and a raised seat along the front. Each wagon pulled by two huge horses. The horses themselves, a mixture of brown and black fur. Emric had explained they are bred for size and strength, and can pull very heavy loads of long distances. A wagon full of men will be a light workout for them. Cheers from all the men could be heard when the Captain spread the word that they would be riding the rest of the way.

Once again, all squads had their own wagon and there was plenty of room on the flatbeds of the wagons to sit ten men, and their packs. In fact, there was so much room that the men could sit with their legs stretched out in front of them. The wagon drivers of course did not speak the same language, so communication was hard. Corvin had ordered all of his corporals to sit on the front seat with the drivers and practice the language of Lena. They'd had their lessons on the ship on the way over, now it was the time to put those lessons into practice.

Corvin sat next to a driver in a supply wagon that was between his section's wagons and the wagons of the Second Section. Conversation was very hard for the first few days. The man's accent was very different to the man that was instructing them on the Bloodchild. The driver thankfully was patient and spoke in one or two-word sentences. By the seventh day, he was exchanging more in the way of a conversation and was starting to understand better. Lorka was speaking the language of Lena well. Irikson struggled but was starting to catch up and Torin like Lorka, was doing well.

At the end of the seventh day, all the wagons had parked up in a large open field. Cook fires where lit and the evening meal was being prepared. Corvin and the Third Section had gone for a light run to stretch themselves. Not a hard workout, just enough to get a sweat on and keep them alert. Corvin had invited Yelix and his squad from the Second Section. Yelix had accepted. In fact, not only did Yelix and the Fourth Squad join them, but also Corporal Yoran and his Fifth Squad did. Fifty men all running as a pack through the fields. There was small chatter between the men. All of the squads had separated, and the men were running as a group. Corvin increased the pace a few times so the men could really stretch their legs. On returning to the camp site, they passed the Captain, who nodded and smiled at Corvin.

Once the men had stretched, they all dispersed back to their squads and got ready for the evening meal. Corvin had gone off alone, a small distance away, to get some solitude. He had just sat down when he heard someone approach.

"Sorry to disturb you, Sergeant."

Corvin turned around and saw Corporal Geren standing there. He looked around to see if Dolac was anywhere near, noticed he was not and stood up.

"Yes, Corporal."

"I have a favour to ask, sir."

"Go ahead."

"Next time you go on a run, I would very much like the Second Squad to join you if that is possible," said Geren.

Corvin was very surprised.

"You are more than welcome. However, after the tension between Third Section and the First Section, how is that going to be seen?" asked Corvin.

"I don't care. I was not happy with what happened. I certainly did not want to cause the problems I did," said Geren, looking at the ground.

It was clear to Corvin now that he was put up to it.

"Was not your idea, was it?" stated Corvin.

"No Sergeant, but I can't say anymore. I admit, I was jealous and upset when you were made a Sergeant, but that is no excuse for the problems I caused."

Corvin did not know how to react, so just smiled.

"How is the wrist?"

"Still strapped as you can see. I have started taking some weight on it and within a few days, I will be able to hold a sword again."

"A broken wrist does not heal that fast," said Corvin.

"It is not broken, Sergeant, just sprained"

"We were told it was broken!" said Corvin.

Geren said nothing.

"I see. Well, your squad are more than welcome to join us. We will be running again tomorrow night. Will it cause problems?"

"I don't care. Also, I would like to say I am sorry for the problems I have caused. It was out of character and when I get the chance, I would like to say sorry to Torin too." It was genuinely said and Corvin accepted it.

There was no game being played here and he knew Geren was sincere.

"Accepted. I am sure Torin will welcome an opportunity to talk to you. Next time, aim for the jaw. The top of the head is the hardest part of the head and the worst place to punch someone," said Corvin with a smile.

Geren returned the smile.

"Thank you, Sergeant. I would ask for some fight training, but I think that would be pushing my Sergeant Dolac a little far. Running with your men, I could get away with, training? No, he would make my life miserable."

Corvin placed his hand on Geren's shoulder.

"You're a good man. If you do not mind me saying, you belong anywhere but in the First Section," said Corvin.

"Truth in that, sir."

Corvin had told his corporals of the conversation that he had with the corporal of the Second Squad. They were all surprised, just as he had been, but warmed by the story.

"I am more than happy to make peace with him," said Torin.

They all nodded.

"Ensure it is out of sight from Sergeant Dolac," said Corvin.

"That's not how it should be. We should not have to hide conversations with other corporals," said Jorga.

"No, we should not," said Irikson.

"No, but for now, just run with it. It also would not hurt if our men were encouraged to start talking to more of the First Section. They may scowl at us or be rude, but that does not mean we cannot try and fix the damage Dolac has done," said Corvin.

They all nodded.

"I'll pass along the word," said Torin.

The others agreed.

"Good. Also, Torin if you want to invite the squads of the Second Section to join us again on our run tomorrow night, that would be good," said Corvin.

"Aye."

The next day had been like all the other days. Warm, no wind and much laughter coming from the wagons as the men bantered and laughed with each other. Much to the Captain's surprise, the eighth day saw the men from the Second and Third Sections completely integrate and share wagons. The divisions between squads gone, with all the men intermixing and sitting in the wagons together. Sharing jokes, spreading laughter and the men telling their story. The former slaves found themselves extremely popular and they were happy to share their story of escape, leaving out the painful memories, of course. When the wagons stopped for the night to make camp, Corporal Geren was true to his word and his Second Squad joined the Third Section squads for their evening run. Along with them, the entire Second Section joined in; seventy men all running together. Once again, mixed together out of squads. Lorka, of course, was helping bridge the gap and running with Geren and some of his men. Making them feel welcome by telling them stories. In fact, Irikson's run in with the cook was once again shared. All of those in hearing distance laughing as they jogged.

"You bastards," Irikson swore from the back.

Corvin looked around and saw the Second Squad laughing and at ease. This was brotherhood, he thought to himself. Two more days and they would be at their destination, then Corvin knew it would be time to show the Captain the faith he had placed the former slaves, was not misguided.

The men were eating together. Second Squad had returned to their section, Corporal Geren not wanting to push the limits too far. Corvin had already received a dirty look from Sergeant Dolac as the men arrived back at camp, smiling and laughing.

Corvin had just finished his bowl of porridge when one of the men from the Fourth Squad he did not know approached him.

"Sir, the Captain needs to speak to you."

Corvin got up and made his way to the Captain. On reaching him, he joined the Captain and the other two sergeants.

"Corvin, change of plan. We've just received a runner

from Kor'Mor. The Sul'Lenans have attacked the wall there; we are needed now. Tell the men to pack up and get back in the wagons. We are traveling through the night," said the Captain.

"Sir," said Corvin, turning around and running back to his men.

On arriving, he stood in front of his men.

"Everyone pack up and climb back in the wagons. The Captain has just received a message. The town of Kor'Mor has just been attacked and we are moving, now. We are traveling through the night, so get your stuff packed and get to it."

Corvin then rushed to his own gear. He could hear the corporals rushing the men.

"You heard the Sergeant, get to it. You can finish your meal in the wagons," he heard Torin shout.

Corvin threw his pack into the back of the supply wagon he travelled in, then ran forward to find out any more information he could.

"My men are almost ready, Captain. Is there anything else I need to do or should know?" asked Corvin.

"No, Corvin. All I know is the Sul'Lenans have constructed wheeled towers and will attack the wall with them soon."

"Wheel towers?" asked Corvin, obviously confused.

"Yes. Massive wooden towers built to the height of the walls and has large wheels. The inside has steps, and the top has a ramp that can be lowered onto the wall, gouging the enemy straight onto the wall. They build it out of range of the wall, then push it right up to the wall. You will see them soon enough. Get back to your men and we should be at Kor'Mor by mid-morning. We will not be stopping, so tell you men to eat in the wagons," said the Captain.

"Yes, sir," said Corvin.

Running back to the Third Section, he passed the word to his corporals, then climbed in beside the driver of the supply wagon.

The driver looked at him and smiled. "Action at last, boy."

Corvin had come some way with his understanding and nodded back. "Yes. Action."

Corvin looked over his shoulder as the wagon got underway and saw all of his section were back in the wagons and had settled themselves. He turned back to the road ahead and smiled. He could not believe he was looking forward to battle. He felt the same rush of anger he felt in the pits. He shook his head and tried to relax but could not. He smiled and closed his eyes, whispering under his breath.

"Is this the excitement before battle you mentioned all those years ago, Smith?"

Chapter Eight

As the Captain had said, they arrived at the gates of Kor'Mor mid-morning. The wagon ride through the night had been at a quicker pace. Some of the men in Corvin's section managed to get some sleep, but most could not relax with the expected action just down the road. Corvin himself found he was on edge and could not focus. He sat in the darkness on the seat next to the wagon driver, lost in his own little world. Many thoughts swirling around in his head; thoughts of the trainer fights he had and, of course, the Smith. His thoughts, always returning to the Smith.

When the sun started to slowly make its way out of the darkness, with dawn arriving, Corvin shouted back to his section. Jorga sitting in the seat on the wagon behind him, hearing the instructions, passed them along the line. All the men dumped their travel blanket, any water skins they had in their hands and packed up their travel pack. The travel pack was put at their feet whilst the men got their weapons ready. Corvin wanted the men fully armed and ready to jump into the thick of it, if they needed to. It would put the men a little more on edge, but that was a small price to pay to make sure they were ready.

The town of Kor'Mor was not much smaller than the capital Iriksec, but it was perfectly square with tall walls completely enclosing the town. The only gate in the main wall of course was in the town, but as they approached the city, Corvin had noticed a large stone staircase that ran down from the Dark Wall to the ground. He could see men standing a top it.

The wagons had parked across from the main gates in a grassy field. The grass was green and knee height already, spring growth well and truly taking over. The men jumped off the wagon as soon as they stopped. Corvin raced forward to the Captain and reached him the same time a runner from Kor'Mor had. He could not understand the runner as he was speaking way too fast. He managed to grab the occasional word from the lean youth, but that was it. As the runner ran back, the Captain gave the orders.

"Right, arm the men and get to the bottom of the staircase. The attack has been underway all morning. It will take us a bit of time to get ready but get the men moving! The soldiers of Kor'Mor are being put under pressure and the Colonel has asked for urgent assistance," shouted the Captain.

Sergeant Emric and Sergeant Dolac nodded and returned to their men with haste.

"Captain, my men are ready now, sir," said Corvin.

The Captain stood up on his wagon seat and looked back. The Third Section was indeed ready and standing in their squads, whereas the Second Section and the First Section were just now getting organised.

"Permission to get straight up that wall, sir? If the soldiers are facing pressure, my section can help a little whilst the other sections get there," announced Corvin.

The Captain did not have time to think so nodded.

"Go Sergeant! Do not take any risks but get up there and help where you can!"

"Sir."

Corvin did not bother running back to his men, he instead ran towards the left side of the city where he saw the large staircase.

His corporals saw him, and he heard the shout go out from Jorga.

"FOLLOW THE SERGEANT!" Jorga yelled.

The Third Section ran after their Sergeant, all packed together and staying in close formation. They ran at a half run, their weapons still in their sheaths. Corvin reached the bottom of the stairs at the same time his section did. They were right on his heels as he started climbing. The steps all made of dark grey stone, but all smooth from the years of feet that had ran up them and down them.

"Plan, Sergeant?" asked Jorga.

"Help where we can, relieve pressure," replied Corvin.

"It's been a while," said Lorka, from a few men back.

Corvin smiled.

"Yes, it has," he replied as much to himself as to Lorka. He felt a surge of excitement as he pounded up the stairs, heading for the wall. He could hear the clash of steel on steel as the battle raged. A thought entered his mind.

"Pass the word on, do not attack anyone in grey uniforms. They are our allies, everyone else slaughter them where they stand!" yelled Corvin.

He could hear the corporals yell out his instructions. They were only a few steps from the top when he shouted out another order.

"Weapons free!" he yelled, drawing his sword and hand axe. He took a quick glimpse at the silver shine on his hand axe. Memories of the Smith and Son-of-angry man went through his mind. He cleared those thoughts quickly. He'd left his shield at the wagon, never feeling comfortable with it.

The Third Section reached the top of the stairs and almost stopped; the carnage was unbelievable. To the right, the Sul'Lenans had made the wall. How, Corvin was not sure but they were up. The Kor'Lenans were battling furiously, their dead lying on the ground everywhere. Corvin tried to estimate how many men were fighting but could not.

"Third Section! Get at them!" He yelled and ran into the fray.

The wall was a full twenty Lai wide, and the Third Section had room to all squeeze in close together.

Jorga shouted out a warning to the Kor'Lenans, Corvin did not know what he said but the Kor'Lenans moved to their right and made way for the newcomers. The surprise on their faces as the newcomers in red tunics came rushing in. Naturally, the Sul'Lenans burst through the gap that had been made, straight into the Third Section. The Sul'Lenans all wearing light leather armour much like the Bloodchildren, their tunics are dark green.

Corvin had no more time to issue orders. No time to think as he hit the line, using a move taught to him by Trainer, he shouldered the first Sul'Lena he came across. The Sul'Lena fell to the ground and Corvin sliced his axe across his throat. His left hand came up catching a sword from another Sul'Lena. He blocked another sword with his hand axe. Suddenly, both Sul'Lenans were dropping to the ground, sword wounds in their chest courtesy of Torin on his left side, and Lorka on his right.

"For the snow-weasel," came the shout at the back as the Third Section piled in.

Corvin battled furiously, block, cut, then look for another

target. His eyes were constantly moving. The Third Section was now spread across the width of the wall, containing and blocking the Sul'Lenans from getting down the stairs. The Kor'Lenans were on the right side of them, preventing them getting into the city through the other stairwell. Corvin turned in time to see Lorka stab his sword through an eye of one Sul'Lena. Lorka's sword got trapped in the skull and for a few moments, he was weapon less. This did not stop him as he grabbed the next Sul'Lena, pulled him into a head-butt and then lifted him above his head. He threw the man into his comrades. Corvin stopped a sword from going into Lorka's side with his hand axe, then sliced the attackers face with his sword. He had been aiming for the throat, but the attacker leaned forward a little and Corvin's blade cut into his jaw, slicing right through his mouth and out the other side. Lorka had managed to grab his sword and was now battling furiously. Either slicing a man or knocking him senseless with his shield. Lorka would prefer to use his two-handed axe, but in the confines of the wall with so many men, there was just no room.

Corvin could see the Sul'Lenans stepping back from the attack and making their way slowly backwards towards the edge of the wall. Now was the time.

"THIRD SECTION! SEND THEM HOME!" he yelled.

The Third Section pushed harder and started battling whilst moving forward. Irikson could be heard giggling from somewhere and it distracted Corvin, who almost lost an eye as a sword thrust came at him. He ducked at the last possible moment; the sword slicing against his helmet. He swung the axe down and up, straight into the man's groin. He yanked the axe clear, and the man dropped to the ground, to bleed out.

He took another step forward, sliced a Sul'Lenan's arm,

and then followed up with his hand axe, straight into the man's chest. The axe went straight through the armour and buried itself into the Sul'Lenan's chest. The axe got caught in the body, and as the man dropped, Corvin had to let go. He drew a dagger and went searching for another target, but there was none.

In a short order, the battle was over. The Sul'Lenans were already on the back foot, but the arrival of fresh troops of the Third Section had finished them. Corvin was breathing hard, as was the men of Third Section. The shout went out and soon, all the men were chanting.

"Snow Weasel! Snow Weasel! Snow Weasel!"

Corvin grabbed his hand axe and ripped it clear. He cleaned it off on the uniform of the last man he had killed and sheathed his weapons. He felt a hand clap him on the shoulder and as he stood up, the Kor'Lenans were congratulating the Third Section. Corvin looked over the heads of the Kor'Lenans and saw the smiling face of the Captain who raised his sword in salute. There must be another set of a stairs on the other side of the town, and that is how the rest of the Bloodchildren must have come that way. Corvin smiled, unsheathed his sword and raised it back. The Captain turned his sword towards the wagons and nodded his head in that direction. Corvin understood, but first called out another order as the chant of "Snow Weasel' died off.

"Third section, throw out the trash!" yelled Corvin.

The men of the Third Section sheathed their weapons and started picking up the bodies of the dead enemy. The bodies were thrown over the wall, to the ground where they had come from. Within moments, the wall was cleared of enemy bodies. Corvin noticed some Kor'Lenans trying to hack through the many thick ropes of the Sul'Lenans.

"Lorka, ropes," said Corvin.

Lorka grinned and finally took his two-handed axe off his back. The Kor'Lenans saw the huge, dark skin warrior move towards them with the massive axe in his hands. They stepped back with fear in their eyes; Lorka smiled and swung. The axe severed one of the ropes in one hit. He continued until all the ropes had been cut. Once done, he bowed to the Kor'Lenans, smiled and turned back to his men.

The Kor'Lenans cheered.

"Off the wall and assemble by the wagons," shouted Corvin.

The Third Section moved off, running down the stairs in a half run. The short battle was had been easy and although they, the Third Section was breathing a little hard, adrenaline still surged through their systems. They made the wagons and stood around talking and laughing. Not one of them had been lost in the first small skirmish, and for that, Corvin was happy. He saw the Captain approach.

"Stand to for the Captain," shouted Corvin.

The Captain arrived and stood in front of the men; he smiled.

"Well done, men. You have faced your first battle with the Bloodchildren and you have done us proud. Relax and get some lunch.

"Corvin, with me," said the Captain.

"Sir," said Corvin.

Corvin followed the Captain until he was at the lead wagon. The other two Sergeants were already waiting.

"Good work, Corvin," said Emric.

Dolac just nodded. Well, that was something anyway.

"Yes, good work, Corvin. Your section held the left side of the turret well. Any injuries?"

"Not that I am aware of, Captain. I have not had a chance yet to look over all the men," said Corvin.

"Of course not. As I said, good work. However, next time, I will not grant your request. It was reckless," said the Captain.

Corvin looked at the Captain, shock written all over his face.

"Don't misunderstand me, Corvin. The mistake is mine; I gave you permission. However, the Bloodchildren have learnt that we do not rush into action. Too easy for the company to get itself into trouble."

Corvin nodded and understood. It still pissed him off, but he hid it well and continued to listen as the Captain continued.

"The Colonel of the City has explained where we will be stationed," said the Captain.

"We are not stationed here?" asked Dolac.

"No. We are at the very end of the line where the Dark Wall meets the mountains. It's not far from here. On our left is Kor'Lena Infantry, on our right the mountains. Expect heavy fighting, as from memory there is a forest just south of the mountains, a small one," said the Captain.

"Yes. They call it the 'Darkwoods' from memory," said Emric.

"Who are we fighting with?" asked Dolac.

"Sea Wolves," said the Captain.

"Sea Wolves are solid fighters," said Dolac.

"Yes, they are, and they love a good fight. Beside them are the Fire Hawks, a company from Nedia Isle, which I have never heard of," confirmed the Captain.

"How big are the other companies, Captain?" asked Corvin.

"The Sea Wolves run at two hundred men, Fire Hawks, the Colonel said, have just over five hundred. There is also some three hundred Kor'Lena Infantry. With us, that is eleven hundred men on this end of the wall," stated the Captain.

"Is that enough?" asked Corvin.

"Plenty. This section of the wall only has room for roughly three hundred men," said Emric.

Corvin nodded.

"The Colonel said he suspects the Sul'Lenans are using the Darkwoods as a large camp for stores and men. In charge of that end of the wall is a captain called Tulnor. He is in charge and we answer to him," added the Captain.

The three Sergeants nodded.

"Go check over the men and get them loaded into the wagons. It's only a short ride over to the end of the wall from here. It's just after midday now, so we should be there, unloaded and organised by dinner time," stated the Captain.

The three Sergeants left to get their men loaded up and ready. Corvin was still a little pissed off at the Captain, and realised it was the first time he had felt that way. He moved off to his men and tried to focus his thoughts.

The wagon ride was even shorter than the Captain had said. Corvin thought they could have run it quicker, but they did have supplies to cart, so said nothing. The Dark Wall was right beside them now and as they rode along all of the men watched the wall and the men upon it.

Arriving at the camp, Corvin looked around. There was

one staircase like the one they had used earlier going from the wall to the ground, but there was no turrets or fortifications, only the Dark Wall itself. Also, there was no town, city or even a village. Surrounding the wall was what could only be described as a tent village. Corvin did not even bother counting the tents; there was too many. All the same, large size, fully enclosed walls with a door flap at the front. A mid-grey colour with many ropes anchoring the support poles to the ground.

The wagons stopped on the outside of the tent village. Corvin could see there was road though the middle of it, leading to the stairway. On closer inspection, the stairway was identical to the one they had run up earlier in the day. He climbed down and made his way to the front to see the Captain. On arrival, he noticed the Captain talking to a man. As he approached, Emric called him over. He walked up to the Second Sergeant.

"Hold off, Corvin lad. Let the Captain talk to Captain Tulnor. We will get our orders soon enough," said Emric.

Corvin nodded and looked over at the Kor'Lenan Captain. He was wearing the grey shirt of the Kor'Lenans and wearing black leather armour. He was short, looking around the same size as Irikson's five and half feet. He was a large around the middle, one would almost say fat. He had no hair and Corvin could not tell if he was bald, or he shaved it. His grey trousers where loose and face was round but strong. *He did not look like soldier*, thought Corvin.

"He does not look like a fighting man, does he," observed Emric,

echoing Corvin's thoughts.

Corvin smiled. "I was just thinking that."

"Here, they fight a little differently. Their officers do not fight in the line like ours do. They stand back and give orders.

Their talents are in their thinking, knowledge and experience; not their fitness or strength," Emric advised.

"So much to learn," muttered Corvin.

"They are soldiers when younger?" asked Corvin.

"Yes. They start from a young age here in Kor'Lena, much like yourself. Then, they slowly rise through the ranks. Once they get to Captain, or above that, they are no longer in the fighting line," said Emric.

"So, it is usually the older solders that hold rank?"

"Yes, but not always. If someone is talented, they rise quickly, much like yourself."

Corvin felt uncomfortable. He was not used to compliments, none of the former slaves were. It was something they were learning to deal with but had a way to go before they are comfortable with them.

"You have done pretty well, considering the rough start you had," praised Emric.

"I suppose. The former pit-rats and I do not know any other way. We have made a life around what we know," replied Corvin.

"You enjoyed today?"

"Yes. I have missed the fights and that concerns me. I will talk it over with some of the others, as I know they have also missed it. After the fight, they were all smiles."

"Understandable Corvin, especially since fighting is all you know. It's no wonder you take enjoyment out of a battle. I saw you briefly and the way the men were right beside you on the line. The Third Section would follow you into the fires of hell," admired Emric.

"That is what the Captain is probably worried about," said Corvin.

Emric laughed.

"For such a young man, you have an old head on those

shoulders of yours. You certainly understand a lot more than I did. When I was your age, all I cared about was getting paid and then going out to drink."

Corvin smiled.

"I do not feel young. Eighteen years old, nineteen once summer arrives. Yet I feel I have been here battling here in this life for twice that. At least, it has not been dull," said Corvin, his half little smile returning to his face for the first time in a very long time.

Emric noticed the smile and laughed loudly.

The Captain arrived with Dolac in step. The Captain had an expressionless face and Dolac his normal blank stare.

"Captain, what news," said Emric, recovering from his laughing fit.

Corvin stood up a little straighter. He was still amused from Emric's laugh that he smiled and nodded at Dolac. Dolac returned the nod, but of course, did not smile.

"We have this night off so we can get some rest. We enter the rotation of troops at first light tomorrow," said Captain Joren.

"Any surprises?" asked Emric.

"No, pretty standard. The wall holds three hundred men at a time. So, our entire company will be on the wall at the same time. Shifts are a half day. If there is battle, then Captain Tulnor will change the men himself when it looks like we are becoming tired. Two days on, one day off, when there is no action. With all the men here, he has placed everyone into three groups. That way one group is always resting. However, when the horn blows, everyone is to run to the bottom of the wall and wait," informed the Captain.

"Tenth Squad?" asked Emric.

"They are included in the rotation for now. There is no elevated area for them to shoot over the top of our own men.

If the enemy is sighted, they will shoot, then when the enemy gains the bottom of the wall, they are to hang back," said the Captain.

"I saw we have spare swords for them?" asked Corvin.

"Yes, and spare shields. Corvin, I will place the Tenth Squad under your command for now. They need to get up to speed with their sword work."

"Certainly, Captain," replied Corvin, pleased to be trusted with the task at hand.

Dolac shook his head before speaking.

"Who are we with?"

"In our rotation, Tulnor has placed us with the Sea Wolves. It's a good match. I'll have words with Captain Noro and see how things are shortly. I know the old raider well," replied the Captain.

"Sleeping arrangements?" asked Emric.

"That is the good news. There are tents allocated for us. Each Squad gets its own tent, ten men per tent. I am sharing a tent with Captain Noro. You Sergeants are to choose a squad and squeeze in. There should be plenty of room and the tents are built to sleep fourteen men. Also, there has been sleeping mats placed for the men. It is a bit more comfortable than sleeping on the ground," advised the Captain.

"Good," said Dolac.

Corvin laughed, and even Dolac smiled.

"Here is our guide now by the look of it. He will lead us to our tents," said the Captain.

The men of the Bloodchildren had settled in. Their tents where to the right of the stone stairway leading up to the Dark Wall. Their tents had the cliff face on the right side, the road and staircase on the left side, the Dark Wall at their rear and then, more tents in the front. It was almost cosy.

As soon as the men had settled, Corvin had the Third Section off on a light run to stretch their legs. Tenth Squad had joined them, since they were under the command of Corvin now and he had told them, not asked them. All of the squads from the Second Section had joined in the run as well. However, this time Corporal Geren's squad from the First Section did not. Corvin was a little bitter but no doubt Dolac had not allowed them.

They ran slowly through the fields to the North of the wall, amazed at the flatland all around them. Apart from the mountains, it looked like a table, it was that flat. Once the run was finished, Jorga led all the men in stretching exercises. This was finished quickly and most of the men went to relax and have a look around, except Tenth Squad, of course. Jorga and Lorka had taken them into the grass fields opposite the Dark Wall to test their sword skills. He could see a few of the archers already losing patience with getting whacked with practice swords. Corvin smiled and went to look from the top of the wall.

Arriving on top of the wall, he was quickly approached by Captain Tulnor.

"Your business?" he asked in the language of the Outlanders.

"Apologies, Captain Tulnor. I am Sergeant Corvin of the Bloodchildren. I wanted to come up and take a quick look at the ground before the wall, to get a feel for it if I am allowed," said Corvin.

Captain stood and assessed Corvin. Up close, Corvin could see he was in fact quite overweight. The Captain smiled.

"You are the Sergeant that led the charge at midday in

Kor'Mor? Then did the courtesy of throwing the bodies over the wall?" said Captain Tulnor.

"Yes, sir. That was my section."

"Fine work. You want to have a look at the ground?" asked Tulnor.

"Yes, Captain, if I can. I like to have as much information as possible. This is my section's first time in the field. I wanted to assess all the different approaches to the wall and see how far this 'Darkwoods' goes," said Corvin.

"A thinking man," replied Tulnor.

Normally, he would tell the upstart to bugger off, but he was interested to see what the young man thought.

"I'll give you a quick tour, follow me."

Corvin smiled and followed Captain Tulnor to the front of the wall.

He looked out and was amazed at the view. The land was flat, as far as he could see. Forests broke up the landscape but nothing in the way of cover. He mentioned this to the Captain. The Captain laughed.

"That is the point, Corvin. When the wall was built, all trees within five Melai were cut down so there was no cover."

Corvin could just see the enemy camps in the distance. He estimated it would not take long for a force to run the distance to the wall. He could see large wooden structures being assembled.

"Are those the towers on wheels?" asked Corvin, pointing to what he saw.

"Yes, they're nasty things. It takes a week to set them up. Then, a full day to wheel them to the wall. Once they are at the wall, they are bloody hard to deal with," said Tulnor.

"What is the plan to deal with them?"

"Fire. We throw small jugs of strong spirits against them, then shoot fire arrows at them."

Corvin nodded his head, then looked over at the forest, not far from the wall.

"So that is the 'Darkwoods'," asked Corvin.

"Yes. Less than eight hundred Lai from the foot of the wall," said Tulnor.

"It would not take much time to run that distance, although our archers would have a field day. Unless, of course, the Sul'Lenans had large thick wooden shields, then archers are useless," said Corvin, as much to himself as to the Captain.

The Captain looked and listened. He could see Corvin's brain was running all through the different scenarios as he was asking these questions. The Captain was a little impressed. This young Sergeant had a good grasp of things.

"Is it possible to climb those mountains on the forest side?" asked Corvin.

"No. Lucky it is high cliffs with no hand holds. Even with ropes, I have been assured by our rangers in the mountain that it can't be done," replied Tulnor.

"Rangers?"

"Scouts. We have a few squads throughout the mountains keeping an eye on things. They have an unrestricted view from the top. They send messages down every few days when they have new information."

"Interesting. Is it possible to climb down into the forest?" asked Corvin.

"Climb down?" asked Tulnor.

"Yes, Captain. If we wanted to, could we get down the mountain and into the forest?"

"Why would you want to?" asked Tulnor.

"Currently, we do not know what's in the forest, do we?" asked Corvin.

"No, we suspect they have a supply dump further back."

"Okay, just curious, Captain."

"It would be a suicide mission. We do not know how many soldiers are in the forest. I suppose it would be possible using long ropes but any one that got down would be slaughtered," advised the Captain.

"Thank you, Captain. That was all, I wanted to see the lie of the land and have a look. Those towers will be a concern, especially as the enemy will no doubt soak them in water before they get anywhere near the wall."

Once again, the Captain was impressed. That is exactly what the Sul'Lenans did. It always came down to a battle between how much water was used to soak the towers, and how much spirits were thrown on to them.

"You're welcome, Sergeant," replied the Captain.

"I best get back to my men," said Corvin and left.

Captain Tulnor watched him go, he would have to watch this one.

The day off went very quickly. When they woke in the morning, they were given a cooked breakfast of eggs and salted ham. Fortunately, Kor'Lena had always kept their supply of food high, just in case the Sul'Lenans came knocking. Which, of course, was exactly what they had done. Captain Tulnor had called a meeting of the senior men. Corvin had entered a meeting tent, larger than the others that was filled with maps hanging on the walls. He spent some time studying these and wished he could show his corporals. In the centre of the tent was a long oak table with many chairs around it. Once the call to be seated was called, Corvin took a seat next to Sergeant Emric at the bottom left side of the table. On the right side of Emric was, of course, Sergeant Dolac, then Captain Joren. After Joren, filling up the left side was three sergeants of the Kor'Lenan Infrantry. Along the other side was four sergeants of the Sea Wolves and their Captain Noro. Directly across from Corvin was seated the Captain Janoor of Jo's Cutthroats and one of his sergeants. At the foot of the table was three more sergeants from Fire Hawks company. Of course, at the head of the table, Captain Tulnor himself and his aide.

Corvin was a little nervous sitting around so many senior men. The fact he was the youngest in the tent did not help. Luckily, everyone spoke in the Outlander language, so it was agreed this is what they would use. Apparently, the Sea Wolves and Fire Hawks did not speak Kor'Lenan very well.

"Right, men. The first tower is up. We expect it will be pushed into position tomorrow. That is when the real work starts. We have only had two skirmishes so far, but now that the towers are under construction, and as I said one has been completed, we expect more fighting from this point on," said Tulnor.

He looked at the room and in turn, looked at everyman sitting there.

It was Captain Noro that broke the silence.

"So, fire arrows as normal then?" asked Noro.

"Yes. We have no other way to deal with them," said Tulnor.

Corvin had mentioned the towers to his corporals last night before bed and they had discussed it at length. They had thrown ideas around, but he was reluctant to say anything.

"Bloody towers," said Janoor.

His accent in the Outlander language being terrible.

"It's the only way we can deal with them, unless you have any ideas?" enquired Tulnor.

Corvin leaned in and quietly spoke to Emric, but before he could talk to him, Captain Joren jumped in.

"Out with it, Corvin. It's an open discussion, let's hear what you have to say," commanded Captain Joren.

"Do the Sul'Lenans water down the inside of the towers?" asked Corvin.

"The inside, lad?" asked Noro.

"Yes, the inside. They no doubt water down the outside to stop fire arrows, but what about the inside? Where the men climb up. Is that bit watered down?" asked Corvin.

"Not sure, I doubt it. The men water themselves down, so if any oil or spirits splashes on them, they don't go up as well," said one of the sergeants from the Kor'Lenan Infrantry.

"Janoor, you have faced these before and seen the inside of one. Do they water the inside?" asked Captain Tulnor.

"No. Not that I am aware of," answered Janoor.

"In that case, we fire it from the inside," said Corvin.

"What do you mean the inside?" asked Dolac.

"We wait until the ramp comes down and fire it from the inside," said Corvin.

"Not a bad idea, lad," said Captain Noro.

"Unfortunately, when the ramp drops, hundreds of men come pouring out very quickly," continued Noro.

"Maybe. I was throwing around some ideas with my Corporals," said Corvin.

"Go on, Corvin," said Tulnor.

"We see what line the tower is coming on. We line up as many archers as we can so they will be looking straight on the inside of the tower when the ramp drops. As soon as the ramp drops, the archers unleash hell, shooting as many arrows as possible into the inside, to hold the enemy, slow them down or even pause for a few moments. If we can get them to stall, my section run right down their throat," said Corvin.

The idea coming clearer, as he spoke.

"What do you mean right down their throat, lad?" asked Noro.

"My section is hiding, crouched down in front of the archers. As soon as the enemy stalls, my section stands and charges straight into the tower," said Corvin.

A few of the sergeants looked shocked, some whistled in surprise. Tulnor just looked at Corvin.

"Then what? There will be thousands of men at the bottom of that tower. Your section will be destroyed," said Tulnor.

"No. We are not charging down to the ground and taking the battle to them. Although, it's tempting," answered Corvin with his half smile.

He looked at Captain Janoor.

"Captain Janoor, there are many levels in the towers, are there not?" asked Corvin.

"Four," he replied.

"We run down to the second level and hold the doors. We do not need many men for that. Whilst we are holding the door, some other men run inside behind us with your flammable spirit, soak the inside and get out. Once we hear the retreat signal, my section gets out, fast. Soon as the last man is out, the archers shoot their fire arrows into the inside. That should do it," said Corvin.

Emric smiled and slapped Corvin on the back.

"There is enough room for thirty men on each level. You will still be taking on roughly a hundred and twenty men. Your section of thirty men could not handle them," said Janoor.

"I am sure I could find a couple of squads to come with the lad. My boys like doing daring attacks," said Noro, rubbing his chin and smiling at Corvin.

"I am sure Fourth and Fifth Squad would go with you. In fact, I don't think I could stop them. Sixth Squad could hold the containers of spirits," said Emric.

"The towers usually have hatch doors over the openings between levels. If you could get to the second level, you could close the hatch and lock it," said Janoor.

Corvin looked at his Captain.

"With your permission, Captain, I would like to try," said Corvin.

"Bloody risky, Corvin, but I cannot see any other options. Who would you use to fire the tower?" asked Captain Joren.

"Tenth Squad. They know my men and I would trust only them. No offence to the other men here but Tenth Squad know who I am and would recognise me or my squads. Would hate to be mistaken for the enemy and be shot full of arrows," said Corvin.

The sergeants around the table nodded and laughed.

"In fact, the more I think of it, the more I am sure it will work," said Corvin after a few moments of silence.

"Why are you sure?" asked one of the sergeants of the Sea Wolves.

"Because it's the last thing the bastards would expect," said Corvin.

There were chuckles around the room from some of the men. Corvin looked down the line at Noro and nodded his thanks. Noro smiled and nodded back before speaking.

"I like it, Captain Tulnor. It's actually quite simple and I think the risk is minimal. If there is only perhaps thirty men per level, it would be easy to control how many enemies are coming at us," added Noro.

"The men inside would not have to hold for long. It would only take moments for the boys to soak the inside. We would want to do multiple levels on the inside, make the thing go up faster," said Emric.

"If Captain Tulnor agrees to the plan, Corvin, you have my permission. Which squads?" Captain Joren asked.

"With me, Fourth, Fifth, Seventh, Eighth and Ninth Squad. Tenth Squad ready to fire their arrows and Sixth Squad on running duty," said Corvin.

"You want some of my squads, Sergeant?" asked Noro.

"Tempting Sir, but I will have fifty men with me, many more will be too many. We will be bumping into each other as it is, but I thank you for the offer," said Corvin.

"Well, I'm happy to give it ago, Joren. If you are happy, of course. It is risky," said Tulnor.

"Yes, I am happy, but I will want the rest of my company to be either side of the tower on the wall as a rear guard in case the plan goes south. I would also suggest having no more men on the wall except archers. Whilst my men are inside the tower, there will thousands of men on the ground trying to get in. Be good practice for your archers," said Captain Joren.

The men around the table laughed.

"We will do it then. The rest of you get prepared, Corvin and Joren please remain behind. The rest of you dismissed," said Tulnor

Emric got up and once again slapped Corvin on the shoulder as he left. Even Dolac nodded his head.

The men left and he was left with the two captains, talking through the plan. They did not have long, but soon, very soon, they would have another small victory.

Chapter Nine

Captain Joren, Captain Tulnor and Corvin spoke for some time. They were interrupted when a solider came running into the tent. He spoke quickly and Corvin got a basic idea of what was being said. The first tower was on its way. The soldier left just as quickly as he had arrived.

"The first tower is on its way. Apparently, the Sul'Lenans have learnt a thing or two. The towers are being pushed by many oxen. It will be here by midday," said Captain Tulnor.

"Pushed?" asked Captain Joren.

"Yes. Apparently, they have built some sort of harness or contraption that lets the oxen push the tower," said Tulnor.

"With permission, Captains. I better brief the men," said Corvin.

"Go lad," said Joren.

Corvin nodded his head and left.

"He is one to watch. He will go far," said Tulnor.

"Yes. If I can stop him killing himself," said Joren.

"Yes, but sometimes you need to take risks," Tulnor reminded Joren.

"Agreed, but he has such a hold on the men around him, that if he does something risky, half the company will follow him," said Joren.

"Good leader, then?"

"Yes, and he does not even know it. The men in his section worship him. If he jumped into the sea in the middle of a shark feeding frenzy, his men would jump in as well. Not only that, I think the other squads would now follow," said Joren.

Tulnor laughed.

"You're just cautious after last season," said Tulnor.

"Yes. Fifty men were lost. Half of our company," said Joren.

"A disaster. What is the lad's story?" asked Tulnor.

Joren told him a brief version of it.

"Amazing. No wonder his fellow former slaves worship him, and they fight like Demons, all of them," said Tulnor.

"Yes, they do. Also, the fighting ability has been rubbing off on the other squads. With training bouts on board the ship on the way over, and the fact that he takes part during his training runs, other squads are lining up to join him. The Bloodchildren will be the better for it. The company is certainly the fittest and strongest it has ever been," said Joren.

"Your replacement for when you retire perhaps," said Tulnor with a smile.

Joren laughed.

"Yes, that thought has been in the back of my mind for some time now. I am ten years off retiring. That gives me ten years to install some caution in him. My Sergeant Emric suggested the same thing," said Joren.

"This plan of his is reckless, but it is a bold one," said Tulnor.

"Yes. Corvin and his Corporals are starting to show a different way of thinking," said Joren.

"What do you mean different?"

"They have a way of looking at problems in a different way, then coming up with solutions others would not think of. My corporal Jorga, one of the former slaves once explained that they were used to constant change. He said if a slave can't adapt quickly, they die," said Joren.

"Very true. Outlander bastards," agreed Tulnor.

Joren laughed.

"Indeed. I'm just scared that if Corvin was in charge of the company, the Bloodchildren would be off to war against the Outlanders," said Joren with a smile.

"I would join them," Tulnor smiled back.

"We are actually going to do it?" said Irikson with some shock.

"Yes," said Corvin.

"It was just a half jest, I did not think you would actually listen," said Irikson.

"Next time, keep your mouth shut and don't suggest good ideas," said Jorga.

They laughed.

"Who are you taking?" asked Torin.

"Down their throat?" asked Corvin with a grin.

"Yes," confirmed Lorka.

Lorka was not a Corporal, but Corvin always included him.

"Seventh, Eighth, Ninth Squad. Joining us will be Fourth and Fifth Squad. Tenth Squad will be waiting with fire arrows. Sixth Squad will be the mules, running in the strong spirit they brew here. The Sea Wolves will have a couple of squads on standby to pull our arse out of the fire. Other than that, the wall will be full of all of the Kor'Lenan Infrantry that can use a bow," said Corvin.

"Fire down on the waiting enemy," Jorga said, nodding his head.

"Exactly," said Corvin.

"What do we need to carry?" asked Torin.

"Small, close combat weapons only; swords, hand axes and daggers for the close work. Sorry Jorga and Lorka, you will need to leave your two-handed weapons behind," instructed Corvin.

Both nodded.

"We should all leave our shields behind. They will slow us down and hamper us when in the confines of the tower," suggested Jorga.

"Good idea," confirmed Corvin.

All the others nodded. Irikson started giggling.

"This should be interesting," said Irikson.

"Interesting?" queried Torin.

"Fun. Imagine the look on the bastards faces when we charge in?" said Irikson.

They all smiled

"That is why it will work; it will be the last thing they expect," said Corvin.

"Can I make another suggestion?" said Torin.

"Of course," said Corvin.

"Ask the Captain if we can have a couple of long ropes further down the wall, ready to throw over for us. If the fight goes badly and we get blocked from getting back up the tower, we may have to make a run for it," said Torin.

Corvin thought about it.

"I'll ask. If that happens, we will be facing a few thousand men down there, and I doubt we could make it," said Corvin.

"Better that than no options at all," said Jorga.

"True. I'll make sure it happens," replied Corvin.

"We will inform the men. When do we expect the tower?" asked Jorga.

"Midday," answered Corvin.

"Okay, we better get to it. I'll pass on to all men the signals and the information," Irikson confirmed.

They all nodded and departed.

Corvin stood on the wall, watching the tower move slowly closer and closer. The oxen had been disconnected out of bow range. Hundreds of men got in behind the tower and were now pushing it. Further back, it looked like a thousand or so men were waiting. As soon as the tower touched the wall, the Sul'Lenans waiting would come running. Lining the men who were pushing, were men holding up large shields.

"All set, Corvin?" asked Captain Joren.

"Yes, Captain," said Corvin.

"The ropes have been organised but hope like hell you do not need them. If you need them, getting to them will be near impossible," said the Captain.

"Yes, it will be, but it is always good to have a backup plan," said Corvin.

Corvin was focused on the tower. He could feel the anger build in him, an anger he had not felt since they arrived at the border of Irik. Captain Joren patted him on the shoulder.

"Luck, lad," said Joren, then walked away to the very end of the wall to stand next to Captain Tulnor.

Corvin looked at the floor of the Dark Wall. Crouched

down were his men and the men of the Fourth and Fifth Squad.

"We ready, men?" asked Corvin.

They all nodded.

"When the signal is called, we go in. We hit them hard, we hit them fast. You know the plan; we do not stop until we are on the second level. You know the retreat signal and the backup plan. If we find ourselves having to go out the front, we slaughter the bastards until we get to those ropes," reminded Corvin.

He could see the look of determination on the face of his men. He looked across at Corporal Yelix of the Fourth Squad. He was grinning.

"We will give them hell, Sergeant," said Yelix.

"That we will. Look to your brothers, protect them, protect yourself and most of all show these ugly bastards what the Bloodchildren can do," said Corvin.

The former slaves started beating their fists on their chest, a slow beat that was taken up by everyone in the Third Section, then spread to the Fourth and Fifth Squad. Corvin took his time to look at all of the men that he could. They all nodded at him. He looked up and saw the tower was only one hundred Lai from the wall. He gave the signal to be quiet. The archers started shooting. Most of the arrows hit nothing but the large shields. A few managed to get through and strike flesh, but only a few. Corvin crouched down with his men, controlling his breathing as he felt his excitement grow. Lorka slapped him on the back.

"Are you ready, Snow Weasel?" asked Lorka.

"Never more so brother," confirmed Corvin.

When in battle, or about to do battle, rank was often forgotten by the former slaves. Brotherhood being more important to them. Corvin looked at Corporal Mika of the

Sixth Squad. All of his men were crouched down holding large jugs with cloth rammed into the ends. These jugs filled with what he had been told a very flammable spirit that the Kor'Lenans brewed from a local vegetable. The Corporal nodded to him. Corvin nodded back. He had only spoken to Mika a couple of times, but according to Emric, he was a solid man. A career corporal and would never go further, but a solid man and very dependable. Corvin looked at the ground and slowly started to tap the stone floor of the wall with his fist. He closed his eyes and thought back to the Smith.

"Be like the Snow Weasel, boy. Once you latch on, do not let go."

The memory of the Smith's words bringing a dark smile to his face. He continued to keep his eyes closed and beat at the floor of the wall. Anger is a gift.

The signal from the Tenth Squad came before he was ready for it. He was not sure how long he waited.

"WEAPONS FREE, DOWN THEIR THROATS!" yelled Corvin as loud as he could.

He jumped up and was first to jump on the ramp. The archers had done a good job, the enemy had indeed stalled and were standing holding their large shields, protecting themselves from arrows. Corvin's feet hit the ramp and he felt Lorka and Irikson beside him. The ramp was wide enough for four men abreast, but with Lorka's size, three at the front would have to do. Time slowed for a fraction as the three brothers charged at the enemy, hiding in the shelter of the top level. From beside him, he heard Irikson call out.

"Feet first!" yelled Irikson.

As the three of them reached the line of enemy, they jumped and flicked their legs forward, feet together. At the same time, the three of them hit the shield wall, impacting against the four large shields blocking the doorway. The four men holding the shields were thrown backwards with great force. The man holding the shield that Lorka flew into, hit the side of the tower and was knocked unconscious, so much was the force of his body hitting the shield wall. The three of them came down and landed on the floor of the ramp. It was not a comfortable fall.

"UP AND OVER!" shouted Jorga and men jumped over the three on the ground and charged into the tower.

Corvin could hear yelling, clashes of steel. All of a sudden, there was arms under him, lifting up. He saw Irikson and Lorka had already been lifted up. They charged forward into the tower. There had only been twenty men in the first level of the tower and they were quickly killed. Corvin was about to shout for the men to go down to the next level, but saw Seventh Squad had already gone down, Irikson their Corporal, not far behind.

The third level had no one in and the men kept going down. However, the second level was packed; forty men trying to get up the internal ladders. Lorka screamed a battle cry and launched himself down the hatch, landing on top of the enemy and knocking them to the ground. Torin and the rest of Ninth Squad followed and recklessly threw themselves down on top of the enemy, stabbing out with daggers in a frenzy. Within a short time, the second level was clear. The fifty men of the Bloodchildren had occupied the second and third level of the tower. Corvin nodded to Jorga and Jorga shouted out as loud as he could.

"TOWER CLEAR!"

That was the signal for Sixth Squad.

"We all accounted for?" asked Corvin

The corporals nodded. Good, so far so good with no loses.

"Lorka, when we get back to camp, you will have to

convince me that you diving on top of forty enemy was a good idea," said Corvin.

The men laughed. Not for long as the enemy below in the ground level of the tower were banging axes against the wooden hatch that covered the ladder. Lorka and Jorga were standing on it, holding it in place.

"As soon as we get the signal, we move! Should not be long now," Corvin said, reminding them all.

Time moved very slowly with the banging and cracking of the hatch becoming more urgent.

"Torin, can you see what is taking so long?"

"On it," said Torin.

Torin climbed the ladder and stuck his head up to see what was going on. A fire arrow narrowly missed his head. He fell down the ladder just as the top level was engulfed in flame.

"Who the fuck fired that?" screamed Torin

Almost as he said it, the retreat signal came. Three blasts on a horn. Corvin's heart sunk. That was the signal for out the front and get to the wall. His men looked at him. Anger was rising in Corvin faster and harder than ever before.

"Some archer is about to feel my wrath!" he said under his breathe.

"OUT THE FRONT! WE TAKE THE BATTLE TO THEM! MOVE!" screamed Corvin.

Watching from the end of the wall near the cliffs, to the right of the approaching tower, were the senior men. Captain Tulnor, Captain Joren, Sergeant Emric, Sergeant Dolac and also Captain Noro and Captain Janoor.

They all watched the tower hit the wall, the ramp dropping. The archers did an amazing job. Fifty arrows hitting the opening of the tower as soon as the ramp dropped. Many men fell until they could get their shields up. Captain Joren was full of pride as he saw Corvin jump up and lead his men. They were right on his heel as he charged the shield wall. The archers straight away moved to the front of battlements and started aiming down, firing on the men waiting to get into the tower. There was only a couple of hundred and even though they had thick shields, the archers were still able to pick off many.

All of the assembled men nodded when Corvin, Lorka and Irikson flew through the air, feet first to bust open the shield wall.

"That's different, I will have to remember that!" said Captain Noro.

The other senior men nodded. Captain saw his men follow in, and within moments, the fifty men had run into the tower. Screams and insults could be heard as the men under Corvin fought. Emric laughed.

"They certainly are having fun," said Emric.

The others laughed, except Captain Tulnor.

"Quiet," he said.

Sixth Squad could be seen charging into the tower with their jugs, filled with spirits. Tenth Squad had lit their arrows and were waiting. Within heart beats, the Sixth Squad had delivered their jugs and returned. As soon as they got back to the safety of the wall, fire arrows were shot into the tower.

Yells went up as the assembled senior men could see the Tenth Squad dropping their bows, and charging into the squad of archers beside them, laying into a squad of Kor'Lenan archers.

"WHAT?" yelled Captain Joren, spinning on Captain Tulnor.

"They will have to get out the front. We can't risk the

Sul'Lenans getting back into the tower, putting out the flames and gaining the wall," said Captain Tulnor.

"YOU PLANNED THIS? AND PUT HALF MY COMPANY AT RISK?" screamed Joren.

"Calm yourself, Captain," said Tulnor.

"This is not over, Tulnor!" said Captain Noro, dropping his title as an insult.

Noro ran off down the wall. He yelled at his men and all of the Sea Wolves on the wall joined him, heading for the ropes.

"SOUND THE DISTRESS SIGNAL!" yelled Joren at the horn blower.

The horn blower put his horn to his lips and blew three short, strong blasts.

Captain Joren looked over the wall. There was over two hundred men still at the bottom of the tower with shields. He looked over and saw a thousand or so enemy sprinting towards the tower. It would be not long before they arrived. He looked over and saw Captain Noro had separated his Tenth Squad and the squad of archers for Kor'Lena. The archers from Kor'Lena were picking themselves up off the ground, with blood all over their faces. Tenth Squad had picked up their bows and had run to the battlements. They were now firing into the men at the bottom of the tower, as fast as they could.

"ARCHERS TO THE FRONT!" yelled Captain Tulnor.

All of the Kor'Lena archers, all two hundred of them walked to the front of the wall.

"Fire on the men at the base of the tower, as soon as you see the red tunics come pouring out, take aim at the oncoming soldiers," yelled Captain Tulnor.

The archers joined the Tenth Squad, firing as fast as they could into the men at the bottom of the tower.

"This will not be the end of this," said Captain Joren.

His anger was building, and he had to stop himself from punching the Captain.

"Control yourself, Captain," said Tulnor.

"You do not understand, do you arsehole?" said Dolac.

Tulnor spun, not being used to be talked to in such a manner.

"No, he does not understand," said Joren.

"Understand what?" said Tulnor.

"If those men make it out of that, especially Sergeant Corvin, they will come for you. I will laugh as Corvin slices you apart, fat arsehole!" said Dolac walking away.

"You get back here now, Sergeant," said Captain Tulnor.

"He does not answer to you, he answers to me. If Corvin does make it out and come for you, I will not stop him," said Joren, as he also walked away.

For once, Captain Tulnor was not so sure of himself.

As Corvin gave the order, the hatch to the bottom level was open. Corvin was about to jump straight on top of the waiting soldiers but was pushed out of the way by Lorka.

"That's my job, brother," said Lorka, as he dived feet first through the hatch.

All the men followed, and the bottom level was a mess within moments. Corvin had been fifth or sixth man down and very quickly. Daggers were the only option and the first thirty men down were all former pit-rats. As comfortable with daggers as they were with their other weapons. The bottom level was cleared quickly. The men who had hit the bottom had many cuts but thankfully, and luckily, none were serious. Lorka and Irikson was holding the enemy at the front door of the tower, and fortunately the enemy did not have any archers.

"We ready?" asked Corvin.

The fifty men had squeezed into the bottom level; many nods.

"We will follow the Snow weasel," said Torin with a smile.

"We get out, break left, fight hard, fight fast and get to the ropes," said Corvin.

The men readied themselves. It was going to be a tough fight.

"NOW!" screamed Corvin.

On the wall, they heard the call. The archers on the left side of the tower, where the ropes were, stopped firing. They faced up and waited for the main force of Sul'Lenans to arrive into range.

Lorka and Irikson burst out into the Sul'Lenans waiting. They were frenzied, striking out fast and hard. Irikson, his short strong body, powering into the Sul'Lenans with his two hand axes. Lorka had sheathed his dagger and picked up a short-curved blade from one of the dead enemies, with swords in each hand he was right beside Irikson as they made for the left. Corvin was out next, focusing on the men coming at Irikson's right. His hand axe causing mayhem and ending lives as his sword was used for mainly defence. Jorga was beside him and behind, protecting Corvin's right side. Torin had managed to get to the left of Lorka, using all the skill he had to keep up with Lorka and Irikson, helping lead the way. It was fast, it was furious and very brutal. Sul'Lenans died and dropped lifelessly to the ground. Members of the Bloodchildren also fell, but no one would notice until much later.

From the wall, Captain Joren watched as the men under Corvin burst out. He had never witnessed such fury as he was witnessing now. His men were fighting like maniacs, like berserkers, desperate to get to the wall and the waiting ropes.

"They might just bloody make it," said the Captain under his breath.

"Yes, but they will have no way of protecting their rear when they get to the ropes," said Emric.

The Captain realised what Emric was saying.

"Permission to take my section down the ropes sir. We can charge in and help, then be able to help them get back to the wall. The archers can give us cover as we climb back up," said Dolac.

The Captain turned to look his First Sergeant in the eyes. "Really, man?"

Dolac nodded before continuing, "We can do it, sir."

"Do it, we will speak of this later," said Joren.

Emric knew what he meant, Dolac had no love for Corvin and the former slaves. In fact, he had hated them since the day they arrived.

"I'll bring some men and go with you. We have ten ropes over the side now," said Captain Noro smiling.

Captain Joren nodded.

"Be quick, the rest of those bastards running at the wall will be here before we know it," instructed Joren.

Joren looked up. The thousands of Sul'Lenans were running with all their speed to reach the bottom of the wall and join battle. They were only a Melai away and would be able to cover that distance very quickly. When he looked over the First Section and a few squads were already scaling down the ropes.

Corvin had taken a cut to his cheek and had a wound on his right arm on the bicep. It was not deep and could have been worse. It was flowing freely with blood but luckily, he had managed to deflect the blade before it went too deep. He was now at the front with Irikson on one side of him, Lorka and Torin on the other side. All of the Bloodchildren were fighting hard, although they had not been battling for long, they were swinging their weapons so fast that they were chewing through their energy. All of the men, whether former slave or an Irik man, were superb.

Corvin was facing forward, and they were slowly walking backwards towards the wall. They had been surrounded by the Sul'Lenans, trying to block off their retreat. Many Sul'Lenans had fallen, and over forty bodies now lay on the ground, food for the crows to feast on. Corvin could not see and had no way of knowing how many Bloodchildren had also fallen. It was inevitable some would, fifty men could not face over two hundred and all survive! Bloodchildren or not.

Corvin dropped to one knee and sent his axe straight up in the groin of a Sul'Lena, on his way up stabbed him in the neck with his sword. A blade came at him and he blocked it with his axe. A sword from someone on his right sliced the man's throat, blood squirting out and over Corvin's face.

"You're slowing down, Corvin," said Irikson from his left.

Corvin took the time to quickly wipe the blood from his eyes. His men had finished off the men in front of them, he could see the ropes only fifty or so away.

"Turn and form a rear-guard," shouted Corvin.

All his men who had been facing the front turned quickly, joining the men behind them. They slowly started walking backwards, fighting off the hundred Sul'Lenans still facing them. Corvin knew his men were tired, he himself was almost at his limits. Fights in the pits had been fast, but no relentless like this. His throat was dry and he needed rest. Hatred drove him now and memories of the battles he had faced. Remembering Angry-man and other Outlanders that had been responsible for the death of Smith, a new energy filled him. He charged through his men and arrived at the front. His axe singing, his sword weeping as Sul'Lena after Sul'Lena went down before him. Jorga was on his right side, using all his skill, taking out soldiers with his easy and economical style, not overusing energy, with a clam look on his face. To his left was Yelix, grinning as he stabbed, blocked and slashed his way through the enemy soldiers.

No matter how much hate they could muster, their bodies were soon to drop. They could not keep this up. Some of the Bloodchildren started to fall back towards the wall, soon they could not have enough energy to climb the ropes. Then it happened, fresh bodies arrived and smashed into the Sul'Lenans. Corvin knew straight away that the pressure had been eased. He had time, so looked around. He saw members of the First Section had charged in and were now battling hard against the Sul'Lenans. Members of the Sea Wolves had also charged in. When did they get here, he thought to himself?

"Get your men back to the wall, Corvin. We will hold them until you're up," said Dolac.

Corvin looked over and saw him battling hard beside him. He had not time to be surprised. He called out the order.

"Third Section, Fourth and Fifth Squads, back to the wall now. AWAY!" he yelled.

As one the men under Corvin retreated back to the wall, they got to the ropes, sheathed their weapons and began to climb. Some of them struggled, as all their energy had been used in the fighting but were spurred on by those behind them and those above. Corvin looked over at Dolac and his men, fighting for all they were worth. Beside them, two squads of Sea Wolves, led by their Captain. Corvin had time for a quick smile.

He spoke to Lorka before Lorka jumped on the rope.

"Once you get up, organise the strongest men to man the ropes. The last ten of us will need to be pulled up, it's the only way," said Corvin.

"You are not staying here alone, brother!" said Lorka.

"I need you up there, your strength alone will mean the difference. Go. Now!" said Corvin as he watched the last of his men jump up on the ropes and start climbing.

Once they were all on, he turned and ran back to the fighting, he joined in on the end of the line and laid into the Sul'Lenans again. "My men are up. I hope you have an idea how we are going to get out of this," Corvin yelled at Noro.

Noro just smiled and continued to fight, narrowly avoiding a sword to his right eye.

"Move back slowly now," shouted Noro.

Slowly they walked backwards until the back of the wall, fighting as they went. On the ground was fifty-one mercenaries and what looked like over seventy Sul'Lenans.

"It won't work," said Corvin. "You need to start sending them up by squads, the rest of us will hold them off."

Overhead the archers had started firing at the oncoming Sul'Lenans, they were almost upon them.

"Second and Third Squad break," shouted Dolac.

The squads retreated back to the ropes. Corvin ran back around and jumped in beside Dolac, mustering as much energy as he could. Noro also sent one of his squads back but continued to fight. There was no room for fancy moves now, as Corvin's body had come to the end of its stamina, he slashed, cut and blocked. He thought this may be the end, as he blocked another cut aimed for his throat. He knew his sword was blunted from all the use, his axe however, being made by the Smith, sharp as ever.

They had walked within twenty Lai of the wall and still they battled. Dolac sent his last squad up and so did Noro. It was the three of them now were holding off twenty; Corvin in the middle, Noro to the right and Dolac on the left. Some of the archers on the wall, the Tenth Squad to be exact, had ignored orders and had fired down on the Sul'Lenans facing their Sergeant. This had even the odds and the Sul'Lenans not fighting the three men, had their shields raised protecting themselves.

Suddenly, Dolac went down to a nasty cut to the face. His own blood was blinding him, and he could see nothing. Corvin saw this and yelled at Noro.

"Captain! Get him out of here now!"

Noro grabbed him and hauled him to the ropes, getting him to hang on as he could not see. It was clear he did not have the strength to hang on, so Noro shook his head and grabbed on, holding Dolac.

Corvin was by himself, battling off the last seven Sul'Lenans. His brothers on the wall could only watch in despair as he fought for his life. A chant was slowly taken up by the former slaves, then picked up by the rest of the Bloodchildren, then eventually all of the Sea Wolves as well.

"SNOW WEASEL, SNOW WEASEL, SNOW WEASEL!"

Corvin heard this and focused, dodge, cut, then block again. He is the Snow Weasel; he would not let go. He would latch on and take the bastards with him. He would not let the Smith down. One after another, Corvin dropped the remaining Sul'Lenans. The Kor'Lenans on the wall were amazed at the man on the ground, killing men, destroying men as the mercenaries chanted. They knew they were watching a man die, watching his last actions, and could not look away. He was facing the last three when arrows flew from the wall, killing the last three. He stopped and looked, the rest of the Sul'Lena force were almost at him. He resigned to his fate and vowed to kill a few more before they took him, but he knew he had no chance.

"Get back to the wall, you crazy bastard!" yelled Irikson.

His voice cutting through the red mist of Corvin's emotions. He turned and ran, sheathing his weapons as he reached the roped. He jumped up and grabbing it, holding on as the rope was quickly pulled up. Four men, being directed by Lorka, pulling with all their strength. His body was being scraped as it brushed past the stone, but he did not care. He just hung on! He reached the tops and was pulled over. He flopped to the floor of the wall, breathing hard. The chant was still being yelled out.

"SNOW WEASEL! SNOW WEASEL! SNOW WEASEL!"

The archers all moved to the front of the wall and fired down, peppering the Sul'Lenans with arrows. They raised their shields and retreated. The tower was an inferno and there is no way they could use it; the ropes had been pulled up and they had no way to gain the wall. They walked backwards, shields raised and waited for another day.

Corvin was picked up and hoisted up onto of someone's shoulder. The chant was still going.

He opened his eyes and saw the smiles on the faces of the men. He raised his hand and smiled.

"I told you he was fucking crazy!" declared Irikson to no one.

Corvin would have laughed but could not spare the effort. All he could say as the chant died down was "I need a piss, then a drink."

The cheers went up.

Corvin was sitting on his bed, a medical orderly stitching his wound in his arm. He had been helped to his tent. His men were being seen to as well and he continued to stare into space. On the way to the tents, he had been told of who got left behind, which men of his did not make it. Also, Corporal Neelan from Tenth Squad had come running up to apologies and explain the situation. The Kor'Lenans had fired on the tower at Tulnor's order. Corvin had thanked Neelan and been helped to his tent. As Corvin stared into space, his face was like a winter storm. Tulnor was responsible for the deaths of seven of his men and three from the Second Section. Yes, they had done well, and the situation could have been worse, but that was not the point. He breathed slowly to calm himself, but it was not working. He stared across at the medical orderly, saying nothing. He knew the situation and would not look at Corvin in the eye. As he finished, the orderly instructed, he should lay back for some time and relax. Corvin just looked at him and shook his head. After the orderly left, Corvin slowly raised himself. He would deal with Tulnor, but first he had other important matters to tend to. He picked up his hand axe. He saw his reflection in the silver finish of it. He put it back in to his belt.

He got up and slowly walked to the First Section's area. The pain was not the worst he had felt, but neither was it pleasant. He did not take the pain paste all the men carried. He walked over to the tent that Dolac shared with his First Squad. He walked in and saw Emric, Captain Joren standing over Dolac. Dolac was lying down on his bed mat. Dolac was smiling as Corvin walked in. Corvin noticed the wound on his face. A straight cut had been stitched. It ran from his left ear, down across his cheek and ended at the bottom of his jawline.

"Crazy bastard," mentioned Dolac smiling.

"Corvin, are you fine to be up?" asked the Captain.

"The cut was not deep, and I am fine, just exhausted," said Corvin.

Emric came up and placed both hands on Corvin's shoulders.

"Dolac is right, you are crazy, but it was magnificent to watch," said Emric.

"You have heard what happened?" asked the Captain.

He was referring to why the tower was fired, making Corvin and his men have to escape out the front.

"Yes," said Corvin between clenched teeth.

"Well, we need to talk of this before you do anything," said the Captain.

"No, we don't, sir. Not yet," said Corvin.

He got down on his knees and held out his arm for Dolac.

"You saved my arse, First Sergeant Dolac. I did not expect it of you, all of the men and I on the ground owe you, thank you," said Corvin.

Dolac smiled and gripped Corvin's arm in the warrior fashion.

"You saved my arse at the end, so how about we call it even?" smiled Dolac as best he could.

He was right. Corvin had almost sacrificed himself so Dolac and Noro could get up the wall.

"Done," said Corvin.

Both were smiling. The relationship was not fully healed, but they would now share an understanding and things would get easier.

Captain Joren started talking.

"Now that's out of the way, Captain Tulnor," Captain Joren suggested.

"Needs to die," said Corvin, cutting him off.

"Yes, he does," agreed Dolac.

Emric said nothing, he knew that politically they were in a tight spot.

Finally, the Captain spoke.

"Maybe, but not here and not now. We are surrounded by one hundred thousand Kor'Lenan soldiers. We cause problems, then we are dead. I have no doubt you would give your life, Corvin, but would you gamble the lives of your brothers?"

"No," said Corvin.

"I will handle this; I need you to trust me. You and the former slaves have proven yourselves many times over. You're a strong, disciplined, amazing fighters and have been loyal to the brotherhood of the Bloodchildren. Give me the chance to return and reward the loyalty. Trust me," said the Captain in a half request, held command.

Corvin looked into his eyes and saw something he had never seen before from the captain. Anger.

"Will you trust me?" asked the Captain.

"I will, Captain. I and the other former pit-rats owe you and yours so much. I will trust you. We will trust you," said Corvin.

"Good. You owe us nothing. Whatever you thought you owed us was paid back by your actions today, you crazy bastard," said the Captain with a smile.

All four of them laughed.

"The Captain now has to come up with a way to get this dealt with, without Tulnor losing too much face," Emric said, thinking out loud with the other Sergeants.

"Oh, the fat bastard will lose face alright, and more," said the Captain with feeling.

"Now that's the Captain I know and miss," said Dolac.

Emric laughed.

Corvin was about to ask a question when Captain Noro of the Sea Wolves entered the tent.

"Good, you are all here. I would suggest getting yourselves ready. The Colonel has arrived," said Noro, smiling.

"What the bloody hell is he doing here?" asked the Captain.

"He could be sightseeing, but I think it is because a nameless mercenary Captain sent a runner and told him to get here quick as the mercenary companies are about to revolt," said Noro.

"You threatened that?" said Emric.

"I bloody well did. That fat, worthless piece of shit is not going to get away with this," said Noro.

"Whatever you decide to do, you have the full support of the Sea Wolves. We will follow you," said Noro.

All of the men looked at Noro.

"That was amazing to watch, lad. We will share the cup soon and talk of it," said Noro smiling at Corvin. Corvin smiled back.

Chapter Ten

"Stand guard, and do not let anyone in," said a voice from outside the tent.

Noro smiled.

"Too late."

The tent flap was opened and in walked the Colonel. He stood there looking at the assembled mercenaries. He was a sight to behold, wrapped in his authority. Standing the same height as Corvin, with slightly more weight on him, but in no way was he as fat as Tulnor. He had short cropped grey hair, was clean shaven and had a seriousness in his eyes. His uniform was spotless! A grey tunic that fit perfectly. Over that, large black leather armour; large because it was thicker than the armour Corvin wore. It was longer and covered the groin completely. Corvin had not really noticed him at the fort over the days before. He stopped his inspection when the Colonel spoke.

"Who is the brave Captain that wrote this?" he said with a controlled anger.

He was holding up a small scroll.

"That was me, did it get your attention then, sir?" stated Noro, more than asking.

"You are threatening to leave the wall. That is mutiny!" declared the Colonel.

"No, it is not. Mutiny if we were of your country, mercenaries are not bound by the same rules. You know that," said Noro.

"What the hell is going on?" the Colonel demanded to know.

Noro outlined what had happened. Corvin was impressed with this Captain. He had been impressed with him on the ground, seeing him fight with his men. He was impressed now, seeing him stand up to this Colonel.

"This happened?" questioned the Colonel in surprise.

"It did," said Joren.

"He almost sacrificed, on purpose, half of my company. Men die in war; that is understood. Mercenaries know they are thrown into the thick of it and always lead from the front; that is our life. Never in my thirty years have I seen this happen. A Captain intentionally endangers mercenaries in that manner," reported Joren.

The Colonel nodded, taking it all in before speaking.

"I see I have much work to do to get to the bottom of this," frowned the Colonel.

"No, you have a lot of work to do to stop Sergeant Corvin here from killing the fat bastard and anyone that gets in his way," replied Noro pointing at Corvin.

Corvin grinned that evil little half grin of his and looked at the Colonel. The look was not lost on the Colonel.

"It was you on the ground I saw battling for his life," said the Colonel.

Corvin nodded.

"Yes, it was Corvin's idea that saved the wall from the

tower and the Sul'Lenans. It was Corvin that lead the fifty men into the tower, then out the other side, almost losing his life and all of the life of his men," said Joren.

"What do you mean you saw?" asked Dolac.

"I was watching from the wall of Kor'Mor. I have a viewing glass that helps to see further than the eye can see," replied the Colonel.

"Then you saw the Sergeant here only just made it, and it took a few squads to get into the thick of it to protect his back as his men made the escape," said Noro.

"Yes, I saw that. I also saw this young man standing alone against the last of them, ready to throw his life away. It was reckless, and we will not even talk about how it is our rule of engagements NOT to get down off the wall," responded the Colonel with both admiration and disdain.

"Well, your fat arsehole of a Captain did not tell us that, he did not tell us a lot of things," responded Corvin, with an edge of attitude.

"You will watch your language when speaking of an officer! Show some respect!" demanded the Colonel.

"Respect is earned Colonel, not given," said Corvin.

Corvin was ready to knock this Colonel on his arse, when Emric laid his hand on the shoulder of Corvin.

The Colonel was used to mercenaries, but not used to being talked to this way.

"I will start an investigation and will have to talk to everyone involved," said the Colonel.

"Yeah, you do that. The Bloodchildren have the full support of the Sea Wolves. Considering we had to endanger ourselves to help out," said Noro.

"What does that mean?" asked the Colonel.

"It means that unless you get to the bottom of it, and do something about Captain Tulnor, the Bloodchildren will be leaving, and the Sea Wolves will be coming with us," said Captain Joren.

"You would damage your name if you left, who would hire mercenaries' companies that did not complete their contracts," offered the Colonel.

"You have that backwards. What companies would ever work for Kor'Lena again if word gets around that your officers recklessly feed the mercenaries to the enemy," replied Noro.

The Colonel knew he was correct, but was still furious. He knew this conversation was going nowhere.

"Your men will not be needed on the wall for the next three days. Take some rest and tend to your wounded," said the Colonel.

"Not needed?" questioned Joren.

"We had some reinforcements arrive last night, so I brought fifteen hundred infantry with me. They will man the wall over the next few days to give you all some rest," informed the Colonel.

"Good," said Noro. "I need a drink."

"As you were," said the Colonel, and then he turned and left, walking out of the tent and leaving the four of them standing alone.

Corvin held out his arm to Noro. Noro took it and they shook in the warrior fashion, hand to elbow.

"Thank you, Captain. You saved my arse and the collective arse of my men," said Corvin.

"No need to thank me, lad. Us mercenaries need to stick together and watching you on the ground, it was impressive," said Noro.

Corvin smiled.

"Your Captain is right, you and your men are crazy. Will you tell me what the hell is with everyone chanting Snow

Weasel?" asked Noro.

Corvin laughed. Dolac also wanted to know, Captain Joren already had a pretty good idea.

"When I was getting ready to fight in the slave pits, a mentor…" Corvin said, then paused.

He smiled as he recalled the conversation with the Smith, before he continued.

"My mentor was trying to work on my fighting style. He suggested I be like the Snow Weasel. Have you seen a Snow Weasel?" asked Corvin.

"Yes, vicious little bastards. I have seen them take down a goat. They latch on and don't let go," said Noro.

"Exactly. My mentor used it as an example how to focus my anger. It was starting to be used as chant when we were escaping. It grew from there, then the men start using it in battle," said Corvin.

"Escape? Slave pits?" asked Noro.

"It is a long story, Noro," said Joren.

"It's one I want to hear. I need to see to my men. Since we are not on the wall, I suggest you join the Sea Wolves for a few drinks tonight. I want to hear this story," said Noro

"Deal," said Joren

"Yes. I need to see to my men and we have the dead to talk of," said Corvin.

"I certainly could use a drink. You have drink with you, Captain Noro?" asked Dolac.

Captain Noro smiled.

"Of course, I have drink. We brought three wagons of Firemer!"

They all smiled.

"Did you not bring any drink?" said Noro.

"No," Joren smiled back.

"You bastards are mad," laughed Noro, as he left the tent.

Dolac, Corvin and Captain Joren were left behind laughing.

"See to your men, Corvin. As I said… trust in me and calm your men down. We will join you after dinner, then go and have some drinks with the Sea Wolves. I hope your head can handle the drink, because the Sea Wolves drink better than they fight," said Joren with a smile.

"I will, Captain and thank you."

Corvin left the tent and headed straight to his men. He found his men sitting on the ground. Dinner was not far away and the sun was just starting to set. All of his men had taken cuts and tomorrow when the sun comes up, all of them would be covered in bruises. Corvin knew it could have gone a lot worse and was grateful the Third Section was not wiped out. He reached a small area by the cliff face beside the tents where a fire was being lit. Lorka, Jorga, Irikson, Torin and Yelix were talking. As Corvin walked towards them, the men of his section and men from other sections banged their fists on their chests and nodded. Corvin nodded back. He knew his men had started to become more popular and accepted by more and more of the Bloodchildren. This show of respect and popularity would take some getting used to.

He arrived at the fire of his friends. One by one, they hugged him. Even Yelix, not wanting to be left out wrapped his arms around him and gave him a hug.

"You are one crazy bastard, Sergeant," said Yelix proudly.

They all smiled.

"Well, let's hope we do not have to try something like that again," said Corvin.

"You have been with the Captain?" asked Lorka.

"Yes," said Corvin.

"When are we leaving then? Or are we allowed to kill that fat bastard?" said Irikson.

Corvin had just seen them smile at his arrival, now he could see the pure look of hate on all of them.

"What do you know?" said Corvin.

They all took turns at talking, sharing their knowledge and gossip about the situation. They knew it all then and there were a few things Corvin would fill them in on. Corvin always told his corporals everything. It was a part of the brotherhood of being a former slave. He did not believe in hiding information from his brothers.

"So, you all know then," said Corvin

"The whole bloody camp knows, Corvin," confirmed Torin.

Corvin smiled, it was the first time he had addressed Corvin by his name and not rank. Corvin had told him time and time again, that when they are in these informal situations, to leave rank out of it.

"Yes, I am sure the whole camp knows," said Corvin.

"We are being watched constantly. There is fifty Infrantry men standing idly just out of sight at the bottom of the stairs leading to the wall. There is another hundred around the tent of that fat bastard. How they can afford to take men off the wall like that, I don't know," said Jorga.

"Yes, I saw the men. They are here to stop us doing something about Captain Tulnor," responded Corvin.

Before Corvin filled them in on what had been said in the tent with Captain Joren, there was more pressing information to be talked of.

"Who did we lose?" asked Corvin.

"Many but could have been a lot worse. We got very lucky," said Yelix.

"We lost enough," said Irikson.

'Who?" Corvin asked, even though he really did not want to know.

"Seventh Squad lost Morg and Jamonth. Eighth Squad Moren and Selix. Ninth Squad Liok and Jamik," said Jorga.

"One from Fourth Squad, three from Fifth Squad, including Corporal Seakor," said Yelix.

"Eleven in total. As it has been said, could have been a lot worse," said Jorga.

Corvin was silent. He wanted to lose no one under him. Even though he was now close to all of the Irik men, it was the loss of his brother slaves that hurt the most. Liok, Jamik and Pula were three former slaves that had made it out of Hura. Corvin looked at Irikson. No wonder he was so quiet. Pula was his drinking buddy, and after Corvin, his best friend. He knew the silence would not last long. Very soon, the rage would take over and Irikson would go looking for someone to kill.

Corvin filled them in on all that had been said in the tent with the Captain, including the meeting with the Colonel. No one said anything, they digested the information. Finally, it was Yelix that broke the silence.

"Thank you for letting me know. I'll keep the information to myself."

"No, brother. The Third Section does not work that way. You share the information with as many people as you can," said Torin.

Jorga, Lorka and Corvin nodded.

"We do not hide information from each other. We share all," said Jorga.

"We certainly owe Captain Noro. He saved our arse and by the sounds of it, did it twice by getting the Colonel involved," said Irikson.

"Yes. He certainly fights well. It was good to see him on the ground with his men. That weapon of his certainly makes a mess," said Lorka.

Corvin thought back to the fight and nodded. Noro favoured a weapon Corvin had never seen before. He would have to ask him about it.

"Injuries?" asked Corvin.

"Luckily, nothing serious," said Torin.

"Yes. Many cuts and scrapes and I am sure a lot of us will be black with bruises tomorrow, but the men just need rest. Your wound, Corvin?" asked Jorga.

"Was not deep. It was cleaned and has been stitched," said Corvin.

"So, what now? What are we going to do to that fat Captain?" asked Irikson.

"Nothing is going to be done. The Captain has said he will deal with it," said Corvin.

"You believe him?" asked Yelix.

"His words were 'you have been loyal to the company and proven yourselves. Let the company repay that loyalty and trust me'," said Corvin.

"You trust him?" asked Jorga.

"Yes. I saw in him something I have never seen since we first joined the company," said Corvin.

"What was that?" spat out Irikson.

"I saw anger in his eyes," said Corvin.

They all looked at him.

"I have heard the stories. Captain Joren used to be quite the hot head when he was younger. He was always fighting duels. When he was made Captain, he slowly started to calm down, but from what the stories say, he was quite vicious when he was younger," said Yelix.

"Hard to see or believe," said Lorka.

"Yes, but trust me on this brothers, if the Captain has said to trust him, then trust him," said Yelix.

Corvin saw the conviction in his face and how he said it. He nodded.

"Then trust him we will. Besides, there is more important things to do right now," said Corvin.

"Like what?" asked Irikson.

"We need to eat, then the entire Company has been invited to share drinks with the Sea Wolves," said Corvin.

This brought a small smile to all of their faces, except Irikson. He had lost his drinking companion and Corvin would have to keep an eye on him.

"Best get to it then," said Lorka.

The night had gone well. The tension of the day slowly leaving everyone as they consumed Firemer. Corvin had told the Third Section to spread themselves out amongst the Sea Wolves and have fun. He knew it would be hard to have fun with over five hundred Kor'Lena Infrantry watching them. They were not obvious, but it was clear to see that they had been spread out in certain places, in case the mercenaries decided to take action. The Fire Hawks were invited to share the cup, but since they did not speak the same language, they were nowhere to be seen.

The entire Bloodchildren company spread themselves out and enjoyed the night. In the early evening, Corvin had found himself with Captain Noro, Captain Joren, Sergeant Dolac, Sergeant Emric and all of the senior men from the Sea Wolves. He knew Noro would want to hear all the stories of the former slaves, so he brought Irikson and Lorka with him. Jorga and Torin were off with Yelix somewhere. Lorka being the storyteller, told the entire story of their escape, including some of the life they had when slaves. He told of the death bouts they all faced, the Trainer and the Smith. All of the Sea Wolves were amazed and listened intently. No one interrupted Lorka as he was speaking.

Corvin was amazed at his friend. He was called Funny-boy in the slave camps as he was always quick with a joke. But tonight, his story telling ability shone through and was amazing to hear. He added in funny tales where needed. He did not shy away from the tragic tales either. Once Lorka was done, the men surrounding the former slaves nodded their appreciation.

"A wondrous story, Lorka. No wonder the Demon-child here fights so well," said Captain Noro.

Irikson looked at Corvin. Not many people could get away with calling Corvin that; the name he had been given by the Outlander bastards, but Corvin was smiling. Captain Noro had such an easy way about him, it was easy for him to get away with what other men could not.

"Irikson, how many death bouts did you have?" asked Noro.

"Don't recall. It blurred into one beating," said Irikson with a smile.

Lies of course, Irikson knew exactly how many death bouts he'd had, but there were some details even the former slaves would not share.

"I think his biggest fight was actually amongst the cabbages, was it not Lorka?" said Corvin.

Diverting the question neatly.

"You bastard. Who asked you, Sergeant?" said Irikson.

Lorka and Corvin laughed.

"Cabbages?" asked Dolac.

Lorka launched into the tale once again of Irikson and the

cook. At the end, as usual, all the gathered men were laughing hard; even Irikson was smiling.

"I should have said yes, but I don't always follow where the Demon-Child leads," said Irikson, with a wink in Corvin's direction.

The men laughed harder, as did Corvin.

"Almost as good a story as Dolac and the baker," said Captain Joren.

Everyone looked at Dolac who was smiling. He launched into his tale.

"I meet a lovely Coin-Wife one night. She was special. Naturally, I went home with her. After a night of fun, I was lying in bed when her husband came home," said Dolac.

Everyone listened.

"And?" said Emric

"He had a sword in hand, and I was very drunk, so I jumped out the window and took off down the street," said Dolac shaking his head.

The men giggled

"Yeah, but he caught you, the husband, didn't he?" said Emric.

"Yes. I was running down the street with my trousers down my ankles, I was struggling to pull them up. He must have jumped out the ground floor window as well because he caught up with me. Bastard baker!" said Dolac.

"You fought?" asked Captain Noro.

"Not quite," laughed Joren

"Before I knew he was there, he stabbed the sword into my arse," said Dolac.

The men erupted in laughter.

"The city guard thankfully pulled the baker off our friend here, who was so drunk, I am surprised he managed to run, let alone spend time with the baker's wife," said Emric.

"That caused me problems," said Joren.

Captain Noro was wiping away the tears from his eyes.

"Problems?" asked Noro.

"He was the only baker in town. For three years, I had to ship in bread from the Capital of Iriksec," said the Captain.

The men all laughed again.

'Well, it could have been worse. At least now, you have a scar on your face to match the one on your arse," said Joren.

All the men looked at Dolac.

He smiled, stood up and turned his back to the men. Then dropped his trousers and showed everyone the scar that was jiggered and in the centre of his butt cheek.

The men erupted in laughter again. Lorka was laughing so hard, he fell of the pack sack he was sitting on.

Corvin laughed along with everyone as Dolac adjusted himself and sat back down.

"He was off duty for two months. The wound got infected," said Joren.

"Bastard baker," said Dolac.

The men laughed again.

The night continued with all the men drinking far too much. Corvin eventually found himself sitting next to Dolac, chatting away and swapping stories. Eventually, it was all of the Third Section Corporals. Corporal Geren of Second Squad and Corporal Yelix of Fourth Squad. Lorka had left with Captain Noro. Noro wanted Lorka to share the stories with his men.

"Thank you, Sergeant Dolac, for what you did today," said Irikson.

Corvin was surprised. He knew his corporals all viewed Sargeant Dolac in a different way now. One night of drinking and one battle would not completely fix the ill feeling between the two groups, but it was a start. However, the surprise was that it was Irikson that thanked him.

"I had to. Who else in the company can I pick on if the Third Section is wiped out?," said Dolac.

Irikson lifted his head and looked at him, intensely. Then a smile creeped over his face before he started laughing. The rest of the men joined in.

Dolac looked at Corvin and winked. Corvin laughed as well.

"Very true," said Jorga.

"Also, if we got wiped out, the First Section would no longer have someone to show them the high standard of the Bloodchildren," said Jorga with a straight face.

Dolac laughed again.

"Agreed. Stick with us and we will teach you and show you how to protect your arse from being stabbed," said Corvin.

The men laughed again.

At the changing of the wall guard at midnight, the men called it a night. All the Bloodchildren returned to their tents as did most of the Sea Wolves. Some of them still continued to drink. Corvin and Dolac slowly walked back to their tents, with Irikson on the other side of Dolac.

"Trust in the Captain?" asked Corvin.

Even though the night had been an enjoyable one, Corvin still had the troubles in the back of his mind.

"Yes Corvin. Trust him," confirmed Dolac.

"What is he planning, Sergeant?" asked Irik.

"Buggered if I know," said Dolac.

"We will have to wait until the investigation is finished by the Colonel. Who knows when that will be complete," said Corvin.

"Yes. We need to wait. Trust in the Captain," repeated Dolac, as he moved off to his tent.

Irikson echoed his words.

"Trust in the Captain," repeated Corvin to himself.

They did not have to wait long. The morning horn was sounded just after sunrise. Many men with sore heads rose from their beds. It was an overcast day and Corvin hoped it would not mean rain. He made his way to the Captain's tent. Eager to find out what was happening.

He had arrived at his tent and found the Captain talking to a runner from the Colonel. He stood back until the runner had left before approaching.

"Captain," said Corvin.

"Corvin. How's the head?" said the Captain.

"Fine, sir."

"Good. I have just heard from the Colonel. Apparently, he has finished his investigation and all the senior men are to meet in Captain Tulnor's tent at midday. No weapons allowed and the tent will be surrounded by Kor'Lena Infantry," said Joren.

"No weapons? Sounds like a trap," replied Corvin.

"On the surface it does, but the Colonel would not risk taking us. Mercenaries are in need."

"Okay. Did the runner give anything away?"

"No."

Okay. If you have no problem, I want to get the Third Section on a light run to stretch after yesterday," said Corvin.

"That will piss the men off," said Joren.

"Don't care. The men will be full of bruises and be sore, a light run is needed to stretch the body and focus them," said Corvin.

At that moment, Dolac arrived.

"Morning Captain, Corvin."

Captain Joren filled him in on what was happening.

"Okay. What are we doing until then?" asked Dolac.

"Relax, get breakfast and wait," said the Captain.

"I'm taking the Third Section on a light run; your section is welcome to join," suggest Corvin.

"My head is too bloody sore to do anything this morning, but it would be good for the men. I'll tell my corporals to report to you shortly," said Dolac.

"Also, once we have dealt with the Colonel, we will need to meet to discuss the shuffling of men. Although we were very lucky, we still have holes in the squads," said the Captain.

Dolac and Corvin nodded.

"I'll get the men out on a run. See you at midday," said Corvin.

Midday arrived and everyone of rank from Sergeant and higher had assembled in the meeting tent of Captain Tulnor. More seats had been placed and everyone was told to sit down. The table had increased in size over night. The difference from the first meeting was that all of the mercenary captains and sergeants were seated down the left side of the table, all of the Kor'Lenan men down the right side of the table. At the head of the table was the Colonel and his scribe. At the door stopping people from leaving, two Kor'Lenan Infrantry. The largest Kor'Lenans Corvin had seen. Slightly taller than himself and by the look of it, well-muscled. Of course, the tent was surrounded by the Colonel's guard. It was clear no one was coming in or out until the Colonel wanted them to.

At the top of the left side of the table was Captain Joren. Then Emric, Dolac and Corvin. Beside Corvin was Captain Noro followed by three of his Sergeants. After that, Captain Janoor and one of his sergeants. The opposite side of the table at the top was Captain Tulnor, then four of his sergeants, then five sergeants that were under the Colonel.

The Colonel spoke, "Accusations have been made by the Bloodchildren concerning the actions of Captain Tulnor. The accusations have been backed up by Captain Noro of the Sea Wolves."

Corvin noticed that the Fire Hawks had not been mentioned.

"Captain Tulnor has, of course, denied the accusations along with all of his men. Captain Janoor of the Fire Hawks has remained neutral and says he does not know enough of what happened," said the Colonel.

Captain Noro looked at Captain Janoor. Janoor just stared back saying nothing.

"This had to be investigated. We cannot be fighting each other when the Sul'Lenans are at our doorstep," said the Colonel.

All was silent as the Colonel's scribe wrote down what was being said.

"My investigation is complete. The Bloodchildren are correct, Captain Tulnor did act in a manner we would not expect our officers to act. Now we need to discuss how we move forward," said the Colonel.

That was quick. Corvin was expecting this to be drawn out.

"How we move forward?" asked Joren in a shocked voice.

"Yes, how we move forward and continue to fight this war," said the Colonel.

"And Captain Tulnor? He stays in charge of us? When we no longer trust him?" said Noro.

"Yes. Our laws here are clear. Unless he has recklessly endangered the lives of Kor'Lenans or committed treason or mutiny, he cannot be removed," said the Colonel.

Corvin looked at Tulnor. He was smiling. Corvin could feel his rage rising.

"I have the authority, so I am offering the Bloodchildren and the Sea Wolves an extra hundred gold coins each for the loss of their men, payable at the end of their contract," said the Colonel.

It was slap in the face and everyone knew it. Corvin looked across at his Captain, his face was like a dark storm rolling in. It was about to be unleashed.

"Not good enough," said the Captain, between clenched teeth.

Dolac was smiling, as was Emric. They knew the Captain was not about to accept this.

"Well, what more can we offer?" asked the Colonel.

"What are the laws surrounding duels in this country of yours? A country that hires mercenary companies, then betrays them?" said the Captain.

The insult was not lost on the men.

'Careful, Captain," said Tulnor.

Corvin smiled. Please Captain, he thought to himself, do not be careful.

"The law on duels is clear. Any man of equal rank may duel to first blood if honour has been questioned," said the Colonel.

Equal rank. Corvin's heart sank.

"Honour has indeed been questioned," said Noro.

"Equal rank Captain. Even if you promoted Sergeant Corvin to Captain, it would not be recognised by us as he has not held the rank for long.

"I was not thinking of promoting him. Even if he were a Captain, he would forget first blood and cut your throat, Captain Tulnor," said Joren.

The tension, which was high when they arrived, was now very thick in the tent. Everyone could feel it and it felt that fighting could erupt any moment.

"Then what are you thinking, Captain Joren?"

Joren stood with all eyes on him.

"Captain Tulnor. You are gutless and have no honour, I challenge you to a duel," said Joren.

There were many gasps in the tent. Corvin was shocked. Emric and Dolac smiled and were nodding their heads. Even Noro was surprised, but a smile quickly formed on his face. Janoor of the Fire Hawks nodded to himself. All of the others down the opposite side of the table just stared at Joren.

"Captain Tulnor?" asked the Colonel.

Captain Tulnor stood and looked at Joren.

"I will duel with you once certain conditions are met," said Tulnor.

"Those are?" asked the Colonel.

"If I win, the Bloodchildren fight under me for the rest of the war and do not receive their bonus," said Tulnor.

Corvin wanted to tell the Captain not to take it. He knew the Bloodchildren would once again be fed to the enemy if Tulnor won. They would not last long. Corvin knew this, in fact everyone in the tent knew this.

"Agreed. If I win, Captain Tulnor resigns from his role as Captain and leaves military life behind. The Colonel then appoints someone else to be in charge of this end of the wall," said Joren.

Everyone was silent as they waited for Tulnor to reply.

"Agreed," said Tulnor.

The Colonel sighed.

"The duel will take place tomorrow morning after dawn. We will journey from the camp and have it away from the men," said the Colonel.

"No. We have it here in the camp. Everyone saw the start of this and deserve to see the end of it," said Noro.

"Agreed," said Captain Janoor, speaking for the first time.

"We have it today. I have much work to reorganise my squads and have rite for the dead to be organised," said Joren.

"Done," said Tulnor.

The Colonel shook his head. Duels were such a waste of talent. He knew honour was important, but still a waste.

"Alright then. I will get an area cleared and set up presently. Sergeants here, spread the word and tell the men who are not on the wall to assemble," said the Colonel.

Everyone continued to stare at the two Captains who looked at each other across the table with such hate in their eyes. Two captains that had only just met and seemed to work well together.

"Dismissed," said the Colonel.

Everyone left to get things organised.

In a very short time, a flat area across from the camp was arranged. Ropes from the wall joined together and laid in circle on the ground to mark out the area and hold back the crowd. All of the men in the camp were seated around this circle. The men at the very back stood to get a better view. There was just over a thousand men, sitting right on top of each other to witness the duel. The Colonel had changed the watch with fresh men from the ones he brought with him. Five hundred stood on the wall, a lot of them turned and facing the duelling area across from the wall. The other thousand men surrounded all those watching the duel, weapons ready. The Colonel was expecting trouble, it seemed.

Emric, Dolac and Corvin spoke with the Captain as he got his body ready. He moved his arms slowly and did stretches of his own.

"You sure, sir? It is a big price to pay if you lose," said Emric.

"Very sure," said the Captain.

Corvin could hear the anger in his words and his face looked like it was ready to explode.

"It's a shame you do not have an axe, Captain. From memory, you are better with an axe than you are with a sword," said Dolac.

"True," said Joren.

Without even thinking, Corvin drew his hand axe, reversed his grip and offered it to the Captain. The Captain looked at Corvin in surprise.

"It was crafted by our mentor and father, the Smith. It is a good weapon. Myself and the Third Section would be honoured if you carried it," said Corvin.

The Captain took it, felt the weight of it and smiled.

"Thank you, Corvin," said the Captain, as he stepped into the arena.

He was loosening his shoulders and getting the feel for the axe.

"How will he do?" asked Corvin.

"Trust the Captain," said Dolac and smiled.

"Trust the Captain," said Emric with a smile.

Corvin sat down next to Lorka on the ground and waited.

He felt tension in him. It was very familiar to him. It was the same nervous tension he felt before fighting in the pits.

"He is carrying your axe?" said Lorka.

"It felt fitting," said Corvin.

"It is fitting," said Jorga from behind Corvin.

The gathered men, whether Kor'Lenans or mercenaries, knew the reason behind the duel. They knew what was at stake, gossip spreads very quickly. Most of the Kor'Lenans were backing the Captain of the Bloodchildren. They knew what Tulnor had done was not honourable and everyone in Kor'Lena from children to the old, valued honour highly. They could not voice their opinions in front of the other Kor'Lenans, as many of the men were still loyal to the Captain Tulnor; not the squad of archers that had fired the tower, however. They had already approached Corvin and apologised. They did not want to do it but had to follow their orders. Corvin and his corporals had appreciated the effort and thanked them, explaining it was not their fault. These archers where firmly behind the Bloodchildren's Captain.

Fat Tulnor entered the arena. He, as the rules stated, was not wearing armour. Tunic, trousers and boots is all that was allowed. Without the armour, his size was there for all to see. Yes, he has a fat, but the rest of him was large muscle. His shoulders, his arms and judging by the tight-fitting trousers he now wore, so was his legs. He swung his sword.

"A longsword? For a duel," said Irikson.

"Trust in the Captain," said Corvin.

The Captain stood in his blood red sleeveless undershirt and his black trousers. His arms showing many scars from years of fighting. His long chestnut hair with many streaks of grey, tied at the nape of his neck. The Captain looked very fit still, and Corvin was impressed with the way he swung the axe.

"Yes, trust in the Captain," said Corvin again.

Both Dolac and Emric heard the exchange and smiled.

The shout went out from the Colonel.

"BEGIN!"

Joren transferred the axe to his left hand, then lunged into action, crossing the small distance between himself and Tulnor. Tulnor stepped to his left side and swung his great sword at Joren. Joren ducked and stepped in. He came up back handing Tulnor across the face. He then circled back around to his left and took a step back. Tulnor's face was red with fury. He stepped in and threw his shoulder into Joren, trying to use his greater weight to knock him off balance. Joren had braced himself and took the charge. He threw his head forward and butted Tulnor full in the face. Tulnor's nose exploded with blood.

Those watching stayed quiet. Corvin was on edge. His Captain moved well, very well and it was clear he was a brawler, like most mercenaries were. Years of experience teaching him the fastest and most effective way to lash out. No finesse or style, just a quick way to deliver pain. Dolac was smiling along with Emric. They were among the few here that had seen the Captain in action. They knew what was coming.

"Looks like our old Captain is back," said Dolac.

Corvin heard Dolac but said nothing, too intent in watching the duel. Tulnor had moved better than was expected. He was able to move his weight faster than could be expected.

Tulnor stepped back, blood running down his face.

"We are just getting started, you fat bastard!" said Joren.

Tulnor did not even wipe the blood from his face. He swung his great sword up, trying to get between the legs of Joren. Joren stepped back and knocked the sword away with the axe in his left hand. The duel was a brawl and the Colonel wondered if Tulnor would risk his own life by killing Joren. That last move was a killing stroke.

The great sword came back, this time aiming for the gut of Joren. Joren was about to block when the swing was stopped. Very quickly, Tulnor stopped the swing, pulled the sword back and stabbed straight. Corvin was impressed. A sword that large was hard to stop and change direction, it showed how much muscle Tulnor had in his upper body. The blade slid past Joren's side and he had leaned away from it. He clamped his left arm to his side, trapping the sword. He swung a fast right hook that connected with the side of Tulnor's head. Tulnor was groggy and tried to draw his sword across the side of the ribs of Joren, but Joren slapped the blade away with his axe and stepped back. Tulnor followed quickly with the hilt of his sword, aiming for the nose of Joren. Joren stepped to the right and brought his knee up into the groin of Tulnor. Tulnor dropped to the ground. Joren stepped back. The Bloodchildren cheered the move. Tulnor slowly got to his feet.

"One more time, you honourless scumbag," said Joren between his clenched teeth

The Colonel watched. Joren was making a mockery of Tulnor, clearly just playing with him. Tulnor was good with that great sword of his, but he was not used to the unorthodox street brawling moves of Joren. Tulnor screamed and charged. Joren was waiting for this move and had planned for it. He threw himself forward. Tulnor aimed his sword directly at Joren's head. Joren's head, however, was not there when they reached each other. Joren had dived, his right foot shooting out to connect with the left knee of Tulnor. His head and body had gone under the sword of Tulnor, and Joren had hit the ground hard. Everyone heard the crack of Tulnor's knee as the foot connected. Tulnor fell to the ground as Joren rolled away and got to his feet. Tulnor was screaming, a scream that went through all the assembled men's bodies and made them cringe. The Colonel stepped forward to stop it.

"First blood you said, Colonel" shouted Captain Noro.

The Colonel stopped in his tracks. Joren walked forward and slashed down, his axe slicing through the cheek of Tulnor, opening a wound identical to Dolac's.

"First blood is mine," said Joren.

Corvin felt instant relief. A small smile formed on his face. He started a chant that was taken up by the former pit-rats, then by the Bloodchildren.

"Snow Weasel! Snow Weasel! Snow Weasel"

The chant was loud and reached those standing on the wall watching. The Colonel yelled for orderlies to come. He waved to the men to quieten the chant. The Bloodchildren kept going. They answered to their Captain. Joren smiled, then waved his own hands to quieten them. The chant stopped instantly.

"I declare first blood to Captain Joren. Honour has been satisfied. Captain Tulnor will resign from his position and leave this place as soon as he is able," he said in a clear voice that carried to everyone.

"Not too long, I hope," said Joren.

"CORVIN," yelled Joren.

Corvin stood up and took a step forward. Joren cleaned the blood from the axe on Tulnor's tunic. He called out.

"SILVER DEATH!"

He then reached back, and his arm shot forward, launching the axe through the air.

Even though Corvin was across the other side of the quickly assembled arena, a distance of fifteen lai, Joren threw the hand axe at Corvin. It sailed end over end as it flew through the air. Corvin smiled. He moved his head to the left and brought his right hand up quickly and caught the axe mid-flight. He sheathed the axe and stood there with a smile. The assembled mercenaries cheered and roared.

The Colonel went with the orderlies as they carried Tulnor on a stretcher towards his tent. Corvin, Dolac and Emric approached the Captain. They reached him and Emric threw him a waterskin, which he took and drained.

"A good axe, Corvin. Thank you," smiled the Captain.

"Silver Death?" asked Corvin.

"Good axe like that needs a name. Trust me, Corvin?" said the Captain.

"Always, sir."

Chapter Eleven

The spring had gone fast for all of the men defending the wall. The attacks had increased to the point where they were getting attacks most days now. The Sul'Lenans sending wave after wave of men to die on the Dark Wall. Thousands and thousands of lives wasted on both sides of the wall, the larger number coming from the invaders. Yet, summer had arrived, and the Dark Wall still held. They had not seen another tower come their way yet, but news from further down the wall was that the towers had indeed been reaching the walls. The Colonel had passed on Corvin's idea of how to deal with them, and the Kor'Lenans were using the plan to great success. Of course, the idea had been Irikson's, but Corvin got tired of trying to convince the men around him of this.

The Bloodchildren, although the smallest of the forces holding the wall, killed more than their fair share of Sul'Lenans. They had earned a reputation for fierceness, hard fighting and being relentless. No enemy gained the wall where they held it. Captain Joren was pleased with his company and very happy that so far, the company had not lost further lives.

The name of the Bloodchildren was now spoken with extreme respect. The former pit-rats building on their reputation as truly great fighters. After the duel, Captain Joren also found himself now looked at very differently, a respect that was not there before. Sure, he was looked upon and respected before the duel, but now it was a respect of thanks, a respect of slight fear. Not only was he a mercenary Captain, but now like his men, he was not to be messed with.

The Colonel, before he left, had promoted one of his own Sergeants to Captain and left him in charge of their end of the wall. Captain Brenik was the complete opposite of the Captain Tulnor. He was in better shape physically and more quietly spoken. He was shorter than Corvin and from a distance, looked skeleton thin. On closer inspection Brenik had good muscle on his arms and shoulders, but compared to Tulnor, he was skeleton thin. The first time Corvin meet him in a meeting, he watched him for the duration, coming to the conclusion towards the end that he was a better choice. Captain Brenik listened to anyone that could add their ideas to a problem. Once he had heard from all those who wanted to speak, he would suggest the best way forward by cutting directly to the heart of the problem and choosing a solution. He treated all those around him with respect and only once spoke of the previous problems with Tulnor, in their very first meeting he mentioned what had happened.

"Now that we have sorted our problems, I am sure we will work well together, and I can personally guarantee that no lives will be thrown away," said Captain Brenik.

All those gathered had nodded their heads and got straight down to business. Before the Colonel had left to go back to the city of Kor'Mor, he had pulled Corvin aside in a private meeting.

"I could not say before I had other things to deal with, but a brilliant effort in getting that tower taken and getting your men back to the wall. I know you lost men and I am sorry," said Colonel.

"Thank you, Colonel," was all Corvin said.

"Remember that I watched from Kor'Mor, you fought amazingly as did your men. Those of my men around me that could see, you have inspired them by what you have achieved, Sergeant. The feeling on the wall among my men is now of hope. They have seen what fifty men can achieve and it has given them heart," praised the Colonel.

Corvin had been taken aback by the comments.

"Thank you, Colonel. I was just trying to get the tower destroyed, then when things fell apart, I had to get my men back to safety," said Corvin.

The Colonel smiled.

"Well, Corvin, you impressed the hell of me, my men and anyone else that hears the story. So much in fact that I am offering a favour to you," said the Colonel.

"A favour, sir?"

"Yes. If there is anything I can do for you, let me know. I think with the problems you faced, a favour is the least I can offer you," said the Colonel.

Corvin thought about it. There was nothing he needed but he knew the men under him and quickly came up with an idea. He smiled.

"One thing, sir."

"Yes?" asked the Colonel.

"The first day of summer is coming."

"Yes, it is not far away," said the Colonel.

"As you know a lot of my men, like myself, are former slaves. During our early life, we never knew when our birthday was. Because of this, we all celebrate it on the first day of summer. I ask that we are given the day off and the day after so we can do this," asked Corvin.

A smile slowly built on the weathered face of the Colonel.

"Done. Not only will you have those two days off, but I'll provide you and your men with a healthy supply of Volic, the spirit we drink here," said the Colonel.

Corvin smiled.

"That will make the men very happy, sir. Thank you," said Corvin.

"I'll send a supply down closer to the time and I will also mention it in my next message to Captain Brenik," said the Colonel.

The Colonel left and Corvin got on with reorganising the new squads with Dolac, Emric and Captain Joren.

"How did you want to do this?" Dolac asked the Captain.

"Carefully. I am sure Corvin here does not want to upset the balance," said the Captain.

"I have some ideas for the Third Section, Captain," said Corvin.

"Oh, I am sure you do lad!" laughed Emric.

They all smiled.

"Go ahead, Corvin," said the Captain.

"I wanted to reduce my section down to two squads. The squads would have eleven men each instead of ten. This would make sense to me. I would give Torin Seventh Squad and Jorga would keep Eighth Squad. I would use what's left of the Ninth squad to fill out Seventh and Eighth Squads," said Corvin.

"Interesting," said Emric.

"Yes, but your numbers are wrong. You would be left with one man left over," said the Captain.

"Yes. I would use Irikson as sort of an aide. He would be by my side, running orders and jumping in where needed. He lost one of his best friends during the tower attack and I want him close to me," said Corvin.

"Done," said the Captain.

"For myself, I will run Fourth and Sixth Squad with one less man, so two squads of nine men. However, Fifth Squad lost three men, one of them a corporal. Unfortunately, I have no one I would look at promoting within my section. Any ideas?" said Emric.

"I do. Even though I will miss him, I can give you Corporal Geren. He trained under you and I am sure he would not say no to coming back. I will also run one of my squads at nine men and send someone over with Corporal Geren. I'll let him decide," said Dolac.

"That's sorted then. I do not like having squads at less than full strength but there is nothing we can do about that. You had just make sure you come up with no more crazy ideas, Corvin," motioned the Captain.

The men smiled.

"I best go make these changes then," Corvin responded.

The changes had been fine and the men of the Third Section had accepted them. Even Irikson had not been unhappy. Corvin explained he was still a corporal, but just currently had no men. Corvin had expected anger or resistance but Irikson just accepted it and moved on. Which was a concern in itself, Irikson wore his heart on his sleeve and always had something to say. After the Colonel had left, the Bloodchildren had held a small death rite for the men they had lost. The job of getting the bodies from below the wall had been difficult, but the new Captain had let them do it.

Small teams climbed down ropes and tied the bodies to spare ropes, then the dead Bloodchildren were hauled up. Once all the bodies had been raised, they were taken to the fields. The armour was stripped off and what weapons left, a few had been taken by the Sul'Lenans. The bodies were burned, which was the mercenary way. Corvin had spoken briefly thanking his fallen brothers and telling them he would see them after.

With the more regular attacks on the wall, the Bloodchildren were seeing more action. Fortunately, the Colonel had left more men to reinforce the position. There was now over fifteen hundred men on this stretch of wall. The Sea Wolves were down to one hundred and eighty men, the Fire Hawks down to four hundred and sixty. The Bloodchildren now ran with eighty-nine men and of course, the Colonel had left another five hundred infantry. With the number in men rising meant that everyone got more time away from the wall to rest.

The Bloodchildren, even though they were the smallest force, handled their share of the workload in defending the wall. Although, as the Captain had said, defending the wall was easy, it still took its toll and the men under Corvin started picking up small injuries from the constant fighting. Many men had sprains, with a few having broken bones. Of course, these men were removed from the wall and given time to heal. The new Captain had added a new idea and three hundred men now stood at the bottom of the wall as a reserve force, ready to rush in if they were needed. So far, they had not been used and it was considered an easy task.

The fitness to defend the wall was also different. It was clear to see that the Bloodchildren were the fittest men at this part of the wall, but they still suffered. Corvin and Jorga had spoken of it. The Third Section of the Bloodchildren, especially the former slaves, were beyond fit. Their endurance was better than anyone's, but after the constant attacks, they themselves were empty. No energy, no strength left, no nothing.

"I don't understand it, brother," said Corvin.

"Understand?" asked Jorga.

"Because of our previous life, we are generally fitter and stronger than anyone here. I do not speak from over confidence. We are some of the best here. Yet, when the attacks stop, I feel as weak and tired as everybody else," said Corvin.

"We are fit, brother. We are not perfect, look to the last attack," said Jorga.

The last attack had seen close to three hundred Sul'Lenans briefly gain the wall to the right near the cliff faces. The Bloodchildren, following the Third Section had charged in from their section further down the wall. With the help of the Sea Wolves, they had managed to drive them off the wall. The Kor'Lena Infrantry that had been on the wall also had fallen back, no more energy, no more desire. They were just tired bodies with no life, walking back from the attack and almost gifting the wall to the enemy.

"Yes. It was a close one," said Corvin.

"Well, our strength won the day. After a full half day of fighting without rest, we still had it in ourselves to charge in," said Jorga.

"True, but I still felt bloody buggered," said Corvin.

"Of course, we did. We had just spent the most part of a day fighting," said Jorga.

They had said nothing more, then Jorga finally spoke.

"We are very good at what we do, but we have out limits," said Jorga.

At that moment, Sergeant Emric had arrived. As was his habit, he had overheard most of the conversation.

"You have to understand, your men are extremely fit, but almost a full day fighting with no relief, is not easy. No matter how well you train. It gets to a point where it is your mind that holds you, keeps you fighting, not your body," said Emric.

"Sergeant Emric," nodded Jorga.

"Corporal," said Emric.

"It's just difficult to understand why I feel so drained," said Corvin.

"When is the last time you trained as hard as you did when you were in the pits?" asked Emric.

"The last time?" asked Corvin.

"I would say, Sergeant, it would have been when we were in the pits. No offence intended to the Bloodchildren, but the training is not as hard," answered Jorga.

"Yes," nodded Corvin.

"I know your section trains harder than any other in the company, but clearly you are not as fit as you once were. Even if you were as fit now, you would still struggle," added Emric.

"How?" asked Corvin.

"You may be a Sergeant, Corvin, but you are still young. Think about it, how long were your bouts in the pits?" asked Emric.

No one else would have the courage to ask for such details. Even though the former slaves had opened up to the rest of the company on many experiences they had, they had not revealed all. Emric, however, was the only one in the company that could ask in such a way that it was taken without insult.

"Honestly, sir? I would say no longer than sixty to one hundred heartbeats," answered Jorga.

"Exactly," said Emric.

Corvin worked his way through it and then agreed.

"We train hard," said Corvin under his breath.

"We do, brother, but not as hard as before. Then, there was always the threat of death hanging over us to train harder," said Jorga.

Emric nodded and ignored the fact Jorga had not called Corvin by his title. He gave much leeway to the former pit-rats.

"Makes sense," said Emric finally.

"Yes, it does. I am thinking we need to train harder, if we can find the energy," said Corvin.

Corvin thought through what he had just said. How would they find the time to train? Rest days were spent sleeping, eating and maybe a few stretches.

"Your section is doing amazing. Noro from the Sea Wolves has already talked about changing up his training over the off season. Do not be surprised if he comes to you with questions," said Emric.

"Thank you," said Corvin.

"Get yourselves some food, then rest. You are back on the wall tomorrow at dawn," instructed Emric.

"Yes, Sergeant," replied Corvin

The Second Sergeant made sense, however Corvin still felt they were not fit enough. A problem for another day, and a problem to think on some more.

The spring came to an end, along with the spring rains. Another thing the former slaves had to get used to, rain. They saw it, of course, during their early lives, but not as much and as often as they had in the lands of Kor'Lena. A steady rain that started and never seemed to end. Fighting in this rain was tricky, but the Irik men from their company had showed the former slaves little tricks on how to stay a little dryer and therefore more comfortable. The tricks were rubbing animal fat on their bare arms, face and any exposed skin. This obviously stunk, but the water hit the layer of fat and ran straight off their skin. They also learnt to rub the same fat onto their armour. Wet leather became heavier than normal, sucking the warmth and energy from their bodies.

The former slaves looked forward to their birthday's celebrations. Corvin had previously informed the Captain but had not told his men. He thought a surprise would keep them on their toes. The news when shared was welcomed. All of the men assembled had cheered. Dolac said he was not sure if they were cheering for extra days off or more spirit to be drunk. The Colonel had been true to his word and sent a wagon of Volic. It was a refined version of the base spirit they brewed for defence. Apparently much easier to drink and not likely to make you blind or die. As there was so much, the entire company was invited to celebrate, which of course they did. Corvin had invited Captain Noro plus a few of his sergeants and corporals as well. All the men looked forward to it.

The first day of summer arrived with much excitement. Captain Brenik was invited but declined. He said someone had to stay sober and defend the wall. Luckily that day, the Sul'Lenans choose not to attack.

The day started with a company run to keep the men sharp; even Captain Joren joined in. Once the run was completed, a light midmorning meal of porridge was had to take the edge of the men's appetites. Then around midday, they started drinking, except for the Tenth squad who were given leave to go hunting. Captain Brenik had told them of large animals called deer roamed the plains and gave them permission to go hunt a few. Irikson had gone with them.

They returned with several of these beasts and Corvin and the rest of the Bloodchildren were amazed at the size of them. Larger than a horse, with massive bones coming out of their heads. Apparently, these were call antlers. The cook had followed the hunters at a distance with the wagon. Each time beast was killed, its carcass was manhandled onto the back of the wagon. The cook could be heard saying he was interested to see how good the leather from the animal skin would be.

Whilst the Bloodchildren sat around drinking and laughing, the cook, Tenth squad and even Irikson got the deer skinned, gutted and roasting over large fire pits.

For the day, the enemy at the wall were non-existent. The men celebrating did not care. However, Captain Joren being the smart man he was, had organised another feast with more drink for two days later so the men on the walls watching or getting ready to take over the watch, also got a chance to feast and relax. Captain Brenik was impressed and made it happen. Joren and Brenik were working well together.

The celebrations had gone well. Even some of Kor'Lenans that had the day off joined in and laughed along with the stories being told. Apparently, the language of the Outlanders was easy to learn and many of the Kor'Lenans had learnt quickly. It helped when speaking the language got you invited to feasts. Many stories were shared and of course, Lorka was in full voice. The Kor'Lenans learning of the former slaves and how they escaped. Corvin found himself sharing a drink and food with the Captain.

"You and your lads are becoming quite well known," said the Captain.

"Yes, we are," said Corvin.

"You do not like the fact?" asked Dolac.

"I do not really have a choice. Lorka's stories make us sound like young gods," said Corvin.

Dolac and the Captain laughed.

"I think if I asked him to stop telling the stories, the men listening would try and kill me," said Corvin with a smile.

"He tells them well," said Emric.

"Yes, too well," said Corvin.

Long into the night, they drank. Many speeches were made after the sun had gone down; many stories shared. Corvin realised that he had drank too much. In fact, he did not think he had ever been this drunk before. He found himself and Irikson walking away from the feast with a jug of Volic in each hand. They were walking towards the only forest in this area. It was not too far away and they both walked in silence, with the occasional giggle and laugh. After a time when the moon was at its highest, they stopped at the edge of the woods.

"Shall we?" said Irikson.

"Yes, we shall," said Corvin.

Both Corvin and Irikson slowly walked into the forest. It was dark with a little mist about, hanging to the trees like it belonged there and blanketing the forest floor like a thick woollen rug. Both knew mist well, but not in summer. It was cold for a summer night but since they both grew up as slaves in the Outlands, it was warm. Before long, they were singing loudly and out of tune. Neither of them had sung before and were trying their best to sing the last song they heard around the campfire. A song the Kor'Lenans had tried to teach them. They could not remember the words but still laughed and giggled as they stumbled along a path. They both carried a jug of Volic in each hand and stopped every so often to stop singing and take a swig.

After some time, they came across a clearing and stopped. Standing on their left side of the small clearing were three men they did not know. The three men were dressed differently but you could easily see they were soldiers. They all wore dark blue tunics with chain mail shirts covering them. If they had not been so drunk, they would have taken more interest in the chain mail shirts. They had been told of them, but never seen them. The three men had their swords drawn. Opposite these men, twenty Lai from them, stood another group of men; ten in all. They all work dark cloaks with their hoods up, protecting their faces. They also had their weapons drawn. It was clear they had stumbled onto something. With a loud shout, Irikson spoke first.

"Why is your face covered? Are you that ugly?"

This set Corvin off laughing, spitting out the mouthful of Volic he had not quite swallowed. The men in the dark cloaks tensed but their leader shouted to them and they relaxed. The leader then shouted something at Corvin and Irikson, who of course had no idea what he was saying.

"What is he saying?" asked Irikson.

"No idea. Maybe he thinks we are Coin-Wives looking for work," said Corvin.

This set them both off laughing again. The leader of the cloaked men started to walk towards them. He yelled something at them, waving his sword.

"Now what the fuck is he saying?" said Irikson.

"My turn," said Corvin.

"Go ahead," said Irikson.

Corvin cleared his throat and blinked to stop the world spinning. He thought of what to say in the Sul'Lena language and spoke.

"Sorry, my friend. I do not find you attractive. If you walk back to where we have come from, you will find some cows that would be more suited to you!"

The three men that had been standing there tried their hardest to hide their smiles but failed. The man in the middle of the three, slightly taller with grey in his beard, chuckled.

The dark cloaked men understood what was said this time and started walking towards them. The leader was shouting abuse of some sort and swinging his sword.

"Shit. Maybe they want to fight?" said Irikson with enthusiasm.

"Maybe," replied Corvin with a huge drunken smile.

"Ask them, just in case. I would hate to piss off the Captain," said Irikson.

"You want to fight us?" yelled Corvin with a grin.

Irikson was also grinning. The dark cloaked leader was shouting abuse now and walking fast. He was within ten Lai when Corvin looked across at the three men. The taller, older one in the middle nodded a yes, then nodded in the direction of the dark cloaks. Corvin knew instantly and carefully put both his jugs down, then drew his weapons. Irikson with a small laugh, set down his jugs and drew his weapons as well.

"Since you got first go at the Sul'Lena that climbed over the wall yesterday, can I have this bastard?" said Irikson.

"Certainly, brother!" said Corvin with a giggle.

"Thank you," said Irikson.

Irikson sprinted forward, exploding from standstill to movement so quickly, the three men could not believe their eyes. Irikson was at full stride and singing as he reached the dark cloaked leader. The leader swung his long sword at Irikson's head.

"*The lady did not know me, and she was not free,*" Irikson sang as he ducked the longsword and stepped behind the leader.

"*I had coins to pay her, so she called me a sir.*" Irikson sliced the leader across the arse with his axe, the leader of the dark cloaked men yelling with pain and fury.

Corvin laughed loudly and also exploded into action, heading for the oncoming dark cloaked men who had broken into a charge.

"I undid my trouser and let them fall, she then saw the boil on my balls," Irikson continued to sing as he ducked a backhand swipe.

Quicker than the three men thought possible, Irikson exploded into action once again. Slicing and cutting the leader with his axe and sword. Within a heartbeat, the leader was dropping to the ground. The three men stared at the body as it hit the ground and did not notice as Irikson had once again moved into action, following Corvin towards the other dark cloaked men. Corvin was almost at the group when he threw his arm back and then shot it forward and released his hand axe. The hand axe sailed through the air and landed squarely into one man's face. Before his body dropped, Corvin had reached him and ripped the axe out of the face. Side by side, they both charged into the group, ducking and weaving, slashing and cutting as they went through the men like a shovel through soil. The three men stood motionless watching, too stunned to join in. All they could do was watch these two men carve a path through the men that had ambushed them.

"She did not like what she saw, the boil was blue and very raw," Irikson continued to sing

as he head-butted one ambusher and shoved his sword into the man's throat, raising his axe in time to block a long sword that was aimed at his side.

He was off balance and about to step back, when he saw a blur of motion as Corvin ran past on his way to his next victim, slashing this man across the back with his own axe.

"Got to move faster than that, brother!" said Corvin as he launched himself forward into a tumbler roll.

He landed on his feet and as he rose drove his short sword into the groin of another man. As the man bent over, he finished him with his axe, the axe smashing into his jaw and up into the brain.

Irikson laughed and almost took a sword to the back, but he swung in time to catch a blade on his sword. His right hand coming around and burying his hand axe in the face of the man.

The three men watched as Corvin and Irikson, laughing and singing, wiped out the men that had ambushed them. The taller and older of the three, was very impressed. He had never seen warriors move so fast, kill so quickly. He had also never seen a warrior sing whilst he slaughtered. He looked at the men on either side of him and saw them smiling.

Irikson dispatched the last man with a sword to the chest, his short sword going all the way up to the hilt. As the body dropped, he hung onto his sword and retched it clear. He looked around and saw all the bodies. He walked all the way back to his Volic jug, picked it up and took along drink. He then walked over and offered the jug to Corvin.

"Entertaining fight. Think we will be in trouble?" said Irikson.

"No doubt," said Corvin.

They looked over and the three men they had saved were walking towards them.

"They want to fight as well, you think?" asked Irikson.

"Hope not. This drink is not sitting well in my gut after that."

"You speak the language better than me. Tell them we are not in the mood," said Irikson.

Corvin got his thoughts straight once more and as he was

wiping his blades clean on one of the bodies lying beside him, called out.

"Sorry. We do not want to play anymore," said Corvin in the language of Sul'Lena.

The three men looked shocked. Corvin and Irikson headed back the way they had come, ignoring the three men standing there with surprised looks on their face. As they reached the forest, neither of them gave the fight another thought. They were more sober now, which irritated them both. Corvin had gone to grab his jugs, picking them up, he took a swig

"Glad you did not drop those jugs, I would not want to share mine," said Irikson.

"You are a selfish bugger," said Corvin.

"True."

"Who the hell was that, sir?" asked Horen.

"Not sure. They both were speaking the language of the Outlanders, so I assume they are mercenaries from Irikson," said the Duke.

"Well sir, they certainly saved our arse!" said Horen.

"Yes. I have never seen any warrior move so fast," said Jimny.

"No. Neither have I," replied the Duke.

Keran walked to one of the bodies and flicked open the hood. He did not recognise the face so proceeded to the next body, and the next, until all the bodies had been rolled over and their faces exposed.

"I do not recognise any of these men, sir," reported Keran.

The Duke strolled over and looked at all the faces. He recognised none of them until he got to the last body.

"I recognise this one. I'm certain he was a part of a group of delegates sent to me once, but I cannot be sure," said the Duke.

"Delegates from where?" asked Horen.

"DuNoor," said the Duke.

"Well, he is the only one that would send assassins after you. Bastard of a goat!" said Keran.

"Unfortunately, we cannot pin this on him," said the Duke.

"You could return the favour, sir!" said Jimny.

"No. I do not play those games, as you well know," answered the Duke.

"We best get back to the camp, sir, to report what has happened," said Horen.

"Yes, we will. Jimny, when we get back to camp you need to go and look at the hired men. See if you can recognise the colours you saw on those two men. I want to chat with both," instructed the Duke.

"Will you be bringing a charge against them, sir?" asked Horen.

"No. I was thinking of offering them a job," said the Duke with a smile.

"I will, sir," replied Jimny.

"Good. Now let's go through the bodies and see if we can find anything that will tie them to Duke DuNoor," said the Duke.

"The assassins would not be that stupid, sir," said Horen.

"No, they would not be, but you never know," said the Duke.

As Horen and Jimny started going through the pockets of

the dead, the Duke replayed what had happened over in his mind. The two warriors were fast and deadly; he smiled.

"Yes, I should offer them work," mused the Duke as he joined in the search of the bodies.

The sun had risen and Corvin opened one eye. He was lying under a tree and could feel a body beside him. He moved his head and saw it was Irikson. His head pounded and his body ached. In fact, it ached so much, it felt as he had done hell runs the day before and not stretched. He opened his eyes wider and was rewarded with a sharp pain being his right eye. He closed his eyes and tried to blink out the pain. With his eyes shut, the world was spinning.

"What the hell is wrong with my head," groaned Corvin.

"Shut up," said Irikson.

Corvin opened his eyes again and used his hands to rub his eyes and face. As he brought his hands down, he noticed something out of place. He moved his hands up and looked again. Blood; covering his arms and hands was blood.

"Where the fuck did that come from?" questioned Corvin.

"I said be quiet," said Irikson.

"Wake and get up, now!" said Corvin.

Corvin slowly picked himself up off the ground and the world started spinning. So much, he dropped back down on the ground. He was now sitting with his back against the tree, his legs out in front of him. He looked at is legs, these too had blood splattered on them. Irikson finally sat up, rubbing his face.

"I have this bloody horrible pain, right here in my forehead," said Irikson.

He continued to rub his forehead when he noticed the blood on Corvin.

"You cut yourself?" asked Irikson.

"No. It is not mine," said Corvin.

"Not yours? We were drinking, how did you get covered in someone else's blood?" asked Irikson.

Corvin buried his head in his hands, his head throbbing painfully.

"The question brother, is why are WE covered in blood!" asked Corvin.

"We?" asked Irikson.

Irikson finally looked over himself. He was covered in blood as well. In fact, he more than Corvin.

"What the hell did we do?" asked Corvin.

Before he could answer, a voice rang out.

"Hold. Do not move you two," said a strong voice.

Corvin looked up. In a half circle around them, stood twenty men, swords all drawn watching them. Twenty Kor'Lenans looking at them, and from what Corvin could make out, concern in their eyes.

"What the hell is going on?" said Irikson trying to get to his feet.

"STAY DOWN!" shouted a voice.

Corvin looked over and saw Captain Brenik stroll forward, flanked by Captain Joren and another ten Kor'Lenans.

Corvin and Irikson stayed sitting.

"What the fuck have we done?" asked Corvin.

"I think we are about to find out," said Irikson.

Chapter Twelve

"Unbuckle your weapons and throw them in front of you," said Captain Joren.

The Captain's face looked like thunder. Corvin looked at him, not knowing what was going on.

"What is going on, Captain?" asked Corvin.

"I have given you an order. I will not repeat myself," said Joren.

Irikson and Corvin undid their weapon's belt and threw it on the ground in front of them.

"Now stand up and walk over here," said Captain Brenik.

Irikson looked at Corvin in confusion and stood. His head was pounding, the bright morning sun not helping in anyway. Irikson helped Corvin to his feet. On shaky legs, they slowly walked forward towards their Captain. They stood in front of him. He could see they looked confused, and he could also smell the Volic on them.

"Follow these men. They will place you in my tent. Warm water is awaiting you with fresh tunics. Strip yourselves, wash yourselves and put on the fresh tunic. Stay in the tent and do not leave. The tent will be surrounded by my men. They have been instructed to kill you if you even show yourselves. Is this understood?" said Captain Brenik.

Corvin looked at him. What the hell was going on? Corvin looked at his Captain, who was staring through him as if he were not there. Corvin could see the jaw muscles in his face moving, his nostrils flaring open and closed as he breathed.

"Is that understood?" repeated Captain Brenik.

"Aye, it is" said Irikson.

"Move it then," said Captain Brenik.

Corvin and Irikson moved off, following the Corporal they did not know. The twenty infantry men surrounded them; swords still drawn. As they moved, they saw other members of their company looking on. Corvin saw the surprise on Lorka and Jorga's faces. The other Bloodchildren, led by the former slaves were taking a few steps forward. Corvin shook his head to Jorga.

"Stand fast," yelled out Jorga.

The Bloodchildren stood and took their hands off their weapons. It was clear they were about to intervene. They reached the tent and moved inside. Irikson sank to the ground, moaning.

"What the hell did we do? Why the fuck is my head pounding so much?" said Irikson

"I don't know," replied Corvin.

He saw the large buckets of heated water. As instructed, he stripped off his armour, tunic and trousers. He grabbed the soap and a clean rag that was sitting beside the bucket. He started to wash himself down. He had smelled himself on their walk to the tent, the smell could drop a cow. Irikson slowly stood and did the same.

Once they were washed and had dried themselves with a large towel that had been provided, they dressed themselves in the simple brown cloth trousers and brown tunic. Corvin felt a little better, although he needed food.

He sat on the bed and with the remaining water, started to wipe down his armour of the blood that was splattered all over it. Corvin remembered nothing of last night. His last memory was of eating around a large fire sitting next to Dolac. His memory ended there. He shook his head and continued to clean his armour.

"Bloody Volic," said Corvin to himself.

"This will not do, Captain Joren!" said Captain Brenik.

They were in the tent set aside for their meetings. Captain Brenik with his aid at the head of the table, Captain Noro on one side of the table, Captain Joren on the other side with Sergeant Emric beside him.

"No Captain, it will not," said Joren.

"Your men have fought well. Your Third Section under Sergeant Corvin saved the wall many times over the spring. Your men have proven themselves time and time again. Then, we find them sleeping off a drunken night covered in blood. In the woods to the North, ten dead bodies, slaughtered," said Captain Brenik.

"I have got to know the Sergeant in question over the spring, Captain Brenik. He is not a murderer," said Noro.

"No, he is not," agreed Sergeant Emric.

"Then explain the bodies. Ten of them," said Captain Brenik.

"I cannot, until I have talked to my men," said Captain Joren.

"I doubt they will remember much. Volic is a good drink to share with a comrade, but it has a way of washing away memories. According to some men I have already talked to, those two drunk jugs of the stuff. They are drunks, Captain. To be honest, the only outcome is seeing them hang," said Brenik.

"We do not know what happened. They could have been defending themselves," said Emric.

"I agree with that," said Noro.

"I sent a message as soon as the bodies were found to the Colonel. He should be here soon," said Brenik.

All those around the table nodded. Captain Brenik was a sound man and had done a good job, but this was above him. A murder like this needed to be dealt with by the Colonel.

"It was him that sent the Volic in the first place, although I would hardly blame him" said Noro.

"If he had known what would happen, he would not have sent the wagons of Volic," said Brenik.

"I want to know what happened and want to talk to them. The last time I saw them, they were singing with your troops around the fire, Captain Brenik. The next time was under that tree covered in blood," said Emric.

"We may never know the truth" said Brenik.

"Yes, we will know," said a voice from the door.

All in the tent turned their heads as the Colonel walked in with another man. All at the table stood up.

"Welcome, Colonel," said Brenik.

All the others in the tent nodded a greeting.

"Please, sit. I think I have some information that will fill in the blanks," said the Colonel.

They all took their seats. The Colonel and the man with him sat at the foot of the table. The man although wearing a standard mail shirt, had a look of authority about him. His long brown hair tied at the nape of his neck.

"I present Duke Eason from Eastmoor in the Kingdom of

Ex'Na," said the Colonel.

All the men round the table stood again and nodded a greeting.

"Please seat yourselves, gentleman" said Duke Eason in perfect Outlandish.

"As I said, I may have some information for you. I assume you are here discussing the bodies that were found in the forest?" asked the Colonel.

"Yes, Colonel, we are. Although the conversation has more been about the guilt of my two men as they now stand accused of murder," said Captain.

"Murder?" said the Colonel.

"Yes, Colonel. Sergeant Corvin and his Corporal Irikson were discovered shortly after we found the bodies. They were sleeping off last night's drinking session. They were covered in blood, stank of Volic and clearly had no idea where they were," said Captain Brenik.

The Duke roared with laughter. The Colonel also smiled and shook his head.

"I do not think, sir, that murder is a matter to be laughed at," said Captain Brenik.

Joren, Emric and Noro just looked at the Duke. The sudden laughter taking them by surprise.

"It is not murder, Captain," said the Colonel.

"It is not?" asked Captain Brenik.

"No," said the Duke.

"Would someone tell me what the hell happened then? I know both of the lads. Yes, they are murderous fighters, but neither of them are cold bloody murderers," said Noro.

"May I?" the Duke asked of the Colonel.

The Colonel nodded, the smile still on his face.

"I am here with a few men to check on how the war is going and see in what way I or my fellow countrymen of

Ex'Na could help. Two of my guards and I had wondered off on spot of hunting in the wood. That is where we were ambushed," said the Duke.

"Ambushed? By who?" asked Captain Brenik.

"Not sure, although I am fairly certain it is from a rival Duke in Ex'Na," said the Duke.

"A rival Duke? Who?" asked Noro.

"I am not prepared to share that information. However, as I said, we were ambushed by ten men. They were about to attack when your two men stumbled into the clearing, drunker than I have seen men in a long time," said the Duke.

He was still smiling as was the Colonel.

"I still do not see why you are smiling!" said Emric.

"If you had seen those two, you would be smiling as well. They insulted the men, who took offence and attacked your two men. Your men, Captain Joren, tore into them and killed them quicker than I have ever seen men killed before. I was impressed!" said the Duke.

"So, it was self-defence?" asked Captain Brenik.

"Defence of themselves and they saved myself and my men. They should not be facing charges and I would like to thank them. My men and I would not have survived," said the Duke.

The Colonel giggled.

"The Duke here told me all that happened. He described your two men, and I knew who they were instantly. The Duke here described Corvin well, and when he told me of a short, yet strong young man singing whilst he killed the ambushers; who else could that be but Corporal Irikson," said the Colonel.

Emric and Noro both laughed. Even Captain Brenik had a small smile on his face.

"That would be something Irikson would do, yes," said

Captain Joren.

The Duke started to laugh again.

"I have never heard singing as bad as that," said the Duke.

'So, sir, no charges?" asked Captain Brenik.

"No, Captain," confirmed the Colonel.

"A happy accident. However, I will still have to do something. They did not know they were saving the Duke here. They got drunk and killed ten men on a whim. I will deal out some sort of punishment," said Captain Joren.

"I have a suggestion," said Noro.

"Go ahead," said Joren.

"No more drink for the rest of the season," said Noro.

"It is not a bad idea," said Emric.

"Will it be enough?" asked Captain Joren.

"Well, I was going to give them a reward," said Duke Eason.

"No. No reward. That and no more drink for the rest of the summer," said Captain Joren.

"Seems fair," said Emric.

All the other men gathered nodded.

"I will see they are released then," said Captain Brenik.

"I will come with you as well," said Joren.

"As will I" said Duke Eason.

Everyone looked at the Duke.

"I still need to thank them for saving my life," said the Duke.

"You two, get out here!" said Captain Joren.

He was happier the two had not committed murder but was still not exactly happy with them for their drunken behaviour.

Corvin and Irikson emerged from the tent. They looked better now they had washed, and they both definitely smelled better. They approached the Captain and said nothing.

"You two were facing murder chargers," said Captain Brenik.

The look of surprise on their face was total.

"Murder? Who did we murder?" asked Irikson.

"No one, thankfully" said Captain Joren.

Corvin could still not read his face. It was blank!

"Ten bodies were found in the woods to the North of here. You two, found covered in blood,' said Brenik.

"Sorry, Captain. I do not remember a thing," answered Corvin.

"No. You'd think I would remember killing someone!" said Irikson with feeling.

"As I said, it was not murder. According to Duke Eason here, you came to his aid, saving him and his men," said Captain Joren.

Corvin looked at the stranger for the first time. He was smiling. A small light of recognition flicked inside Corvin; he vaguely remembered the face, but that was all.

"Yes. You both saved me and my men. I would like to thank you both," said the Duke.

"Saved you?" asked Irikson.

"Yes. Those men were there to kill me, I am certain of it. However, you both showed up and took care of it. I was going to reward you," said the Duke.

'Reward us?" asked Corvin.

"Yes, reward you, but as punishment for getting drunk and attacking men who you did not know, and killing them all, you will not be getting a reward. Also, for the rest of the summer you are not allowed to drink spirits, ale or wine," said Captain Joren.

"What? We saved this man, and are getting punished?" said Irikson.

Corvin was also pissed off. He still had no idea of what happened, but to be punished for saving someone, Corvin was not happy.

"Yes, punished and if you argue further, I will be happy to give further punishment. Remember, you were to be hanged. You're both good fighters, and fine Bloodchildren members, but we cannot have you getting into drunken fights. We cannot have you slaughtering people. Yes, in this case, you saved someone's life, and for that I am proud, but you did not know that at the time, did you?" said Captain Joren.

Both of them stayed quiet.

"DID YOU?" yelled the Captain.

"No, Captain" they both said in unison.

The Duke could see both the young men were pissed off, anyone within distance could see that. Still, he smiled.

"As I said, thank you both. I thought it was over and I would not make it home," said the Duke.

He held out his arm to Corvin, who took it in the warrior fashion. Then the Duke and Irikson shook as well.

"I may not be able to reward you, but I can say this. If either of the two of you get bored of the mercenary life, find your way to Eastmoor in Ex'Na. I will happily offer you a job," said the Duke.

Neither of them were listening. Corvin was looking at the ground. His anger pushing past the hangover and his mind working clearly for the first time since he woke. Irikson just nodded, but like Corvin, was not really listening.

"Get yourselves back into clean uniform. Your weapons are in a sorry state, so clean them off and then I suggest you go for a long run and clear your head," said Captain Joren.

They both nodded and left. Joren and the Duke watched

them go as Captain Brenik left them to return to his duties.

"They are amazing fighters, Captain," said the Duke.

Captain Joren took a few long breathes to calm down. How could they be so foolish? He will have another chat in a few days, to remind them of how close they came to being hung. Finally, he looked at the Duke.

"Yes, they are and usually more disciplined. However, they are far from perfect and even though they saved your life sir, I am still pissed off," said Joren.

"They are mercenaries, and young ones at that," said the Duke.

"True, but Corvin is what I would describe as an old head on young shoulders. He is more mature than his nineteen years, usually," said Joren.

"Nineteen? Amazing," said the Duke.

"In what way?" asked Joren.

"He is a sergeant in a company of mercenaries. One of the best fighters I have seen and yet still only nineteen year of age," said the Duke.

"Yes. I keep forgetting how young they both are," said Joren, relaxing a little.

"Were you any different at their age?" asked the Duke.

"No. I was worse," said Joren.

"There you go," said the Duke.

Joren said nothing. He was breathing easier now, but still mildly pissed off with Corvin and Irikson. He realised now he was angry for the fact they could have been hung for their actions, and he would lose two very good men. It had nothing to do with what they had done, although he was still a little shocked they managed to kill so many when drunk. He shook his head.

"Why do you shake your head, Captain," asked the Duke.

"They have had an interesting life, those two," said Joren.

"In what way?" asked the Duke.

"Too long a story, and I need some breakfast," said Joren.

He wanted to be away and deal with anything else that would arise from the actions of the two former slaves, but he would not be so rude as to dismiss the Duke. As the Captain of a mercenary company, he always needed contacts for further work. A Duke from Ex'Na, was not one you wanted to dismiss.

"Easily solved, Captain. I offer breakfast. It should be done and would invite you to share it with me in exchange for their tale," said the Duke.

Joren wanted to refuse, but this is too important contact to refuse.

"Done. What are we having?" asked Joren.

The Duke laughed.

"I have some smoked bacon from my home and fresh eggs," said the Duke.

"I have not had smoked bacon in years," said Joren.

They walked off together, heading for a breakfast and a long conversation. A conversation where Captain Joren would share all he knew of the former slaves. He would feel a little guilty after the conversation, of course, but the opportunity for more work for the company outweighing the need for privacy.

Corvin and Irikson had told their brothers what had happened. Of course, they could not remember the fight, but told all they knew, including the punishment that had been dealt out to them.

"You being punished?" said Torin.

"Yes. No more drink for the rest of the summer," said

Irikson.

"Well, that makes sense," said Jorga.

"What?" asked Irikson.

Even Corvin looked at his brother, Jorga.

"You got drunk, killed ten men and then feel asleep drunk under a tree," said Jorga.

Irikson looked at Jorga, then finally his actions came rushing home.

"I never looked at it that way, and of course, you are right brother," said Irikson.

Corvin was not so quickly calmed; he said nothing. The others chatted but what they said drifted past him as he rolled what had happened around and around in his head. He was working himself up but could not stop it. He was about to say something when the horn went.

"Shit. An attack!" said Jorga.

"Yes. We have this day off but get the men ready and stand them at the bottom of the wall, to the left of the stairs," said Corvin.

"Your weapons," said Lorka.

He handed them over, clean and sharp. Corvin's mouth curved into his little half smile.

"Thank you, brother," said Corvin.

Jorga ran off to see to his men, as did Torin.

"We best get into our armour," said Irikson, shedding his brown tunic and trousers.

"Yes."

The Sul'Lenans deciding that it was time to throw everything they had at the wall and they did! From when the first horn blew, all day and into the night. The Bloodchildren were not on duty this day, but had gathered at the foot at the stairs. By midday, not long after the horn had been blown, they and the Sea Wolves were called to the wall to relieve those that were there. On gaining the wall, they saw the carnage. Hundreds of dead Kor'Lenan Infrantry lay on the dark grey stone, eyes lifeless and their blood stopped. There cannot have been more than one hundred left fighting, with roughly the same amount of Sul'Lenans on the wall, and more gaining it every few heartbeats when the Bloodchildren and Sea wolves arrived. Lead by Captain Joren, they charged in.

"Bloodchildren! At them!" yelled Joren, as he led them in.

The Sul'Lenans did not have time to position themselves when they were hit by the three hundred mercenaries. The battle was not over quickly. Corvin with Irikson on his left fought recklessly. He was still pissed off at what had happened and was throwing himself at the Sul'Lenans, with no regard to defence or his life. He cut left as an axe came at him. He caught the axe on his left-hand sword and head butted the wielder. He followed up with upswing with his axe that connected with the Sul'Lenans jaw. The Sul'Lena dropped. Irikson darted into the gap that had been left and started swinging, his twin axes striking out in every direction at once, it seemed. Corvin jumped in beside him as the Third Section backed them both up. The Sul'Lenans slowly being pushed back to the edge of the wall.

"Stupid bastard!" Corvin muttered under his breath.

A Sul'Lena had thrust a spear at him, which he dodged then using his right armpit, trapped the spear. His sword in his left hand coming around in an arc and slicing through the Sul'Lenan's neck. He swung left, then blocked another sword that came at his head.

"Not today, scum," he muttered again.

His axe swung down and then up, straight into the groin.

With a scream, the Sul'Lenan dropped. As he stepped forward, his sword swung down, stabbing into the Sul'Lenan's throat.

"THIRD SECTION, PUSH!" yelled Corvin.

As one, the Third Section pushed forward into the remaining Sul'Lenans. There was no more room to move, and the Sul'Lenans were not the type to climb back down the wall.

The First and Second Section to the right had also pushed forward, trapping the Sul'Lenans up against the merlons of the wall edge. As the Bloodchildren battled the last remaining Sul'Lenans, the Sea Wolves pushed sideways, between the Bloodchildren and the wall merlons.

"SEA WOLVES! SEND THEM HOME!" shouted Noro as his men charged straight into them.

The Sul'Lenans got slaughtered. Some were seen trying to get off the wall but did not retreat to the ropes quick enough. The Sea Wolves took great pleasure in pushing them off or stabbing out at the Sul'Lenans as they tried to climb over.

Noro himself killed the last Sul'Lenan on this section of the wall before coming face to face with Captain Joren.

"Fine work, Noro," said Joren.

Noro smiled.

"No time to rest," said Noro, looking out over the ground in front of the wall.

Joren joined him, looking out. He swore to himself.

Approaching were three wooden towers. Behind the towers pushing, looked to be over three thousand Sul'Lenans.

"This is not good, Captain," said Dolac.

"Emric. Send a runner to the Captain Brenik. Tell him, we need him now!" said Joren.

Emric sent the runner off and approached the Captain.

"Three is going to be bloody hard, Captain," said Emric.

"Yes. Corvin, I'll have your word now, no silly ideas," said

Joren.

Corvin had approached, still in a dark mood, his bloodlust from the battle still up. He just nodded, thinking it best to say nothing.

Within moments, Captain Brenik had arrived. He took one look at the three towers and started shouting orders at his own sergeants.

"I want archers called, all arrows and spirit pots stacked at the back of the wall," he ordered.

One sergeant ran off.

"I want every man in this camp able to fight, to be organised and at the base of the wall now," he said to another sergeant.

That sergeant ran off, and Brenik turned to Joren.

"Fine work, Joren. Get your men back to the ground, watered, some food in their bellies and wait at the bottom of the stairs," instructed Brenik.

"Captain, we only just got here."

"I know, but trust me, Joren. This looks serious. I want your Bloodchildren and the Sea Wolves to be our reserve force for the rest of the day. You are perfect shock soldiers, able to get in quickly and do-good damage. You are the best reserves," said Brenik.

Joren nodded, then issued the orders. The Bloodchildren and the Sea Wolves left the walls and retuned to refresh themselves. Joren had no idea how they were going to hold. He saw what he thought was over three thousand men. To face them, they had just over twelve hundred combined forces. He had looked further down the wall and could see the heavy fighting along its length, at least as far as he could see.

Once the Bloodchildren had taken water and a light snack, he raced back up the wall to see Captain Brenik, Noro joining him.

"Not looking good, Joren," Noro said as they took the steps, two at a time.

"No," Joren agreed.

They got to the top and saw Brenik had things organised. Three hundred archers were placed at the rear of the battlements. At their feet, braziers with fires burning. Crouched below the merlons were just over two hundred Kor'Lena Infrantry, all holding small jugs of rough Volic; the spirit they brewed that burnt well.

"Captain Brenik. The Bloodchildren are refreshed and waiting at the bottom of the stairs," said Joren.

"The Sea Wolves also," said Noro.

"Good. Did you lose many men?" asked Brenik.

"None. Just a few cuts that are being seen to," said Joren.

"I only lost one, one of my Corporals got dragged down over the wall with a Sul'Lenan," said Noro.

Brenik nodded.

"I lost over a hundred and fifty men in that attack. I think from now on we will have a reserve force on standby night and day. Although we will discuss once we have time to breathe and have dealt with those wooden bastards," said Brenik.

"You have an idea?" said Noro.

"As your man Corvin came up with, we will fire from the inside. If that fails, we soak the outsides in spirit and fire them. They may have wet the walls, but enough Volic on them and they will burn regardless," said Brenik.

"Good. You do not mind if we wait here with you?" asked Joren.

"No. Stand with me and it will be good to have you," said Brenik.

The Towers hit the wall, with the Sul'Lenans screaming and abusing those that waited on the walls. The archers had done their best to thin the ranks, and even though roughly three hundred bodies on the ground across the battlefield, the Sul'Lenans still hit the wall. Brenik had said they faced closer to thirty-five hundred men. He had also said that he sent a messenger for reinforcements, but the runner was sent back quickly. The Colonel had no more to give.

As soon as the doors had opened, the jugs of Volic were flying through the air, impacting on Sul'Lenans and the inside of the towers. The flame arrows followed but did nothing. There were a few flashes when the Volic ignited, but it was doing no damage to the towers, or the men inside. With a battle cry, the Sul'Lenans came pouring out of the towers. The archers kept firing as the infantry raised themselves up and engaged. Corvin had snuck up the stairs and saw the problem. The fire arrows were doing nothing, he called to Jorga who ran up.

"Ideas?" he asked.

Jorga looked at the scene before him, the previous way of dealing with the towers was clearly not working and the Kor'Lena Infrantry were being hard pressed.

"Maybe," said Jorga.

He ran to the right, heading toward as the cliff face that the wall butted up against. It would be the only place where there was no fighting. He ran past Captain Brenik, Captain Joren and Captain Noro with Corvin close behind him.

"Sorry sir, need a quick look," said Corvin as he went past the three Captains.

Jorga was looking over, mindful of any enemy archers, and looking at the mass of Sul'Lenans. The Sul'Lenans were all around the base of the towers, waiting to get into them. Their shields all locked together to prevent easy picking from the

Kor'Lena archers, not that the archers could hit them. They were still at the back of the battlements, firing into the doorways of the towers.

"We need to kill the men at the bottom of the towers," said Jorga.

"That is the idea, yes," said Noro.

Jorga turned to Corvin.

"Volic."

"The firewall the Smith spoke of," said Corvin with a half-smile.

"Exactly," said Jorga.

"You need to get back down to your men," said Brenik.

He was still clearly angry with what had happened and not happy with Corvin at all.

"We have an idea, sir," said Jorga to Captain Joren.

"Speak it," said Captain Joren.

"We need to kill the men at the base of the towers, not the ones inside. We can deal with the ones inside but if those on the ground make it to the wall, we are finished," said Jorga.

"Yes. We know this," said Brenik losing patience.

"Arrows won't work, but a firewall will," said Corvin.

"A what?" asked Captain Brenik.

"A firewall, sir," said Jorga.

"Yes. We throw all of the Volic we can into the men at the foot of the tower then light it up. If we can get enough of a fire going, it will prevent the men getting into the towers. We create a wall using fire," said Corvin.

"Where the hell did you learn that lad?" said Joren.

"Long story, which we do not have time for Captain," said Jorga.

"It could work," said Noro.

Brenik thought about it. It was a good idea, in fact a great idea. He was pissed off at himself for not thinking of it.

"Do it. Get all the reserves to grab as many hand jugs as possible," said Brenik.

"Every man only needs two each. If all the reserves do this, we can have over five hundred jugs of Volic going over the wall," said Noro.

"Yes, exactly, but you need to clear out the archers as we would need to line up along the backside of the battlements," said Jorga.

"Get about it, Corvin," said Joren.

Corvin ran off with Noro and Jorga and it was not long before they had themselves ready. Two hundred and fifty mercenaries lined themselves up along the backside of the Dark Wall. The Fire Hawks took over the reserve duty. Corvin looked at Dolac, who had a sick smile on his face. He looked to the left and saw Emric, concentrating on the Kor'Lenans battling just in front of him.

"LET THEM FLY!" screamed Corvin.

As the Sea Wolves and Bloodchildren let fly, two hundred and fifty small jugs of Volic went over the wall, then within a few hearts beats, another two hundred and fifty followed. Corvin waited a few heartbeats, then signalled the Tenth Squad. The Tenth Squad raised their fire arrows, and with a half draw, let them go. The arrows sailed up and then came down sharply. At first, there was nothing, and Corvin could not run to the front to see what had happened as the battle was still raging. He waited and looked at Jorga, who shrugged his shoulders. Then with a bright flash and a huge noise, the Volic ignited. Even though the Mercenaries were at the back of the wall, they could feel the heat from the flames, then within heart beats, they could see the flames. The battle at the front of the wall stopped, as the men on both sides ducked to escape the heat. Corvin breathed, their throws had been perfect and landed close to the wall. Just past the wooden towers. The battle in front of them resumed and became uglier. That is when Noro screamed out again.

"SEND THEM HOME!"

All the mercenaries drew their weapons and ran in, fitting into any spot they could in order to get at the remaining Sul'Lenans. The fight stopped quickly. Men panting and still shielding themselves from the flames that were still burning fiercely. Corvin managed to grab a quick look over the wall and saw the devastation. Hundreds of Sul'Lenans had been burnt alive at the foot of the towers, others behind them burnt horribly before running back to their camp. Of the thirty-five hundred Sul'Lenans who had attacked the wall, fourteen hundred lay dead or dying on the ground. On the wall at his feet, a further four hundred.

It had worked. Jorga joined Corvin and looked out over the battlefield. The Sul'Lenans had regrouped out of arrow range, and what looked like more ropes were being handed out.

"They are waiting for the fires to die down before trying again," said Jorga.

"Yes. Let's go see the Captain," said Corvin.

"It worked, Corvin. Good idea but the smell is horrible," said Captain Joren.

The smell was horrible. Corvin had never smelt burning flesh before, and he could do with never smelling it again.

"Yes Corvin, good idea. How much Volic did you use?" said Captain Brenik.

"Five hundred small jugs, sir. So, should not have used much of your supply," said Corvin.

"Is that all? No, you still have much more if that is all you used," said Captain Brenik.

"Another suggestion, sir," said Jorga.

"Go ahead," said Joren.

"We can get more Volic and store it on the wall. If they try to come again, and it looks like they are going to, all we need to do is fire more of the spirit onto the already burning flames," suggested Jorga.

"Good idea, Corporal," said Brenik.

"It will give us time to deal with the towers," said Captain Joren.

"Leave them there, sir. We can put in traps," said Corvin.

"Traps?"

"Yes, Captain. We flood the lower parts of the towers with more Volic. Whilst down there, I will cut a small hole in the side. If the Sul'Lenans make the wall again, they will head for the towers. That is when one of our archer's fires an arrow straight through the hole and burns anything on the inside," said Jorga.

Noro let out a whistle and smiled.

"You boys are really enjoying using fire, aren't you?" he said.

"No, but it is doing a lot of the work for us," said Corvin.

Brenik thought about it, he wanted to object but could not see anything bad with the idea.

"Carry on then, Corvin. I'll get my men to throw the bodies of the Sul'Lenans back over and get rid of our dead. Thank you Joren, thank you Noro. Once again, the Bloodchildren and the Sea Wolves have won the day," said Captain Brenik.

"The day is not over yet," said Noro.

As the sun started to rise and its fingers of light stretched across the sky, the battle had still not ended. Two full days and two full nights, the fight had lasted. The firewall had done better than expected and even though the Sul'Lenans had tried everything they could, soaking themselves in water, using large shields also soaked in water, nothing they did could get them through the flames. It was not until past midnight when they had broken through. They had run straight into the towers. Captain Brenik had waited until they had started coming out the top of the tower, onto the wall, before he gave the order. Fire arrows were fired at the holes that Corvin and his men had made, the towers erupted into flames. Hundreds of Sul'Lenans had lost their lives, dying of the heat and smoke, well before their bodies were burnt. The defenders of the walls had lost no one since the firewall, and Brenik was impressed. Of course, he had sent a runner along the wall to the next position to inform the Colonel of what they had done. Within short order, flames outside the wall further down at the city of Kor'Mor could be seen. There had been a brief respite before first light, as the Sul'Lenans retreated. Brenik was not sure how many had lost their lives, but even if they lost thousands, he knew there was thousands more. As the sun rose, he looked out over the battlefield. In his life, his long career as a solider, he had never seen so many dead bodies; they were everywhere. He looked further out as the sun lit up more of the ground. His heart sank, standing in ranks upon of ranks was more Sul'Lenans. He started counting, a rough count that junior officers were taught in order to gauge enemy strength. He lost count at 3000. Where the hell were these men coming from? He shook his head.

"We are going to either have to come up with something very clever or perhaps something very dangerous. If we don't, we are going to lose this wall," said Captain Joren from beside him.

All he could do was nod in agreement.

Chapter Thirteen

Corvin from his part of the wall looked out across the battlefield. Well out of arrow range stood the Sul'Lenans. He had never seen so many people in his young life. He would count them, but he could not count that high. He was lost in view, the view of the enemy that would soon be attacking.

Sergeant Corvin, you are wanted by the Captains. They are standing at the cliff face," said a young runner.

Corvin noted the nervous look on his face and doubted the young man with sandy blonde hair had ever seen that many people before either. Corvin nodded.

"Jorga, with me," he said as he walked towards the cliff face. The cliff face was the name they had given to the end of the wall where it meets the Black Mountains. There was space there set aside for the senior officers to meet. This way, they didn't have to walk all the way to the command tent to meet each other.

"Where are we going?" asked Jorga.

"Officers' meeting," said Corvin, whilst walking between the soldiers on the wall.

"I am not an officer."

"I know, but I think I need you to help me explain a plan," said Corvin.

"What plan?"

"The one we discussed when we first got here," said Corvin.

Jorga stared at his brother's back, shocked at what Corvin was thinking of suggesting.

"Hearing that has just ruined my day," said Jorga.

He could not see but Corvin had his half grin on his face.

"No doubt I have," replied Corvin.

"Corvin," said Emric as he nodded.

Captain Joren was looking at Jorga, then looked to Corvin for an explanation.

"Sorry if I overstepped my bounds, Captain, but Jorga often has good ideas and insights," said Corvin.

The Captain nodded.

"He is welcome if you think he has something to offer Corvin," said Captain Brenik.

"Thank you, sir," said Corvin.

Standing there was Captain Joren, Sergeant Emric, Sergeant Dolac, Captain Noro and of course, Captain Brenik.

"We were just discussing what the next plan is," said Captain Brenik.

"In other words, what are we going to do about that shit storm about to hit us?" said Noro pointing.

"The firewall you came up with will work again, and we have a good supply left," said Brenik.

"How much?" asked Dolac.

"If we use as much as we did the last time we tried the firewall, we would have enough for two more attacks only. We get resupplied every few days," said Captain Brenik.

Jorga was standing against the Merlon looking out at the Sul'Lenans. He looked back to Corvin, smiled and then spoke.

"Sergeant Corvin, I think you may be right. It will be the best way to save many lives," said Jorga.

"What are you two thinking of?" said Emric with a smile.

"I hate to think," said Captain Joren.

"You are not going to like it, Captain," said Corvin.

"I don't like the sight of all those Sul'Lenans much either," said Joren.

"Out with it, Sergeant," said Brenik.

"When we first got here, Irikson, Jorga and myself talked over a plan. We thought it would be good if we get desperate," said Corvin.

"I am really not going to like this, am I?" asked Joren.

"No Captain, you are not," said Jorga.

"We need to get over the wall and attack them," said Corvin.

All of them except Jorga were shocked. Brenik was standing wide eyed, Emric and Dolac shook their heads and Captain Joren's face went blank. Even the usually open Noro was shocked.

"We do not go over the wall, Sergeant. That would defeat the purpose of having a wall," said Captain Brenik.

"Which is why the Sul'Lenans would never expect it," said Corvin.

"May I?" asked Jorga, looking at the Captain.

Joren nodded his agreement.

"When we first got here, we asked if using ropes, we could get down the side of the cliff, further round the mountains. We were told 'yes' but it would be suicide," said Jorga.

"As it would, lad," said Emric.

"No, Emric, it would not. The Sul'Lenans would never expect it. We could be down and into the forest very quickly.

If done quiet and at night we could get quite a few men down into the forest," said Corvin.

"They would have scouts in there. Not looking for people coming over the wall or down the cliffs, but for just watching the walls," said Dolac.

"Yes, they would Sergeant Dolac, but we are confident we could take them out," said Jorga.

"What do you plan on doing once you are down?" asked Brenik.

"The original plan was to take a few hundred men and make for the rear of their position. Once there, lay down our supplies and perform hit and run attacks wherever we can. Attacking, causing as much chaos and death a possible, before running off to our next target. With the supplies we can carry, we could keep that up for two weeks. Once we run out of supplies, steal what we need and continue on," said Jorga.

The Captain's eyes went wide.

"I would not authorise that, sorry. A few hundred men behind enemy lines would be destroyed," said Captain Joren.

Emric and Dolac agreed.

"Which is why we have changed the plan slightly, sir," said Jorga.

"Instead of hit and run tactics, we clear the forest and wait," said Corvin.

"Wait for what?" asked Dolac.

"The next attack on the wall. We would wait for them to charge and then hit them with an arrow storm from the forest. We could fire at them the whole way to the wall," said Jorga.

"Yes, and we would take fighters to form a small line in front of the archers to protect them. We would be hiding a little way back to stay hidden, but close enough to see them. If they send in a small force, the fighters can take them out. Then the archers keep firing," said Corvin.

"They would send in most of their men," said Captain Joren.

"No, sir, think about it. You are about to storm the wall with a small army. On your approach, arrows appear out of nowhere and kill fifty to one hundred of your men. You know the archers on the wall are too far to hit you. You would be wondering where the arrows came from, and as you were wondering, another storm of arrows hits your force. More men go down than before because you had called a halt. If you don't work out where the arrows are coming form, you would be hit quite a few times before you realised. Once you realised, you would send how many into the forest?" said Jorga.

"If I had as many men as they have now, I would send in two hundred," said Captain Joren.

"Yes. Your two hundred would be fired at the entire way in. You would see your two hundred men disappear into the forest, and never come out. Then in a short time, more arrows would take out more of your men," said Jorga.

"And if he sends in his whole force?" asked Noro.

"He wouldn't," said Corvin.

"Why?" asked Emric.

"There could be more men in the forest than he has, and it could be a trap," said Jorga.

All of the senior men looked at each other. Noro was smiling. The other were not.

"You do remember our conversation after the first attacks with the towers, Corvin? The one where I explained I would not go along with any more dangerous ideas?" said Captain Joren.

"I remember, Captain," said Corvin.

"Although," said Jorga.

All looked at him. He felt a little out of place. He was not an officer after all, and should not have been there. Jorga looked at Corvin, who nodded for him to continue.

"We could change it slightly, that would make it safe," said Jorga.

"Go on, lad," said Emric.

"We don't hit them on the way to the wall. We hit them when they are at the wall," said Jorga.

Corvin was smiling.

"The meat grinder?" said Corvin, with a huge grin across his face.

"Yes," said Jorga with a smile on his face also.

They both remembered a lesson the Smith had given, a lesson where he described grinding up a small force against a tall wall. They never forgot that lesson.

"Meat grinder?" questioned Captain Brenik.

"Yes. A tactic our mentor once told us of," said Jorga.

"The Smith? The one who you took your name from Corvin?" asked Dolac.

"Yes," said Corvin.

"Of course, the archers fire at them as normal. We wait until the force is at the wall, then, our archers hit them from the forest. They will still be confused, and they will come to a stop as they throw their ropes and grapples onto the wall or the ladders. If they send a small force out to meet us in the forest, we take care of them and continue firing arrows at them. If they look like they are about to send a larger force at us, that is when we start another firewall," said Jorga.

"Yes, but this firewall would be further out, as far as the men can throw. We would want to catch them between the Dark Wall and the fire wall. They would have nowhere to go. At that point, the archers in the forest fire everything they have got, the archers on the wall fire everything they have got. If you have more Volic, throw it right on top of them. If any get through the flames, the fighters in the forest charge out and greet them," said Corvin.

They all thought. Captain Joren looked out over the Sul'Lenans again, as his brain worked overtime. Captain Brenik was nodding. He did not trust the idea but knew it was a good one. Captain Noro, of course, was what could be derived as bloody excited, but Noro loved a dangerous fight.

"How many would go, Corvin?" asked Dolac.

"We would ask for volunteers as this is what the Captain Joren would say as bloody dangerous," said Corvin.

They all laughed, even Captain Joren smiled.

"How many?" asked Captain Joren.

Corvin looked at Jorga.

"I would suggest around three hundred. One hundred archers, carrying as many arrows as possible, and two hundred fighters," said Jorga.

"Three hundred?" said Emric.

"Yes. Anymore would not help and to be honest, we could not spare them from the wall," said Corvin.

"All of the Bloodchilren?" asked Dolac.

"No, Sergeant Dolac. The Third Section and then find other volunteers from the Sea Wolves, Kor'Lena Infrantry and the Fire Hawks. There is not enough Bloodchildren and we cannot risk wiping out the company here," said Jorga.

Emric and Dolac nodded their appreciation. Jorga would go far, they both knew.

They were all working through the details as a runner ran up to Captain Brenik.

"Sir, they are turning," said the young runner, the same one that had fetched Corvin.

All of them looked at the Sul'Lenans. They were moving back from where they were standing and heading back to their camp, which could not be seen from the wall as it was over the other side of a small hilly area.

"Sergeants," shouted Captain Brenik.

His sergeants down the line looked over at him.

"Get the men watered and fed. Reserve group on the wall with watchers. If they assemble, blow the horns," said Captain Brenik.

The sergeants started to get their men off the wall to make way for the reserve force, which was waiting at the bottom of the stairs.

"Gentlemen, get your men seen to and meet in my tent. We will share a light breakfast and discuss this further. It is a huge risk but, the plan has appeal," said Captain Brenik.

All assembled officers, including Jorga, nodded and moved off.

"Corporal Jorga, feel free to join us for breakfast," said Emric.

Jorga smiled and nodded.

"Sergeant Emric, can I ask you bring Corporal Geren with you? He often thinks of things that others do not," asked Corvin.

"I second that. He is a bright lad," said Dolac.

"I will," said Emric.

In the meeting tent was the Bloodchildren group of Joren, Dolac, Emric, Corvin and of course, Jorga. Jorga sipping a mug of water and feeling very out of place. Corporal Geren had also joined them, he was happy to be included. The Sea Wolves consisted of Captain Noro and three of his Sergeants. Across the other side of the table was the Fire Hawks, which was led by Janoor and beside him, three of his own Sergeants. The head of the table was Captain Brenik and his aide. The foot of the table was two of the more senior Sergeants of the Kor'Lena Infantry. Neither Corvin knew well, but had seen them in action and knew they could fight.

"A plan has been put forward by the Bloodchildren and we are here to discuss it," said Captain Brenik.

"Jorga, would you outline the plan, please," requested Captain Joren.

Jorga stood and spoke. He was nervous, he did not like talking that much and in front of so many more senior to him, he was a little intimidated. He outlined what Corvin and he had suggested, going through every point slowly and making sure to not miss anything out. He himself was sure the plan would work and the more he had thought about it, the more he was convinced that it would work with minimal loses. Once he finished, he sat down.

"So, you are asking for volunteers?" asked one of the Sergeants from Kor'Lena Infrantry.

"Yes," said Corvin.

"My men are out. We are paid to hold the wall, not climb down and fight," said Captain Janoor.

Corvin nodded. Emric had warned him that Janoor would not take part.

"I will not order any men over the wall or down the cliff as it were. It will be volunteer basis," said Captain Brenik.

"Three hundred?" asked Noro.

"Yes," said Jorga.

"Who have you got so far?" asked a Sergeant from the Sea Wolves.

Corvin had shared a few drinks with this man before, but he could not remember his name. He always thought of him as the toothless one. A youngish man, not much older than himself. Thin muscle covering his body; a bald head and of course, the man was missing three teeth from his top row.

"We have the Third Section of the Bloodchildren, so twenty-two men so far. We need one hundred archers and another one hundred and eighty fighters to complete the force," said Corvin.

"You not taking any more of your men, Joren?" asked Janoor with a sneer.

Captain Joren ignored the way it was said.

"No. We are a small company and I do not want to be completely wiped out. Although I will give Sergeant Corvin one more squad to take. Corvin, you now have thirty men," said Joren.

"Thank you, Captain. If Emric agrees, I would like to take Fifth Squad under Geren, if he agrees, of course," said Corvin.

"Done," said Emric.

"If the Captain agrees, I will also give you one squad," said Dolac.

"That is half our company, Sergeant Dolac," said the Captain.

"Yes, but I believe the lad will get through this with minimal losses," said Dolac, nodding at Corvin.

Corvin returned the nod.

"Which squad?" asked Emric.

"I will give First Squad under Kalin," said Dolac.

"Thank you, Sergeant Dolac," said Corvin.

"So that is forty men," said Captain Joren.

"Sergeant Molich, do you think you could find one hundred archers that would do it?" asked Captain Brenik.

"Sir, I am sure I could," said Molich, the Sergeant of archers.

Corvin had seen him about but had never talked to him.

He was a short man, with not much weight on his body. He looked like a strong breeze would blow him over. He had a thick brown beard that matched the short brown hair on his head. He did not look like much but Corvin looked at him and saw a calm, strong intelligence in his eyes.

"Who would you have lead the archers, Molich?" asked Captain Brenik.

"I would lead them, sir" said Molich.

"You would?" asked Noro.

"Yes," was all Molich said.

"Okay, all we need is another one hundred and sixty men as we have the numbers," said Jorga.

"I will volunteer the entire Sea Hawk company," said Captain Noro.

A few shocked faces looked back at the likeable Captain.

"All of them, Noro?" asked Captain Joren.

"Yes and I'll go with them," said Noro with a smile.

"You are happy to lead this force?" asked Emric.

"No. It is the lad's idea. He can lead," said Noro.

"He does not have the rank!" said Captain Janoor.

Noro shrugged.

"That is three hundred and twenty men," said Jorga.

"Well, Captain Brenik? Are we doing this?" asked Noro.

Captain Brenik looked at those assembled. He looked over to Captain Joren.

"Joren. What do you say?"

"I cannot think of anything else that would work. I hope I do not regret this, but I agree. The question is when?" said Captain Joren.

The meeting had broken up quickly and the officers participating ran to get their men prepared. Corvin and Jorga had suggested going that night, so all the men got their gear ready and then returned to their tents to try and sleep or rest. It would be a long night. Once again, Corvin had been surprised when he was named the senior man in charge of the force, especially since Captain Noro was going. Captain Brenik and Captain Joren had pulled him aside when everyone had left.

"Corvin, I am giving you the temporary rank of Commander. It is not a rank we use very often and it is only a temporary one. This will make it clearer as to who is in charge," said Captain Brenik.

"Sir?" said Corvin looking at his own Captain.

"Makes sense, lad. Noro will agree," said Captain Joren.

Corvin did not know what to say, so thought of it no more. He had got all the men together, and along with Jorga and Noro outlined the plan. The Third Section was, of course, excited. Corvin knew it was due to the fact they would be getting off the wall and taking the fight to the Sul'Lenans.

The archers under Molich, although did not share the same enthusiasm, had volunteered to a man. Of course, Noro's Sea Wolves were also excited to get over the wall.

The plan had been outlined. Jorga, who had been made temporary Sergeant in charge of the Third Section, outlined what to carry.

"Keep you packs light. You want three water skins, food that will be handed to you soon, one sleeping blanket and your weapons. Archers, you are to carry as many bunches of arrows as you can. The rest of us will also be carrying as many arrows as we can as well, so we have a good supply. Every man will also carry one small jug of Volic. Apparently, there is a stream not far into the forest that we will have to clear first, if there is enemy there, of course. This will keep us with fresh water," said Jorga.

Corvin had explained where along the mountains they would be coming down. Not far from the Dark Wall, there was a path that led into the mountains and made its way up. A few Melai along the path, it dropped down to a ledge. The ledge was according to Captain Brenik, roughly seventy-five Lai high. This was the lowest point along the cliffs which they could reach the bottom with ropes, which had been recycled by being tied together from the ones the Sul'Lenans had left behind.

"Once we have all we need, we will head out. We were going to rest here but I want us moving along the path in full daylight, then finding a spot to get some rest. We will rest until sometime past midnight when we'll make our way down the ropes. Any questions?" asked Corvin finally.

No one said a thing. Just took in the information.

"You know what we are doing once we are down. We break their backs, then make for the wall and get back up by ropes thrown down to us. If I am killed, Captain Noro will take charge. If he is also killed, Sergeant Jorga here will then take command. Get yourselves to the food tent to get the food we need. You will all be given enough food to last us three days. After that, we are eating whatever we can find or steal. Understand?" said Corvin.

A sea of faces nodded.

"Good. Get your gear and meet back here," said Corvin.

The men all moved, and Captain Noro approached.

"Looking forward to this, Commander," said Noro with a huge grin.

"Why is that, Captain?" said Corvin.

"Wall work is boring, and when I saw you and your sections storm the towers, then come out of the towers into the teeth of the storm, I was impressed. A mercenary's life is always uncertain, but if I could choose my end, it would be doing something crazy like this," said Noro.

"Well, hopefully not too crazy. I plan on surviving!" said Corvin.

The trip down the cliff face had gone off smoothly; the men were quiet and quick. The ropes they had recycled from the Sul'Lenans, long enough when joined together, reached the ground. The men had to be reminded to climb down, not slide down. Corvin did not want the men to get rope burn on their hands and then not be able to hold their weapons. Corvin and Irikson were down first. Irikson had a way about him when it came to scouting. He could move quickly and silently. They quickly scouted the area in the forest next to the cliff face, then returned to the ten ropes now hanging down. Irikson pulled on the rope three times, the arranged signal, and the men started their climb down. Once all the men were down, the rope was tugged again three times, and the ropes gathered and pulled back up. Twenty Kor'Lena Infrantry had accompanied the force in order to bring up the ropes, then take them back to the wall.

"Jorga, send Seventh and Eighth Squad to scout all of the forest. It is not large, and they should be able to do it and get back here quickly. Noro, please take a few of your men and take up position near the forest edge. We need a good position to see the wall from and I want you to keep an eye out for the Sul'Lenans, just in case they want to attack by night again. The rest of us will wait here for the scouts to return," advised Corvin.

The men moved off quietly. Corvin and the rest of the

force waited at the edge of the forest, sitting down on the ground, ears and minds alert. As predicted, it was not long for the scouts to get back to Corvin.

"The forest is empty," said Corporal Torin.

"We found nothing either," said Irikson.

As Jorga had been made a temporary Sergeant, Irikson had been given Eighth Squad.

"We did, however, find a large hollow under a large tree near a stream. We can use it to stash our gear," continued Irikson.

"Good. We will do that now. How far is it?" said Corvin.

"It's only about two hundred Lai from the forest edge, near where Noro is keeping watch," said Torin.

"Perfect. We stash our gear in that hollow, cover it up and move to where Noro is," said Corvin.

The men all moved to the hollow and relaxed. Corvin sent Seventh Squad off to stand guard and watch the approaches from the south. Corvin did not want to be surprised. Corvin left his men sitting, some sleeping, around the hollow and made his way to Noro.

As he got to Noro, he saw the position was better than he had hoped for. The trees stopped on the edge of the forest, and the forest had plenty of dense bushes that came to a man's waist. Looking into the forest and seeing anyone would be difficult. He reached Noro and crouched down beside him.

"Good view?" asked Corvin.

"Yes. We can't see the wall in this dark, but it can only be just over there," said Noro, pointing.

"Good. I have left the men resting. We will not move them up until we see the Sul'Lenans," said Corvin.

"Good idea. I have five men along the edge of the forest to warn us," said Noro.

"Good. I have Seventh squad watching our backs. Luckily, the forest is not so large."

"Yes. You nervous, commander?"

"Not nervous, just concerned," said Corvin.

"Concerned?"

"Yes. My main concern is the sun comes up and there are more Sul'Lenans than we expected," said Corvin.

"That would be a shit day out," said Noro with a grin.

"If it is, I may be leading these men to their deaths,"

"I am sure they would follow you," said Noro.

The sun started to rise, its small light slowly lighting the horizon. The Dark Wall could just be seen and as the light grew, Corvin could see the Kor'Lenans where standing, waiting. As his eyes adjusted and he could start to see further, he finally saw a glimpse of the Sul'Lenans. They too were assembled, standing together in one mass. Corvin still had problems with his counting and could not estimate how many Sul'Lenans there were. He knew there was more than expected and swore.

"My thoughts exactly," said Noro.

"Can you send a runner back to the men, I want Molich here," said Corvin.

Noro nodded and sent a runner back. In a short time, Molich came running up and crouched beside Corvin.

"Shit!" said Molich as he saw the Sul'Lenans.

Noro smiled.

"How many?" asked Corvin.

Molich took his time, doing a rough count.

"I would say roughly forty-five hundred Sul'Lenans," said Molich.

"That is more than yesterday," said Noro.

"Yes," said Noro.

"Can someone go and get Jorga," said Corvin.

"No need, Commander. I'm already here," said Jorga.

He had made his way to their position and was crouching down beside Noro, Molich and Corvin.

"Fuck!" said Jorga.

"Yes. Molich says forty-five hundred of them," said Corvin.

"Does not change anything," said Jorga.

"It doesn't?" asked Molich.

"No. This plan is still the best one to hold the wall. The only difference is it makes our surviving a little harder," said Jorga.

"How hard?" asked Molich.

"We won't survive," said Corvin.

The four of them were silent. Molich certainly did not want to throw his life away. He only came as he was confident, they would win, and survive.

"Stick to the plan, Commander," said Noro.

"Yes," said Jorga.

Corvin nodded.

"I'll tell the men," said Corvin.

Full dawn had arrived and the early morning sky with reds and yellow lit up the battlefield. The Dark Wall could be seen clearly and so could the Sul'Lenans. A wide line of five hundred men, with nine more ranks behind them. They were tightly packed, walking shoulder to shoulder. Corvin had told all of his force about the numbers and told his men that if any choose to sit this out, they were welcome to. He would not look down on anyone. None had wanted to sit this out.

"They are all crazy," said Corvin.

"No. They trust in you," replied Jorga.

All of the force under Corvin were now in position. Four lai back from the forest edge, hiding behind the thick bush were the two hundred and twenty fighters from the Sea Wolves and the Bloodchildren. Five lai behind them, the one hundred Kor'Lenan archers. Corvin was convinced the Sul'Lenans would not be able to see them, and confident they could cause some real surprise damage. The archers knew they could not fire until Molich said so. Corvin had discussed this with Molich at length, that the arrows could not start flying until the Sul'Lenans were at the bottom of the wall.

Slowly, the Sul'Lenans were walking forward. The front row of Sul'Lenans holding large, oversized shields, held tightly together so no arrows could get through.

"Never seen a shield that big," said Lorka.

"Tower shields. Good protection but very heavy. It is a strong man that could carry that all day in battle," said Noro.

The second rank was also holding these shields.

"They will protect from arrows?" asked Corvin.

"Aye. Nothing will go through those, not even Lorka's huge axe. They are two layers of aged wood with a small layer of thin steel. As I said, good protection but very heavy," said Noro.

Only the first two rows were carrying these shields. As the enemy came abreast of the men waiting in the forest, Corvin noticed the shirt colour of the enemy was different from the normal Sul'Lenans colours. Sul'Lenans wore a mixture of colours, every solider wearing a different shirt. These men, however, were all wearing dark blue shirts. Corvin did not know what this means, he whispered to Molich.

"Solanum Guard. They are the guardians of the capital. They look good, but from what I have learnt, they are all good individual fighters, but not so good in fighting in a unit. The mayor of the city, which is a word for someone in charge, is quite vain. He picks the largest and most vicious fighters to join the guard. They all wear those pretty blue shirts, have the armour but as I said, throw them in a unit, and they fall over themselves," said Molich.

"Good to hear. Irikson, spread what Molich has just told us, they will give the men a little heart," said Corvin.

Irikson ran off, spreading the word.

"On my order," said Molich.

The Sul'Lenans had reached the wall and were throwing their ropes up and passing forward ladders. The men holding these tower shields were blocking any of the arrows from the top of the wall. The Sul'Lenans were completely safe from anything the defenders could throw down at them, but not safe from behind.

"NOW!" yelled Molich.

One hundred arrows went flying and Corvin watched as they flew. Before they had hit the target, a second group of one hundred arrows was in the air. The first lot slammed into the backs of the Sul'Lenans, all scoring hits and many killing men. The Sul'Lenans looked around in confusion. In fact, a lot of them were looking back towards their own camps when the second group of arrows hit them, more men dropping.

"Five quick shots, NOW!" yelled Molich.

The archers fired off five lots of arrows. The Sul'Lenans were getting agitated and yelling at each other when five hundred arrows hit them again. Many men went down, arrows stuck in their bodies. Some dead instantly, other wounded.

"Hold!" said Corvin.

Molich gave the signal to hold. The Sul'Lenans finally realised where the arrows were coming from. The order was given and five hundred of them broke off and ran towards the forest. As they broke ranks, Corvin could see the number of dead at the bottom of the wall, before he could ask Molich, Molich was already speaking.

"Looks like over two hundred dead, and five hundred on their way to greet us," said Molich.

"Hit the ones coming our way with everything," said Corvin.

"Aim at the newcomers. FIRE!" said Molich.

Arrow after arrow was sent at the Sul'Lenans heading for the forest. They only had six hundred Lai to cover before they reached the forest. The archers on the Dark Wall also fired. The five hundred charging Corvin's force now had arrows from in front and behind. The archers decimated the oncoming men so much that when Corvin gave the order for the archers to stand back and the fighters to stand up, only two hundred were left. The two hundred remaining Sul'Lenans charged into the forest, right into two hundred and twenty pissed off and angry mercenaries. Corvin drew his weapons and yelled out.

"Welcome them with weapons," he said, charging into the nearest Sul'Lenan.

The force responded. Corvin was surrounded by the Bloodchildren, the Sea Wolves split evenly to the left and right. The archers ran back twenty lai and held with their bows ready. Corvin dispatched his first opponent with a swift sword stab that went into the Sul'Lenan's neck. He went to follow up with his hand axe but somehow slipped and almost fell over, Lorka who was beside him stepped into the gap. He had drawn his double handed axe and was laying into the Sul'Lenans as they came at him. The first went down as Lorka stabbed his axe head straight into the face of dark haired Sul'Lenan; the Sul'Lenan's teeth and jaw smashing under the impact. The second went down as Lorka pulled his axe back and up, before winging down, straight through the armour and into the shoulder of the next Sul'Lenan. Corvin had gotten up and was engaging another Sul'Lenan when he heard Irikson in full voice.

"BASTARDS!" screamed Irikson as he rushed into the middle of them. He had broken the line and stepped in between two enemy. He slashed his axes left and right, blocked, pivoted and slashed out again. In the thick of it, surrounded by enemy, was just the way he liked it. He smiled; he threw insults as Sul'Lenan after Sul'Lenan died at his feet. He took a cut to his cheek, and if he had not stepped back, would have died. He was starting to be overwhelmed when Corvin heard a second voice.

"TO THE CORPORAL!" yelled Torin.

The Seventh Squad and Eighth Squad rushing into the gap Irikson had created. The Sul'Lenans were now cut into two, the Bloodchildren holding between them in the middle. The Sea Wolves slowly pushing forward and holding the line. The archers now joined in, taking careful aim and shooting when they had a clear shot. The Sul'Lenans never stood a chance. Corvin dispatched an opponent and stopped. They were all dead. He looked around and saw Irikson being helped up. He was covered in blood and Corvin walked over.

"Any of it yours?" said Corvin.

"Some," said Irikson.

Corvin shook his head. He looked around and saw the Sea Wolves finishing of those Sul'Lenans that had not quite died yet. He looked over the bodies, spotting a few of his own. He did not have time to check who it was.

"This is not over. Reform the line," he said in a voice that carried.

The force moved back into their original formation, and Corvin and Noro crept forward. The wall defenders had held. No Sul'Lenan had yet reached the top of the wall. Judging by the dead on the ground, there must have been at least a thousand dead Sul'Lenans.

"I lost a few, you?" asked Noro.

"A few, but have not counted yet," replied Corvin.

Corvin's eyes were fixed on the battle below the wall.

"It is time to throw the plan to the wind. We need to hit them from behind, and now!" said Corvin, standing up

Noro said nothing, just smiled.

Corvin called the men and they all moved from the forest together, fighters in the front, archers in the back. They ran out into the open ground and stood facing the wall, a line of fighters one hundred wide with two ranks, and one hundred archers standing at the ready. They were standing five hundred Lai from the wall when Corvin shouted the orders.

"Fighters crouch, archers loose," yelled Corvin.

The fighters along the front kneeled down, the archers started firing their bows. Wave after wave of arrows hit the Sul'Lenans in the rear. Sul'Lenans dropped to the ground, arrows in various parts of their bodies.

"Looks like they are learning," said Jorga.

The Sul'Lenans formed into ranks under the wall and started to march towards Corvin's force. The rear ranks of Sul'Lenans carried the large tower shields to stop the defenders on the wall hitting them with arrows as well. A fine gesture, if you were in the back rows. Not so good for those in the front rows. Arrows rained down from the defenders of the wall, arrows came thick and fast from Corvin's force. The Sul'Lenans were caught in an arrow storm from which there was no escape.

"Now would be a good time to throw some Volic," said Corvin to himself.

As soon as the words escaped his lips, jug upon jug of Volic flew from the wall, sailing over the heads of the Sul'Lenans, and landing many Lai in front of them. Corvin watched hundreds of jugs smash before a few fire arrows hit the flammable liquid. The explosion of heat knocked Corvin's force to the ground.

"GET BACK!" yelled Jorga.

All of Corvin's force got up of the ground and ran back a further two hundred Lai. They reformed and watched. The wall defenders went berserk, raining arrows and more Volic down upon the Sul'Lenans. Corvin could still feel the heat from the firewall and could just see the Sul'Lenans retreating closer to the walls to get away from the flames.

"Archers, FIRE!" ordered Molich.

"Good man," whispered Corvin.

The archers from Corvin's force fired, time and time again. They exhausted their supply and had to stop. They had more arrows with their stashed gear but none on them now. Corvin looked but could not see much beyond the firewall.

"Back to the camp!" Corvin yelled.

The force stood and ran back to the forest. As they reached the green bushes Corvin turned. The firewall was going out and beyond it all, he could see was Sul'Lenans. Thousands of dead Sul'Lenans. Looking at the sun, it was not even mid-day yet. The plan had worked wonderfully.

Geren approached Corvin and laid his hand on Corvin's shoulder.

"A good win, Commander," said Geren.

"Yes. We need some food and a quick rest," said Corvin.

"And then, Commander?" asked Geren.

"Then it is time to ignore my orders," said Corvin.

Geren grinned.

"You're going to get yourself in trouble again, Commander," said Geren.

Chapter Fourteen

Captain Brenik and Captain Joren had watched the ground force run off back into the forest.

"That worked better than expected," said Brenik.

"Yes, it did," said Joren.

Joren was watching the firewall burn down and looking at all the corpses on the ground below the wall. His men had done well. Corvin and Jorga's plan had worked so much better than he expected. It was a risk to send men over the wall, but once again, Corvin and his men had saved the day.

Brenik had changed the guard on the wall with fresh troops. He was also looking at the corpses below, not looking forward to the smell. The bodies were usually cleaned up at night when he sent small cleaning crews over the wall. They were dragged back from the wall and put in piles, then burnt. According to his teachers, in the last war, the clean-up crews did nothing else. No guard duty, no fighting, no anything. They slept all day and at night, climbed down if it was safe and cleaned up the day's mess. It was the only way to stop the spread of smell and disease.

However, since the Sul'Lenans had been attacking nonstop for the last three days, his clean-up crew had not been able to get over the wall. The smell was starting to get bad. The fire they used as a defence helped, but there was still one hell of a mess to clean up.

Brenik and Joren watched the battlefield. Apart from the still burning bodies, there was stillness. They could hear fighting from further down the wall to their left, but only just.

"Why did the Sul'Lenans never attack the entire length of the wall at once? They have the men for it," asked Joren.

"They do have the men for it, but probing certain areas of the wall is the way they have always done it. Also probing the way they do, this as a good way to concentrate their men on one section at a time. Even though they have the greater number, I think even they would be spread thin," said Brenik.

Joren looked over and saw the Kor'Lenan archers leaving the forest. They were gently jogging towards their position.

"They are returning now," said Joren.

"DROP THE ROPES!" called Brenik.

The ropes were quickly dropped for the returning men. As the force got close to the wall, Joren noticed Noro and Corvin running with them.

It was not long before the archers were climbing the wall, to applause and cheers. Joren smiled as he saw Corvin climb over the wall, with Noro not far behind. The cheers for Corvin were loud and as he made his way to the Captain, many a man slapped him on the back. However, Corvin was not smiling, he had a determined look on his face.

"Okay. This does not look promising," said Joren.

"No," said Brenik.

Corvin reached his Captain and slapped his fist in his chest in greeting.

"Well done, Commander!" said Brenik.

"Thank you, Captain. Can we have a word in the command tent, please? We have an opportunity and I do not want to miss it," said Corvin.

"You want to what?" asked Joren.

"Their camp is now almost empty. If the force under me leaves now, we can hide out until dark. Then, we hit the camp and destroy it, move on to the next camp, and repeat," said Corvin.

Emric, Dolac, Captain Joren and Captain Brenik where all in the command tent, listening to the request.

"That was not the plan," said Brenik.

"The original plan, yes. The plan you approved, no it was not," said Corvin.

"As Corvin said, we have an opportunity now. The force they sent was wiped out. The camp will be virtually empty. We want to get in, cause as much damage as we can, then get out," said Noro.

"Yes. Then, we move to the next camp along, wait for them to move off to attack the wall, make sure there is no large force, go in and do the same," added Corvin.

"I said 'no' the first time for a reason, Corvin," said Captain Joren.

"You did, sir, and you were right. It was too greater risk going into their camps as we did not know how many soldiers we were going to face, but now we have just destroyed over four thousand Sul'Lenans. We can get there and check to see how many men are left. If it is too many, we return. If it is defenceless, we hit it," said Corvin.

"Which is why your men are still in the forest and have not returned with the archers?" asked Captain Brenik.

"Yes," said Noro.

"You agree with this, Noro?" asked Captain Joren.

"Yes," said Noro.

"It's too good an opportunity to let slip, Captain," reminded Corvin.

Once again, Joren knew that Corvin was right, but he was reluctant to let Corvin off the leash. Too much at risk and after last year's disaster where they lost half the company, he did not want to risk it again.

"How many men did you lose?" asked Dolac.

"Not as many as I thought. First Squad lost one man; Fourth Squad lost three men," said Corvin.

"Four men?" asked Brenik.

"You are right, not as many as we expected," said Dolac.

"I lost sixteen men; they were all of the newer men I had," said Noro.

"Twenty in all? That is all we lost in the defence? I would say we have been bloody lucky," said Emric.

"Yes, we are. Convince me, Corvin! Convince me, I should let you off the leash to attack the camps," said Joren.

"First and Fourth Squad will return to the wall. For the plan, I'll take the Third Section only along with Noro's Sea Wolves. One hundred and eighty men should be more than enough for the fast attacks. If we can burn that camp to the ground before the reinforcements arrive, which will not be long, they will have to spend time building it again. Also, they will need to resupply which takes more time and effort. If we can move onto the next camp and destroy that, it will buy more time. We will not change the outcome or win the war, but it will provide breathing space for the forces on this section of the wall and hopefully further along. It will also provide us with information on what is going on in their camps, information that will be very useful," said Corvin.

"Information of their numbers, positions and morale. That alone makes the risk worth it," said Noro.

Brenik thought about it. He was not worried about wasting the lives of these men, they are mercenaries and paid to take risks. He was more concerned that Corvin was in charge and although impressed with the man and the things he had achieved, he did not trust him. Also, if they fell into the enemy hands and were tortured, there was too much information they could give away. He looked at Captain Joren.

"What do you think, Captain Joren? The information would be very valuable, wouldn't you agree?" asked Brenik.

"He has almost convinced me," said Joren.

"Captain, I trust Corvin to get the Third Section to the camp, do some damage and get back here; no one else could do it. Remember, it was Corvin and his fellows that made it across the land of the Outland bastards, living off the land, defending themselves and making it to our borders. It is not a case of should he go, it is a case of why he has not already gone," said Emric.

Captain Joren turned to Brenik.

"Captain, if I allow this you will need to convince the Colonel that the Bloodchildren, and the Sea Wolves, are worthy of a much larger bonus at the end of our contract," said Joren.

"The contract is the contract. You know this," said Captain Brenik.

"Then the answer is no. The contract is to defend the wall, not go down and take the fight to the enemy. We have already gone further than we have needed to. The towers we destroyed, whilst my men were over the wall. The recent action, my men hiding beyond the wall and hitting this force from behind. You said yourself, we have gone further than our duty. Convince the Colonel to make our bonus larger and I'll let them go," said Joren.

Captain Brenik knew it would be a hard battle to convince the Colonel to let more money go. It was not that Kor'Lena was a poor country, but they were very strict with their spending. This war could go on for years, just like the previous ones. However, the information would be very useful.

He pulled out a charcoal pencil and a piece of parchment. He spent some time writing a large note. He then folded it, tucked it into a leather pouch, wrapped it with string and tied it tight.

"RUNNER!" he yelled.

A young man, no older than fourteen appeared in the tent door.

"Sir?"

"Get this to the Colonel. Do not come back until he has given an answer," said Brenik.

The runner took it and left.

"I have just outlined the plan and what you expect in return, Joren. It is in his hands now," said Brenik.

It did not take long for the messenger to return. The young man was out of breath. The next section of wall at the town of Kor'Mor was not far, but he had run all the way, got the answer and ran back. Captain Brenik opened the letter and read it.

Let them go. I'll double their end of year bonus.
Colonel Kora

"You can go, Corvin, just get those men back here safely. Listen to Noro and Jorga," said Captain Joren.

"Also, take Molich and one squad of archers with you. They may come in handy," said Brenik.

"They will come?" asked Corvin.

"Yes," said Brenik.

Corvin along with Molich and one squad of archers left. They grabbed more packs of supplies, food mainly, and got themselves over the wall. As they ran back towards the forest, Corvin looked over his shoulder and saw the ropes being lifted back up. He grinned and continued. Open space, an objective and surrounded by men he trusted. This is where he belonged. He looked over at Noro jogging beside him. He also had a grin on his face. Noro and he had more in common than he realised.

"Good to be out from behind that wall, eh?" said Corvin.

Noro laughed. "You have no idea! Give me an open battlefield any time."

The force under Corvin got organised very quickly. Jorga had already stripped the dead men of armour, weapons and supplies. The armour and weapons were stacked neatly, free for anyone to replace their own tools that had seen better days. The food had been distributed amongst the men. The dead had been buried. The four bodies of First and Fourth Company that had died, were taken back to the wall by their own squads. Corporal Kalin and Geren were not happy about missing the raids, but the order had been confirmed by Captain Joren to return. Corvin had not told them it was his idea. The men of those squads were good fighters and the Third Section had been impressed by them and respected them, but they were not trained for what was about to happen. Corvin realised Noro's men were very similar to the former pit-rats. They enjoyed hit and run tactics, and were good at them. The Sea Wolves dead had been buried by their fellow company members.

"I have stacked all the weapons there, for us to replace what is broken or worn out. Once we have resupplied, we will stash them and come back for them. Too valuable to leave lying around," said Jorga.

"Good work, Sergeant. We ready?" asked Corvin.

"Yes, Commander. There was very few injuries apart from the large cut through Irikson's face. It has been stitched by one of the Sea Wolves and smeared with some sort of paste," said Jorga.

"Merlot paste. It helps the healing and stops the wound going bad," said Noro.

"Good. It should improve his looks," said Corvin.

Jorga laughed loudly along with Noro.

"Good. I don't like competition," said Noro.

Out of the forest in the south, 186 men moved out. It was late afternoon as they kept low and moved through the tall grass plains. Everyman carrying a backpack with plenty of food and water. Jorga said they had enough food to last roughly four days. Water should not be a problem as they passed many streams. Sea Wolves had taken on scouting duties, and Noro had sent two full squads out as a screen and extra eyes. The men in pairs surrounding the main force as they moved steadily. Corvin looked at the men around him. The former slaves all had slight smiles on their faces, with eyes of determination. Corvin had not realised how bad it had been stuck on the wall until they had been out in the open. The wall seemed to remind him of his former life, and he realised all of his brother slaves felt the same. Corvin nodded to himself again. Yes, out here running in the open, is where they belonged.

The light had faded. The force was hiding in the long grass of the plains, most were lying down and resting before the night was at its darkest, others sitting and eating. Fortunately, unless someone was standing right on top of them, they would not be seen. The main force was over two Melai from the encampment. Noro, Jorga and Corvin had carried some food and water forward to another position within six hundred Lai of the camp. They were on a slight rise and had a good view. They watched the encampment as the light faded. There were only a few people here and they had seen no soldiers.

The encampment was large. It looked roughly twice the size of the Bloodchildren's home camp back in Irik, except there were no walls. The first thing he noticed were large wooden buildings. These Corvin thought would be meeting halls, food halls and the like. Surrounding the rest of the camp looked like to be small huts. These were wooden frames and walls, with canvas as the roof. By the size of them, they looked like they could sleep ten to twenty men each.

"How many do you think those huts could sleep?" asked Corvin.

"Ten men, maybe more like fifteen," said Jorga.

"How many of those huts are there?" asked Noro.

Jorga counted. "Roughly three hundred."

Noro did the numbers in his head. "So that is roughly between three and six thousand men this camp could hold," he confirmed.

"I'll take your word for it," replied Corvin.

Corvin only had a basic understanding of numbers.

"They have these camps back from the wall, right across the country?" asked Jorga.

"Apparently, yes. The Colonel once said the count was up

to forty-five of these camps. That is potentially enough room to hold one and a half million men," added Noro.

"That number is too big for me to understand it, sorry," said Corvin.

"Agreed," added Jorga.

They continued to watch, noticing all movement and as many details as they could.

"Empty," Corvin finally said.

"Yes, seems that way. I have seen a few women that look like they are preparing hot food for their soldiers when they return," commented Jorga.

"Yes, but those soldiers won't return," said Noro.

"No, and it surprises me. It has been most of the day and you think they would send someone to check," added Jorga.

"You can't see the action from here and can only just see the wall. It took us all afternoon running to get here," said Noro.

"Yes it has. I have counted what looks like to be twenty different women so far," said Corvin.

"Yes, as well as what looks to be ten children who are treated no better than slaves," added Jorga.

It was true. Corvin had seen a few of the children treated roughly. He did not know what they had done, but they had been smacked upside the head or kicked.

"We need to be careful here. We won't kill woman and children," said Corvin.

"Neither will my men," agreed Noro.

"We get to the edges of the encampment and start some fire in the first buildings. Then once they are well alight, we make as much noise as possible and hopefully the woman and children will realise it is the enemy and not their men returning. Once they are out of the way, we help ourselves to some hot food, then we burn the rest of the camp. The problem is going to be using enough Volic to burn the camp quickly but saving enough for the next camp," offered Jorga.

"Yes, this makes sense. I think we get the men to tip a little Volic on burnable objects and not waste a whole jug. It will take longer, but it will still burn quick enough before the next camp realises and sends men," said Corvin.

"Which way do we go?" asked Noro.

"Further south for a few Melia, then turn and head towards the next camp in the east. That will avoid anyone from the next camp," Jorga said.

"Won't we risk running into them?" asked Noro.

"Yes, but it is the last thing they would expect. The natural thing for us would be to run north at speed, getting back to the wall. The last thing they would expect is us to hang around and have more fun," smiled Corvin.

Noro and Jorga chuckled.

"Midnight then?" asked Jorga.

"No. We hit the camp as soon as the sun sets. I want that hot food," said Corvin with a grin.

The raid had gone off perfectly. The force had run in quietly, covering the distance from their hiding spot in the grass, to the camp in a short time. They had left their packs hidden in the grass and only carried their weapons and a jug each of Volic. As planned, they had set fire to the first large wooden building they came across. Then with much banging of weapons and yelling, made as much noise as they could. The women and children came running from wherever they were, saw what was happening, and ran for it. They took off to the east, Corvin knew they were running for the next camp.

Once the woman and children had run, Corvin called everyone in.

"Everyone into that eating hall," Corvin said, pointing to the large hall in the middle of the camp.

"Grab some hot food, grab any supplies you can, and we will bun the rest of this place to the ground. Only use a small amount of Volic," instructed Corvin.

"Then, we head back to our packs, stash the supplies and head further south. Take only fresh food, if you can. We eat that first. We can't survive on hard food alone," added Jorga.

The men chuckled, then headed for the food hall. Noro, Jorga and Corvin stayed back and kept an eye out. A few of the Kor'Lenan archers had also started checking the other buildings on Molich's command.

"We don't eat goat, which is what these savages usually eat," said Molich.

Corvin nodded. He knew the Kor'Lenans thought these Sul'Lenans where savages, but meat was meat and he had eaten worse as a slave. He also saw Lorka searching the buildings as well.

"What is Lorka doing?" asked Corvin.

"He said he was checking for drink," said Jorga.

"I could bloody use a drink," said Noro.

"Yes, although we cannot afford to have your head muddled with drink," said Corvin.

"Especially not you or Irikson. No knowing who you will kill!" said Noro with a straight face.

Jorga roared with laughter. Corvin smiled.

"Bastard!" said Corvin muttered under his breath, which set Jorga and Noro laughing together.

He was headed to the cook house when he heard a shout go out. A voice he recognised all too well. It was Lorka, and he heard rage in his voice. Corvin turned and sprinted towards the sound. Jorga and Noro were with him. They ran around a small supply shed to see Lorka attacking a few of the Kor'Lenan archers. One Kor'Lenan archer was on the ground out cold, another was holding a broken nose and sitting on the ground, blood everywhere. The third one was trying to hold Lorka at bay. The Kor'Lenan was abusing Lorka and trying to throw a punch, which he could not. In the end, Lorka pulled him into a sickening head-butt, which dropped the archer onto the ground.

"HOLD!" yelled Molich who was drawing his weapon.

"Put up that weapon," said Corvin as he and Jorga and Noro arrived.

"No, Commander. He attacked my men!" said Molich.

The noise had brought most of the men from the eating hall, some still holding bowls of the stew and eating, whilst others had drawn their weapons and headed towards the sound. Molich was walking slowly towards Lorka, the remaining archers had drawn their bows and notched arrows. Seven of them, all of them pointed at Lorka, who had a murderous look on his face. He had taken his two-handed axe off his back and was standing there, looking at Molich with hate in his eyes.

"That was an order!" shouted Corvin.

"I don't take orders from slaves," said Molich.

"PIT-RATS DRAW WEAPONS!" yelled Jorga.

All of the pit-rats along with the Third Section drew their weapons and surrounded the seven archers. Irikson stood behind Molich.

"Slaves we may have been, but we still saved your arse a few times scum," said Irikson.

Corvin knew on his word, these men would be torn to pieces. The Third Section were very protective of each other.

"Lorka. What happened?" asked Corvin.

Lorka's face was hard, he spoke between clenched teeth and as he was angry, spoke in Outlandish.

"These scums were about to kill to children. CHILDREN!" said Lorka.

Corvin looked into the doorway of a hut. He could just see a small face, hiding and watching what was happening through the doorway. He felt his anger rise.

"They did what?" said Noro.

"I came across them, Commander. They found two children in the hut. I heard a scream and found them holding them up against the wall. I stopped them, you saw the rest," said Lorka.

Corvin turned to Molich. "You happy for your men to do this, Sergeant?"

"Sul'Lenans are not human, we do what we want with them!" said Molich.

"I knew they hated the Sul'Lenans but did not realise it was this bad," whispered Noro.

"There is never an excuse to harm a woman or a child, you scum," said Irikson.

Molich turned around and faced Irikson. He then saw all of the Third Section, and a number of Sea Wolves with their weapons drawn. His arrogance got the better of him.

"Your man will be punished for this. It is against the mercenary's code to strike a solider on the same side, especially the soldiers paying you," said Molich, with a sneer on his face.

Corvin looked at Noro. He had never heard this.

"Maybe, maybe not," said Noro.

"What is the penalty for killing these scums who breathe the same air as the rest of us, even though they do not deserve to?" asked Corvin.

"You would hang," said Molich.

Corvin looked over at Jorga. Jorga nodded slightly. He looked over at Lorka, who also nodded back at him. He had no need to look at Irikson. He knew what he was about to do, given half the chance.

"Lorka," said Corvin.

"Yes, Commander," said Lorka.

"Take his head," said Corvin, pointing at the one on the ground in front of Lorka.

"NOOOOOOO!" yelled Molich.

Too late, very quickly Lorka's axe came up and then down, severing his head in one blow from his axe. The head rolled towards Molich and stopped just before his feet. Corvin as always, moved with astonishing speed. He rushed the other two on the ground and cut their throats. Molich went to charge Corvin, but was foot tripped by Irikson.

"Move and I'll end your life," said Irikson.

Irikson's hand axe was resting on Molich's throat.

The remaining archers raised their bows with arrows ready, they were about to fire when the Third Section completely surrounded them. It was Torin who spoke.

"Put those bows down, or never leave this place," said Torin.

The archers lowered their bows.

"You will hang for this," said Molich.

"I hope so. Better to hang than fight for a people that treat others no better than animals. You are no better than the slave masters we used to be beaten by. You act more civilised, but the truth is you have the honour of worms. I thought your previous captain was an exception, turns out you are all the same," said Corvin.

Corvin wiped his swords on the dead archer at his feet before sheathing his weapon. The only noise that could be heard was the crackling of the burning buildings. Corvin looked at Noro, Noro nodded. Good Corvin thought, he agreed with what has happened. He did not care if he hung.

"Molich. Take your men and your packs, and head back to the wall. You are no longer needed or trusted. I am sure, we will continue the conversation of what you are, when I return. The rest of you, burn the rest of the camp and we go back for our packs," commanded Corvin.

All of the Sea Wolves ran off, laying some Volic on the wooden buildings before using the torch to light them. The Third Section also took off, putting the torch to everything they could find. Molich got up and walked off with his archers. He turned around and looked at Corvin.

"I would not say anything else, lad. The Commander may change his mind and kill you and yours where you stand, and I would love to watch it," said Noro.

Molich looked at Corvin and then with his men beside him, took off to get their packs before the run back to the wall. As they left, Corvin approached Lorka.

"Thank you, brother," said Corvin.

"For what?" said Lorka.

"Reminding us of who we are," said Corvin.

Lorka did not smile as he usually would. He was still worked up and Corvin could see the veins in his forehead pulsing under the growing firelight. Lorka just nodded.

It did not take long for the camp to be put to the torch. The Force moved off and returned to their packs they had hidden. They found them and found their gear had not been touched; this surprised Corvin. He had expected Molich or his men to tamper with them, but they hadn't. The men grabbed their packs and started jogging to the south. The night was dark, but the moon was up and of course, the flames from the burning camp could be seen from many Melai. They ran faster, time to put a little distance between themselves and the burning camp. They would run for some time before turning East and coming up behind the next camp.

As they jogged, Noro spoke to Corvin.

"Well done, lad. We will both be punished for this, but it will be well worth it," said Noro.

"Tell me that when we are both swinging," said Corvin.

Noro laughed. "That won't happen, lad."

"How you can be sure?" asked Corvin.

"Well, it may happen to you, but I'm pretty sure I am safe," grinned Noro.

Corvin smiled and continued to run; another problem to deal with, which Captain Joren would not be pleased about. Perhaps this is what the bad feeling Irikson had experienced before they came to this country. Time would tell.

They had approached the next camp and hidden in a small group of trees that was hardly big enough to be called a forest. The force all sat closely packed together throughout the night to stay hidden. They had run for most of the night, heading south then before midnight, turning east to come up behind the next camp. One of the scouts had found the small wood and said they would all just fit. Once into the trees, they had all eaten and rested. There was no need for scouts to watch as the group of trees was so small, no one could creep up on them without being seen. Noro and Corvin as well as Irikson and Jorga had sat at the front facing the next camp. This camp was only roughly nine hundred Lai from the trees. The four of them had watched the camp throughout the night and when the sun started to rise, it roused the men. They had all eaten some of the fresher food they'd found at the last camp, gotten water into themselves, then stashed their gear. All they carried once again was their weapons and a small jug of Volic, bound to their weapons belts with some leather straps found at the last camp.

As they kept watch, they slowly discussed and came up with a plan.

"The camp is exactly as the last camp," said Irikson.

It was true. If they had not spent half the night running here, they would have sworn they were looking at the same camp as the one they had just burned. The centre of the camp held a few large wooden buildings and surrounding this centre was more of the sleeping huts with canvas roofs.

"So, we wait until the men leave to attack the wall, then we go in?" asked Noro.

"Yes, although we need to be sure that they do not leave a reserve force," said Jorga.

"Also, we need to be weary of the men they sent to the camp we destroyed," said Corvin.

As they had reached the trees, they noticed a group of roughly five hundred men leave this camp and head in the direction of the camp they had attacked. The sun was now coming up, spreading its light across the land and the men they had watched leave, had not returned.

"There." Jorga pointed.

Corvin looked in the direction Jorga was pointing. He could see the Sul'Lenans force gathering. It looked larger than the force that had attacked the wall.

"How many?" asked Corvin.

Noro spent some time counting.

"I would say around four thousand men and add that to

the five hundred that left, and I would say we could be in for a bad day if they hang around," said Noro.

'We wait," said Corvin.

"Yes. No need to get excited," said Jorga.

They continued to watch as the force started moving north out of the camp. Luckily, the camp was in a hollow and they could just see over the building from where they were hiding. The force of men stopped outside of the camp, waiting.

"What are they waiting for?" said Irikson.

Noro pointed. "There, to the west."

They all looked over and saw the men that had left last night, fast walking towards the main force.

"They have returned," said Jorga.

The smaller force of men joined the larger one.

"I would love to be able to hear what they are saying," said Corvin.

"That would be handy," said Irikson.

They continued to watch.

"Finally, they are moving," said Irikson.

The main force was moving off towards the north, at an easy lope to conserve their energy for the fighting. However, a small group had turned and re-entered the camp.

"They are leaving a guard," said Jorga.

"Looks like two hundred men as a guard force," said Noro.

"We can take two hundred," said Irikson.

They all nodded.

"Tell the men. We wait a little longer to see if anyone else arrives, then we go in. This will be a hard fight, but we will get in, kill every man we come across and burn the place. We will reassemble here," said Corvin.

Corvin was going to mention the women and children they may come across but knew the men under him would not need to be reminded. Word was passed back, and a lot of the men stood, started stretching their arms. Corvin looked over all the faces he could see. No nerves or worried faces looked back at him. Strong, determined faces is all he saw. He looked at Lorka, who was holding his large two-handed axe in his hands. He looked pissed off. Corvin stood and approached him.

"Okay, brother?" asked Corvin.

Lorka shrugged his shoulders.

"What is it, brother?"

Lorka said nothing but just looked at the ground.

"Last night?" asked Corvin.

Slowly Lorka nodded.

"You have done nothing wrong," said Corvin.

"I know that, brother," said Lorka.

"Then what?"

"I did not want to get the rest of you in trouble, but no one does that to a child if I have anything to say about it," said Lorka.

Corvin put his right hand on Lorka's shoulder. Looked comical, Corvin standing close, his arm reaching up to reach Lorka's shoulder.

"We would have all done the same. Do not worry about what will happen when we get back. What have you told me before about worrying?" said Corvin.

"Let tomorrow look to itself," said Lorka.

Corvin smiled. So many times, in the slave camp, Lorka had calmed Corvin down and stopped him from worrying. Now it was time to return the favour.

"If we get into trouble when we get back, we get in trouble together. If they try to hang one of us, we all go down fighting, together," said Corvin.

Lorka smiled finally.

"If there is any justice in this shit world, I'll get to cut Molich's throat!" said Corvin.

Lorka's smile grew bigger.

"Get in line, brother," said Lorka.

Corvin chuckled, squeezed Lorka's huge shoulder, then moved back to the front.

"No change?" asked Corvin.

"None," replied Noro.

Corvin looked at the sky, the sun was now up almost fully, and the dark had gone from the land.

"We move now," said Corvin.

The force charged. As instructed, they sprinted, as fast as they could. There was no time for a steady jog to save their energy. They had to get in, wipe out the guards left, burn the place and move on. The men were instructed to do not bother looking for supplies. Get in, do the damage, then get out.

They all stayed together; 186 men all standing at each other's shoulders. They hit the centre of the camp, right into the reserve force of what looked closer to three hundred men rather than two hundred. There was no time for thinking, quick plans or strategy. The guard force had been waiting. They stood in tight ranks, shields to the front. If they had archers, Corvin's force would have been wiped out

"CHARGE THEM!" yelled Corvin.

As one, they all ran in. Lorka had shot forward a few Lai, eager to be first to hit the line. Irikson and Torin ran to join him and were just behind him when he hit the shield wall. He used his large axe, held across his body at waist height as a ram. He hit the wall, his size and weight knocking over three of the Sul'Lenans. He jumped over the three that had fallen and was amongst them. His axe in hand, swinging left and right, jabbing out and causing death wherever he struck. Torin and Irikson were just behind him, preventing him being surrounded.

"You crazy bastard, that's my job," yelled Irikson as he blocked a spear coming at his throat with his right-hand axe.

He brought his left-hand axe up and cut the spare in half. He surged forward and brained the wielder with his right-hand axe. Torin chuckled and blocked a spear on his shield, his sword locking out at the wielders throat when he stepped forward to close the distance.

Corvin blocked a sword with his left-hand sword, then sent his hand axe in a straight jab that connected with wielders head, knocking him out. Corvin felt something was wrong and turned behind them. Charging in from behind them was another fifty men.

"Fuck!" was all Corvin said.

Chapter Fifteen

"THIRD SECTION, BEHIND YOU!" screamed Corvin as he turned to the rear.

The Third Section had heard and disengaged where they could. Torin, Lorka and Irikson were in the midst of the battle at the front, and were stuck. As the Third Section disengaged and ran to join Corvin, the Sea Wolves jumped into the gaps the Third Section had made and fought furiously.

"SEA WOLVES! PUSH THEM BACK!" screamed Noro.

Noro knew the Sea Wolves had to hold the men in front while Corvin dealt with the ones at the rear.

As Corvin reached the small force that had come in from behind them, the Third Section were at his shoulder and behind them.

"SNOW WEASEL!" yelled Jorga as the forces hit each other.

Corvin dived forward into a tumbler roll, as he came up, he led with his sword; his sword lancing into the groin of the first Sul'Lenan. The sword got stuck and Corvin stepped past him, drawing his knife. Sweat was coming down his face and he wanted to wipe his brow but had no chance. He blocked a sword that was coming for his throat with his dagger, his hand axe coming round and straight into the side of the Sul'Lenan, cutting through his leather armour and sticking into his side. He pushed the sword away and his dagger came straight across the Sul'Lenan's throat. As the body fell, he tugged his axe loose, in time to block an axe that came for his own neck. His axe had stopped the Sul'Lenan's axe only a fingers width from his own throat. Corvin snarled and went to follow through with his dagger, when a large sword went straight into the side of the Sul'Lena. Jorga was at Corvin's right shoulder.

"Take my short sword!" yelled Jorga.

As Jorga stepped in front of Corvin to take on the next Sul'Lena, Corvin sheathed his dagger and grabbed the short sword from Jorga's right hip. Corvin stepped to Jorga's right and engaged again. He stabbed out with his sword, slashing a Sul'Lenan across the face, his sword going through the cheek of the man. He had been aiming for the throat, but his aim was off. Corvin's hand axe went down and then up, straight into the groin of the Sul'Lena. The Sul'Lena screamed once as the axe went in and screamed louder as Corvin pulled the axe clear. Corvin then shoulder charged a Sul'Lenan, knocking him to the ground. Youst came running in and slashed his own sword across the throat of the man on the ground, before stepping into another Sul'Lenan. Corvin then stepped back and to the left, as a spear came at him fast. The spear went past Corvin's right ear. His hand axe battered it away before Corvin's left hand sword went straight through into the stomach of the Sul'Lenan. His hand axe came up quickly again as another spear came at his face, but the spear never reached him as Youst had intercepted the wielder and head-butted him before slashing his sword across the wielder's face.

"Thank you, brother," said Corvin as he dragged his sword free.

Youst smiled and engaged another target. Corvin moved again but with more urgency. They needed to end this rear force and re-join Noro. He surged into action, two Sul'Lenans dying under his attack. He engaged another, killing him with a sword stab to the chest, his axe almost taking the arm of another that had got to close. He pulled his sword clear and finished the man off with a long slash across the face. Youst was at Corvin's side and stopped a sword going straight for Corvin's neck. Youst then stepped in, kicked the Sul'Lenans in the balls, and stabbed him in the chest as the man was going down. Corvin stopped and realised the force was finished.

"BACK TO THE FRONT!" shouted Corvin.

As one, the Third Section turned and sprinted back to the front, where the Sea Wolves were battling hard.

"HIT THE FLANKS!" yelled Jorga

The Third Section split and ran to the left and right of the Sea Wolves. Corvin could see many dead, Sea Wolves and Sul'Lenans. As he hit the side of the Sul'Lenans, he heard Irikson in full voice, screaming his insults. Corvin was tired now. A night without sleep had not helped. He shifted his body to the side as a Sul'Lena thrusted a sword at him. The sword brushed up against his armour and Corvin slammed his axe into the Sul'Lenan's neck. As he pulled his axe free, he felt his head explode. As he fell, the last thing he remembered hearing was Lorka's voice.

"DEMON-BOY!"

Corvin woke and found himself lying on the ground, with a blanket over him. He looked up and saw the stars, it was night. He looked around and saw himself surrounded by his men. All were either lying down sleeping or sitting and eating. He tried to get up and a pain shot through his head. He felt dizzy and laid back. His head was spinning.

"You are awake," said Noro coming to sit beside him.

"Just," said Corvin.

"You had me worried, lad," said Noro.

"What happened Noro?" asked Corvin.

"A Sul'Lena smacked you in the side of your head with the flat of his axe. Luckily, it was the flat and not the blade," said Noro.

"It does not feel bloody lucky," said Corvin.

Jorga sat on the other side of him laying his hand on his chest.

"Rest, brother," said Jorga.

"What happened?" repeated Corvin.

"Open your mouth and take this," said Noro.

Corvin obeyed and open his mouth. Noro slowly poured water from a cup into his mouth as Jorga supported Corvin's head, holding it up so he could swallow. Corvin went to spit it out.

"No, lad. Trust me, swallow it. It will help with the pain," said Noro.

Corvin forced himself to swallow it all. Jorga laid Corvin's head back down.

"The water had some pain paste in it. Rest, we are safe and hidden. We will talk when you wake," said Jorga.

Corvin wanted to know what was happening but trusted in Jorga. He closed his eyes, and it was not long before he was fast asleep again.

"How much pain paste did you put in it?" asked Jorga.

"A lot. He needs a full night of sleep. As you said, we are safe here. He needs the rest, and so do the rest of us," said Noro.

"Did he wake?" asked Lorka, who had moved over to them.

"Yes, briefly. We gave him some pain paste and he fell asleep again," said Noro

"He will be fine. He has been through worst," said Jorga.

"True," said Lorka.

Corvin slept through the night. He slept without dreams and when he woke in the morning, his head pounded. The pain in his head was worse than the hangover he and Irikson had suffered on their binge, that saw them kill the men in the forest. He opened his eyes and the bright sun hurt his eyes. He sat up and wished he had not. The pain behind his left eye making him almost whimper. He sat with his hand over his left eye and breathed deeply.

"Drink this, brother," said a voice.

Corvin looked to the left and saw Lorka holding a jug with a smile on his face. That warm smile that had gotten Corvin through many hard times.

"More pain paste and water?" said Corvin.

"No. Some sort of juice that the Sul'Lenans make from fruit. It is sweet and very refreshing," said Lorka.

Corvin took it and sipped slowly. It was sweet and as he swallowed a mouthful, he smiled.

"That is good. Where did you get that from?" asked Corvin.

"Jorga found it before we put that camp to the torch. The small storeroom full of the stuff. Jugs of it stacked from the floor to the roof. After Jorga tried it, he commanded all of us to grab as many as we could. We made off with quite a bit of it," said Lorka.

"Tastes good," said Jorga as he and Noro came to sit down in front of Corvin.

"So, what happened?" asked Corvin.

"We lost a few," said Jorga.

"How many?" asked Corvin.

"More than we wanted," said Noro.

Corvin looked at Jorga and saw the pain behind his eyes. He knew in that instance things had gone wrong.

"Who?" asked Corvin.

"Youst, Celix, Benik, Bordix, Meron, the two brothers Goro and Jimny, and finally Ceron," said Jorga.

Corvin's heart broke. Four more former slaves were dead and four of the Irik recruits under him who he had become close to.

"Forty-one Sea Wolves are also dead," said Noro.

"I am sorry. I should have guessed they would leave more soldiers behind," said Corvin.

"It's not your fault, Demon-child. We escaped, the camp was put to the torch and we got clear," said Lorka.

"Yes, we are lucky we did not lose more. It was a tough fight," said Noro.

"So how many left? I cannot think," said Corvin.

"The Third Section has sixteen left, not including yourself," said Jorga.

"The Sea Wolves have 123 left," said Noro.

"Too many," said Corvin.

They all stayed silent as Corvin worked through his own emotions. Finally, it was Noro that spoke.

"When we saw you go down, we fought harder. Not has

hard as Lorka here, who charged through everyone to get to your side. Then he carried your body here," said Noro.

Corvin looked up and into Lorka's eyes.

"Had to," said Lorka.

"Thank you, brother. You saved my life," said Corvin.

"Once you went down, it did not take long to finish the rest off. We stripped our men of their armour and weapons, put all the bodies into their eating hall and set fire to the place," said Noro.

"Where are we?" asked Corvin.

"After what happened, we were not sure whether we run north to the wall or hide out. Jorga, however, came up with a plan and we ran to not the next camp, but the one after that. We hid in the small woods, where our gear was stashed. We waited until it was dark and then ran through the night. We made it not long after midnight and thankfully found this thick bush to hide in," said Noro.

"So where are we exactly?" asked Corvin.

"Fourth camp along," said Jorga.

"Fourth camp?" asked Corvin.

"We hit the first camp, then the second, we missed out the third and are now roughly four Melai away from the fourth camp, which looks like a major supply camp for them, from what we can see," said Jorga.

Corvin smiled, then spoke.

"Do what the enemy least expects," said Corvin.

"As always," said Jorga.

"What's the plan now? Where is Irikson?" asked Corvin.

"Irikson is on watch, and as to what we plan? It is up for discussion," said Noro.

"Jorga. What is your assessment?" Corvin asked.

"From what we have seen, the amount of enemy at this camp

is smaller. We have seen roughly two thousand soldiers. However, the amount of supplies that they hold looks like much more. The size of the wooden building in the centre of this camp is double to what was at the first two camps. I think we wait another day or two, then hit it. Once we do this, we make our escape and head back to the wall. We have done and lost enough," said Jorga.

"Agreed," said Noro.

"It sounds like a long way back to the wall," said Corvin.

"Four to five full days of running," said Jorga.

"How many if we head straight north, to the wall?" asked Corvin.

"Half a day, but why would be risk that?" asked Noro.

"Because the Sul'Lenans would not expect it," said Corvin.

"Correct. They know we are out here somewhere, and only our habit of hanging around close to their camps has kept us safe. I think they have horseman out looking for us but are looking too far out to find us. Perhaps we hit this last camp at midday when the sun is at its highest, we then look for a hiding place between the two camps but further to the north. As soon as the Sul'Lenans return at the end of the day, we head north at speed," said Jorga

"Yes, hopefully we do not get shot full of arrows from the Kor'Lenans when we reach the wall," added Corvin.

"No, we head to our end of the wall. It would mean a longer run, but worth it," said Lorka.

"Yes," agreed Jorga.

Corvin's head was still throbbing, but not as bad. He drank the jug of fruit juice and asked for more. Lorka brought him another jug of the juice and also some food they had taken.

"How are you feeling?" asked Noro.

"Head is throbbing, like a bad hangover," said Corvin.

They nodded.

"Give me another night and I'll be ready to move," said Corvin.

Corvin had spent the day slowly walking around talking to the men. He had visited every single one of the men from the Third Section and held a conversation with them. The former pit-rats were, of course, devastated at the loss of more of their number. Even though all of the former slaves were proud to be a part of the Bloodchildren, more than once the comment was heard that if they continued as they were, there would be no pit-rats left. Corvin agreed with them and made the promise to himself to have a long conversation with Jorga when they get back to the wall.

Corvin's head started to feel better throughout the day. He continued to drink the juice that was sweet on the tongue and refreshing, just as Jorga had said it was. Jorga and Corvin spoke at length about Youst. The youngest of the former Pit-rats who had been killed. Youst had saved Corvin twice in the last battle, and now Corvin would not be able to thank him or return the favour. Jorga was hiding it well, but Corvin knew he had been hit hard by the loss of the Youst. A pit-rat that Jorga had watched over and trained.

"You trained him well, brother. He saved my life twice in that battle," said Corvin.

"Not well enough," said Jorga, who was clearly blaming himself.

Corvin said nothing. He knew nothing he said would help right at this moment, so he just sat in silence beside his brother.

"They are leaving," said Jorga.

"How many?" asked Corvin.

"All of them. Looks like just over two thousand men," said Noro.

"Do you have someone in your ranks that is, how would I describe it, a sneaky bastard?" asked Corvin, looking at Noro.

"Yes," said Noro.

"Send him in. Get a good look at the place and report back to us," directed Corvin.

The sun had come up but was not fully up. Corvin hoped a runner could sneak close, make sure there was no more surprises and get back to them.

"Megen!" called Noro.

A small man with fire orange hair came running.

"Noro, sir?" asked Megen.

"Can you get to the camp, have a look and get back here safely?" asked Noro.

Megen looked over the approach to the camp. He looked over the ground, judged the best route and then turned to Noro.

"Yes, sir. I can."

"Get in there. Normal signals, stay safe," said Noro.

Megen ran off. He was running in a half crotch but still managed to cover the ground quickly. Within a short time, he was standing with his back to the wall of a sleeping hut. He was hiding in the shadow of the building, with the sun not fully up, he was almost invisible.

"Impressive," remarked Jorga.

"Yes. Used to be a thief," said Noro.

They all watched in silence as Megen ran from shadow to shadow, having a good look. After a while, he stood up straight and walked out from the shadow that he was hiding in. He walked past all the sleeping huts.

"What is he doing," asked Corvin.

"Does not look like anyone is home," said Noro.

Megen then walked back to the perimeter and gave Noro the signal.

"Done. The place is empty," said Noro.

"Alert the men! We move now," said Corvin.

Jorga ran off back to the camp. When he returned, all of the men were running with him, and all of them carried their back packs.

"Packs?" asked Noro.

"We are heading north, no point running back to grab our things," said Jorga.

"Good point," said Noro.

The men moved quickly into the camp. They stopped and looked around, and could see no one. Megen came running back.

"Enemy?" asked Noro.

"No, sir, but a good surprise. Follow me," said Megen.

"The rest of you pour the remaining Volic on every building you find, but do not light it yet," said Jorga.

All of the men set off in every direction. Corvin, Jorga, Irikson and Noro followed Megen. Megen ran to a large building that looked like it was storage. They all entered and when they saw what was in there, all of their mouths dropped open.

"Is that what I think it is?" asked Noro.

"Yes, sir. I tasted it," said Megen.

They all looked at the building and the tall shelves that went from floor to roof. All of those shelves packed with jugs of Volic.

"That will make a nice fire," said Irikson.

"Yes, it will," replied Corvin.

"It looks like at least a couple of thousand jugs of the stuff!" said Jorga.

"Yes," said Megen.

"Irikson, you and Jorga start smashing some jugs on the ground. Maybe 100 jugs should do," said Corvin.

Jorga and Irikson started smashing the jugs on the ground. The smell of the spirit filled their nostrils. Corvin left with Noro in tow. Megen joined in the smashing of jugs and Corvin could hear giggling. He smiled.

"I don't think we will ever grow up," said Corvin.

"I hope not," said Noro with a chuckle.

Before long, all the men had returned to the centre of the camp. All of their Volic now gone as everything was soaked. They had all taken the time to eat some fresh food and refill their water skins. They grabbed a small amount of food but did not stock up like they usually did. In theory, they were running straight for the wall and wanted to be light as possible. The sun was now up fully and Irikson had sent a few men to keep watch in all directions.

"Are we ready?" asked Corvin.

"Yes. We will light all of the buildings except the large Volic storage building and then leg it," said Jorga.

"Why not the large Volic building?" asked Irikson.

"The other fires will eventually reach it, and I am hoping it will be a rather large bang when it goes up," said Jorga.

"Noro, you had some men out scouting for a position to hide?" asked Corvin.

"Yes, but they are not back yet," said Noro.

"Okay as soon as they are back, we move. As soon as the flames take, run like hell. We want to be as far away as possible when the Volic storage goes up. It will attract a lot of attention," said Corvin.

They all nodded. Noro walked away as he saw two of his men running in hard.

"Found something?" he asked.

"Yes, sir. A deep hollow about two Melai from here towards the north-west. It's deep enough for us to lie in with our blankets over us and not be seen. We would have to keep a few men on the lip to keep watch," said the man.

"No bush or woods?" asked Corvin.

"No, Commander. Nothing," answered the second man.

"The hollow ground it is. MOVE!" shouted Corvin.

All the men scattered throughout the camp. Corvin led the men without torches away from the camp, they stopped five hundred lai out into the open and all crouched. Corvin looked towards the wall but apart from the outline of the wall, could not see much. Certainly, he could not see any Sul'Lenans. Of course, they would be fighting and trying to get over the wall, but best to be careful. His head was still a little sore, but not enough to stop him running.

The men that had fired the camp came running. Beyond them, small stacks of smoke could be seen coming out of the buildings. As the men crouched next to the main force, Corvin spoke.

"We move quickly and we move quiet. What's left of Seventh Squad are our scouts and will move out around us. Noro's scouts will lead us to the hollow. Once there, we rest up. As soon as the sun goes down, we make for the wall," instructed Corvin.

The men were tired and all of them effected by the loss in the last battle. However, they all had determination written all over their faces.

"Move," Corvin said.

As one, they all stood up and followed Noro's scouts, not a

flat out run but not a jog either. Corvin wanted to get there quickly, but not for them to tire themselves out.

"Here they come now," whispered Corvin.

"Not many left," said Noro.

There was roughly nine hundred men running towards the camp they had put to the torch.

"No. They must have lost a few when they tried to disengage from the wall," said Jorga.

"The small fire must have got their attention," said Noro.

Corvin and Jorga laughed.

The small fire had been spectacular and not small at all. All of the men had been lying and resting under their blankets. Except for the senior men that were keeping watch on the lip of the hollow. The hollow was as deep as Corvin was tall, at its deepest point and there was more than enough room for the men to all lie down and relax. Noro had his men watching the south, and west side of the hollow. Corvin, Jorga and Noro had been on the Northeast side to watch for the returning soldiers. They were watching the open grass land when there was large boom. All eyes turned to where they had come from. The men under their blankets threw them off and made their way to the lip. All could see the massive firewall that had shot into the sky and the smoke that followed it.

"Burns well," laughed Noro.

As Corvin watched the Sul'Lenans running to get back to their camp, he noticed what looked like more men coming from further east.

"Is that more men?" asked Corvin.

Jorga looked to where Corvin was pointing.

"Looks like it, yes. A lot more than that lot that will pass us soon," said Jorga.

"Make sure the men are well hidden but have their weapons ready. They will only pass us by four or five hundred Lai," said Corvin.

Jorga moved off to inform the men.

"When are we going to move?" asked Noro.

"I'm tempted to wait for night, harder to see us, but would rather arrive at the wall in full light and not get fired at," replied Corvin.

Jorga returned with Torin with him.

"Torin, your eyes are better than mine. How many men does that look like?" asked Corvin.

Torin looked and quickly answered.

"About four or five hundred roughly," said Torin.

"What about the other group farther east and behind those?" asked Noro.

Torin raised his head and looked out at the second group that was perhaps one Melai from them

"Fuck!" said Torin.

"How many?" asked Corvin.

"Over a thousand!" replied Torin.

"They must really be pissed off," said Noro with a huge smile.

"Inform the men. As soon as all of those Sul'Lenans reach the camp and start fighting the flames, we make a run for it," said Corvin.

Torin and Jorga crept back from the lip and went to inform the men.

"We are only two Melai from that camp. They may catch us if they see us," said Noro.

"Yes," said Corvin.

"How far to our section of the wall?" asked Noro.

Corvin looked over to the north and saw where the wall meets the cliffs. He could only see the outline but was growing in confidence with estimating distance.

"I would say four or five Melai," replied Corvin.

"I don't mind a good fight, but all this bloody running," said Noro.

Corvin chuckled to himself.

"Keeps you fit," said Corvin.

"You do realise that if we are seen, it will be a race to the wall?" asked Noro.

"Then, they better not see us," said Corvin.

"We can't outrun them?" asked Noro.

"We could, you can't, old man," said Corvin.

That earned him a slap across the shoulder.

Corvin laughed.

"Murdering savage," muttered Noro.

Corvin looked over at the men in the hollow. They had strapped their packs on, that were empty, and stood ready. Jorga had got all the men to have a light snack of the food they had left and throw the rest. They also had a small drink and tipped the rest of their water out on the ground. No one can run on a full stomach. Corvin watched as the Sul'Lenans made their way past and got closer to the camp that was well and truly ablaze.

"PICK UP THE PACE. WE HAVE BEEN SEEN!" yelled Corvin.

They had all left, he followed and made good time for the first Melai. After that, Corvin had eased the pace a little. No sooner had he done that, a call went up from the back. They had been spotted and were being chased. All of the men increased their speed. Not a flat-out sprint but what trainer would have called a good pace. They were still three Melai from the wall.

"How far back?" asked Corvin.

"They have just left the camp. I would say three Melai," said Jorga.

"They won't catch us then. We have to run the same distance and they can't outrun us," said Irikson.

"HORSES," yelled one of Noro's men from the back.

"You had to say it, Irikson," said Lorka.

"They will catch us and quickly. Can we make it to the wall and be with in arrow range before they catch us?" asked Noro.

"No. We will still be just over a Melai away from the wall when they get to us," said Jorga

"Shit!" responded Noro.

"Spread the word. When I give the order we stop, turn and wait for them," instructed Corvin.

The word spread quickly.

"Jorga. You make the call," said Corvin.

Jorga nodded his head. As he ran, he looked back over his shoulder now and then to gauge the distance of the riders.

"There's 150 of them," said Jorga.

"Won't be when we are done," said Irikson.

Corvin breathed heavy as they continued to run. He slowed the pace again slightly and waited for Jorga to give the call. It would be a fine line to draw but he trusted his brother. Corvin concentrated on his breathing, feeling the anger build in him. They had done what they set out to do, lost many men whilst doing it and could not even catch a break when they were heading towards home. He was bitter. From the behaviour of Molich and his men, the loss of more men and now the horsemen.

"Bastards!" said Corvin.

Jorga knew the sign. His brother was starting to enter his

fight rage. He knew he would not make the best decisions when his blood was up.

"Commander. Can I run this battle?" asked Jorga.

Corvin looked at Jorga, looked into his eyes as they ran towards the wall. He saw a seriousness in his eye. He did not know why he had asked, but once again trusted him.

"SERGEANT JORGA NOW COMMANDS THE FORCE!" Corvin shouted.

All of the men heard but did not understand. The former pit-rats did. The only reason Corvin would hand over command is if he knew he was unable to command himself. The only reason he would be unable to command was if he were injured or going into one of his black moods. One look at Corvin's face and the former pit-rats knew what the reason was this time.

Irikson was smiling and muttering to himself. He knew the mood Corvin was working himself into, and he welcomed it.

"Fucking horsemen trying to get us. Bastards are about to learn," muttered Irikson.

Lorka looked at Jorga. Jorga nodded at Corvin. It did not need to be said. Lorka knew his job was now to keep up with Corvin and protect him.

Corvin's head would not stop, around in circles his thoughts flew. Smith, Trainer, the bastard Outlanders and every other thing in the world that upset him or pissed him off came flashing into his brain. Corvin was now lost into his anger, he was speaking to himself and even ignored the singing coming from Irikson:

> *The lady did not know me, and she was not free,*
> *I had coins to pay her, so she called me a sir.*

Jorga was continuing to look over his shoulder, and ignoring Irikson and Corvin for now.

"The defenders on the wall will not be able to help us, but they will be able to see us, they will watch us, and they will judge us," said Jorga in a loud clear voice.

Corvin felt his pace quicken. Soon. Soon, he would unleash.

"LET THEM JUDGE US!" shouted Jorga.

A loud war cry went up from the 139 men running towards the wall. If the defenders could not see them, they certainly heard that war cry and the screams that followed it. Corvin was now chewing on the inside of his cheek. His jaw clenching and unclenching as he barely held himself in check. Soon.

"What the hell was that?" asked Captain Brenik.

"War cries," said Emric.

"From where?" asked Brenik.

Dolac pointed in the distance to a small group of men, running towards them. The distance was far too great to see who they were, but they could see outlines of men running towards the wall.

"Who are they?" asked Brenik.

"Shall we see?" asked the Colonel.

"Colonel. When did you arrive, sir?" asked Brenik.

"Just now, Captain," said the Colonel.

The Colonel took out his viewing glass, extended the tube and looked through it. He laughed loudly before handing the tube to Captain Joren.

Joren took it and looked through it.

"Corvin," said Captain Joren.

The Bloodchildren around heard who it was and started cheering.

"Quiet. He is not out of danger yet," said Joren.

Joren handed the viewing glass back to the Colonel.

"If I am not mistaken, that is a very large dust cloud further back from them. That could only mean horses," said Joren.

"Yes," said the Colonel.

"We go over the wall and wait for them, sir?" asked Dolac.

"No. No more men over the wall," said the Colonel.

Dolac looked at the Colonel and said nothing.

"It is a race then!" said Joren.

"Yes Captain, it looks that way," said Dolac.

"No. It is not a race," said Emric.

"What do you mean?" asked the Colonel.

Emric turned to his Captain.

"Remember Corvin and his men when they first arrived at the wall of Irik, at the border town of Bordix," said Emric with a smile.

Captain Joren and Dolac both laughed.

'What?" asked the Colonel.

"Do not want to ruin the surprise for you, Colonel," said Captain Joren.

"They will be fine, sir," Dolac said to the Colonel.

Dolac moved off to stand with his section; Emric went to stand with his.

It was just Captain Brenik and the Colonel standing at their part of the wall now.

"You got the message I sent then?" asked Captain Brenik.

"Yes. That is why I have come," said the Colonel.

"They killed three of my men," said Brenik.

"Yes, and if they make it back to the wall, they will face a trial and then hang for it," said the Colonel with a blank look. Such a waste, he thought to himself.

"STOP AND TURN!" yelled Jorga.

The force stopped and turned. They all stood catching their breath. Corvin had moved to the front. His weapons were in his hands, and his chest was moving up and down as he breathed hard. All of the others had done the same.

"On my word, we charge the bastards," said Jorga in a voice just loud enough to carry over the force.

Irikson stood on Corvin's left, on his right the powerful figure of Lorka.

"You ready, Snow Weasel?" asked Irikson.

Corvin did not reply. He watched as the horsemen rode fast towards them. No sound did Corvin hear, just the throbbing of the blood in his veins. The rage had taken him.

"What are they doing?" yelled the Colonel.

"Fighting your war for you," said an unknown voice from amongst the Bloodchildren.

There was much chuckling throughout the company. Captain Joren would normally quieten down the men, but this time, he let it slide. It is not as if whoever had shouted out was wrong. Corvin and his force where indeed fighting the war for the Kor'Lenans. He had grown to dislike the Kor'Lenans and their lazy attitude to war, to fighting and to honour. He had heard the rumours of Corvin and his men killing someone they were not supposed to but did not have all the details. He knew that is why the Colonel was here. Dolac, himself and

Emric had spoken about it last night. There was nothing they could do until Corvin returned, if he returned. Now here he was again on the wall, watching the best Sergeant he had ever seen, about to do battle in front of him. Once again, he was powerless to help.

Corvin and the men around him waited. The horsemen were within five hundred Lai now and would be on them within heartbeats. Corvin did not need to look at the men around him to know they were not nervous. He knew they were like him, determined and pissed off. Irikson was still mumbling to himself but Corvin could not hear it. His anger was there, right under the surface and ready to explode on his next victim. The people he killed today were indeed victims, and not enemy soldiers. Enemy soldiers would have some chance of surviving. These victims on horseback had no chance. Corvin blinked and the horsemen were within three hundred Lai. He started clenching his jaw, his arms were almost shackling as the rage started to come out. He needed to let it out, he could not wait any longer. Jorga behind him knew Corvin was over eager. He also knew if he did not give the order soon, Corvin would charge regardless of timing. The horsemen were at one hundred Lai, then fifty Lai almost on them, when Jorga heard a blood curdling yell.

"ANGER IS A GIFT!" screamed Corvin.

The men standing responded with a howl of their own.

Jorga breathed in and gave the word.

"NOW!" screamed Jorga.

The men responded and surged forward. Not as quick as Corvin who had exploded like he does, and was in the lead, running almost alone at the two hundred horsemen. Lorka and Irikson were trying to catch up with him but had no chance. Corvin would strike the first blow, as was his way.

"Son of a bastard!" said the Colonel.

He had heard and seen Corvin and his men from a distance, but never seen them in action so clearly. He had sworn in fright as the howl from the combined force under Corvin had howled and charged forward.

"He will get them all killed," said Captain Brenik.

"I'll take that wager," said Sergeant Dolac with an evil grin.

"Agreed. Those horsemen are already dead, they just don't know it yet," said Captain Joren.

Corvin may have made a few mistakes in the last few months, but he was inspirational to watch. As Corvin ran ahead of the others, Joren's heart almost exploded with pride of the young man.

As they all watched from the wall, they were all silent. They watched as Corvin had reached the horsemen first, had jumped high in the air and sent his axe slicing through the rider's neck before landing on the ground and moving forward once again. They all witnessed with open mouth astonishment as they saw Lorka charge a horse head on and knock it over as he collided with it, the rider being caught under the beast as it fell. They saw Irikson dodge a horse and then grab the rider and haul himself up onto the saddle, bringing his twin hand axes down onto the neck of the rider before rolling backwards off the horse and searching for another target. Jorga, the big blond giant standing his ground with his two-handed long sword, slicing horses and men alike as he stood in the middle of the battle, the rest of the Third Section standing in line with him, dodging horses and attacking where they could. The watchers on the walls saw Noro and his men swamp riders, three or four men to a horse, dragging the men from their saddles and viciously killing the riders, before moving off and attacking again.

"My god, what a sight! They are, an example of fighting men," said a new voice.

Captain Joren turned to see Duke Eason and two of his guards standing there.

"Welcome, Duke. How are you here?" asked Captain Brenik.

"I invited him," said the Colonel.

"I am glad I came," said Duke Eason.

He watched with open amazement at the battle before him. He had seen Corvin and Irikson in a fight before when they saved him, but now to see them on the battlefield, was truly amazing.

"They fight well," said the Colonel.

"More than that," said the Duke.

All looked on as a chant started up from the Bloodchildren, slowly and quietly at first until Dolac and Emric heard and joined in, encouraging their men to join and chant louder.

"Snow Weasel, Snow Weasel, Snow WEASEL, SNOW WEASEL!" they all chanted.

The Duke smiled.

"They worship him," he said in a half whisper.

"Yes. Yes, they do," said the Colonel beside him.

"You do know that will make what lies ahead very difficult," said the Duke.

"Yes," said the Colonel.

In time, the Kor'Lenans were also chanting. The ones that did not speak Outlander did not know what the words meant, but out of respect, they chanted with their hearts and throats as loud as they could. One squad of Kor'Lenans was not chanting, a group of archers standing to the far left. They watched with hate. Their leader, Molich, standing with a sneer on their face.

"Let them be slaughtered," said Molich under his breath.

Corvin dodged to the left as a horseman came at him. As he moved left, his hand axe went sideways, straight through the front leg of the horse. The horse went down, and the rider went with it. Corvin moved forward, leaving the rider for his men. His anger was now all over his face, not hiding, on display for all of those around him to see. He went forward into a tumbler roll as another horseman came at him. He turned around with his axe poised to throw but saw further on and could see Noro in trouble. He adjusted his aim and threw his axe at the man Noro was struggling with on the ground. The axe hit home and sunk straight into the back of the head of the Sul'Lenan. Corvin changed his sword to his right hand and drew his dagger with his left. He had just done it when another rider that was on foot came at him. This one wielded a long sword like Jorga and used it well. Corvin fended off blows before getting on the inside and gutting the man with his knife. Corvin let out a howl as the knife cut. He turned to look for the next man but there was none. All of the horsemen were dead. He looked to the walls and heard the chanting for the first time.

"SNOW WEASEL! SNOW WEASEL! SNOW WEASEL!"

Corvin just stood there, looking at the wall, breathing heavily. His anger was spent, he was covered in blood and wanted nothing more than to sit down and have a long drink. Jorga approached him. Corvin had calmed down enough to think clearly.

"Losses?" asked Corvin.

"None, brother," said Jorga with a small smile.

"You run a good battle," said Corvin.

Jorga almost laughed. "I did not run anything, brother. You charged in and we followed."

Corvin looked up at the wall and although could not make out faces, knew his own. Captain was watching. He also knew Molich would be watching. He felt his anger rise.

"Are you ready for another battle?" asked Corvin.

"You are thinking of Molich?" asked Jorga.

Corvin nodded.

"I am sure, I could fit one more in," said Jorga.

Irikson, also covered in blood, approached them.

"Good fight," said Irikson.

"More to come," said Corvin.

Irikson looked up at the wall, then back at his brothers. He smiled.

"Good," was all Irikson said.

Noro then ran up with Corvin's axe, cleaned, and handed it back to him.

"Good throw, lad. I owe you," said Noro.

"If you owe me, then take my advice," said Corvin.

"Advice?" asked Noro.

"We are about to do battle again, I am sure. It would not be good for you and your men to be near us. Get up the wall first and make your way to the tents. Leave us be," said Corvin.

The others nodded. It took a few moments for Noro to work out what they are talking about.

"The archers you killed?" asked Noro.

They all nodded.

"No. Fuck that, lad. We are with you," said Noro.

Corvin nodded in thanks.

"Thank you, Noro, but no, trust me on this," replied Corvin.

"SEA WOLVES!" yelled Noro.

All the Sea Wolves and all of the other men on the ground before the wall ran to see what was up.

"Third Section form up around Corvin, Sea Wolves form an honour guard around the Bloodchildren. Once we are on that wall, no one lets anyone get through the lines without my permission," shouted Noro.

"No," said Corvin.

"Blow it out your arse, Commander," said Noro.

Irikson laughed loudly.

Jorga whispered to Corvin and Corvin nodded.

"Forward to the wall," ordered Jorga.

Chapter Sixteen

The remaining mercenaries made their way up the ropes onto the wall. All of them were spent, no energy left and they barely made it up the walls. All of the men had stepped to the front and back of the wall, leaving a huge space down the centre of the wall. Once the mercenaries were up on the wall, they formed up. Corvin, Jorga, Lorka, Noro, Irikson in the middle. Beside them in lines on either side, the remains of the Third Section. On the outside of them, the Sea Wolves flanking each side and the back. Six men abreast, they walked down the wall towards the Colonel, Captain Brenik and the Duke. All of the men on the wall cheered loudly as the brave, some thought insane, mercenaries as they made their way along the wall. All of the men were covered in dust and blood, but they held their heads high. As they walked closer, Corvin caught a brief glance at Sergeant Emric and Sergeant Dolac. Dolac was smiling and cheering, and nodded his head in respect. Corvin smiled back that little half grin of his. Corvin then looked to Emric who shook his head in seriousness. Corvin smiled and winked at him. Emric knew exactly what was coming. They reached the end of the wall near the cliff face and stopped.

"Senior men present," shouted Jorga.

As one, all of the mercenaries banged their right hand against their chest and nodded their heads in respect – except Corvin, of course. Respect was earned, not given. At this moment with his anger still bubbling under the surface, he had no respect for these men.

The cheering died down as the Colonel stepped forward.

"Welcome back, you crazy bloody mercenaries," said the Colonel with a large smile.

The men on the wall started cheering again. The Colonel waved his hands to quieten them down before continuing.

"That was some brave fighting. We have all seen the fires in the distance and the massive explosion this morning. You have done well. The pressure on this end of the wall had been relieved to the point we could almost send the men home," said the Colonel.

There was more cheering from the men on the wall.

"You have done a massive service to the Kor'Lenan people. Go get your men cleaned up and get some fresh food into them. Then, we can meet to discuss the success of what you have done," said the Colonel.

The men all cheered again, yelling until their throats were hoarse.

"No," said Corvin.

The cheering stopped.

"No, Sergeant Corvin?" asked Captain Brenik.

The fact he was called Sergeant and not Commander, spoke volumes to all of the mercenaries. Corvin looked at Jorga for reassurance, Jorga nodded slightly. Jorga knew what was coming and for one, knew the time was not to be careful. Noro leaned over and whispered to Corvin.

"Don't back down, lad. We have learnt all too well what these bastards are. Say your piece," said Noro.

"No. We will not get cleaned up. Before the day is out, there may be more blood on us, and we do not like cleaning off blood twice. A waste of energy that none of us have," said Corvin.

A few moments ago, the wall had been cheering loudly, now there was silence. Enough silence, that all you could hear was the faint sound of fighting further down the wall.

"What are you talking about, Sergeant?" asked the Colonel.

"I am sure your less than honourable Sergeant Molich has spoken to you regarding their behaviour at the first camp," said Corvin.

The Duke raised an eyebrow. This lad had balls, he thought to himself. The Colonel was wild about the eyes but did his best to keep his composure, Captain Brenik, of course, was just wild. His face was dark, and he had no intention or ability to hold back what he was feeling. Captain Joren, with his Sergeants Emric and Dolac listened carefully. They had no details yet of what had happened.

"You murdered three of my men!" said Captain Brenik.

"No. We killed three child killers!" said Corvin, almost spitting the words out.

There were gasps amongst the Kor'Lenan Infantry on the wall. The mercenaries that did not have a good grasp of the language, did not understand. Captain Joren did and his face went white. In that one sentence, his support swung to Corvin.

"This is not the place to discuss, Sergeant Corvin. Get your men cleaned up and meet in the command tent," said the Colonel.

Corvin was about to speak, his anger ready to be

unleashed. The Duke slowly shook his head. Corvin got himself under control, just.

"We will get ourselves cleaned up, Colonel and meet you in the tent as requested," said Corvin.

"Also, eat something, Corvin," said Captain Brenik.

"No. Cleaned up and then meet. This matter cannot wait," said Corvin.

Brenik whispered into the Colonels ear.

"As you were Corvin, we will meet shortly," said the Colonel.

As they made their way down the wall, they talked quietly.

"I'll get the men cleaned up. We will want all of the Third Section with us when we meet," said Jorga.

"They won't fit in the tent," chuckled Irikson.

"They can assemble not far away, all waiting," said Jorga.

Corvin nodded. "Yes. Tell them when they hear my nickname, they come running and kill anyone in their way."

"You have my men, and I'll be with you in the tent," said Noro.

"Thank you, Noro. For your support over the wall and now. It means much," said Corvin.

"Yes, it does. I would be honoured to call you, brother," said Irikson.

All of the others nodded and Corvin stopped midstride.

"I would also be honoured if I could call you brother," said Corvin.

Corvin held out his arm and Noro gripped it in the warrior fashion.

"Brother," said Noro.

Jorga, Lorka, Torin and Irikson all took turns gripping Noro's arm and calling him brother.

"I am honoured to share the battlefield with you all," said Noro.

It did not take long to clean up. They all assembled and walked towards the command ten; 139 mercenaries led by Corvin, Jorga and Noro walked steadily towards the confrontation, 139 men ready to charge their own allies if they needed to. All of the Sea Wolves supported Noro and had the back of Corvin. The Third Section under Corvin would die for him if need be, and probably would. As they got within fifty lai of the command tent, they stopped. Two hundred men, Kor'Lenan Infantry stood guard around the tent. Colonel Kora, Captain Brenik, Duke Eason and Captain Joren stood at the tent entrance.

"That is far enough, Corvin. All senior men are welcome to join us in the tent. We have much to discuss," said the Colonel.

Corvin looked at the assembled soldiers. Noro chuckled.

"As you can see, the tent is well guarded and our meeting won't be interrupted," said Captain Brenik.

Noro roared with laughter; the Sea Wolves laughed with him. Corvin smiled, easing some tension and lessening his anger.

"Why do you laugh, Captain Noro?" asked the Colonel.

"You just saw what the men in front of you did to two hundred horsemen, and you think these scums will hold us if we decide to attack?"

Corvin's smile broadened. The feeling of support he felt was indescribable. Jorga, Lorka and Irikson around him, smiling and ready once more to charge in with no regard to whether they should or not. Noro, his new brother, also ready to leap headfirst into danger. Corvin chuckled.

"Why are you talking of fighting, Captain Noro? There is no hostility here, except for the anger you and the men beside you are bringing. We are allies here," said the Colonel.

"If there is no hostility, Colonel, why the two hundred guards?" said Jorga.

Corvin laughed. His brother had come out of his shell a little when they were beyond the wall and he was now learning to speak up. Corvin's heart willed with pride.

The Colonel could not answer.

"Look to the Duke, lad," said Noro.

Corvin moved his eyes to Duke Eason. The Duke was slowing and subtlety moving his hands in the downward motion for calm. He then nodded the direction of the command tent. Corvin grasped his meaning. Be calm, come into the tent.

"Should I trust this Duke?" whispered Corvin to no one in particular.

"Yes," said Noro.

"I agree," said Jorga.

Corvin thought about it, then acted.

"My last command as your force commander. Stand down and make yourselves comfortable across the way from the tent. We will be back shortly," said Corvin, in a voice loud enough to travel over the men.

The Duke nodded and smiled.

"You hear my name, you charge in," Corvin said to Lorka.

"Rely on it, brother," said Lorka.

Corvin, Jorga, Irikson and Noro headed to the command tent. The rest of the force did as they had been commanded, and moved to the other side of the dirt path, not thirty-five Lai away from the command tent and relaxed.

As the senior men approached the tent, they were stopped by a guard Sergeant Corvin did not know.

"Weapons are left outside, Sergeant," said the Guard Sergeant.

"I thought we were allies, Colonel?" said Corvin.

The Colonel thought about it, then looked to Captain Joren.

"They will not pull them, Colonel. Trust me on that," said Captain Joren.

The Colonel nodded and the Guard Sergeant stood back.

"Come in, Corvin, and welcome," said the Colonel.

They were all seated at the large wooden table, Corvin alone at the foot of the table. At the top of the table was the Colonel and his aide or guard, Corvin could not be sure which one he was. Down the right side from the top sat Captain Brenik, then Sergeant Molich, who was sitting with a smile on his face, followed by two sergeants that Corvin did not know from the Kor'Lena Infantry. He recognised their faces but did not know their names. Then Captain Noro, and Jorga. Down the left side was Duke Eason, followed by Captain Joren, Dolac, Emric and then Irikson. Irikson was staring at Molich and smiling.

"Well, men. Congratulations to Corvin and Noro and the rest for a bloody successful raid. As I said, we saw the fires and are in your debt for releasing the pressure we were facing," said the Colonel.

Most of the men around the table clapped. Sergeant

Molich did not clap, of course, just sat there and sneered. Irikson noticed this and whispered to Corvin.

"I am going to kill him," said Irikson.

"Get in line," replied Corvin.

"We want to chat first about the plans for the wall next and also what information you learnt when on your raids," said the Colonel.

"No. First, we address the tension in the tent and discuss why we are really here. Once that is done with, then we speak on how to move forward and let you know what we learnt," said Noro.

"Agreed," said Captain Joren.

The Colonel was taken back by the interruption. Captain Brenik was not happy.

"It is clear, Noro, you do not intend to make this an easy meeting," said Captain Brenik.

"No. I do not," said Noro.

The Colonel turned to Sergeant Molich.

"You want to lay charges, perhaps you tell us what happened, Sergeant? There will be no interruptions from anyone else," said the Colonel.

"Thank you, sir. On our raid of the first camp, everything had gone well. We had got in and secured the camp. As most of the force went to steal some hot food before we set flames to the place, my men and I searched the camp looking for prisoners. We wanted to bring one back to get information out of them. Three of my men found two youths and were securing her when Corvin's giant friend Lorka, attacked them. He laid them all out when we came across him. The rest of my archers drew their bows and I confronted him. Corvin then turned up with Captain Noro and Corporal Jorga. That is when Corvin and Lorka attacked and killed my men, which were defenceless and without weapons. When I went to defend my men, Irikson foot tripped me and held his weapon to my throat. The entire Third Section, as well as many of Noro's Sea Wolves surrounded my remaining archers. Corvin killed two of my men, Lorka cut the head of the other one. They were murdered, and yes, I want to bring charges against them," stated Molich.

All of the men that had witnessed what had happened sat there with anger and hate on their faces. Corvin stared at Molich.

"You left out one small rather important detail," said Corvin.

"You will get your chance, Corvin, hold your tongue. Sergeant Molich, what happened next?" said the Colonel.

"He ordered me and my men to return to the wall, he said we had no honour and would not fight with us again. A number of the Third Section then threatened our lives, so we ran for it," said Molich.

The Duke knew there was more to the story than what Molich had said. Corvin was still young and had not learnt to hide his feelings, his emotions and certainly did not know how to lie.

"I would like to hear from Noro now," said Captain Joren.

"Why not Corvin next, Captain?" asked Irikson.

"Well, it is clear they dislike our brave Sergeant, and no matter what he says, he will not be believed," said Captain Joren.

Duke Eason nodded.

"Very true, I agree with Captain Joren. Captain Noro?" asked the Duke.

"Most of what that gutless worm says is true," said Noro.

This caused some more tension and the shock on all of the Kor'Lenans was clear on their faces. Corvin, Jorga and Irikson smiled. Yes, Noro was a true brother.

"Careful, Captain. There is no need for name calling. We are all professionals here," said Captain Brenik.

"As I said, most of what he said was true except for one minor detail he left out. We all ran when we heard the yelling from Lorka. On arrival, Corvin questioned Lorka and Lorka informed us that Molich's men were about to execute two small boys they had found. Lorka's words were "They were dragging them out and holding them against the wall, one of them was about to slice their throats. It was clear Lorka was fired up and upset," said Noro.

"You believed him?" asked the Duke.

"Yes. These former slaves do not know how to lie. It is not in them. If they told me the sky had turned black, I would believe them," said Noro.

"Then what happened?" asked the Duke.

"Just as Molich described. Lorka and Corvin dealt with the men in question. Once that had been taken care of, Molich and his men were ordered back to the wall," said Noro.

"Corvin. This is what happened?" asked the Colonel.

"Yes, Colonel. Exactly what happened," said Corvin.

"Molich?" asked the Duke.

"I did not see what they had described, but if it is as they described, they still are murderers," said Molich.

"Killing children is acceptable?" asked the Duke.

"They are not even humans these Sul'Lenans. They are nothing better than animals. If my men choose to kill animals; that is their business!" said Molich.

The shock on the faces of all the mercenaries in the tent, and the Duke, of course, was real. Never had any of them seen this side of the Kor'Lenans before.

"Animals?" asked the Duke.

"Yes, animals," said Captain Brenik.

"Corvin is facing charges of murdering these scums, these child killers?" asked Dolac.

"In our laws, what they attempted to do to the children, who is our enemy, is not a crime," said Brenik.

"What kind of people, are you? I thought I knew the Kor'Lenans and was proud to work for them. Not now," said Captain Joren.

"Unfortunately, it is an old law that we have tried to change before, but more of the traditionalists fight the change. It goes back to the second war with the Sul'Lenans fifty-six years ago. I do not agree with it and do not share the same liking for it, but it is our law, and I cannot go against it," said the Colonel.

"What does this law say?" asked the Duke.

"Sul'Lenans are animals and can be treated as such and done with, as we please," recited Captain Brenik.

"I cannot believe what I am hearing," said Sergeant Emric.

"Neither can I. It is shameful," said Sergeant Dolac.

"Shameful you may think, but it is our law," said Molich.

"Which means that the charges against Sergeant Corvin stand. He is charged with murdering two Kor'Lenans and Lorka is charged with murdering one," said the Colonel.

Colonel Kora did not like it, harming children was shameful and disgusting. But as a Colonel, he had to follow the law.

"Also, this reflects badly on the company of the Bloodchildren and the Sea Wolves. After the trial is finished, if Corvin and Lorka are found guilty, they will hang. I daresay your companies will have ended a very bad reputation and will not be getting much work in the future," said Captain Brenik.

Corvin looked at his Captain. Captain Joren was mad,

pissed off and Corvin could see there was nothing he could do to change the situation. Jorga leaned over and whispered to Corvin.

"Challenge the bastard, Demon-Child."

This brought a smile to Corvin's face.

"Share it with the table, Sergeant Jorga," said Molich.

Jorga smiled.

"Oh, you will share in it," said Jorga.

Irikson, Dolan, Emric and Captain Noro laughed loudly.

"What? What is it?" demanded the Colonel.

"Corvin lad, share what you have to say, and you have my full support," said Captain Joren.

Corvin smiled and stood. Looking at Molich, he spoke, "You have insulted me and my men. Whereas, you have no honour, as does the laws of your land. Sergeant Molich, I challenge you to a duel. Not first blood, but to the death!"

All of the Bloodchildren and Captain Noro smiled. None of the Kor'Lenans did. Duke Eason was puzzled.

"Why do I need to accept? Our law will end your life. Why do I need to endanger myself? I am a good fighter but why accept?" said Molich standing.

"Because I call you a child killer and you have no honour," said Corvin.

Molich's face grew red.

"I am not a child killer," he said between clenched teeth.

"Here are the terms. Myself and Lorka, who has had his honour questioned, against you and nine men of your choosing," said Corvin with a smile.

"All duels must be one vs one!" said the Colonel.

"Yes, it can't be a pitched battle!" said Captain Brenik.

"Corvin just offered a duel where the odds are in Molich's favour. If you turn this down, then it will be clear for the world to see that the Kor'Lenans are not only dishonourable but cowards as well," added Noro.

"The fight has my backing," said the Duke.

"You may be a Duke, but you have no say here, sir," said Captain Brenik.

"Yes, he does. I invited him here to be a member of the trial judges. Our laws call for someone impartial," said the Colonel.

Molich looked over and eyed all of the Bloodchildren one by one. Sergeant Dolac was smiling, Sergeant Emric was smiling, Corporal Irikson was smiling, and Corporal Jorga was smiling. Corvin and Noro were smiling, and it was clear they were holding back laughter. Captain Joren was not smiling but writing on parchment. In fact, he had been writing on parchment the entire meeting.

"Why are you all smiling? And you Captain, what are you writing?" said Captain Brenik.

"They are smiling because they know that either way, you are screwed. If you fight Lorka and Corvin, you will die. If you choose to have these men hung, the notes I am writing, the same message over and over again, will be sent out to all mercenary company on the wall," said Captain Joren.

"What are you writing, Captain Joren?" asked the Colonel.

"A brief note on how the Kor'Lenans betrayed us in the battle of the wooden towers, and what you do here," said Captain Joren.

"What will that achieve?" asked Captain Brenik.

"Once the mercenary companies read the truth of what he has written, they will all leave the wall and go home. They will not fight for someone who betrays them," said the Colonel.

"Correct. I regret not taking my company and leaving then. I thought things would change when Captain Brenik was put in charge. They haven't and I regret staying. Corvin and the men that went with him jumped the wall and took the fight to the enemy. You all stayed safe behind your wall. Someone said that we are fighting your war for you, and I agree," said Captain Joren.

"You are betraying our contract with words like that, Captain," said the Colonel.

"No. The Kor'Lenans betrayed the contract the first time when Corvin and his men were left for dead on the battlefield when attacking those dam towers. I only came here to honour an agreement made during the last war between one of the previous Captains of the Bloodchildren and a council member. But either way, I'll be damned if I stay here to die for the Kor'Lenans when they don't have the courage to take the fight to the enemy," said Captain Joren with feeling.

"You will lose your bonus, Captain Joren," said Captain Brenik.

"When word travels that you don't keep your promise, what mercenary company with ever fight for you again?" asked Noro.

"This is getting out of hand. We need to stay calm and not get ahead of ourselves," said Colonel Kora.

"Agreed," said the Duke, who then stood. "Corvin has issued his challenge, it is unusual but a challenge none the less. Do you except Sergeant Molich?"

Molich knew that Corvin and Lorka were great fighters, but against ten of his men, he was confident in the outcome.

"I accept. A fight to the death, myself and nine men of my choosing against Sergeant Corvin and his man Lorka. Single handed weapons only," said Molich.

"Sergeant Corvin, do you accept the conditions?" asked Duke Eason.

"Yes," said Corvin.

"Done then," said the Colonel, also standing.

"After dawn tomorrow, the fight will commence. If Corvin and Lorka win, they will still be asked to leave our lands. They will no longer be welcomed. If they lose, then it will not matter. Regardless of the outcome, the Bloodchildren and Sea Wolves will finish the contract until the winter. The bonus that was doubled will still be paid, as long as they honour the original contracts," said the Colonel.

"I advise that if Corvin and his man do win, they are paid all coin they are owed, and a bonus is given to them. They led a successful raid and saved this section of the wall, not for the first time, I might add," said the Duke.

"No one company will hire them when they heard what has happened here," said Molich with a sneer, not that they are going to win, he said to himself.

"I agree with that amendment, Duke Eason. Assemble at dawn. Meeting over," said the Colonel.

Corvin stood in a large circle, ringed by all the men not guarding the wall. He was bare chested with no armour on his body. He looked down at the hand axe the Smith had made for him and then looked to his short sword in his left hand. Weapons that had seen a lot of death, blood and violence. They would see more, he knew. He looked over at his giant friend Lorka, who stood with a calm face. A face that usually radiated warmth and caring, but right now, it radiated death. Lorka was watching the ten men they would face with absolute hatred on his face.

"I am sorry to get you into this brother," said Corvin.

"No need for that. I would have chosen to be by your side,

if given the chance. These bastards will learn the meaning of honour, I will teach them," said Lorka.

"How are you feeling without your axe?" asked Corvin.

One of the conditions of the fight was only single-handed weapons were allowed to be used. The Kor'Lenans had a distaste for two handed great weapons, as the Sul'Lenans used them and anything similar to the Sul'Lenans, they hated. Lorka had a standard issue Bloodchildren short sword in his right hand, and a Bloodchildren shield in is left.

"I'll be fine. I need a promise from you brother," said Lorka.

"Anything," said Corvin.

"The soon to be dead scum called Molich, he is mine," said Lorka.

Corvin looked at him. He had wanted him for himself but could not refuse Lorka in anything he asked. He did not ask for much, but when he did, Corvin would not say no.

"He is all yours, brother," said Corvin.

"Thank you," said Lorka.

Corvin looked over at Noro. Noro nodded and slapped his right fist onto his left breast in respect. Corvin looked back to the ten men facing them. Molich no doubt picked the best men he could. All of the assembled looked like fighters. He saw Molich and Molich was smiling. Corvin's rage, which had not fully gone down since yesterday's meeting, was just under the surface. He felt his heart, pumping fast, not from nerves, as the fight about to start. Standing here now, he was taken back to all the fights he had ever been in whilst a slave. His arms started to shake a little as the adrenalin started going through his system. His jaw was clenching. He was not thinking of strategy or tactics. He was thinking back to his very first death bout he ever had in the pits and smiled.

"Anger is a gift," he muttered to himself.

"And we love to give," said Lorka beside him.

The men in front of them stepped forward and Lorka and Corvin did likewise. Corvin got a good look at them. He recognised none of them apart from Molich, who was standing in the middle. They were all bigger and taller than most Kor'Lenans he had come across. All taller than his own six feet. None of them came close to Lorka's size, of course. They were all well-muscled, so trained hard, but they did not have the speed or the skill of the former slaves, and they did not have the anger either.

The two groups stopped at the centre of the circle. They were fifteen Lai from each other, facing each other down. The ten Kor'Lenans smiling broadly, Corvin and Lorka staring with intensity. A loud call went out.

"On my order, fight. Fight with honour, fight with pride," said Colonel Kora.

Corvin felt it, the rage climbing the surface of his being and he welcomed it. His axe hand was starting to shake with anticipation.

"FIGHT!" declared the Colonel.

Corvin as always sprang into action faster than anyone else could. In one step, he had crossed over the path in front of Lorka, his arm with the axe in it went back, then forward again quickly. His axe thrown into the Kor'Lenan to Molich's right. The axe went straight into his face and the man dropped. One down!

Corvin had ran straight across the path of Lorka and was heading towards the men on his left, Lorka had stepped around Corvin to the right and launched himself at Molich. Although not as fast as Corvin, Lorka still moved faster than the Kor'Lenans. Lorka and Corvin had reached their line before the men facing them were ready for it. Lorka swung his shield as hard as he could in a backhand motion, catching

Molich in the chin, dropping him to the ground. He hit the ground and was out to it. He parried a sword from a second man and head-butted him, following up with his sword through the man's chest. Two down!

Corvin had blocked a sword with his own sword, then had to spin around to his left to avoid another sword from a second man. He spun right into a third man but was leading with his sword and gutted him. Three down!

He ducked his head as a sword flew above him. On his way up, he stabbed the man in the groin, the man dropping to the ground to bleed out. Four dead.

Lorka thrusted his sword into the neck of a man and he dropped, taking Lorka's sword with him. Five dead.

Lorka reached down and grabbed Molich's sword, coming up in time to block one sword on his shield and another on the captured sword blade. He kicked one man in the balls, dropping him to the ground, this freed up his shield, which he smacked into the face of the other attacker. This stunned the man and Lorka followed up with his sword, thrusting it into the man's chest and out the other side. He yanked the sword free and turned into time to block another sword. Six down.

Corvin rolled forward into a tumbler roll to avoid two men and they chased him and tried to get to him. As he came back to his feet, he suddenly had his axe in his right hand again. He had grabbed it out of the body of the dead man he had thrown it at, and no one watching had seen it. All they saw was Corvin once again with two weapons. He stepped to the right, his sword going into the heart of the man chasing him, he ducked as the second man launched a sword stroke aiming for his head. As the man's sword went over his head, Corvin stood back up and stepped forward, releasing his sword from his grip and smashing the axe into the man's jaw and up into his eye. This man then dropped to the ground. Seven down.

Corvin gripped his sword still struck in the chest of the man. He was still standing but as Corvin ripped it free, he screamed and fell to the ground. Eight down.

Corvin looked over and saw Lorka battling the last two. Lorka's sword parried a stroke, and he blocked the other man's sword with his shield. Corvin launched his axe. It landed in the side under the arm of one of the men. Lorka blocked the sword again from the other man and smashed his shield into the face of him. As the man stepped back spitting his teeth out, Lorka stepped in and rammed the blade in deep. Corvin had ran at the man crouched on the ground and ripped his axe free, at the same time slashing his sword across the throat of him. Nine down, and dead.

"HOLD!" came the call from the Colonel.

The cheers went up around the circle from all the Bloodchildren and Sea Wolves watching. By now, the word had spread why they were fighting and even many of the Kor'Lenans they showed their appreciation. Roaring and clapping or slapping their weapons on shields.

Lorka and Corvin took a couple of steps back and could see Molich was just starting to stand.

"He is mine," said Lorka.

"Use my sword. It is better than the one you have," said Corvin.

"No. I'll use Molich's sword against him," said Lorka.

Lorka ran forward, faster than Corvin had ever seen him move before. Molich had stood up at the same time Lorka had reached him. Lorka had timed it perfectly and with all his strength, had sung the sword two handed at Molich's neck. The blade connected and severed his head. The body dropped and the head rolled way. Lorka stabbed down and buried Molich's blade into the dead body, leaving it there as he walked back to Corvin.

"Now it's over," said Lorka.

"GUARDS!" shouted the Colonel.

Guards formed around the perimeter had walked to surround Corvin and Lorka.

"No," said Captain Joren.

The Colonel ignored him. Jorga saw what was happening.

"PIT-RATS!" Jorga screamed.

Within moments, all of the former slaves had raced ahead and surrounded Corvin and Lorka. The rest of the Bloodchildren had joined them. The Sea Wolves had drawn weapons and followed Noro and were now at the backs of the Bloodchildren. The Fire Hawks who had been on the wall guarding it, but still watching stormed down and joined the mercenaries.

"What are you doing, Colonel?" asked the Duke.

"My job. I was going to put them into custody until they leave these lands," said the Colonel.

"You stupid bastard. One wrong move and your men will die," said the Duke.

"My men will leave, but you will treat them with respect. They have won their freedom in that fight, not that they had done anything wrong," said Captain Joren.

The Colonel stood still. The Duke was right, one wrong move or one wrong word and a lot more death would happen. He breathed.

'GUARDS! STAND DOWN!" he yelled reluctantly.

Immediately all of the Kor'Lenans stood down and returned to where they were. Colonel Eason, Captain Brenik, Captain Joren and the Duke made their way over to the Mercenaries.

"Bloodchildren stand down!" said Captain Joren.

All of the remaining Bloodchildren sheathed their weapons and took a few steps back.

"SEA WOLVES STANDOWN!" yelled Noro.

The Sea Wolves also stood back and walked back to their place they had stood before.

"Fire Hawks back to the wall or I'll cancel your contract for abandoning you position," said the Colonel.

The members of the Fire Hawks returned to the wall, many of them looking back over their shoulders at the two brave fighters they had watched. Respect in their eyes and their hearts.

The senior men reached Corvin and Lorka. Although the Bloodchildren had stood down, all of the former Pit-rats would not. They stood beside their brother.

"What am I going to do with you, lad?" said Captain Joren as they reached each other.

"I have done nothing wrong, Captain," said Corvin.

"No, he has not," said the Duke.

"Still, he agreed to the conditions of the fight. You now have seven days to leave our lands, never to return. Sorry Corvin, you have done some amazing things here for us, but you cannot be trusted, and you kill too easily," said the Colonel.

"You and Lorka return to the ship and wait for us, lad. We will join you at the end of the contract," said Sergeant Emric.

"No. He needs to leave our lands and cannot sit in a ship in our harbour," said Captain Brenik.

"What are you scared of? He has only ever defended himself and fought your war for you, stupid bastards," said Captain Noro.

"Mind your language," said the Colonel.

Noro shook his head.

"It is the law Joren, and not even I can go against it. If someone gets banished, they have seven days to leave," said the Colonel.

Corvin shook his head in disgust.

"We will leave, sir. I, for one, don't want to stay in this shit country where the men pay others to fight their wars for them when they are too cowardly to fight it properly for themselves. You need to change the way you fight, or the Sul'Lenans will eventually win," said Lorka with disgust.

It was another slap in the face to the Colonel.

He just nodded. He was starting to have doubts about the way they fought himself.

"I grant you an evening to eat, get clean and rest before your departure. I would also ask that you are confined to your tent and Captain Noro here gives his word, he will guard you and make sure you do not leave the camp."

"I give my word," said Noro.

The Colonel looked at Corvin. It looked like he wanted to take his axe and bury it in someone else. Colonel Kora shook his head and walked away.

"I will see you soon, lad. There is much to discuss," said Captain Joren.

With that, he also walked off.

Chapter Seventeen

They had cleaned themselves up and got into clean clothing. Corvin and Lorka had eaten alone in the tent, demolishing all the food that was brought to them. Lorka was hoping for a drink, but all that was brought to them was water; understandable really. True to his word, Noro had put six men outside of the tent. He told Corvin they would never attack them, so please just relax and stay put. Corvin promised they would.

They had been in the tent all morning, lying on the bed mats and talking. They discussed many things from what had happened, mistakes they had made and what not to do in future. All the chat was worthless. They both agreed if put in the same situation, they would do exactly the same. They enjoyed the time together but were a little annoyed none of the others had come to say hello. They did not know that all visitors were being stopped from coming in. It was almost midday when their first visitor arrived in the tent. They both stood up.

"No, please remain seated," said Duke Eason in Outlandish.

They both sat back down on their bed mats. The Duke sat in the only chair in the tent.

"I was not sure if we were allowed visitors," said Lorka.

"You are not, but the Kor'Lenans owe my country a great deal, and as I am my King's envoy, they show a great deal of respect and let me do what I want to," said Duke Eason.

"What's an envoy?" asked Corvin.

"It's like a messenger but more important. I have the authority to make deals and speak on behalf of my king," said the Duke.

"What is a king?" asked Lorka.

The Duke was shocked.

"I am surprised you do not know what a king is, but I should not be. You were raised away from the rest of the world and know nothing of these things. A king would be," the Duke stalled trying the best way to describe it.

"You were held in the Outlands, yes?" said the Duke.

"Yes, sir," said Lorka.

"As I understand it, they have a whole lot of chiefs looking after a certain area. Well, imagine they had a chief of chiefs. One chief that ruled over all the other chiefs. That is what a king is," said the Duke.

"A very important person," said Corvin.

"Yes. I, as a Duke, am like the chiefs you know. However, in the Kingdom of Ex'Na, there are only seven dukes or chiefs. One for every province. Well, there are eight provinces in Ex'Na, but no one really cares about Lands' End," said the Duke.

They both started to understand.

"Well, welcome to our tent then," said Corvin with his little half smile.

The duke laughed with honest laughter and Lorka joined in.

"The fact you can keep a sense of humour amongst all this impresses me even more," said the Duke.

"Have to laugh sir, when you grow up as slaves, you learn to laugh at everything. If you do not, life can wear you down," said Corvin.

Lorka nodded

"It's true, sir. We do tend to laugh at things which are perhaps a little dark. It is the only way to keep yourself going. Perhaps one day you will hear our story," said Lorka.

"Oh, I have already heard it," said the Duke with a large smile.

"You have?" asked Corvin.

"Yes. After you and Irikson saved me in the forest, I learnt all I could about you, mostly from Captain Joren. I am sure there are things he does not know, but he gave me a good picture of how you all grew up," said the Duke.

"Why would you ask about us, sir?" asked Lorka.

"Corvin, I watched yourself and Irikson save me that night in the forest. I had never seen men move so fast and explode into combat as fast as you two and I was impressed. I then watched you and all your fellows in front of the wall, destroy the horsemen in front of you, even though you were outnumbered. You never lost a man, and I was impressed even further. Then the fight this morning, you destroyed those ten men; they never stood a chance. You have to be some of the best fighting men I have seen in a long time and I have seen a lot," said the Duke.

Corvin and Lorka where a little uneasy with the compliments. They looked at each other, then just nodded to each other.

"Sorry, sir. We are not used to compliments. Yes, we can

fight, that is what we have been trained to do from an early age. It's all we know," said Lorka.

"Yes," said Corvin.

"Bullshit," said the Duke.

They both looked at him, with questions in their eyes.

"You know so much more than you realise. You can navigate politics like you were born to it, how you learnt this as slaves, I have no idea. You're moving through the meeting in the tent was masterful, you manipulated Molich into that fight, but you did not know you were doing it," said the Duke.

They both looked blank.

"We both just follow how we feel, sir," said Corvin.

'Exactly, and you followed them to this outcome," said the Duke.

"What outcome, sir?" asked Lorka.

"Being banished from the land of Kor'Lena," said the Duke.

They both stayed silent.

"Look lads, I came here to reoffer what I offered to you, Corvin. I owe you for saving my life. I am offering you employment with me, if you decide that the mercenary life is not for you," said the Duke.

"We are loyal to the Bloodchildren," said Corvin.

"As it should be, but if that changes, you are welcome to return with me to the land of Eastmoor in the country of Ex'Na," said the Duke.

"We won't leave the Bloodchildren, sir. If we did, it would not be just us two, but all of the former slaves. We are a family and will not leave each other," said Lorka.

"You say that as if I would be upset. How many of you are there?" asked the Duke.

"There are ten of us left, which escaped from the Outlands," said Corvin.

"Ten men who all fight like Demons? I would be only too happy to have you all," said the Duke with a huge smile.

"As we said, we are loyal to the company," said Lorka.

"As I said, things change," said the Duke standing up.

They both stood with him.

"Keep it in mind. You never know where life will lead you and working for me will be a lot safer than being mercenaries," said the Duke.

"We will, sir and thank you for the offer," said Corvin.

The Duke left. Once he was gone, they spoke more.

"He has offered that to you before, brother?" asked Lorka.

"Yes. Irikson and I refused. We will not betray the company," said Corvin.

Lorka nodded and lay back down on his bed mat.

"A life with less fighting is not a bad thing, brother. We may be good at it, but there must be more to this life," said Lorka, shutting his eyes.

Corvin looked at his friend. Lorka was not wrong.

They had been summoned to the command tent. When they arrived, sitting there was the Duke, Sergeant Dolac, Sergeant Emric, Captain Joren and Jorga.

"Please sit both of you," said the Captain.

Dolac poured them cups of ale which they gratefully took and sipped.

"I want to say first off, that you have done nothing wrong in my eyes. You both acted with honour and have fought bravely so many times. Your raids were a great success. Unfortunately, our hosts, are stupid and do not see it. They are too stuck in their ways and will not move with the times," said Captain Joren.

"That is for certain," said the Duke with a smile.

"I have called you here for what is a Bloodchildren problem, but the Duke is here as he has good insight and knows the Kor'Lenans laws and customs better than I do," said Captain Joren.

Lorka and Corvin sipped their ale and said nothing.

"Unfortunately, their stupid bloody outdated customs and laws, have or are about to cause a problem for the Bloodchildren," said Emric.

"How so?" asked Corvin.

"Even though you two have been banished from these lands and cleared of all fault, the Bloodchildren's reputation has been threatened. Captain Brenik has said he is threatening to spread the word of what laws the Bloodchildren have broken," said Dolac.

"What do we do when we are threatened?" asked Corvin.

The Duke roared with laughter, Emric and Dolac joined in.

"You can't kill everybody, Corvin!" said the Captain.

This got Jorga and Lorka laughing as well.

"No, Captain, we cannot. How big is the threat?" asked Corvin.

"If word gets around that we can no longer be trusted, then we no longer get work. It is as simple as that," said Captain Joren.

Corvin did not like where this was heading. His heart started to feel heavy.

"What is the best way forward?" asked Jorga.

"We will get you two on a ship that is not the Bloodchild and get you two back to Irik as soon as possible," said the Captain.

Corvin had a flashback to his conversation with Irikson and that bad feeling he had.

"How will that help?" asked Corvin.

"Get you two out of here yes, help our reputation no," said Dolac.

"I don't see where this is going," said Corvin.

'We are going to tell the Kor'Lenans you have been released from the Bloodchildren, then get you away as soon as possible. Not the outcome I wanted, but it will keep them from spreading a bad word about the company," said the Captain.

"They will believe you?" asked Jorga.

"I doubt it. They are simple in many ways, but they will see through that lie pretty quickly," said the Duke with a smile.

He looked at Corvin and winked.

"Bastard!" Corvin said.

The Duke laughed loudly again.

"Corvin?" asked Captain Joren.

"Nothing sir, sorry sir," said Corvin.

"The Duke is right. They will never believe the lie. The company should leave with Corvin and head home. We will find more work next season, and the company is not poor. We can survive," said Dolac.

"I agree," said Emric.

"You will miss out on bonus pay, and they promised they would double if you finished your contract. All the men we have lost so far would have died for nothing," said Corvin.

"True," said the Captain.

Corvin felt like he was being pushed into a decision, and he did not like it. He looked at the Duke who was still smiling. The Duke knew what was going to happen when he had come to see them. Corvin did not know the word for it, but he felt he was being pushed, twisted and forced to going into a direction not of his choosing. He eyes became a little wild.

"There is only one thing for it then," said Jorga.

Clever Jorga had already worked out in a short time what Corvin had struggled with since his meeting with the Duke.

"What is that, Jorga?" asked Dolac.

Jorga looked at Corvin.

If he were being pushed down a different path by events, he would have the final say.

"He means that Lorka and I will leave the Bloodchildren," said Corvin.

"What?" asked the Captain.

"No lad, that is not what we want," said Emric.

"No, it is not," said Dolac.

"We have no bloody choice. If Captain no spine Brenik knows for certain that Lorka and I have left the Bloodchildren, will he spread the information round?" asked Corvin.

"No, he will not," said the Duke.

"You leaving is not on the table, Corvin," said Captain Joren.

"We have no choice, sir," said Lorka.

"No, they do not. Leaving is the only option, Captain," said Jorga.

"I do not want to lose either of you. You are both good men," said Captain Joren.

"No, we do not but I can understand it. It is just a shame; we would lose many good men," said Emric.

"What do you mean?" asked the Captain.

"He means that if Lorka and Corvin go, all of the former slaves would go as well," said Dolac, finally understanding the strong bond between the former slaves.

Corvin smiled and nodded at Dolac.

"All of you?" asked Captain Joren.

"Yes. If Lorka and Corvin go, the rest of us will follow. In fact, stopping the rest of the Third Section following would be hard as well," said Jorga.

"My company, it's being gutted again," said the Captain.

"No. We can impress on the rest of Third Section to stay. Their experience beyond the wall will be too valuable not to share, especially if Torin is made Sergeant of the Third Section," said Corvin.

"I am not letting you go, so stop trying to suggest a new sergeant to replace you," said Captain Joren.

Jorga, Lorka and Corvin were impressed with the loyalty shown by their Captain. He was wrong, but still they were moved.

"Sorry, Captain but it is the way forward," said Corvin.

"Yes, it is. Corvin and I have not always seen eye to eye, but I now respect him and his brothers. I do not want to see them go either, but if Torin and the rest of the Third Section stay, we will be in a good position still," said Dolac.

"How?" said the Captain.

"Waynix, do not forget, has been training new recruits for the time we have been away. You told him fifty recruits this year and we would choose the best replacements when we get back. With the training taught to him by Corvin and the rest of the former pit-rats, the recruits will be superbly fit. Once we get back, they will fill out the Third Section well. With Torin as Sergeant of the Third, and the rest of the Third being spilt between the squads, we will have a good base to work from," said Emric.

All at the table nodded; even the Captain nodded. He knew what Emric was saying. It was still hard to let the newest members go so easily.

"You make sense, but I am still not happy with it," said Captain Joren.

Corvin had accepted it. He also did not like it, but he and

his brother slaves all adapted well to new situations. They had learned to.

"Well, it looks like it has been decided. Where will you go?" asked the Captain.

The Duke roared with laughter and Corvin joined in. Lorka chuckled.

'What is so funny?" asked Dolac.

"The Duke here has already offered us employment, although I have turned him down, twice," said Corvin.

"You have?" asked the Captain looking at the Duke.

"I saw where things were heading and made the offer, yes," said the Duke.

"Have you got room for ten of us?" asked Jorga with a smile.

"I'll make room for ten of you," said the Duke.

"If you can control their drinking and occasional murders, they will work out fine, sir," said Dolac with a smile.

They all joined in the laughter, even the Captain.

"It will be sad to see you go lad, but Dolac and Emric are right. You will leave the Bloodchildren in better shape than they were when you arrived. What about all your gear, you must have clothing and such back in Irik?" asked Captain Joren.

"No. We brought it all with us and thank you. You offered us all our lives when we did not know what to do with our freedom. Some of us still have a long way to go before we are what you would call civilised, but we will get there. Thank you, sir," Corvin said.

Corvin then stood up and walked to the Captain, holding his arm out. The Captain looked at his arm and shook his head. He engulfed Corvin in a hug.

All of them shared a handshake or a hug, then once again settled themselves down. Corvin looked at the Duke.

"If I find out you have manoeuvred events to get the services of myself and my fellows, I'll kill you," said Corvin.

"CORVIN!" said the Captain.

"It is okay, Captain. No Corvin, I have not manoeuvred events. I just took advantage of a situation. We will speak more on the ship ride home, but you will find you and your men will be rewarded well for your services. Also, as soldiers of my province, you will not be in as nearly much danger as a mercenary. I am sure in time, you will all come to thank me," said the Duke.

Corvin only nodded.

"You are not yet in my employ so you can get away with it, but if you threaten me or any man of quality once in Ex'Na, the King will hang you. I doubt you can get away from a few thousand King's guards when they come for you," said the Duke in warning,

"Understood," said Corvin.

"Well, we better get Torin in here and promote him. Also, Jorga if you would go and tell your fellows what has happened and give them the choice of staying if they want to," said the Captain.

"I will, sir, but they will all go," said Jorga.

"I know," said the Captain.

The morning arrived quickly. The former pit-rats had agreed to follow Corvin's choice and enter the employment of the Duke. When Corvin, and Jorga had got them together, Corvin was nervous. He was happy for them to stay with the Bloodchildren, but they were his family and he wanted them all to stay together. Corvin felt selfish for what he wanted, but he needed not have worried, they all agreed to come. When Corvin looked to them, one by one, he could see on their faces there was no question of them not coming. The rest of the Third Section had to be convinced to stay. Most of them wanted to follow Corvin. Once Corvin explained they needed to stay to keep the strength up of the company, and he asked it of them as a favour, they agreed. Torin was not happy about Corvin leaving and Corvin and Jorga had to talk hard to get him to accept the promotion and stay.

All of the former pit-rats had left their armour in their tents along with their Bloodchildren shirts. Captain Joren had let them keep their weapons as a parting gift, the weapons he had given them, of course. Most of them had their own weapons they had arrived with, but a few had Bloodchildren short swords and daggers.

Captain Brenik and Colonel Kora were very surprised when they had discovered that Duke Eason had employed all of the former slaves.

"Why would you employ those murderers?" said Captain Brenik.

The Duke smiled.

"If I get that lot to spend two years training ten thousand men, would you want to face that force?" asked the Duke.

They both went white and shook their heads.

"Ten thousand like them? No," said the Colonel.

"Exactly," said the Duke.

Before they all got into a wagon that the Duke had hired, the former pit-rats said goodbye to the friends they had made. Many sad faces and sad goodbyes. Corvin had spent time with many that morning. Talking, chatting, saying goodbye. It was not easy and something the former slaves had never had to do before.

The Bloodchildren company had assembled around the wagon. Captain Joren got up onto the wagon to speak.

"You came to us as slaves, you are leaving as brother mercenaries. None of us will forget what you have taught us. You have showed us many things and I hope in return you have learnt something from us. I class you all as Bloodchildren even though you are leaving us. If you ever need employment, you know where we are," said Captain Joren.

Great cheers went up from everyone there.

"For Corvin, I have something different. You were the youngest Sergeant the Bloodchildren have ever known. You have led men well and done things most of us would never dream was possible. For you, I have a title that has only been used twice in the History of the Bloodchildren. A title for a former member that has done so much for us, shown us so much and remained loyal. With this title, which you keep as long as you live, comes a gift. Whenever you need us, send for us. Whatever we are doing, we will drop and come to you, wherever you may be in the world. We will even give you a special rate for services," said Captain Joren.

The surrounding men laughed, and Corvin smiled.

"Corvin Demon-Child," Joren stopped to catch his breath.

Everyone was quiet as they listened.

"I name you the Blood Child," said Captain Joren.

The roar of approval from all of the men there was deafening. Corvin was slapped on the back by Dolac and Emric spoke quietly to him.

"No empty offer, lad. You call, we will come. As long as you can pay us, of course," said Emric.

Corvin was invited to get up and give a speech. He declined. He was emotional and was expecting after recent events to leave quietly. He did not expect the praise from his former Captain of the title he was given, nor the benefits that came with that title. He shook everyone's hand one last time, gave Captain Joren another hug and jumped up the front of the wagon with the driver. Standing beside on horseback was the Duke.

"Blood Child? Slightly better than Demon-Child," said the Duke.

"Corvin," called out Noro.

Noro ran up to the wagon and stood facing Corvin.

"I'll leave you two to say goodbye," said the Duke.

'Please stay, sir. This may concern you too," said Noro.

"Okay," said the Duke with honest surprise.

"I should have told you when I met you, but I had not worked it out yet. I have just put the information together in my head last night. Irikson said once that you and he were possibly from DuNoor, the land adjacent to Duke Eason's?' asked Noro.

"Possibly. An old mentor of ours said our accents when we spoke the language reminded him of that place," said Corvin.

The Duke looked on, puzzled.

"I ran into an old pirate a few seasons back. I was talking to him in a tavern. He told me a story of young children being stolen from DuNoor, dragged from small villages and put onto ships and never seen again. Apparently, it was done with the Dukes of DuNoor's permission, as he was taking gold from the Outlanders that took them in some sort of arranged deal," said Noro.

"You can prove this?" asked the Duke urgently.

"I cannot, no, but the old pirate was from somewhere called Lands' End. He said he had planned to open a tavern there. His name was

Poris, an old bugger but quite sharp if you know what I

mean," said Noro.

"I understand, yes," said the Duke.

"Means nothing to me," said Corvin.

"It does to me, lad. We will talk about it on the journey home," said the Duke.

Corvin jumped down and grabbed Noro in a hug.

"Thank you, brother. Sharing this information may be very helpful to finding out about my past. You are a brother to all of the former slaves, and never will I forget the time we spent over the wall. It was quite the adventure, although we lost a few good men," said Corvin.

"You are welcome, lad. Yes, the time over the wall will also live in my memory. Like Captain Joren said, if you never need fighting men, send for the Sea Wolves. We will come without question," offered Noro.

"Brother," repeated Corvin with a smile.

"Brother," Noro said with a smile.

"We will see each other again, trust me on that," said Noro.

As Noro walked away, Corvin looked at his back.

"Yes, we will see each other again," said Corvin quietly to himself.

He then climbed in the wagon as it started to roll off. He sat back and closed his eyes. His mind empty, the sun shining on his face as the wagon creaked along. He heard chuckling from the back of the wagon where his brothers entertained themselves. He smiled.

The journey back to the capital, Kor'Na, seemed to take a lot less time than the last time when they travelled to their posting at the end of the wall. Everything had changed. With the war in full swing, stalls and marketplaces had sprung up next to the camps they had stayed in along the way of the main road. Also, this time they did not sleep in camps on the side of the road. They stayed in proper accommodation in the military towns along the wall. Being with the Duke afforded the former slaves much more luxury that to be honest, they were not used to. Being late summer, the grass was now a golden yellow and tall. The Duke had said fall was not far away and that meant winter. The former slaves had coped better with the warmer climate than expected, but still looked forward to the cooler weather. Many nights in inns they stayed in, Corvin tried to engage the Duke in conversation as to what he and his brothers would be doing. The Duke, however, was tight lipped. He said very little on the subject and said they would discuss on the ship back to his country. All he said was they would be training men to fight.

The ship journey would only take a day, as the land of Ex'Na, was right next to Kor'Lena. He had said they would spend two days in the capital where he would report to his king, then five days by horse to get to his own province. Corvin and his brothers talked about what they would be doing.

"So Corvin, the Duke is staying tight lipped?" asked Norda.

"Yes. He said we would be training men, although he did say when he made the offer, it would be an easier life than one as a mercenary," said Corvin.

"We could use easier. I just hope it is not too easy. A boring life would not suit us," said Irikson.

"I know what you mean, brother. I do enjoy a good fight, and even though I have tried to shake our former life, I think that life has shaped us, and it will be hard to break," said Jorga.

The ten nodded agreement. Corvin looked around at the last of his brother slaves that had made it out of slavery. He thought back to the losses during their escape, and the more recent losses in battle. He was lost in thought.

"Corvin, do you know much about this country we are going to?" asked Lorka.

"No, not much at all. The Duke has said that Dukes, are like chiefs that we know of. They are eight provinces or regions. Seven of these Dukes rule over these provinces like a chief. Then there is a King that rules over all of the Dukes. Kind of like an over chief," said Corvin recalling the conversation he had with the Duke.

"You said eight provinces, but only seven Dukes. Why is that?" asked Thomik.

"The Duke said there is one province at the bottom of their land that is worthless. Not many people live there, and it produces nothing. It is called Lands' End or something. Apparently, it is not worth having a Duke there," said Corvin.

"Interesting. Just annoying we do not really know what we are doing, but I follow where you lead," said Irikson.

Corvin nodded and smiled.

"I will say that staying in these inns is a little much. The beds are far too soft!" said Lorka.

They all laughed. They knew that his main complaint was that he was actually too large to fit on any of the beds. Most nights, he slept on the floor.

"Still, should be interesting to see this new land. Do they speak the same language as the Kor'Lenans?" asked Maddik.

"No. We have to learn whole new language," said Jorga.

"Great. More learning. We already speak Outlandish, and most of us have a good grasp of Kor'Lenan. How many bloody tongues do we need to learn?" asked Mirac.

"The Duke has said that if we can pick up Kor'Lenan like

we have, which he said is not an easy language, then picking up the language they speak in Ex'Na should be very easy," said Corvin.

"Well, Kor'Lenan was not that bloody easy to pick up," said Samik.

They all roared with laughter and Samik shook his head. He had struggled the most of all the former slaves to pick up the language and only understood and spoke a little. It had not been bad as all of the mercenary companies spoke Outlandish. Also, the senior men, including the Duke also spoke the Outlandish.

"We will be getting lessons soon I think," said Jorga.

"As long as there are coin wives, I will be happy," said Irikson.

They chuckled to themselves.

"You never know brother, there may be another old cook," teased Lorka with a grin.

They all roared with laughter.

"Bastard. You will never let me forget will you," said Irikson.

"No," said Lorka.

They all laughed again.

"We best get to our rooms and get some sleep. We arrive tomorrow at the capital again and the Duke has said we will be boarding the ship he has hired straight away," advised Corvin.

They all nodded and got up from the floor they were all sitting on.

"Looking forward to that nice soft bed. Enjoy the floor," teased Irikson.

"Bugger off," replied Lorka.

They all laughed.

Chapter Eighteen

The Duke was not lying when they said they would board straight away. They had reached the capital and rushed straight to the harbour. Corvin thought they had rushed quickly through the Capital when they arrived, but this time was even faster. The wagon, drawn by four horses slowed somewhat, but still went quite quickly. They did not have much more of a chance than last time to look around. They saw the same buildings, but it all seemed a little different. This time they saw the filth, the dirt on the roads, and the people without homes living in the streets. Corvin had asked the Duke about this and his answer was simple.

"You were overwhelmed the last time you were here; all of this was new. The size, the amount of people was all new. You have seen it before and now you notice the things, you did not perhaps take note of before," said the Duke.

Corvin understood, it made sense.

When they arrived at the harbour, they were off the back of the wagon and made their way to the ship they would be sailing on. The name of the ship was written in large white writing and stood out against the dark wood. Corvin could not read as it was in a different language. He had asked the Duke.

"Wave Lady," answered the Duke.

The former slaves did not understand why you would name your ship that, but just shrugged.

They boarded the ship quickly. Corvin noticed how much smaller the ship was, thinner than the Bloodchild, the large ship owned by the Bloodchildren company. It only had two masts, but the Duke had assured them it was a lot faster than the last ship they had been on. There were not very many sailors, even less than the Bloodchild had. Corvin asked about this.

"This ship runs on fifteen sailors. We are only at sea for a day, so they don't have different shifts, just work through the sailing, then rest in port," said the Duke.

When they reached the deck and straight away noticed how much nicer the ship was. At first, they did not notice, but on closer inspection it was the finishing touches that set it apart from the troop ship that had travelled on. The deck they walked on was much smoother, the rails that ran the length of the ship was of a finer wood, shaped and sanded as smooth as marble. The wood on the rails shaped to a curved shape, and not just rough wood secured in place. The steps were of a different coloured wood, a golden light brown, to give a contrast between the dark wood of the ship, and the lighter coloured steps. The sails were a bright white, with no mends in them that Corvin could see.

"This way," said the Duke as he led them down into the second deck. They walked down a corridor that was lit with candles, hanging on candle holders that had been secured to the walls. They reached the bow of the ship and the Duke opened a door. They all walked into a large room that took up the entire bow of the ship. Instead of the hammocks they had slept on during their voyage over, there was simple yet large single beds; twenty of them. Ten down the Port side, ten down the Starboard side. The beds were long and even Lorka would be able to lie on one and not use the floor.

"Here are your beds. Stash you packs here and then feel free to wonder the deck. We set sail soon with the tide. By the time you wake up in the morning, we will be in port. I have to talk to the Captain. We will talk again soon," informed the Duke,

"Is this your ship, Duke, sir?" asked Thomik.

The Duke smiled. "Just sir. If you are referring to me and I am not in the room, then refer to me as 'The Duke'," said the Duke.

"Sorry, sir," said Thomik.

"No need to apologise, Thomik. I was not telling you off, just preparing for life in Ex'Na."

"You know my name, sir?" responded Thomik with surprise.

"Yes. I know all of your names. And no, this is not my ship. It is a passenger ship that was hired by the King to bring me here and return me home. Talk soon, lads," said the Duke as he left to find the Captain.

The men all stared at their room. It may only have been for a day and night but was luxury to what they were used to. Irikson found himself a bed and threw his bag down on it.

"Well, things are looking up. I'm glad we have beds and not those poxy hammocks," said Irikson.

They chuckled.

"You on the floor again, Lorka?" said Irikson.

They all laughed. To prove a point, Lorka choose the bed beside Irikson, lay his pack on the floor and then laid down on the bed. His feet only stuck out a little over the edge.

"No. this will be fine. Now, we just need to organise the

cook to pay you a visit during the night, and we will be sorted."

The men all roared with laughter.

"Look, you big bastard, you have told everyone we have meet about that. Stop it!" said Irikson.

The men all laughed and a lot of tension was released from Corvin. He laughed long and he laughed hard. He looked around at his family smiling.

Lorka smiled and close his eyes, relaxing.

"You lot can stay here; I want to see this ship set sail. She is very sleek, and I would like to see how she handles herself in the water," said Jorga.

"I'll join you," said Corvin.

All of them left to return to the top deck, except Lorka and Irikson. They continued to argue. Well, Irikson argued, Lorka just smiled.

They were seated on their beds. They had indeed watched the 'Wave lady' set sail. The ship seemed to glide over the waves and through the water. Jorga, having grown up on boats, was fascinated. He had spent a lot of time with the Captain discussing the ship they were on. The Captain was a thin rake of a man, late fifties with long grey hair that he tied into a knot at the nape of his neck. The Captain was what the Duke described as a grumpy old man that should have retired long ago, but he knew his business and knew the Wave Lady very well. The Captain was only happy to ask Jorga's questions which was unusual for the man, but he welcomed Jorga's thirst for knowledge on anything to do with the ship.

The men had enjoyed dinner on deck, being handed bowls

of a fish stew with spoons. They stood on the deck, watching the sea as they held their bowl of stew and ate. The cook had also provided a few loaves of bread for them to soak up the soup. Corvin had never had fish stew before but was amazed at the flavours. One large mug of wine was provided with the meal, a red wine that had a little bite to it. They had never tried red wine before and Corvin enjoyed the sour taste on his tongue. They were standing around after their meal, enjoying their second mug of wine when the Duke approached.

"Have a seat, gentleman," said the Duke in Outlandish.

They all looked around and sat on the deck, their legs crossed and waited. The Duke looked around and then started speaking.

"I have asked the Captain to give us some time alone on the deck here and not to be disturbed. Now I know I have not been forthcoming with what you are going to be doing, but I promised Corvin that once we are at sea, I would let you know more information," said the Duke.

All the men listened up with nods. They had been waiting for this and Corvin especially wanted to know if he had made the right choice, not that there had been much of a choice. He was more worried he had dragged his brothers onto a bad situation.

"You will be training men to fight. It is that simple! How you do that will be up to Corvin and Jorga. My province currently has only fifteen hundred men at arms," said the Duke.

Jorga raised his hand.

"Yes, Jorga," said the Duke.

"Men at arms, sir? We don't know what that means," said Jorga.

"Soldiers," said the Duke.

"Sir, that does not sound like many for a chief, sorry, a Duke to have," said Irikson.

"It is not. You need to understand that each Duke only has a limited number of soldiers. The Crown or the King, before you ask, raises the armies himself if there is a war. They are ordinary men trained briefly, then sent to war. The Kingdom of Ex'Na has not been to war for over one hundred years," informed the Duke.

Corvin raised his hand. The Duke nodded.

"Are you allowed to have more men?" asked Corvin.

"We can have as many as we like, as long as we pay for them. As you can imagine, keeping a large army paid and fed is not cheap. The company you came from, only had one hundred men, and those men earned money every season. An army, however, does not go and earn money in the summer season, yet they need to be paid. It can drain my coffers very quickly," said the Duke.

The Duke nodded at Lorka who had raised his hand.

"So, we are training these men you have? Or has something changed?" asked Lorka.

The Duke smiled. "Not just a handsome lad then, eh?"

This got the men laughing and Lorka blushing.

"Correct, something has changed. The men that I have are called the Eastmoor Guard. They keep security within my province, that is all. They are good at what they do, chasing down criminals, settling disturbances and the like. They are not trained for a serious battle. There are some good men amongst them and they may be useful, but I know, I will be creating a new force that can handle themselves in a battle. It won't be a big force to start with, and I have not even thought of numbers. You lot will be responsible for training them. I want them as fit as you, as fast as you and to fight like Demons the way you do," said the Duke.

The former pit-rats took the compliment, most of them smiling. Corvin raised his hand.

"You said that something has changed, which is why you need this new force. So, what has changed?" asked Corvin.

The Duke smiled. Impressed with Corvin's mind.

"Yes, something has changed. Firstly, even though we are further south than other provinces. Your former masters, the bastard outlanders, have started raiding my coastline," said the Duke.

The former pit-rats all sat up straighter, a determined angry look on their faces. All of them! The Duke looked at Corvin and was shocked at the mad look in his eyes. He knew the men would have hatred for their former masters, but what he saw in their faces, what he saw in their eyes, was nothing short of madness. It was Jorga who spoke, calming them all down.

"I am sure, sir, that all of us would be more than happy to deal with that little problem," said Jorga.

The tension started falling away from them, as quick as it had arrived. Some were smiling and nodding. The Duke continued.

"What else has changed?" said Corvin.

A look of madness still across his face.

"Secondly, something has changed but it is private. There is only two other people in the world that know of what I am about to tell you apart from myself," said the Duke.

He looked at all of them, a serious look that they surely would understand.

"We know how to hold our tongues, sir," said Jorga.

"Good, because if you do speak of it, you will lose your lives," said the Duke.

They were all shocked. They did not take threats lightly, but the Duke continued before they could ask questions.

"Then, I would lose my life, my family would be killed and anyone that supports me would also be hunted down and killed," said the Duke.

They remained silent; they understood the seriousness alright.

"You can trust us, sir," Corvin finally said.

"I am trusting you, with my life! There is a civil war brewing in my country. It may not happen next year or five years from now, but it is coming. I cannot tell you of all those involved but I believe they want to overthrow my King. The King always faces problems, jealousy and plots, but never before has it been by open war. That's why I came to Kor'Lena. I came looking for skilled men. The King knows why I came, he gave me permission. He is one of those that knows about this trouble in our country. When my men and I saw Irikson and Corvin, we saw what I had been looking for. Men who do not think, just react when trouble happens. I have never seen soldiers react so fast, strike so fast and strike so hard. After that incident in the forest, I started asking discreet questions. Your Captain Joren, he's a fine man but a man with a big mouth. Over a few drinks, he shared your tale. I know as much as he did. And no, I did not cause the problems you faced Corvin, I just took advantage of the situation when it came up. You men will be invaluable for training my men all you know, over the next few years. Joren told me some of the ways you had changed the training. He told me he had never seen men as fit. So, when you ALL wanted to come, I was very happy indeed. You are looking at me, ten men who are superb fighters, and I do not speak light of your previous lives, it sounds violent and bloody unpleasant. I would not have survived it, but imaging if there was one thousand of you, or even ten thousand of you," said the Duke smiling.

'Sir, if there was ten thousand of us, we would be invading the Outlander bastards and burning their country to the ground," said Irikson.

All the others nodded.

"I bet you would," said the Duke with a smile.

"You want us to train that many?" asked Jorga.

"No, my coffers could not afford to pay you all," said the Duke.

"So, we are getting paid to train men for the civil war brewing, and fight of some Outlanders?" said Corvin.

"Yes," said the Duke.

"Living conditions? Pay?" asked Thomik.

"Before we talk of such things, I need your word," said the Duke.

"Our word, sir?" asked Lorka.

"Your promise," said the Duke.

"Promise on what, sir?" asked Irikson.

"Apart from myself when we are alone, or the King if he ever asks you to, which he won't, you will promise me that you will not ever talk about the troubles in the kingdom, to anyone," said the Duke.

One by one, they promised. They said the words, put their right fist on the left breast, and nodded their heads.

"Good," said the Duke.

"So, what type of force are you wanting exactly, sir?" said Jorga.

"That will be up to you," said the Duke.

"Me, sir?" asked Jorga.

"Well, you and Corvin," said the Duke.

"You are giving us free reign to do as we please, sir?" asked Corvin.

"Yes, before anything is decided, you will spend some time studying the language. Once you all know the language and can speak it well, you will go out around the province, taking a look around and seeing what there is to be seen. Once you have had a good look around and seen what kind of men at arms I currently have, then you can decide what we need," said the Duke.

Corvin looked at Jorga and nodded. They were smiling.

"Thank you for the confidence, sir. Where will the men be coming from?" asked Corvin.

"Wherever you find them. Some may be peasants, mercenaries or former soldiers. However, you will get total control and there will be gold available to help build this force, but I will be keeping a close eye on the money. You will not be able to spend it on anything," said the Duke with a smile.

"You do not trust us, sir?" asked Irikson.

"No, Irikson. I would not want you to hire guards to protect you from unwanted advances from old cooks," said the Duke with a huge smile.

The men all erupted into laughter, no one laughing harder than Lorka.

Irikson went red, from embarrassment and not anger.

"How did you find out about that, sir?" asked Jorga, said with a smile all of his own.

"As I said, Joren has a big mouth," said the Duke.

They were all still laughing.

"There is much work to be done and many things for you lads to learn. There will be lessons on how to ride a horse, history lessons on Ex'Na, information on all the provinces that make up my country, how to behave yourself if you are ever in the presence of the King and much more. You lads will have to hit the ground running as the saying in my country goes," said the Duke

They all looked at each other and nodded. Comprehension of what the next few months had in store for them became clear. Corvin was looking forward to training the men and sinking his teeth into the new role he was now in; Jorga the same.

"That is all, men. I will give you more information once we get you to Eastmoor. The good news, before we left, Captain Joren gave me your owed wages, including some of the bonus you would have got had you lasted the season," said the Duke.

The men stood up and cheered. They all started to disperse and talk amongst themselves.

"Jorga, Corvin and Irikson. Can I have a word, please?" asked the Duke.

They followed him to the bow of the ship.

"Right, you three. I have further information to pass on. What I have is for you alone! You, Corvin and you, Irikson. Jorga, I have asked you here as you will be a senior man in my new force, and your insight will be useful," said the Duke.

Jorga nodded.

"As Corvin has told you by now, Captain Noro passed on some information about the raid on a neighbouring province where both Corvin and Irikson may have come from," said the Duke.

They all nodded.

"I am going to ask you not to ask to any questions or try and track down the lead he gave you, Corvin. I will do it for you. I owe you both my life, and as you will find out, people from my country take owing debts very seriously. The main reason I do not want you asking questions or trying to track this down alone, is that the Duke of Du Noor is at the centre of the problems I just raised with the men," said the Duke.

They all looked surprised.

"If we blunder into anything, it may ignite the fire, sir?" asked Jorga.

"Exactly. I will send a man I trust to follow this lead up. There has been rumours for years that the Duke, when younger, took payment from the Outlanders in exchange for turning a blind eye and not having his own soldiers in areas who may get in the way; a nasty business. Have any of you heard this story before?" asked the Duke.

"I have, sir, I think," said Corvin.

The other looked at him with surprise.

"The Smith said he was working for a mercenary company protecting this Duke's lands from raiders. He said he was captured in an ambush. He said the outlanders had bragged the Duke was feeding them information on where the soldiers would be and giving them the best way to raid his own villages without being caught," said Corvin.

'Really?" asked Jorga.

Corvin nodded.

"And this Smith, would he act as a witness?" said the Duke.

All three of them looked to the ground and stayed silent. The Duke was experienced enough to know he had said something wrong.

"I have spoken something which has caused you deep sadness, haven't I?" said the Duke.

"He was our mentor, and the closest thing we all had to a father. It was his death that drove us to escape. A lot of us still feel numb from his death, even though it was a season ago," said Jorga.

"I did not mean to open wounds," said the Duke.

"You were not meant to know, sir. Once we have reached your province, if you shout us a fine wine and an open fire, we can tell you the rest of the story, the parts you do not know," said Corvin.

"Yes sir, we would," said Irikson.

"You would?" asked the Duke.

"You trusted us, sir. Trust goes both ways," said Jorga.

The Duke just nodded.

"Well, now you know about Duke of Du Noor. As I said, he could be a problem. He has been slowly increasing his men at arms over the last few seasons. He now has just over four thousand men and I cannot work out how he is paying for them. His province although had good silver and gold mines, I doubt they could support such a large force. Also, it is rumoured that he has outlanders in his force as well," said the Duke.

"Really?" said Corvin with surprise.

"So the rumour goes. I have not seen it myself, but he does have at least one. His bodyguard is an Outlander. I can confirm that as I have met him; huge bastard. Not as big as Lorka but still bigger than all of you three. I have seen him wrestle, he is powerful, I have not seen him lose, ever!" said the Duke.

"Then the first thing to do, would be to kill the bodyguard," said Corvin.

"Agreed. That will put him off balance and make him feel less secure," said Jorga.

"Yes, a scared man can make mistakes," said Irikson.

"Woah, you three. We have not even reached my country yet, and already you are planning on killing someone," said the Duke.

"Sorry, sir. It is what we do. We see a problem and we deal with it," said Jorga.

"I appreciate that, but wanton killing is not what you are

here for. Besides, it has more to do with the fact he is an Outlander that you want him dead," said the Duke.

The three of them smiled.

"True, sir," said Corvin.

"Keep this all to yourself. We are nowhere ready to move against the Duke of Du Noor. Your first task is to learn the culture, the language and the laws. Once that is done, build me a new force," said the Duke.

"To kill raiders and protect from this arsehole Duke. Is that correct, sir?" asked Irikson.

"Yes," said the Duke with another smile.

"We can handle that, sir. It will be more adjusting to this new situation, but I am sure we can manage," said Corvin.

"Good. Enjoy the sailing. Once you wake up, we will be in Pulan, the main port city of Pula. If you were impressed by Kor'Mor, wait to you see the home of the King," said the Duke.

"Thank you, sir," said Jorga.

As the Duke walked off, they talked some more.

"So, we going to obey him and not kill this big bastard bodyguard?" asked Irikson.

'Yes, we are," said Corvin.

"Agreed," said Jorga.

'Really?" asked Irikson.

"Yes. We may have fought well in Kor'Lena, but we lost many friends. We need to do more to fit in and not behaving…" Corvin did not finish as he was looking for the right word.

"Unpredictable," said Jorga.

'Yes. If we are told to fight, then we fight, but it sounds like this country is a little stricter," said Corvin.

"So, we just need to be a little more careful? Is that what you are saying," said Irikson.

"Exactly," said Jorga.

They all nodded.

"Are we all happy with where we are going? I know the men are happy to follow, but I would hate to think that my actions have robbed us of a life we were suited for?" stated Corvin.

"No, this way is better. We will lose less brothers this way. We are training men, fighting raiders and learning about this new country. No more needless deaths," said Jorga.

"Yes. Enough of us have been lost," said Irikson.

"Thank you, both," said Corvin.

"One thing," said Irikson.

They both looked at Irikson.

"I will slice the throat of the next bastard that mentions that cook again."

About the Author

Author of *Slave Boy*, the first book in the Democ'Chu Series, Nath always had a huge imagination.

As a small child he was known as the storyteller. He started writing short stories in his early twenties as a way to get his feelings and ideas onto paper.

Life, as it sometimes does, took him down another path away from his creative side and he spent the majority of his life managing bars, hotels and restaurants.

In his late thirties he started stand-up comedy and found this a good outlet for his stories and imagination, enjoying his time on stage and entertaining people. However, when New Zealand went into isolation holiday (Lockdown) for Covid-19 and he was meant to be writing his first hour-long comedy show, he got side-tracked and wrote the first draft of *Slave Boy* instead. He found he had missed his storytelling and found a new love of world-building – which he had been doing his entire life in his head without realising it. He found drive and focus in his life that had been missing for a very long time.

Share the journey with Nath, and get just as lost in reading the story as he got writing it.

If you have purchased a copy of this book, we would love for you to send us a selfie of you and the book on your preferred platform:

facebook.com/RealDawnBates
instagram.com/realdawnbates
twitter.com/realdawnbates
linkedin.com/in/dawnbates

…so we can thank you in person.

With love and gratitude,
From all at Dawn Publishing